THE MINOTAUR'S HEAD

THE MINOTAUR'S HEAD

Marek Krajewski

Translated from the Polish by
Danusia Stok

MACLEHOSE PRESS
QUERCUS · LONDON

First published in Poland as *Głowa minotaura*
by Wydawnictwo W.A.B. Co Ltd, 2009

First published in Great Britain in 2012 by

MacLehose Press
an imprint of Quercus
55 Baker Street
Seventh Floor, South Block
London W1U 8EW

A CIP catalogue reference for this book
is available from the British Library

ISBN (HB) 978 1 906694 94 4
ISBN (TPB) 978 1 906694 95 1

2 4 6 8 10 9 7 5 3 1

Designed and typeset in Octavian by Patty Rennie
Printed and bound in England by Clays Ltd, St Ives plc

THE MINOTAUR'S HEAD

PART I

The Entrance to the Labyrinth

"I know of a Greek labyrinth that is just one straight line. So many philosophers have been lost upon that line that a mere detective might be pardoned if he became lost as well."

From "Death and the Compass", Jorge Luis Borges, 1942

LWÓW, TUESDAY, MAY 9TH, 1939
FIVE O'CLOCK IN THE MORNING

Dawn was breaking over Stary Rynek. A pink glow poured between the miserable huts in which peasant women had begun to arrange their pots of *borshch* and *pierogi*. It settled on the milk churns drawn from Ester Firsch's dairy on a two-wheeled cart by a Jewish trader, and spread across the visors of caps perched on the heads of rogues who stood in gateways, unable to decide whether to go to bed or wait for the opening of the nearby drinking-den, where a tankard of beer would satisfy their burning, alcoholic thirst. The flush of first light settled on the dresses of two girls, who, having had no clients that night, returned in silence from their posts on Mostki and disappeared through gateways on Mikołajska and Smerekowa streets, where each rented a bed screened off in a shabby room. The rosy light shone straight into the eyes of men briskly making their way to the Baczewski vodka factory on Wysoki Zamek, but they ignored it; they fixed their gaze on the cobbled street and quickened their steps, causing the bags of bread and onions to rustle in their hands. None of the street urchins or workers in Lwów admired pink-fingered Eos as she sculpted the triangular roofs of the Sisters of Mercy Hospital; nobody wondered at the cyclical phenomena of nature; nobody analysed the subtle changes of light or nuances of colour.

1

Deputy Commissioner Franciszek Pirożek, like his fellow country-men, was a long way from Homeric rapture. As he drove along Kazimierzowska in a brand-new police Chevrolet, he carefully observed the inhabitants of this working district, looking for signs of any particu-lar unrest, and kept an eye out for groups of people engrossed in lively discussion, or huddled together threateningly, armed with tools. People who might want to lynch a criminal off their own backs. He had not yet sighted anyone suspicious, either on Kopernik or Legionów. Nor did he see them now. Gradually he relaxed and his sighs of relief grew louder. There were no harbingers of riots whatsoever. "What luck," he thought as he passed the Wielki Theatre and parked outside the pharmacy at Żółkiewska 4, "that the horror was discovered by the pharmacist, a sensi-ble rationalist who didn't go ranting about in the yard, yelling and waking everyone in the vicinity."

Pirożek climbed out of the car and cast his eyes around. His throat constricted. The sight of a police constable outside the pharmacy had not gone unnoticed by the locals, who stood around and pondered loudly – even quite impudently – over the presence so early in the morning of a guardian of the law at this particular spot. The latter, on the other hand, glared at them from beneath the visor of his hat and every now and then slapped his hand against the truncheon at his leg. Police officers did not command respect in the area. There had been times when they had been obliged to walk in the middle of the road to avoid being dragged into a gateway and beaten up. The constable from Police Station III was happy to see Pirożek, therefore; he saluted and let him through into the phar-macy. The deputy commissioner knew where to go and made his way behind a counter on which stood an antiquated telephone. He crossed the dark hallway, tripped over a chest containing rusty apothecary scales and entered the kitchen at the back of the apartment occupied by the phar-macist and his family.

While the pharmacist, Mr Adolf Aschkenazy, had behaved very calmly, just as Pirożek had anticipated, his wife had not a single drop of cold blood running through her veins. She sat at the table, pressed her slender fingers into the curlers which hugged her skull like a ski hat and wailed loudly, shaking her head. With his arm around her, her husband held to her lips a glass of what must have been a valerian infusion, judging by the smell. A kettle bopped up and down on the stove. Steam covered the windows, making it impossible for the gawper, whom the constable outside had not managed to chase away, to pry. The air was stifling. Pirożek removed his hat and wiped his brow. Mrs Aschkenazy stared at him with horror, as if she were seeing the devil rather than this rosy-cheeked, corpulent official who generally inspired trust. Pirożek muttered his greetings and mentally recreated the telephone conversation he had held with Mr Aschkenazy half an hour earlier. The apothecary had recounted everything very calmly and in detail. Pirożek, therefore, did not have to ask him the same questions now, in the presence of his terrified wife and with the nosy-parker still glued to the window.

"Which way out into the yard?" asked Pirożek.

"Through the hall and down to the end," Mrs Aschkenazy replied unexpectedly.

Pirożek, not stopping to think about the woman's sudden animation, returned to the dark hall. A loud snoring came from the next room. "Must be children," he thought. "Their sleep is always so heavy, even death going rampant doesn't stir them."

The muddy yard was built up on three sides and cut off from the street by an iron fence, access to which was guarded by police constables. Around it stood dilapidated two-storey buildings with internal galleries. Luckily, most of the inhabitants were asleep. Only on the first floor was there a grey-haired woman sitting on a stool, not taking her eyes off police inspector Józef Dułapa as he stood near the privy smoking a cigarette.

I went out to answer nature's call, Pirożek recreated Aschkenazy's telephone account in his mind, *and found something terrible in the –privy*.

"Good morning, Commissioner, sir," said Dułapa, crushing the cigarette beneath his shoe.

"What are you doing, Dułapa!" yelled Pirożek, making the old woman in the gallery jump. "This is a crime scene! Spit on the fag and put it in your pocket! Don't erase the evidence, damn it!"

"Yes, sir!" answered Dułapa, and bent to look for the cigarette butt at his feet.

"Where is it?" Pirożek felt distaste on saying this. He should not have referred to a deceased human being as "it". "Well, where's the body?" he corrected himself. "You haven't moved him, by any chance? Point to where and give me a torch!"

"In the toilet. And be careful, Commissioner. There are guts all over the place," whispered the worried inspector, and as he handed over the torch he added even more quietly, "No offence, Commissioner, sir, but it's awful. Just the thing for Commissioner Popielski."

Pirożek was not offended. He ran his eyes carefully over the damp black earth so as not to disturb any footprints. Then he stepped over to the toilet and opened the door. The stench took his breath away. The sight he beheld in the pink light of dawn blurred his clarity of vision. Out of the corner of his eye, the commissioner saw the old woman lean out heavily over the balustrade in an attempt to peer into the darkness of the privy. He slammed the door.

"Dułapa," he said, drawing rotten air into his lungs, "get that old woman off the gallery."

The police officer adjusted the fastening constricting his collar and made towards the stairs with a stern expression.

"Come along now, old dear," he shouted to the woman, "inside with you, but *now*!"

"Can't even relieve meself!" screamed the woman, but obediently she disappeared into her lodgings, leaving the stool prudently in the gallery.

Pirożek opened the door again and illuminated the pale mass lying in the privy. The child's body was contorted as if someone had tried to force its head under its knee. The hair on its skull was sparse and curly, the skin on its cheekbone distended with swelling. Guts lay strewn around on the threshold, their slippery surface covered with irregular rivulets of blood. The entire body was covered in lesions. The deputy commissioner felt as though his gullet had become a plug which blocked all breath. He leaned against the open door. Never before had he seen anything like it. A sick child, scabby, broken limbs. It did not look older than three. He pulled himself upright, spat and looked at the body once more. These were not scabs, they were puncture wounds.

Pirożek slammed the privy door. Dułapa watched him with interest and unease. From a distance, from the direction of Gródecka Street, they heard the jingle of the first tram. A beautiful May day was dawning over Lwów.

"You're right, Dułapa," Deputy Commissioner Pirożek announced very slowly, "this case is just right for Popielski."

LWÓW, THAT SAME MAY 9TH, 1939
A QUARTER PAST TEN IN THE MORNING

Leokadia Tchorznicka stepped out onto the balcony of her apartment at 3 Kraszewski and gazed a while at a small corner of the Jesuit Gardens. She did so every day because she adored the invigorating certainty that nothing changed in the neighbourhood and everything was in its rightful place: the chestnut trees, the oaks, Agenor Gołuchowski's statue and the vase depicting allegories of life. That day, however, something was different from the weeks that had gone before; the chestnut trees had blossomed, and students in their final year at the nearby Jan Długosz Gymnasium had appeared. Looking down from the first floor, she watched several young men in school uniform as they walked up the street, cigarette in hand, carrying books bound with a belt beneath their arms and avidly arguing about the relationship – as Leokadia understood it – between tangents and sines. She recalled her own final school exams forty years earlier and the happy years which followed, studying French philology at Jan Kazimierz University where, as one of only four young ladies in the department, she had been constantly surrounded by admirers. She now rested her elbows on the duvet hanging over the balustrade, turned her face to the sun and welcomed the memories of secondary school and her student years. A lorry carrying scrap iron thundered past beneath the balcony. This was something unexpected and Leokadia hated anything unforeseen. When the unforeseen occurred, she reproached herself for having no imagination.

And this is precisely what happened now. She started, quickly returned inside and closed the balcony door. The last thing she wanted was for her cousin Edward Popielski, with whom she had lived for twenty years, to wake at that moment. Throughout all those years the only arguments between them had concerned her cousin being woken suddenly – whether by a draught banging a poorly shut window against the frame, a door-to-door salesman stridently touting his wares in the yard, or the maid singing her prayers too loudly in the kitchen. All such events could violently disrupt the sleep of a man who went to bed at five in the morning and did not generally rise before one in the afternoon. Leokadia anxiously approached the door to her cousin's bedroom, the windows of which gave out onto the yard as did those of his daughter Rita's room and that of the kitchen. She listened carefully for a moment to see whether the dreadful clatter of old iron a few moments earlier had had the result she had feared. Indeed it had. Her cousin was no longer asleep and was standing at the front door holding the telephone receiver. "I shouldn't have replaced the receiver," she reproached herself, "but what was I supposed to do when headquarters kept ringing Edward from six in the morning? He'd have woken up in the end and been unbearable."

Popielski was now standing in the hall staring at the receiver in silence, as if he saw a real person there. All of a sudden he raised his voice. She quickly retreated to the kitchen and closed the door behind her so as not to eavesdrop. Her discretion, however, was pointless. Popielski shouted down the hallway and she heard every word.

"Don't you understand Polish, sir?" She knew now that he was speaking to his boss, the head of the investigative department. "Did I not make myself clear? I refuse to take on this investigation and I refuse to give the reasons for my decision! That's all I have to say to you, sir!"

Leokadia heard the rattle of the receiver being slammed down, the creaking of the living-room floorboards beneath her cousin's feet, and then the characteristic sound of a telephone dial turning. "He's making a phone call," she thought. "Maybe he wants to apologise to that Zubik." His voice was far quieter now. She sighed with relief. She did not like him arguing with his superiors. He never wanted to tell her the reason for their quarrel; it lodged within him like a splinter, making him swell and redden with pent up anger. It might end in another attack. "If only he could overcome the block for once," she thought, "and confide in me the secret of his relationship with that boorish chief . . . that would help!" Why didn't he want to talk about these conflicts when he didn't hold any secrets from her regarding even the most confidential of investigations? He knew she would remain as silent as the grave.

From the larder she brought the gingerbread biscuits she had purchased at Zalewski's that morning, then put some freshly ground coffee beans into a jug and poured boiling water over them. A floorboard creaked and the curtains rustled. "He's stopped talking, gone into the living-room, drawn the curtains against the sunlight and is now, no doubt, sitting beneath the clock with a cigarette and newspaper," she thought as she placed the dishes on a tray.

Nearly all her suppositions proved correct — except about the newspaper which still lay on the little table in the hall. The thick green curtains were drawn in the parlour and the chandelier set in the moulding of the ceiling lit. Popielski sat in an armchair beneath the grandfather clock and flicked ash from his cigarette into a shell-shaped ashtray. He wore a pair of thick felt trousers, leather house slippers gleaming with polish, and a cherry-coloured morning jacket with black velvet lapels. Traces of shaving soap were visible on his bald head, as was one small cut. A closely trimmed, blackened moustache and beard encircled his lips.

"Good morning, Edward," Leokadia smiled and placed the tray on the table. "I must have been on the balcony when you got up and shaved. Zubik phoned, you jumped at the sound of the ringing and cut your head. Is that right?"

"You ought to work with me in the police." The words were not, this time, accompanied by his customary smile. "Is Hanna not here today?"

Leokadia sat down at the table, poured the coffee and waited for him to join her at their usual breakfast ritual: "*primum makagigi, deinde serdelki*", which meant that first he ate biscuits with his coffee, then sausages, horseradish, rolls and butter, and washed these down with tea. But he did not sit at the table and instead continued to smoke his cigarette, the butt of which he had wedged into an amber cigarette holder.

"Don't smoke like that on an empty stomach. Put it out, sit down and have some breakfast. Besides, it's Tuesday today."

"I do not understand" — the cigarette holder knocked against the shell ashtray — "the connection between the two."

By the slowness with which he spoke, Leokadia saw he was in a very bad mood.

"There isn't one," she said. "Today is Tuesday and it's Hanna's day off. I simply answered your question."

Popielski set down the ashtray on the little table beneath the clock. He walked around the dining table and came to a sudden halt behind her. Holding her by the temples, he kissed Leokadia on the head, partially dishevelling her carefully styled hair.

"Sorry about my rotten mood," he said and sat down at the table. "The day started badly. Zubik phoned and . . ."

"You refused to lead the investigation into the case of the boy people say was ritually murdered by Jews?" she asked, not expecting a reply.

"How do you know?" he retorted and swallowed a bite of gingerbread.

"I heard. And even if I hadn't I'd have guessed . . . You always sit beneath the clock, smoke and read the paper before breakfast. Today you didn't. *Slowo* and its supplement are lying there untouched. Either you were so overwrought you didn't want to read or you knew what was on the front page. I deduced the latter."

"True," he answered glumly and did not, as he usually did, praise her correct reasoning.

"Why did you refuse Zubik? You know you can be dismissed for it. But above all, do you want the criminal to go unpunished?"

Such an insinuation would, in normal circumstances, have made Popielski explode with anger. "How dare you suspect me of such a thing?" he would have yelled. Now, however, he said nothing and his jaw moved rhythmically as he ate.

"Zubik asked me the same thing," he said unhurriedly once he had swallowed, "and that's when I raised my voice at him."

"But I'm not Zubik!" Leokadia's slender form stirred suddenly. "And you can tell me everything . . ."

"You're not Zubik," he interrupted her, "and that's why I'm not going to raise my voice at you."

9

She knew that she was not going to learn anything from him as usual. She drank her coffee and got up to go to the kitchen to heat some sausages for him. Popielski leaped up too, grabbed her by the wrist and sat her down again.

"I'd tell you everything, Lodzia, but it's a terribly long story." He inserted a new cigarette into his holder.

With joy she thought this meant the end of his reluctance to talk, and that she was about to learn everything.

"I'd tell you everything but I don't know where to start . . . It's to do with the case of the Minotaur."

"So start *ab ovo*." Leokadia was tense with curiosity. "Best to start with that Silesian city and thick-set Silesian you call your friend, whom I never really liked . . ."

"Yes . . ." he said pensively. "That's where it all started."

BRESLAU, FRIDAY, JANUARY 1ST, 1937
FOUR O'CLOCK IN THE MORNING

Fireworks welcoming in the New Year exploded above the Municipal Theatre as a shaking droschka drew up outside the impressive tenement marked Zwingerplatz 1, in which Abwehr Captain Eberhard Mock lived along with his wife Karen, their German sheepdog Argos and a couple of ancient servants, Adalbert and Martha Goczoll. The droschka shook for two reasons. Firstly, it was being jostled by a gusty wind which vigorously lashed it with snow, and secondly, after a party at the Silesian Museum of Fine Art that was awash with champagne, Mock was filled with an indefatigable male force which he was attempting to relieve in transit, not even waiting to find himself alone in the bedroom with his wife. Caring little about the frost, or about Karen's weak protests and the cabby's garrulousness, he was trying to penetrate the layers wrapped around his wife's body. The results of his efforts were feeble, however, and merely ended with the cabby, who was used to such frolicking in his cab, becoming discreetly silent.

"We've arrived, Ebi, calm down." Karen delicately pushed her panting husband away.

"Good," Mock muttered, evidently pleased, and he held out a ten-mark note to the cabby. "And this is for picking us up punctually." He added another two marks.

Climbing out of the droschka, they were caught in the cold flurries of a wind which had picked up outside the Guildhall and whisked up dry snow from the pavement. The force of the wind was so strong it tore Mock's top hat from his head and the white silk scarf from his neck. Both pieces of attire swirled in the gusts then parted ways, the top hat hopping along the tram tracks towards the Hotel Monopol while the scarf stuck to the window of Fahrig's Café. Half-blinded, Mock decided to retrieve the scarf first, as it had been a Christmas present from Karen. He rushed towards the café window gesticulating to his wife to shelter from the blizzard. A second later he was pinning the scarf to the window pane and looking around for his hat. Karen stood in the gateway.

"Go to the bedroom and wait for me there!" he shouted, tying the scarf in a knot.

Karen did not move. Shielding his eyes, Mock made his way towards the brightly lit hotel from which steam and the majestic rhythm of a Vienna waltz burst forth. He strained his eyes for the hat but could not see it anywhere. He imagined it rolling along the pavement becoming soiled with horse manure, and the image annoyed him greatly. He stood still, looking around; his eyes came to rest on Karen standing in the gateway. "Why in God's name doesn't she go indoors?" he thought. "Is the care-taker drunk, has he fallen asleep? Well, I'll go and wake him up alright!" Gazing at her helpless, huddled figure, he felt disinclined towards

11

bedroom frolics. He opened his mouth and swallowed several flakes of snow. His tongue, parched from an excess of alcohol and cigars, felt like a rough, unplaned block. There was only one thing he wanted: a large, cool jug of lemonade. He turned on his heels and made towards his tenement, leaving his top hat prey to cabby horses.

A tall man with a bowler hat pulled down over his eyes cut briskly across his path. Mock reacted instinctively, dodging an imaginary blow, and squatted to observe his assailant. The latter did not strike, however, but merely extended a hand holding Mock's his top hat.

"Thank you very much," said Mock delightedly, taking his headgear. "I'm sorry, I thought you were going to assault me, whereas here you are performing a good deed . . ."

"It would be a shame to lose such an expensive top hat," said the stranger.

"Thank you once again." Mock glanced at Karen who was smiling as she watched the scene. "A healthy New Year!" he said to the man.

"Criminal Secretary Seuffert, assistant for special affairs to Criminal Director Kraus, liaison officer between the Gestapo and the Abwehr." The man did not reciprocate with good wishes but with an absurd list of his responsibilities, and then held out a business card. "There is an urgent political case, Herr Hauptmann. You have to come with me. On the orders of Colonel von Hardenburg." He enunciated the name of Mock's superior with such accuracy and emphasis, as if he were pronouncing the long and technical name of some disease.

Mock shook the snow off his hat, put the hat on his head and looked at Karen. She was no longer smiling.

There was great commotion at the squalid Warsaw Court Hotel, at Antonienstrasse 16. Two uniformed policemen bore a body on a stretcher covered with a grey sheet stamped INSTITUTE OF FORENSIC ANATOMY; next to the receptionist's lodge Helmut Ehlers, police photographer and fingerprint technician, folded away his tripod; on the stairs raged forensic physician Doctor Siegfried Lasarius as, using one violent gesture after another, he explained to Criminal Assistant Hanslik in a raised voice that he was not in a position to determine a corpse's ethnic identity unless the corpse was male and Jewish. The only person who remained still, other than to bring a long thin cigarillo to his lips at intervals, was Colonel Rainer von Hardenburg, Chief of the Abwehr Breslau Regional Branch VII, who stood on the landing. Mock noticed that the heads of all the men were graced with a top hat; only on Seuffert's elongated skull was there a bowler. The receptionist, swaying behind his desk and trying to sober up by constantly moistening his face with water from a basin, was bare-headed. Except for Mock and Seuffert, who had only just arrived, each of those present was holding a tall glass.

"A good thing you're here, Captain Mock!" von Hardenburg loudly greeted his subordinate, forgoing any New Year's wishes. "Have a glass of soda water and take a look at the murdered woman's body. Show him the girl!" he bellowed at the two policemen who, having conquered the stairs, set down the corpse at Mock's feet.

"This man from Hanover knows me inside out," Mock reflected. "He knew I'd have a hangover the morning after a New Year's ball." Mock walked up to the reception desk on which stood four siphons, held one firmly in his hand and generously squirted some soda water into a glass. He glanced at the receptionist's bloodshot eyes, then at the siphon bottles, and realized he had overestimated von Hardenburg's concern. Who at this

13

time on New Year's Day *doesn't* have a hangover? Everyone's been to some New Year's ball, and everyone's been drinking! Everyone except him over there – he ran his eyes over Seuffert with disdain. The scum from the Gestapo only drink water and don't eat meat, just like their god, that miserable Austrian *Feldfebel*.[†]

"I warn you, Captain!" von Hardenburg's voice electrified the company. "It's a shocking sight!"

One of the uniformed men threw aside a corner of the sheet and covered his eyes. The other left the hotel together with Seuffert and held up his face to the sky, from whence fell thick flakes of snow. Ehlers turned his back to the stretcher and started packing his equipment into a huge leather case as fast as he could; von Hardenburg lit another cigarillo, while Hanslik's patent-leather shoes flashed briefly in the light as he ran to the top of the stairs, heels clattering, and hurried away somewhere. Only Doctor Lasarius leaned over the body and with his ever-present cigar butt pointed out various important details. Mock felt as though his tongue was swelling in his mouth as he listened to Lasarius' deductions.

"It's not at all difficult, Mock," – Lasarius indicated the red flesh between the nose and eye with his cigar butt – "to tear away half of somebody's cheek. A man with a healthy set of teeth can do so with no problem whatsoever. His teeth don't have to be filed sharp like those of the leopard men in Cameroon. Oh yes, he can do it, no problem whatsoever . . ."

Mock drank the entire glass of soda water in one go. It did not help. His mouth was full of splinters.

"What you see here" – Lasarius' cigar wandered towards the vicinity of the girl's crotch – "are fragments of the girl's hymen stuck together with blood."

Mock's eyes followed the doctor's unconventional pointer and sud-

† Equivalent to sergeant.

14

denly felt all the various dishes he had eaten at the New Year's reception fill his mouth. First came the taste of salmon roll, pickled tongue and collared herrings, then fillet of perch, asparagus with ham in aspic, veal and wild mushrooms. All these dishes now took on a hint of rancid butter in Mock's mouth. He grabbed the siphon, put the spout into his mouth and pressed the lever. Water spurted onto his tongue; the siphon gurgled and spat out its last drops. Mock rinsed out the taste of rancid butter, got a grip on himself and looked at the body again.

"These bloodied half-moon abrasions" – Lasarius touched the girl's neck with his fingertip – "were made by fingers and nails. The victim was strangled. She was raped, had half her face devoured, and was strangled. She was probably strangled at the end. Why are you so surprised, Mock?" Lasarius said, misinterpreting the horror on Mock's face. "That can be ascertained even at first glance. You can see the results of haemorrhaging from the cheek and genitals. That means he bit and raped her while she was still alive."

There was a taste of vinegar in Mock's dry mouth. Acid spilled over his tongue. He rushed towards the reception desk and started to shake the siphons. Every one of them was empty. The vinegar demanded a reaction. Spasms shook Mock's gullet. And at that moment he saw the reception-ist run his tongue over his parched lips and, without a trace of repulsion, stare at the thin white body whose face had been prey to some beast. Oil and vinegar flowed back into the depths of Mock's digestive tract.

"What the hell are you gaping at?" yelled Mock, grabbing the recep-tionist by the lapels of his dirty uniform. "Turn you on, does it, you pervert? Get me some soda water or beer. In a flash, you dog!"

The receptionist turned away so as to escape his persecutor, but not without some help from Mock. Mock had aimed well. His patent leather shoe landed squarely on the receptionist's backside, and within a split second the unfortunate man disappeared behind his desk.

"What are you doing, Mock?" Von Hardenburg was beside himself with indignation. "You can't treat people like that! Now follow me, we're going upstairs! I'm going to show you the scene of the crime. Come with us, Seuffert."

As he followed his boss up the stairs it seemed to Mock that it was not the creaking of the old floorboards he could hear, but the symphyses in his brain. The hangover was spilling across his head and stomach. On top of that, he was yawning until his eyes watered. He kept tripping, swearing and glancing to see whether he had scuffed his patent shoes.

In a small room stood an iron bed with a pillow and coverless duvet. Snow fell through an open window, beneath which stood a metal stand with a chipped basin partially hidden by the open door of a wardrobe. Mock went to the wardrobe to close it, in vain. It opened again a moment later with a sound that grated in Mock's skull. He leaned out of the window and looked down. The gas lantern fixed to the wall gave a fair amount of light. The one-way street was so narrow that only a clever cyclist would be capable of slaloming between the over-filled dustbins, pieces of furniture and punctured buckets. Mock looked up. Guttering ran down next to the window. One of the brackets holding it in place had recently been torn from the wall. The captain felt someone's breath on the side of his face; like his own, it reeked of alcohol.

"Yes, Captain Mock," von Hardenburg said, indicating the edge of the roof, "this is how the criminal got in. Along the gutter perhaps. He couldn't have weighed much. Only one bracket broke away. If – forgive me – he's built like you, all the brackets would have come away from the wall and he himself would be lying in pieces among the rubbish."

"Colonel, sir," said Mock as he withdrew into the room, "you and I work for the Abwehr. You're its head in Breslau. And that man over there" – he nodded towards Seuffert who was inspecting his hands – "is from the Gestapo. What the hell are we doing here? Why doesn't the Murder

16

Commission take care of this? Hanslik is the only one who should be in the room, no-one else, yet all the most important officers of the secret services in Silesia are here, with hangovers and, to top it all, dragged from parties. Well, all except the chap from the Gestapo . . . He probably doesn't dance or drink. And the only ball he's ever seen is on a New Year's card!"

"If I were you" – there was amusement in von Hardenburg's eyes – "I wouldn't speak so scornfully of your fellow worker. He's your assistant as of today."

Mock rested his backside on the sill. He could not believe what he had just heard. He had left the police for the Abwehr in 1934. He could not bear to watch scum from the Gestapo penetrate his world like syphilitic pathogens and turn everything upside down. He had not been able to look his two finest men in the eye when they had been obliged to leave their entire professional life behind just because they were Jewish. He had left because he believed that all the dirt which surfaced after the Reichstag elections and the "Night of the Long Knives" would not cling to him in the Abwehr. And all of a sudden, three years later, on the first day of the new year, the slime had caught up with him. "Once contaminated, always contaminated," he thought as he ran his tongue over a palate as coarse as sand.

"It's not my decision." Von Hardenburg was now completely serious. "I made it . . . not without a certain amount of coercion. After midnight the receptionist you kicked in the backside sensed the pull of God's will. He decided to go and visit a girl, a daughter of Corinth, or so he thought. The girl was registered here as Anna. Just that, no surname. Rooms are rented by the hour, and all the receptionist is interested in is whether the client has the money to pay. A guest could call himself Frankenstein's Monster for all he cares. The girl arrived, dragging this lot with her." He pointed to a large cardboard suitcase beneath the bed. "She hardly spoke a word of German. But that didn't bother the drunken receptionist whose intentions were not, so to speak, to chat. So when he felt the will of God he entered her room and saw a corpse. He telephoned the Police Praesidium immediately, saying that the murdered girl was a foreigner but he could not say what nationality. The duty officer knows what to do when a foreigner dies. He telephoned the Murder Commission where Hanslik was on duty, and then the Gestapo. The Gestapo duty officer was Criminal Secretary Seuffert who . . . well, what is it you did, Seuffert?"

"I telephoned Criminal Director Erich Kraus," Seuffert reported stiffly, tearing himself away from contemplating his neatly filed nails. "And he . . ."

"And he," von Hardenburg interrupted him, "first came here and then to the ball at the Silesian Provincial Town Hall, where I was having a wonderful time. He reported that we were dealing with a case of espionage. He suspected the woman of being a spy. A strange spy who doesn't speak German!"

Von Hardenburg grabbed Mock by the elbow and dragged him to the window. He glanced back at Seuffert and added in a whisper:

"Kraus created a real drama. He stopped the music and announced that we had arrived at a bloody settling of accounts between spies. And do you know on whom everybody's eyes rested? On the man who is the expert in espionage in this town! On me! So I had to demonstrate to our Silesian dignitaries that I am a man of responsibility; that despite it being New Year's Eve I was equal to the task and ready to throw everything in. I had to abandon the ball and desert my family so as to take care of some foreign whore! And I" – he was now speaking out loud – "appointed you to this task as my best man, the man with the most police experience. But unfortunately nobody knew where you were spending New Year's Eve, which is why you got here so late. Thanks to you I couldn't get back to the ball!" yelled von Hardenburg so suddenly that his monocle sprang from his eye. "So, to work, Mock! I'm going to bed!"

He left, slamming the door behind him.

A long moment elapsed. Wearing a pair of gloves, Mock opened the girl's suitcase and rummaged through her belongings. Apart from some warm underwear, a few pairs of stockings, a hairbrush, mirror, talc, scented soap and a few dresses, there was a large Torpedo typewriter. He looked at the keyboard. Some keys appeared to have been replaced because they now featured French accents.

Mock sat on the window sill, his mind in shambles. He knew now why Kraus had suspected a French spy network, but he could not concentrate on the thought. The description "foreign whore" rang in his head. He gritted his teeth and regretted not having reminded von Hardenburg that Abwehr chiefs had more than once fallen asleep in the embrace of a foreign whore at Madame le Goef's establishment in Opperau on the outskirts of Breslau. "People should not have to die," he thought, "just so that some high-ranking scum can finish his tango! Gnawed, raped and strangled, the poor thin girl shouldn't have to give up the ghost after terrible torment just because some bespectacled son-of-a-bitch doesn't want to leave his cake half eaten!" He glanced at Seuffert who was once again examining his manicured nails, and felt a surge of fury. In order to control himself, he started to decline in his head the passive present subjunctive tense of the Latin verb *mordere* – to bite. He hoped that the mantra – *mordear, mordearis, mordeatur, mordeamur, mordeamini, mordeantur* – would calm him, that the receptionist would presently arrive with another siphon, and that a good gulp of water would enable him to collect his thoughts.

There was a knock at the door. The receptionist stood on the threshold.

"Unfortunately there's no beer or soda water for you, sir," he said, frightened. "I even went to the Green Pole, but the students had already drunk it all."

Mock pushed himself up from the sill. He brusquely shouldered the receptionist and Seuffert aside, heavily made his way along the hallway and stomped downstairs. There was no-one left at the Warsaw Court Hotel.

"Where are you going, Criminal Director?" Seuffert shouted.

"Home, for a cold drink," Mock said slowly.

"And what about me?" Seuffert was clearly losing control of his voice.

"You conduct the investigation! Those are my orders to you as my assistant!"

Mock snatched his coat and top hat from the hanger and left the hotel. He found himself in a white alley where the rubbish was already covered with a layer of powdery snow and made towards Reuschenstrasse and Wachtplatz and the droschka stand. A few years earlier he might have plunged his head into a bucket of cold water and begun his search for the beast which had gnawed away half of a girl's face. But that was in the past. Now Mock was fifty-four and his hangovers were growing increasingly acute.

BRESLAU, THAT SAME JANUARY 1ST, 1937
SIX O'CLOCK IN THE MORNING

Mock did not reach home. As he neared the droschka stand he glanced down Fischerstrasse and noticed the curtained windows of Café Nicolai-platz on the corner. He felt the strong, stabbing hunger of a hangover. Spurred by curiosity, he peered through the window. The room was empty and tidy; all that remained of the New Year's party were an enormous clock decorated with extinguished candles and red ribbons, and strips of tissue paper hanging from the ceiling. Mock's thoughts returned to his student days, when the dirty drinking-den whose customers were anything but wealthy university youths looked nothing like the present-day, orderly Café Nicolaiplatz. In breaks between lectures he had devoured modest lunches there, generally made up of fried potatoes and sauerkraut, or of herring salad, frankfurters and rolls. The hunger which now drilled at his insides was the same as that of many years ago. This cheered him. He no longer felt like a man on the threshold of middle- or old-age who finds consolation in an absence of needs, but like a youth with strong needs and a desire to satisfy them.

He tugged at the doorbell. Nobody came. He tugged once more with such force that the cord almost snapped. A window opened above the café and an elderly man in a nightshirt and with a black net over his walrus moustache peered out.

"Hey there, why the hammering?" he shouted. "Can't you see we're closed? Is your head still swimming in beer?"

"This is for you" — Mock held up a twenty-mark note — "for the best New Year's breakfast!"

"Just coming, good sir," the man in the nightgown said politely.

A moment later, Mock was sitting in the dining-room as Heinrich Polkert, the manager, having first hung up his customer's coat and top hat, took down his hearty order. The guest was first served coffee in a pot and cream in a milk jug. After a few sips he felt his muscles grow taut and the sand beneath his eyelids dissolve. He undid his bowtie, removed his plastron and collar, then unfastened three shirt buttons. Dishes appeared on the table: first to arrive were slightly stale rolls and a ball of butter decorated with parsley, then scrambled eggs arranged evenly over thick slices of fried bacon. A small vegetable platter appeared with marinated herrings, horseradish and pickled cucumbers, followed by two long serving plates: on the first were rolled ham and tiered little balls of liver pâté and parsley, and on the second, a pyramid of hot Polish sausages and

21

dried *Knackwurst*. Mock was a virtuoso of taste. Methodically he spread a roll with butter and liver pâté then arranged slices of ham on top. He bit off a little of this sandwich, then filled his mouth with scrambled egg, bacon and a piece of Polish sausage or *Knackwurst*. The next bite was of herring, horseradish and cucumber. And so on. In turn. In military order imposed by this pedantic gourmand.

Mr Polkert held out a bottle of rye vodka and a glass; his eyebrows shot up. Mock nodded, devoured the last morsels of this satiating breakfast and a moment later a tall glass stood in front of him. The sharp, burning liquid turned to velvet in his stomach. Mock pointed to his glass, which was immediately refilled. He emptied it once more, sighed and loosened a button on his trousers. From his pocket he extracted a golden case full of Muratti cigarettes, lit one and blissfully blew a cloud of smoke towards the ceiling.

He should have gone home then and fallen asleep next to his wife, but something kept him in the café where he was the only guest. He felt a slight stomach ache which, at any other time, he would have taken to mean that he had eaten his fill, but on that day, that New Year's morning, it seemed to him like an undefined stimulus. He recalled his student days when, after eating dinner in the dining-room, he would rush off to a Latin seminar with the young yet strict professor Norden, during which he would passionately and joyfully parse Plautus' verses. The modest meals had not induced sleepiness in those days, but inexhaustible energy. "I used to take Plautus' poems apart, and now? What am I supposed to do now?" He looked at his table still laden with food. On the edge of a plate lay a bitten slice of dry sausage. The association was immediate. "I bit on *Knackwurst*, the beast bit on the girl's face. I chewed herrings and he chewed skin from her cheek. I drank vodka, he – blood." Mock got up abruptly, scraping his chair across the floor.

"Pack up the rest of the breakfast for me, please," he said, laying a banknote on the table. "Oh, and add about three bottles of Engelhardt!"

"Yes, sir," said Mr Polkert. He ran out to the back and fetched two cake boxes which he quickly filled.

Mock set his attire to rights and stubbed out his cigarette in the ashtray.

"Do you know what, one doesn't need a bucket of icy water to spring into action," he said, taking the boxes and bottles from Polkert. "A good breakfast's enough, and two glasses of rye vodka."

"A blessed and healthy New Year to you, sir, and to your whole family," the owner of the café replied, guessing that his guest had drunk one glass too many.

BRESLAU, THAT SAME JANUARY 1ST, 1937
A QUARTER TO SEVEN IN THE MORNING

The receptionist at the Warsaw Court Hotel, Max Wallasch, was not pleased when the doorbell rang shrilly, tearing him from his sleep. Even less so when for the second time that day he saw the square build of the man with the thick dark hair and a considerable stomach. He still felt the pain in his tail bone where the tip of the dandy's shoe had landed two hours earlier. The dandy's face was not hard now, however, which reassured the receptionist a little. The man hung his coat and top hat on the same rack as before, pulled three bottles of Engelhardt's Brewery beer from his coat pocket, sat down heavily at a table covered in leaflets advertising brothels, and waved to Wallasch.

"Sit down, man," he said and ran his arm over the table like a snowplough, pushing all the leaflets to the floor. "Sit down and have something good to eat. There's nothing better for a hangover than good food."

Wallasch watched in disbelief as the man who had earlier been addressed as Captain opened two cake boxes from which wafted the smell of sausages and bacon. He did not quite know how to behave. The hiss of beer being opened finally convinced him. He sat down at the table and took the bottle from the captain. The frothy liquid was like medicine.

"Eat, man." The captain pushed the two boxes towards him. "Haven't you got a spoon around here?"

Wallasch fetched a spoon from his enclosed lobby and began to eat. The captain watched him with a smile. Wallasch ate everything in a flash, drank the beer, sat back in his chair and belched loudly.

"The stomach approved, eh?" The captain burst out laughing and all of a sudden his laughter set. "And now I'll tell you something. A Latin proverb – *Primum edere, deinde philosophare*. You know what that means? First eat, then philosophize. You've just eaten, so now we're going to philosophize. You're going to tell me everything, right?"

"But what, sir?" Wallasch felt the pain in his tail bone again. "What am I supposed to tell you? I've already told you everything . . ."

"But not to me." The captain tipped back on his chair, which squeaked dangerously. "To others but not to me. So go on, man! From the beginning, everything! From the moment you first saw the girl Anna." He held out a cigarette. "Smoke?"

"Yes, thank you." A moment later Wallasch was inhaling deeply. "This is what happened . . . Last night, it must have been about ten, the little one came in with a damn huge suitcase. She could barely drag it along. She was tired, could barely talk. She took a room for two days under the name of Anna."

"That didn't surprise you? First name only?"

"There's not much surprises me here, sir. I ask for a name so I know what to put in the register. Someone gives me their first name? Fine. So I add a surname. And that's what's in the register: both first and second names. The owner, Mr Nablitzke, demands it. And nothing surprises him either."

"So what surname did you give her?"

"What else?" Wallasch grinned broadly. "Schmidt! That's what I gave her."

"Fine." The captain opened more two beers and pushed one in front of Wallasch's nose. "You say she was tired, dragging a heavy suitcase . . . Fine . . . But if she was tired dragging it the few metres from the door to your desk she couldn't have dragged it before, down the road, otherwise she'd have collapsed on her face from exhaustion, right?"

"Of course that's right! She came by cab! As soon as she walked in the mare clattered away along the cobbles and the cabby left."

"The cabby went off." Mock mused.

"Yes, he left. I even asked why he didn't help her with the chest . . . But she said it was none of my business."

"She spoke German?"

"Only that much. 'None of your business.' Only that much. She didn't understand anything and just gawped goggle-eyed."

"Goggle-eyed, you say." The captain's face changed and he stood up abruptly. "Goggle-eyed like she did when she was dead, or a bit different? And her swollen tongue hung from her mouth, too, eh? Well, go on, you son-of-a-whore, how did she gawp at you with those goggle-eyes? And was there a blue mark on her neck when you stared at her little tits?"

Wallasch pushed back in his chair and at that moment felt his cheek burn. He tumbled to the floor, waving his arms helplessly. The captain leaned over him. The receptionist caught the smell of beer and tobacco.

"You know why you got it in the gob? Lack of respect. You should have helped that poor girl carry her luggage."

Wallasch did not get up but cowered, watching his assailant. The latter walked up to his coat, pulled out a visiting card from one of the pockets, picked up the telephone receiver and dialled.

"Seuffert? Mock here . . . So what if you're asleep!" he said in a raised voice. "I've got a task for you! Get as many men as necessary and question all the droschka and cab drivers. I know there's going to be a thousand of them! You've got a couple of days in which to do it! Find the one who took a girl speaking very little German from the station to the Warsaw Court Hotel on Antonienstrasse at about ten o'clock. I know all the cabbies in Breslau were working on New Year's Eve! So question them all, even if there're two thousand of them! Just do it!"

Wallasch still lay on the floor. As Mock passed him, the receptionist heard his assailant burst out laughing and say to himself:

"Fucking Gestapo! Get to work, you scum!"

BRESLAU, SUNDAY, JANUARY 10TH, 1937
A QUARTER TO EIGHT IN THE EVENING

Mock was not too keen on Pastor Berthold Krebs who, at Karen's invitation, paid them a visit more or less once a month. The pastor was a preacher through and through, and not only from the pulpit of St Paul's Protestant Church but, what was worse, also when drinking herbal tea and eating cinnamon buns. Karen, who was an Evangelist unlike the Catholic Eberhard, would return from morning service at the distant church in a state of elation and describe to her husband in detail all the messages and rhetorical tricks bandied about by Pastor Krebs without restraint. These exaltations and raptures, and especially the information that the pastor was still unmarried, aroused Mock's interest in Krebs in two ways. Firstly, he checked the pastor's police file; secondly, he forced himself to get up early one morning and surreptitiously visit St Paul's Church in order to take a look at the priest. The first exercise brought no results since there was no police file with the pastor's details; the second, on the other hand, proved fundamentally important. When he saw the small, thin man who was desperately trying to paste what remained of his

26

dyed hair to his bald pate, his jealousy vanished without a trace and his wife obtained Mock's agreement to invite the pastor home, something she had been requesting in vain for some time.

And that had been Mock's mistake, because with Pastor Krebs' first visit he found himself gripped by powerlessness. He did not know how to behave when the guest devoutly entered their living-room, sat himself down in the armchair, lay the Bible on his closed knees and began to thunder in a loud, resonant voice. What mattered was that the priest strongly criticized everything that Mock considered normal and legitimate. The consumption of alcohol and meat Pastor Krebs saw as a straight path to the degeneration of body and mind, smoking tobacco and drinking coffee as self-destruction, and the practice of sport as meeting bodily temptation halfway. A praiseworthy exception was made by the preacher for sweet delicacies, the eating of which he justified with a sentence from the Book of Deuteronomy. Bombarded with criticism which he took as a personal attack, Mock could no longer stand being in his own home. When he lit a cigar, he felt like a criminal; when he sipped coffee, he felt a degenerate. So he held back from any discussions and answered in monosyllables, for which his wife later reproached him, calling it an ostentatious demonstration of ill-will towards such a wise man. He was in a spot because he did not want to hurt Karen's feelings as she blossomed spiritually in the pastor's shade, yet he could not do what he most wanted to do, namely to crudely and definitively break off Kreb's moralizing arguments and ask him to leave. He therefore sat with his weak tea and no tobacco and picked at a cake with his fork, counting the hairs pasted down on the pastor's bald pate and the quarter-hours chimed by the grandfather clock.

Now the beautiful handicraft of the Black Forest master craftsmen in Kieninger struck three times, announcing that in exactly a quarter of an hour, "infallibility personified" would stride into their parlour. Martha

Goczoll arranged the pastry plates and a pot of tea on the table. Karen looked at Eberhard with a smile and turned up the radio which was transmitting Viennese waltzes. At that moment the telephone rang.

"Maybe it's Pastor Krebs," said Eberhard. "Maybe he wants to call off his visit because he has to dye his roots?"

"Oh, Ebi, your ill-will towards the pastor bores me." Karen could not help smiling.

Eberhard went out into the hall, sat down by the phone and lifted the receiver to his ear.

"Good evening, Captain. This is Criminal Secretary Seuffert."

"Good evening," he muttered into the speaking tube. "No doubt ringing to say you haven't managed to complete your task, are you?"

"Not quite, Captain. I'm reporting that we've questioned seven hundred and forty-two cabbies and three hundred and fifty droschka drivers. None of them took any girl from any station whatsoever on New Year's Eve . . ."

"What do I need the numbers for, Seuffert?" asked Mock, lighting up his last cigarette before the arrival of their special guest. "I want to know whether you've asked *all* the droschka drivers and cabbies in our beautiful city if they took Anna to the Warsaw Court! *All*, and not how many!"

"I'm trying to be precise," retorted Seuffert, offended by Mock's tone. "Because I've heard that what you appreciate most is exactitude . . . All the cabbies and nearly all the droschka drivers. We've got two left, drivers 36 and 84. Both often park themselves outside Main Station. I haven't had time to question them yet. But I'll do that tomorrow . . . I've got their addresses from the cabby register."

"No need, Seuffert," said Mock sweetly, and hearing that Karen was listening to the radio quickly added: "I'll take care of it. After all, you've done a good piece of work. Over a thousand men in a week! Ha, ha, not bad, Seuffert, not bad . . ."

"I'll just give you the addresses . . ."

Mock hung up without another word, replaced the speaking tube and began to put on his coat and bowler hat as quickly as if someone spurred him on. He stepped into the parlour and kissed his wife. He registered disappointment in her eyes.

"I have to, pet, I have to," he interrupted all protest. "Such is the job, unfortunately . . ."

He bowed most gallantly to Pastor Krebs, who was just mounting the stairs.

BRESLAU, SUNDAY, JANUARY 10TH, 1937
HALF PAST EIGHT IN THE EVENING

Mock nosed his black Adler into the parking bay outside Main Station and turned off the engine. He lit a cigarette and observed the three droschkas standing in front of the huge building. None of them were numbered 36 or 84. He climbed out of his car, pulled on his coat and bowler, then, hands behind his back, made slowly towards the main entrance. As he had thought, the cold had swept all the beggars and newspaper vendors from the approach. Only two women with painted lips were walking up and down outside. Mock stopped in front of them and measured them with his eye. As if on command, both unbuttoned their coats and rested their hands on their hips. One was tall and thin, the other short and curvaceous. He looked at them carefully and decided to help the one which seemed more desirable – meaning the more curvaceous one – to earn some money. He nodded to her and she approached with a dancing step. He looked at her lips, blue with cold, and pulled out two two-mark coins.

"What's your name?"

"Bibi."

"Fine. So now I know you. And do you know me? You know who I am?"

"A dandy like you must be some director . . ." She smiled broadly.

"I'm a police officer," he replied. "Once, when I was young, I dealt with girls like you."

"Oh, sorry." The smile froze on the prostitute's lips.

"Don't apologize, because you haven't got anything to apologize for yet." Mock spat out his cigarette and with the tip of his shoe crushed the butt as fastidiously as if he had wanted to grind it into the pavement. "I'm telling you so that you know you can't fool me. Understood, Bibi?"

The girl nodded without a word.

"You're cold. Want some supper?" He showed her the coins. "Then I'll give you some money to buy supper. Two marks now. You stay here for the time being and keep your eyes wide open. If droschkas 36 or 84 roll up, I repeat 36 or 84, you're immediately to run to the restaurant, buffet or cards club – I don't know where I'm going to be yet – and let me know. Then you'll get another two marks. And you're not going to make an ass of me. Right, Bibi?"

"And what happens" – she looked at him cheekily – "if a client comes along and cab 36 doesn't turn up?"

"My loss." Mock patted her on the cheek. "But then I'll come here again sometime and say hello. I'll go to play cards or have a beer and you'll have to carry on looking out for cabs 36 or 84. You've taken the deposit, you have to follow it through. *Adieu!*"

He made towards the station concourse and was looking around for a newspaper vendor when he heard the brisk clatter of shoes.

"Commissioner," he heard Bibi's voice. "Number 36 has just arrived. So, am I going to get the rest?"

"I'm a man of honour." He handed her a coin. "Don't use it to buy cigarillos or vodka because your pimp will take it from you anyway. Eat a good supper tonight and drink one schnapps to warm yourself up, but remember: only one!"

"And chocolate for the kid? Is that alright?" she asked and, without waiting for a reply, she clattered away down the concourse.

BRESLAU, SUNDAY, JANUARY 10TH, 1937
A QUARTER TO NINE IN THE EVENING

Mock knew that nothing oppresses the interrogated as much as the sudden proximity of the interrogator. The cabby was not, in fact, suspected of anything, but the transgression of a person's invisible boundaries was already in Mock's blood. He walked up to droschka 36, jumped onto the box next to the driver and scrutinized him from a distance of ten centimetres. The fat cabby moved away a little but they were both still crushed. This, however, did not bother Mock in the slightest.

"Name?" he asked, shoving his identification card under the cabby's nose.

"Pohler, Heinrich," answered the driver, looking at Mock carefully. "You've probably . . ."

"Tell me, Mr Pohler," – Mock felt sure he was about to hear a negative reply, and would then be able to nip off for a game of skat or bridge – "did you take anyone from here, from the station, to the Warsaw Court Hotel on New Year's Eve?"

"Yes," replied the driver. "Two young women. Foreigners."

Mock moved away from Pohler and climbed down from the box. He sat inside the droschka and fixed his eyes on the driver, mechanically pulling on his gloves.

"What time was that?"

"About ten at night."

"What makes you think they were foreigners?"

"They spoke to each other in a whisper but I heard some of the sounds."

"And how would you describe the language?"

"*Slonsakisch*," answered the driver without hesitation. "They were speaking Silesian."

"Tell me everything as it happened from the moment they got into your droschka. And describe them."

"Well, they got in." Pohler fixed his eyes on Mock anxiously. "They were young. Pretty? Both pretty. One was older, looked like twenty something – she had those sort of looks . . . Dark . . . Turkish . . . The other was younger, seventeen, maybe eighteen . . . Blonde. The older one showed me a card with the Warsaw Court Hotel on it. We drove there. The younger one got off at the hotel and the older one gave me another card with the word Morgenzeile on it and some number I don't remember. And we left. On Morgenzeile, in front of some residence, she said 'stop'. She rang at the gate. The villa was dark. Only dogs barking behind the fence. After a while a butler arrived and paid for my whole run. That's all."

"What do you mean by 'Turkish' looks?"

"I don't know . . . Dark, sallow, black hair, black-eyed."

The adjective "black-eyed" made Mock think. Rarely used, untypical, literary, stylized. He looked at Pohler. A refined word for a cabby.

"Fine, but something still bothers me. Why didn't you help the younger one carry her suitcase into the hotel? Apparently it was very heavy."

"Because the other one took it. She tore it away and carried it to the door in a flash. Then she jumped into the cab and we left for Morgenzeile. That's all."

Mock lit a cigarette and lost himself in thought. Two young women speaking Silesian, if the cabby's ear could be trusted. One went to a shabby hotel which in truth acted as a cover for a brothel. The other dragged the suitcase from the droschka for her and carried it to the door. Why did Anna need a French typewriter? What was a virgin doing in a brothel anyway? Maybe this really was a case of espionage? Maybe that Hitlerite Kraus was right? And then some thin crook with strong teeth climbed in through the window, raped, murdered and gnawed Anna, although we don't know — as Lasarius put it — whether he did all this in that order. Meanwhile, the other woman ended up in one of the most prestigious areas of Breslau.

Mock roused himself from his musing under driver Pohler's watchful eye.

"I thought you'd fallen asleep, sir," said the cabby with a smile.

"Why aren't we on our way there yet?" Mock looked sharply at Pohler.

"To where, sir?"

"Morgenzeile!"

"Right away!" Pohler raised his whip.

"Wait, wait!" Mock grabbed the whip handle. "The matter's very urgent. We're taking my car!"

He rolled out of the cab so suddenly that the vehicle shook, and then walked briskly to the Adler. Pohler watched Mock in astonishment, his whip still held high.

"Well, come on, come on!" shouted the captain.

"And what am I supposed to do with my cab?" the droschka driver shouted back. "Someone might steal my horse!"

Mock looked around and spotted Bibi smiling at him from the main entrance to the station.

"Hey, Bibi, come here!" he ordered in a loud voice. "Keep an eye on this cab for two marks! And if something goes missing you'll have me to deal with!"

"Alright, just coming, my lovely," Bibi laughed, daintily skipping up to Mock. "And for a tenner I can blow your balloon."

Pohler looked aghast at Bibi, who was supposed to look after his place of work. She smiled, and her alcoholic breath wafted over Mock. It was clear that that evening the girl's child was not going to be eating chocolate.

BRESLAU, SUNDAY, JANUARY 10TH, 1937
A QUARTER PAST NINE IN THE EVENING

The windows of the vast villa on Morgenzeile gave on to the bare trees of Scheitniger Park, their dark panes reflecting the feeble light of street lanterns. Behind railings spiked like flames thrashed two massive dogs of a breed unknown to Mock. Keeping his finger pressed to the bell at the entrance gate, the captain watched the dogs; he was sure he had seen the breed before, but could not remember where. Standing next to Mock, Pohler kept glancing at the two beasts in fear.

A light came on over the villa driveway, where a butler appeared marching stiffly and bearing a large, hanging torch. As he reached the fence and cast light on Mock, the latter imagined the servant's tailcoat bursting under the strain of all that muscle.

"Yes, sir? How can I help you?" said the butler slowly as the glow of the torch settled on his close-cropped hair.

"Is that him?" Mock asked Pohler, indicating the man with his head.

When he saw the cabby nod Mock quickly reached into his inner coat pocket for identification. The movement caused the butler to automatically go for his own pocket and the dogs to leap at the fence, covering it with slobber.

"Get those monsters away, you lackey!" roared Mock, showing his identification. "And then open this manor! I'm Captain Eberhard Mock!"

The butler only obeyed Mock's first order. He whistled at the dogs and they lowered themselves onto their bellies, growling quietly. Their tamer walked up to the fence, leaned against the railings and fixed his eyes on Mock. Cold, scrutinizing eyes.

"This is the residence of Baron Bernhard von Criegern," he said quietly. "The baron and baroness have been at their villa, Villa Clementina, in Schreiberhau for a week now and I do the honours here. I don't want to offend you, Captain, but in order to enter in the absence of the baron and baroness you need a higher rank."

"Well, look at that, Pohler," – Mock turned to his companion – "how nicely he puts it! A true orator!"

The captain's head felt like a vacuum. Usually, in similar situations, he reacted with fury and decision. He either threatened, blackmailed or beat people. But here he could do none of these things and the results of a possible fight would be foregone in favour of the strongman with the crew cut. He spat on the ground profusely. He hated being unprepared for a talk.

"Then I won't go in," he riposted. "We'll talk here. Besides, I haven't come to see the baron and his wife, but you. Would you care to open, Mr . . ."

"And him, he's a police officer, too, is he?" The butler glanced disdainfully at Pohler's old coat. "I'm to let him in too, am I?"

"Yes." Mock did not understand why he said this. "He's a police officer, Sergeant Pohler, my associate."

"Well I'm Bruno Gorsegner and I'm very sorry," Cerberus replied and waved his hand as if he were chasing a fly from his face, "but according to Baron von Criegern's instructions nobody apart from servants, family and authorized persons are allowed on villa territory. And you, Captain, sir and Sergeant," – he smiled faintly – "do not belong to any of the above categories. You are not, after all, either a police officer, prosecutor or even bailiff, but only a high-ranking officer of the Abwehr. If I were to let you in I could just as easily make the land accessible to, for example, a high-ranking quartermaster officer. But I'm going to be polite and ask you once more: can I be of any assistance to you in a situation where a fence stands between us?"

For the first time since he had met Criminal Secretary Seuffert, Mock regretted that the man from the Gestapo was not with him. The eloquent lackey would have been as obedient towards the Gestapo as were those growling beasts. At that moment it occurred to Mock where he had seen such dogs before. They had been tearing rats apart at a riding stables near a horseracing track when, along with some other men, he had been betting on which dog would gnaw the most rats to death. He cast aside the gory memories.

"You can help me, Mr Gorsegner," he said. "Even through the fence. Have you ever seen this here Sergeant Pohler before?"

"No, never," the butler hastily replied.

"That's not true!" shouted Pohler. "You paid me for that woman's ride, the one I brought here in the evening!"

"I've never seen you, sir," answered Gorsegner. "And I won't have you addressing me with such familiarity. The day before yesterday I was here and nobody troubled me or rang at the gate. Nor did I pay any droschka driver for any ride."

"Mr Gorsegner," snarled Mock, "are you saying my man is lying?"

"I'm not saying anything, Captain." – Gorsegner laughed merrily – "I'm just stating that I did not see this man or any woman he apparently brought here. Either on Thursday, or any time before or after . . ." He slapped himself across the arms. "I'm very sorry, gentlemen, but it's getting rather cold and I'm not dressed as warmly as you are . . . Do you have any other questions, Captain? I'm willing to answer."

"No." Mock glared furiously at Pohler, who cowered in fright. "Thank you, Mr Gorsegner. Good night."

"Good night, gentlemen," answered the butler and briskly made his way towards the mansion.

The dogs, bereft of their master, howled and barked as Mock walked away dragging Pohler by the collar. As they neared the car, the captain took a swing like a discus thrower and spun the cabby who collapsed onto the Adler's bonnet.

"Perhaps you can explain that, Pohler?" Mock removed his bowler hat and wiped his brow. "Who's lying, him or you? Are you going to explain or are we going to the Gestapo?"

The terrified droschka driver took off his cap and smoothed his hair. He lowered his head and looked at Mock beseechingly, squeezing and wringing the cap in his hands. He reminded Mock of his own father, a poor cobbler from Waldenburg who had once been summoned by the headmaster of Eberhard's secondary school. The headmaster had yelled and threatened Willibald Mock, saying that his son Eberhard, the school-boy present there, had turned out to be a disgrace to such an excellent institution of learning because he had been caught by the secret police in a house of ill-repute along with two other pupils. The shamed cobbler, dressed in his Sunday best, had stood in front of the fuming headmaster cap in hand, just like Pohler now.

"But you know I wouldn't lie to you, sir," said the cabby through his tears. "Do you really not recognize me, Captain? I know it was many years ago and I was much slimmer and had thicker hair. I was a helper at the theatre . . ."

"Well, I think I do," replied Mock. He flashed through his memory but could not find Pohler's face there, let alone associate it with any theatre. "And so what if I recognize you?" He was furious again. "Even if I do, how am I to know you're not lying?"

"That woman was a misfit," whispered Pohler.

"Meaning what?" Mock put on his bowler and leaned over the cabby. "Whisper in my ear!"

"A misfit, dressed up," replied Pohler a little more loudly. "I drove him to that butler. He's a misfit, too, a queer. Hides it . . . You know what it's like now . . . The Gestapo, concentration camp . . . It's not the golden twenties."

"And how do you know that woman was a man in a dress? Because what? Because she carried the suitcase herself? How do you know that butler's a queer?" Mock felt as excited as a dog following a scent.

"I know them. I recognize them all . . . But you know, you know me . . . In those days many years ago, you were a criminal assistant, not a captain like now . . . You treated me like a human being."

Mock lost himself in thought, gazing into the darkness of Scheitniger Park. Wind stirred the bare branches. Somewhere beneath those trees stood a public convenience where perverts met . . . The captain suddenly remembered a certain operation in which he had taken part. But when in the hell was he going to remember where he knew Pohler from? He sighed. As a matter of fact he did not really want to know. He did not want to listen to another trivial, painful and entirely predictable story. He just wanted to go home, where Pastor Krebs would definitely no longer be, and sit down at his desk with a glass of cognac to gather his thoughts. Later, far into the night, he would spread out his chessboard and recall the different variants of closed games, which he liked most of all.

"Alright, I believe you, Pohler," he muttered. "Get in or Bibi might catch a client and what'll happen to your cab then?"

He fired up the motor. Pohler did not dare sit next to Mock and curled up with cold in the back seat. The captain was cold, too. Passing the park, Fürstenbrücke and the Church of St Peter Canisius which could be seen beyond the naked trees, he glanced into the large windows of art nouveau tenements where lights were already going out. When home, he would first sit down by the stove and spend a long time warming himself. Next, he would eat a late supper. Liver and onion. And then he would pour himself a glass of cognac.

He skidded a little on Kaiserbrücke but that was the only unpleasant surprise on the snow-covered roads, where night carts with sand were only now appearing here and there. He side-slipped a second time by the station, but the skid was intentional. The manoeuvre caught the attention of one lone sleepy cabby and Bibi, who was sitting on the box of the droschka with a man.

Mock turned to Pohler.

"Goodnight, Pohler!"

"Goodnight, Captain, sir." The cabby grasped the door handle but a few seconds later let it go. "I know you don't remember me, sir. You were pretty tipsy at the time. I want to thank you, Captain."

"But you've already thanked me!" replied Mock in a tired voice. "For treating you like a human being. You've already said that . . . Go on or Bibi's going to turn your cab into a bordello!"

"Not for that, Captain," Pohler went on as if he had not heard Mock's words. "Not for that but for not now going on about where you're supposed to know me from, how we met and so on . . . You knew that talking about it would be torture for me. That I've got a wife and children. That's what I'm thanking you for."

Mock laughed and held out his hand to Pohler.

"Good luck in the New Year!"

"Thanks, and the same to you, Captain!" The cab driver squeezed Mock's hand firmly.

"But don't think, Pohler," he added with a smile, "that I'm as considerate as I appear. I didn't ask you because all those grubby stories bore me now. The private history of this city's inhabitants is a history of sin and shame. My head is so full of such goings-on there's no room for any more. God be with you, Pohler, and go on sinning, but do so on the quiet and don't catch the eye of any Gestapo."

"You treated me like a human being today, too. You even told that gate-keeper that I work for you. And let me tell you — I can work for you if you want. There's always a lot going on here by the station and my eyes are wide open. But only for you."

"Listen then, Heinrich," said Mock after a moment's thought, as he handed Pohler his business card. "If any sort of pervert appears on Morgenzeile, let me know, alright? Regardless of whether he talks Silesian or Apache, understood?"

"Of course." Pohler opened the car door. "Good night, Captain!"

"Good night, Heinrich."

Mock laughed even louder. And once again his joyful voice echoed in the car. Despite everything, today had been his lucky day. First, he had managed to avoid Pastor Krebs, then he had found a new informant. Not bad for one evening! To hell with some impudent lackey! A good spirit, Eudaemon, had prompted him to do two things: firstly, to tell the butler Gorsegner that Pohler "worked" for him, and secondly to refrain from uttering a certain sentence when the cabby kept testing whether Mock recognized him. He refrained from making a certain comparison out loud, and thanks to that reticence had gained a new and valuable informant. Had he spoken out loud he would most certainly have lost Pohler's good-will. The maxim was to have been: "Why are you so surprised that I don't recognize you? Do you think it's easy to distinguish one piece of shit in a dunghill from another?"

BRESLAU, SUNDAY, JANUARY 10TH, 1937
HALF PAST TEN AT NIGHT

Mock did not go home, even though Pastor Kreb's visit must certainly have come to an end. Sitting in the car, he mindlessly watched a group of youths carrying skis and backpacks, a drunken Bibi bantering with Pohler, and a sausage vendor who kept opening his cauldron to entice travellers with its appetizing smell while he warmed himself over its hot steam. Mock knew that these moments of vacuous gawping would presently set a chain of images in motion. It was not original ideas or some revelatory solution he had in mind; no – his ambitions were, at that moment, considerably more modest. He simply wanted to catch hold of a thought which had come to him as Pohler was about to get out of the car, and which had been stifled by the cabby's prolonged expressions of gratitude. Two officers in black coats and visor hats caught his eye as they approached the station. He slapped his brow. He could not explain why precisely this sight had recalled the other thought.

He climbed out of the car and made towards the station, paying no attention to the smiling Bibi, her thin colleague or the sausage vendor. Casting his eyes around the concourse enclosed by a hemispherical vault, he saw his objective – a pole from which hung timetables of stiff, varnished cardboard attached lengthwise to a moveable ring. He approached the boards and began to flick through them. The noise as they thwacked against each other aroused the curiosity of a man whose foolish smile and bloodshot eyes showed he had not yet stopped celebrating the New Year. Mock found the relevant board of afternoon and evening train arrivals at Breslau's Main Station. His gaze quickly fell on the underscored itineraries of trains coming from abroad. Only one train pulled into Breslau just before ten in the evening, round about the time cabby Pohler had picked up his two mysterious passengers – an express which arrived every other day at half past nine. Mock took out his notebook bound with a rubber band and, on a ruled page, carefully noted all the information concerning the train. Ignoring the drunkard who clearly wanted to borrow some money for a beer, he approached another pole marked DEPAR-TURES. After a long search he found the number of the express train he was looking for. It departed every other day in the early hours of the morning. Mock jotted down all the intermediate stations, underscored one and wrote "border" next to it. Remembering his momentary intellectual

41

blackout in the car, he added *expressis verbis* what he was to do the following day: "Phone the border crossing in Morgenroth."

As he left the station he saw Pohler whipping his horse. He waved, but the latter must not have noticed him. "Ah well," thought Mock, amused, "it is not every day a cabby has the chance to drive Hitler's praetorians."

Sprawled out nonchalantly in the cab, cigarettes in hand, sat the two SS-men who a few minutes earlier had walked past Mock's car.

LWÓW, MONDAY, JANUARY 11TH, 1937
SEVEN O'CLOCK IN THE EVENING

Few of Lwów's decent, moral inhabitants knew that in the heart of the city, among the beautiful old tenements not far from Rynek, almost beneath the dome of the Dominican church, was a place which had little in common with high morals. The Sea Grotto tavern was located in the inner courtyard of the splendid tenement at Dominikańska 4. A visit to this temple involved two quite different hazards. The first of these – the danger of spraining if not breaking a leg – lurked in the unlit gateway leading to the minuscule yard. The second danger was the den's drunken regulars. With alcohol running through their blood, they either declared their love to the whole world, or attacked their neighbour. Furthermore, the drunken rogues were quick to reach into their pockets for flick-knives or razors.

Commissioner Popielski was neither a decent nor a moral citizen. He knew the rogues well and always carried a torch with him when he went to the den, not to mention a Browning revolver in his pocket. Today, however, he had forgotten both and consequently felt quite insecure. He kept close to the wall as he struggled to see anything at all in the feeble flickering of a lantern hanging in the yard over the dive. He walked slowly, step by step, feeling for the slippery surface with his feet, and anxiously glanced at his left arm which he still could not straighten having broken it very badly at the elbow two years earlier. He was far less worried by the fact that he had no weapon; he knew his presence in one of the worst drinking-dens would immediately be known to all the ruffians east of Halicki Square, that is, in Łyczaków. Unfailing word of mouth operated here and the characteristic figure of the bald Commissioner in his bowler hat and white scarf was known to every child. During his sixteen years in the Criminal Police he had often seriously incurred the anger of Łyczaków's daredevils, but no Lwów bandit in his right mind would risk an attempt on the commissioner's life.

Popielski passed through the treacherous gate without slipping, but did not manage to avoid a quite different hazard. As soon as he found himself in the yard he felt his polished Salamander brogue, his beautifully stitched, aerated shoe which had cost fifty złotys, sink into a soft, sticky substance.

"Damn it!" he yelled. He wiped the sole against the cobbles in disgust and cursed his tendency to dress like a dandy. "If I had worn thick winter shoes and not these elegant brogues," he thought, "there'd have been no problem."

He scraped the sole of his shoe for several metres over the cobblestones until he found himself beneath the only lantern in the yard, which feebly illuminated the entrance to the cellar which housed the drinking-den. Popielski lifted his foot and studied his shoe. The sole was relatively clean whereas the sides were wet and soiled with brown gunge. He knew perfectly well what he had stepped into. The inhabitants of this tenement frequently complained to the police about excrement left in the yard by den regulars. He looked around. The only thing to wipe his shoe on was the rough wall, but this could mean scuffing the elegant leather of the uppers. Popielski opened the door to the tavern. A shaft of light fell from the interior into the yard. An old cabbage sack lay on a beer crate. Although it too was rough, it did not risk ruining the leather, and Popielski could find nothing better. As he cleaned his shoe, he gazed at the clouds of smoke wafting up from the dive. Slowly he descended the steep stairs and found himself three metres below the surface of Lwów's pavements. With each step the Sea Grotto grew increasingly silent. He stood at the threshold, removed his bowler hat and for a moment relished the silence which had descended and the heat which radiated from the stove. Here and there he heard a hiss. He knew the thieves and bandits were quietly repeating his nickname: Hairless-s-s.

He walked unhurriedly through the centre of the tavern and surveyed what he knew so well: dirty fingernails rapping the table; eyes looking askance from beneath cloth caps; gnarled fingers holding lit roll-ups of the vilest tobacco; greasy, plastered-down hair. He picked up the smell of steaming greatcoats, unwashed shirts and sodden felt boots. He did not study the faces; he knew the bandits sought by the police – warned by word of mouth – had long since scampered to their hovels. He approached a table where three men were sitting. All had their elbows and forearms on the table and did not take their eyes off Popielski. An accordion player began a lively melody and sang:

> *On Kołłątay Street*
> *Fayduli, fayduli, fay,*
> *An old hag a policem'n beat,*
> *Fayduli, fayduli, fay,*
> *Punch his gob, and kick his balls,*
> *Fayduli, fayduli, fay,*
> *Down the old policem'n falls,*
> *Fayduli, fayduli, fay.*

Popielski applauded the accordionist for a few moments, and although his applause was unduly loud, the musician did not show the least gratitude. The police officer hung his overcoat on the back of a vacant chair at the table of the three men, adjusted his black jacket and bowtie and sat down without removing his bowler hat. He rested his arms on the table like the others, then suddenly extended them to both sides, knocking two of the men's elbows off the table. The men pushed their chairs back, ready for a fight. The third, sitting opposite Popielski, motioned to them to remain calm.

"Don't you know the rules of good manners, boys?" asked Popielski, noticing with horror that he had stained the sleeve of his suit in a pool of liquid on the table. "You don't sprawl your weight around like that!" He breathed a sigh of relief when he saw the remains of some vodka in front of the men – a drink which "did not stain uniform or honour" as his deceased uncle, an officer in the Austrian army, was wont to say.

"Calm down, you idiots" said the man sitting opposite the Commissioner. "He's only playing at being fancy! Such a fancy man!"

"Over here, old chap!" Popielski was now in a better mood and clicked his fingers loudly. "Here, old chap! A pork cutlet, some cucumbers and a quarter bottle of vodka! But don't spit under the cutlet" – he laughed, slamming the table – "because I'm going to be eating with these here citizens!"

"We're not hungry," replied the man sitting to Popielski's right.

"Keep it down, damn it," Popielski hissed at him and grabbed him tightly by the arm. "You're not going to gorge on my food, but he" – with his eyes he indicated the waiter who was emerging from behind the counter – "doesn't have to know and then he won't spit into it! Hey, Gum" he said, turning to the man opposite, "calm your pals down so they don't butt in!"

The waiter, hair slicked down with pomade and wearing a stained dinner jacket and collarless shirt, approached the table and whacked it a few times with the rag which always hung over his forearm. He stood a small bottle labled Pure Monopol Vodka in front of Popielski along with a glass and a plate on which lay a roll, a cold schnitzel and four pickled cucumbers. Then he slid a stand of napkins across the table.

"Pay up front," muttered the waiter gloomily.

"Old chap!" called Popielski, handing him his bowler hat and a one-złoty coin. "And glasses for my friends?"

The waiter thanked him for the considerable tip and returned behind the counter as if he had not heard the request. He hung up Popielski's hat and began to wipe down the counter. The man whom Popielski had addressed as Gum spoke out, and his voice resonated powerfully in the silence.

"No offence, Commissioner, sir, but we don't eat with police. We're not informers. We won't eat with you. Either Walerku, or Alfonik, or me. You want something, I listen. And Walerku and Alfonik are going to listen too."

Popielski was familiar with the practice of having a witness present during informal talks between police and underground crooks. These talks always took place in a crowded tavern and the witnesses were the thickest and most hard-line of outlaws who never lied to their collaborators, and who reacted violently if accused of deception. They acted as guarantee that the crook was not a police informer, and everyone believed them.

"Very well." The Commissioner glanced at the bloated, pimply faces surrounding him. "But only these two citizens are to be witnesses." He stood up abruptly, swept his eyes across the room and yelled: "And not the entire tavern! Well? Heads down to your plates!"

A hostile murmur and hissing rumbled through the smoky atmosphere. Popielski sat down and extracted a silver watch from his waistcoat pocket. At about seven every evening his body invariably sent signals that it was time for dinner. He skewered the cutlet on his fork, examined it carefully, then bit off a large mouthful. Tavern food served only one purpose: to temper the taste of vodka. The Sea Grotto's all-in-one cook and barman, who arranged eggs in mayonnaise, cold sausage with equally cold cabbage, herrings, fried pork and pickled cucumbers on the bar counter, did not heed fashionable modern diets. No, he wanted only to make the consumption of alcohol more enjoyable, although many of his customers had not caught on and were drinking without nibbling on anything at all. The delicacies displayed beneath glass covers, and never fresh, made Popielski think of the girls who stood out on bridges; those prostitutes were no longer at their freshest, and they were rarely taken on either.

He poured himself a glass of vodka and swallowed it, helping it down with a piece of cucumber. A moment later he crunched the cutlet's thin batter between his teeth. He adored the food in sordid taverns, even if he knew that he risked an upset stomach. He spent a long time savouring the taste of the meat. Downing another glass, he looked around the room. It was noisy, but the hubbub was more muted than it had been when the commissioner had first entered. It amused him that the thieves and bandits could not broach their usual subjects now. He bit off half a cutlet and this time devoured it greedily. He wiped his mouth with a napkin, pulled out his cigarette case and lit up an "Egyptian", without offering one to his companions at the table. He knew what their response would be.

"Right, Gum, let me tell you why I've come to see you. What do you know about the assault on the old Jewish woman on Gęsia Street?" His eyes pierced the man sitting facing him. "That was not the work of an ordinary pickpocket. Someone robbed her and beat her up."

"I don't know anything about it. But I know something else . . ."

47

"Like?"

"It's gonna be sad news to you, Commissioner." Gum lit up his own shag. "It's about your daughter. She's in with some rough company."

A curious defence mechanism switched on in Edward Popielski whenever he heard that someone was about to say something bad about seventeen-year-old Rita. A scene from the mid-twenties would immediately appear before his eyes: a peaceful evening, the city quiet beneath a thick cover of snow, vespers at the Church of St Mary Magdalen near the Baworowski library. He is standing in the congregation with three-year-old Rita, pleased that the child is exceptionally calm and not running up and down the church or shouting and subjecting him to the unpleasant glances of women as old as mortal sin, as Bolesław Prus had once put it. He does not hold it against his little girl that she is not singing the Latin responses to the Mass which he has just taught her, or the carols as they had so entreated her to at Christmas Eve dinner. Despite a severe hangover resulting from his New Year's celebrations, he is happy because Rita is standing obediently, not even demanding to sit in a pew. And then "Silent Night" begins, a carol he always sang softly to Rita throughout the year as she lay in bed at night, regardless of whether it was Lent, Advent or Easter. It was the little girl's favourite song. As the organist draws out "in heavenly peace", Popielski feels the girl huddle up to him. A moment later she is in his arms, pressing her burning face to his freshly shaven cheek. She is not singing, not playing up, but kissing her father on a cheek wet with tears.

Whenever this recollection thrust itself upon him, Popielski was prepared to forgive his daughter anything, even her first poor marks at school, one of them for Latin what's more, and given by a teacher with a heart of gold who was a good friend of her father's. This moment long past, one of the most beautiful in his life, allowed him to adopt a defensive attitude; whenever he suspected someone was about to criticize Rita, he would recall the scene. It was his shield. Up until now, however, the grievances had come from teachers, tutors, the school catechist, possibly from a shopkeeper at the local delicatessen to whom Rita had made a rude remark. At such times this image from the past had power. It muted the attacks, filtered complaints, extinguished all speculations. It appeared again now, but it was blurred, distorted, foggy, barely visible. In this current recollection Rita was not kissing her father. Instead she came close to his face in order to give him a hard bite. What he heard was no ordinary complaint, of which there had been many over the last few years. This accusation came from the mouth of Felicjan Kościuk, alias Felek Dziąsło, known as "Gum", a dangerous criminal suspected of drowning his own illegitimate child in a cesspit. Popielski felt rivulets of sweat run down the smooth skin on his head and looked at the men around the table. They were smiling maliciously. They knew what Gum was going to tell him. They watched with satisfaction as Hairless wiped his head with a napkin and turned purple.

"Well, go on, Gum." Popielski pushed away the plate with the half-eaten cutlet . "Tell me everything, one thing at a time."

"I'll describe everything as if I was in a confessional." Gum looked at Walerku and Alfonek who nodded. "It was Thursday. We'd knocked them back that day and then evening came, what a hangover! And a hang-over wants more of the same, eh? Hair of the dog." He laughed, echoed by his friends. "Right, so we're off to Wacki in Zamrstynowsk. There's these three circus strongmen, you know, from the one that's come for Christmas, and two chicks, sorry, two young ladies with them. All dolled up, like. And there's this giggling, squealing and screaming behind the screen . . . Well, Alfonek, am I right?"

"The strongmen really had the chick thrilled," muttered Alfonek.

"One of those young ladies," said Gum slowly, "right there at the table and not behind the screen, was the commissioner's own daughter, like."

49

Silence fell. The crooks stared at Popielski, smiling. It seemed to him as if everyone around was raising a glass to drink the health of the degenerate seventeen-year-old Rita Popielska. He poured himself a third glass, emptying the bottle, and sipped at it. He wanted the vodka to burn him; he wanted the raw taste scratching his throat to act as a substitute for the punishment he deserved for all the sins he had committed as a father. He lit another cigarette even though the previous one had only half burned down. The tobacco was as sour as vinegar. And at that moment Popielski picked up the stench of excrement. He pushed himself away from the table, held up a candle and studied the sole of his shoe. A stinking clod was lodged behind the heel, where he had not wiped the sole properly. Shit. He carefully set down the half-empty glass, wiped the wet rings on the surface of the table with a napkin, and then lunged across the table.

He heard a faint crack and saw blood spurting from the nose and onto the plate with what was left of his meat. Alfonek and Walerku leaped away and reached for their pockets. Popielski did not even glance at them. He grabbed Gum by the hair, pressed the man's face to the table and pushed against his head with his entire weight. If the crook's nose was not damaged before, it most certainly was now. Felek did not utter a peep but lay silently on the table with blood slowly pouring around his face. He felt the commissioner's alcoholic breath in his ear.

"And now take back what you said," hissed Popielski. "Say it's not true. That my daughter wasn't there with those circus types. Say it in a complete sentence."

Despite his violent reaction, the commissioner's thoughts were now clear. He knew what would follow. He knew he would not hear anything from Felek because there was one thing he had not taken into account. Gum, a strong-willed rogue, would never withdraw what he had just said in front of his pals. Popielski could mould Gum's death mask in the table-top, yet he would not hear a retraction of the words he had spoken. It was a question of honour. On the other hand, he himself could not now leave, or he would lose whatever respect these men had for him. This, too, was a question of honour.

He grasped Felek by the collar and dragged him to the exit. The latter offered no resistance as they climbed the stairs. Popielski held him well away, so as not to soil his suit with blood. Eyes filled with hatred followed him out, but this did not surprise him. These thugs had all been humiliated by him today because they could not help their pal, who had been brutally attacked by the untouchable Hairless.

Once in the yard, Popielski grabbed Felek by the throat and pressed him against the tavern wall.

"You got drunk out of your mind on Thursday, did you?" He purposely used precise Polish grammar which the rogues disdained.

"Uh-huh," agreed Gum and sniffed.

"So much so that you slept through the entire day and did not wake up until late at night, right?"

"No," croaked the rogue. "'Wasn't night, it was evening."

"It was dark, was it not?"

"It was."

"So it could have been night? You do not have a watch and you see it is dark. So it could have been night, could it not?"

"It could."

"So it was night." Popielski's resonant voice carried in the well of the yard. "It was night and my daughter is always at home at night! At *home!*" he yelled to a woman who leaned out from a built-in balcony. He turned to Felek who was wiping his nose on the sleeve of his jacket. "Go back to the tavern and bring me my coat and hat."

When had Felek disappeared, Popielski walked over to a sack lying in the porch. Wiping his heel, he thought about the consequences of the day's events. Firstly, he was sure the crook had lied to him in order to harass him in front of everybody. Secondly, he realized that by leading Felek out he had sown a seed of doubt among the rogues. They were going to start wondering: did that chancer Felek crack out there in the yard or not? Did he bark back or not? A rift, a crack was going to appear between them, and they particularly despised representatives of the law who infringed upon the eternal solidarity of rogues.

Gum emerged and handed Popielski his coat and upturned bowler. The commissioner peered into the hat to check whether anyone had spat into this exquisite product of the Skoczów hatmakers. There was no spittle, but a pig's ear pierced with a nail. It represented a stool pigeon, but also a cop. And the meaning of the nail was unequivocal.

"Tell everyone, Felek" — he brought his face close to the swollen nose — "that I'm not frightened, but thank you for the warning. And that next time I'm going to bring a can of petrol. And burn you all out." He sniffed. "You stink. Wash more often, you slob, don't be a beast! You sleep in a pigsty or what?"

Suddenly he felt a pain in his chest and a spasm in his diaphragm, but this was not a heart attack. It was the thought of Rita sitting amongst circus strongmen, bandits and whores. "Smoking? Drinking? Did she step behind the screen? Did the stench emanating from Gum ever reach her delicate nostrils? Impossible," he thought, "after all, the thief had denied it all!" He told himself that he woke up at night and Rita had not as yet — thank the Lord! — spent a single night away from home!

He heaved a sigh of relief, donned his hat and coat and made his way across the small, dark yard followed by Gum's gaze. He even nodded as he left. He had understood the crooks' message. It was, in the end, a matter of honour.

Rita Popielska, already dressed in her pyjamas and dressing gown, was sitting at her desk in her room. The bright light coming from beneath a green lampshade fell on scattered text and exercise books. It illuminated a schoolbook of Polish–Latin exercises, a small exercise book full of handwritten Latin vocabulary and a school selection of Cicero's speeches, including explanatory footnotes. Nearby lay a trigonometry textbook, a compass and a set square. The lamp also illuminated an open drawer in which lay two pages covered in a girl's rounded script and giving off a faint scent of perfume. It was a letter from her friend, Jadzia Wajchendler. Rita's entire attention was focussed on this letter, which she was reading for the hundredth time that day. With every reading her anxiety grew.

. . . I am certain, dear Rita, that when we were leaving that horrible place in Zamarstynów on Thursday we were seen by an acquaintance of my father's, a man called Szkowron who works in sanitation and often orders hats from us. He was riding in a droschka; I think he was a bit drunk, but he did see us. I'm scared he's going to tell my father everything. You absolutely must talk to Miss Deskur and beg her (and even bribe her with something, brrr . . . how awful!) to swear to your papa that you were having lessons with her on Thursday! I've already got an alibi. Should the need arise, Beanpole is going to back me up by saying that I was helping her with her French. She got a whole tin of Zalewski cakes from me in return. She has to eat them on the quiet because what's she supposed to tell her mama? Where would a poor thing like Beanpole get the money to buy cakes at Zalewski's? If only we could trust your Hanna, then everything's going to end well. Admit it was worth it, my dear Rita! We hadn't seen a world and people like that before! A real thrill of the unknown!

Rita reflected once more on the danger posed by their servant, Hanna Półtoranos. "No," she shook her head, "that decent woman's not going to give us away! She loves me too much and she's known me since I was little! How many times have I entrusted her with secrets! No, she's not going to tell Papa that I went to the circus – and not wearing school uniform at that! And Auntie? But she wasn't here. She went to play bridge at Assistant Judge Stańczyk's. And at the circus? Oh, well . . . Maybe somebody did see us, but we'd already had time to paint our lips and put on so much make-up that the old cow in the front row spat at the sight of us, thinking we were harlots! Nobody would have guessed that the two young made-up women were schoolgirls from Queen Jadwiga's, that's for sure! Everything would all be alright if it weren't for that cursed sanitation worker! But maybe he was drunk and can't remember anything?"

She shuddered as the sound of a key grating in the lock reached her from the hallway. Quickly, she pulled herself towards the desk and closed the drawer. Of course, it must be gone ten and Papa was back.

Familiar voices resounded in the hallway: Auntie joyfully greeting her father. Such joy it made you sick! Always the same! "Edward! One can set one's clocks by your habits! Hanna's already asleep but she's left you a roast as a snack. Do you want some tea? It's hot and waiting. Or maybe I should heat the roast up for you?" And more bantering between her father and auntie; he feigned anger at the Russian custom of setting up the samovar, she – laughing and pleased – criticizing her father's "Austrian twaddle". Now he would go and put on his smoking jacket, remove his bowtie, come to his daughter's room, kiss her on the head and ask about her day at school and she would reply the same as always: "Everything's fine, Papa!" Then her father, reassured at having fulfilled a father's duty, at having devoted an entire minute of his busy day to her, would sit down with Aunt Lodzia in the parlour and start talking in German so that she, Rita, would not understand what they were talking about. No doubt he would tell her about some terrible things that had happened in the suburbs, unaware that his daughter also knew these mysterious and foreboding places!

And they were sure to keep throwing in those cursed Latin sayings all the time!

Rita's conjectures proved only partially right. Her father did indeed banter a little with Aunt Lodzia, but only very briefly, and a moment later he was already in her room, wearing his smoking jacket. He did not, however, kiss her, nor did he ask what had happened at school that day.

"Good evening, Rita," he said and sat down in the other chair.

"Good evening, Papa," she replied, a little worried by his atypical behaviour.

Her father looked at her strangely for a while, then started to examine various odds and ends in her room: photographs of film stars, the teddy bear she had found beneath the Christmas tree when she was three and had loved madly ever since, dried flowers hanging from the shelves of her escritoire, shells found on the beach in Wielka Wieś, and a chocolate box with pieces of paper on which were written quotations. His bald head reminded her of the head of the strongman who had so admired her a few days earlier. Her father's ears, however, were not as deformed as those of the other man. She looked at his hand and its signet ring adorned with a cabbalistic symbol. He did not have such massive and dirty paws as the other man; her father's hands were strong, cared for and tipped with convex nails. This observation warmed her heart. She stood up, approached her father and, without a word, kissed him on the brow. She was met by the odour of alcohol, eau de cologne and tobacco, and when she sat at her desk again, she saw that his face had changed.

"I was at a meeting of the Polish Society of Philology today," said her father quietly. "And I met Professor Sedlaczek there."

"Ah, Claudius the Blind!" Rita slapped her forehead. She always forgot the name of the Latin teacher who owed his nickname to his habit of taking off his glasses and staring at the giggling girls with the bulging eyes of someone who is short-sighted.

"You're going to get the lowest marks in Latin this term, and from a pretty undemanding teacher! How do you explain that?"

"Don't worry, Papa!" Rita bit on a pencil with her pretty little teeth. "I'm definitely going to improve next term. I simply loathe having to translate those stupid texts into Latin! I even prefer Cicero! Look, Papa, this idiotic letter from Bronisław to Stanisław, for example."

She got to her feet, picked up a book with one hand, raised the other like a Roman orator and began to recite:

"'Dear Stanisław!'" – she lifted her eyes to heaven – "'We went to Italy with our beloved teacher. Oh, what raptures we experienced there!' It's so stupid it makes your teeth ache!"

Rita broke off and laughed brightly. Popielski admitted to himself that the present-day texts in the book were pompous and pretentious. He looked at his daughter still posing as an orator. "She has her mother's talent for acting," he thought. "She ought to be performing in the theatre rather than translating texts about Bronisław and Stanisław." Professor Sedlaczek had complained that Rita aped him when he wrote Latin sentences on the blackboard, and that he had had to punish her accordingly by testing her on the *consecutio temporum*. Her shameful ignorance of consecutive tenses immediately became evident and, as a result, he had been obliged to give her the lowest marks, which had proved decisive in her end-of-term assessment. Popielski could imagine Sedlaczek tapping at the dictum "*Errare humanum est*" on the blackboard with his nicotine-stained yellow finger, and in his squawking, slightly stumbling voice exploring the maxim while adding appropriate *exempla* from Ancient Rome. All of a sudden he remembered the great enthusiasm Rita had shown when he himself had started to teach her Latin after lunch on Sunday afternoons. He could still picture her underscoring dictums in her exercise book. How pleased she had been when, in return for her conjugating correctly, her father had given her some ginger biscuits! But later he had neglected it; he had preferred to read newspapers rather than devote time to his daughter. Sometimes he had been treating a hangover with a beer. It was all his fault, all of it!

He clenched his teeth and approached Rita to kiss her on the head. He picked up the same scent of her dark hair as he had many years earlier when – or so it seemed to him – he had rewarded her with a kiss as she ran through the declensions and bantered with him at the table: "*Primum philosophari, deinde edere.*" He clenched his teeth even harder and as he left his daughter's room, he heard her say: "Good night, Papa!"

LWÓW, THAT SAME MONDAY, JANUARY 11TH, 1937
HALF PAST TEN AT NIGHT

Leokadia Tchorznicka interrupted her game of patience while Edward finished telling her about his meeting with the bully boys from Łyczaków. She had listened to him carefully and understood everything, even though she disliked German and much preferred French. Edward's German was so rich and refined that she generally took great pleasure in listening to it, but now the pleasure had been considerably spoiled and tainted with bitterness by the contents of his account. Her game of "galley-slave" patience had not worked out for Leokadia, as usual, so she set aside the cards and looked at her cousin.

"Listen, Edward," she said, taking care to find the appropriate German words. "You don't know girls and you've never been a seventeen-year-old girl yourself. But I have. And I was just as curious about the world as Rita is. Let me tell you a story. It happened in Stanisławów. At the time, I was a year younger than Rita is now. I remember secretly slipping out at night in order to watch hussars drinking wine through the window of the Mikulik Restaurant on Ormiańska. They had looked so beautiful parading down Sapieżyńska in the day! One of them stepped out into the yard to take a leak." Leokadia used this crude description, which sounded vulgar coming from a lady's lips. "He saw me at the window and invited me to his table, offering me cakes and dancing. And I agreed, even though it was almost two o'clock in the morning and the hussars were drunk and very much aroused. And do you know why I agreed?" Leokadia slowly gathered the cards. "Because I really did think – and I must emphasize this – that I'd only be eating cakes and dancing. I believed it, forgetting that there weren't any cakes at Mikulik's at that time of night. I fancied that hussar so much I believed in those cakes of his!"

"And what happened?" Edward asked, a little concerned.

"I didn't eat any cakes, of course." Leokadia smiled. "Nor did I dance. And if it weren't for Mikulik and his son I would have left there a dishonoured woman. I never believed any man after that and maybe that's why . . . I'm alone today. Well, I apologize, I'm with you – Rita, yourself, Hanna . . . Don't worry," she said in a reassuring voice after a moment, lost in thought. "When I returned from my game of bridge at Assistant Judge Stańczyk's, Rita was already home. There were traces of lipstick on her face but I thought she'd only been playing with make-up. I told her to wipe it off, said you'd be angry if you saw it. She did and we talked for a long time. She was especially friendly towards me which, as you know, does not happen all that often. She was laughing and larking about. That's not the way a seventeen-year-old girl from a good home behaves when she's just got out of a stinking rascal's miserable bunk – excuse my language."

"So Rita believed in cakes, too?" asked Popielski, calmly stroking his Spanish beard, which Lodzia called "Tartar". "Believed who? The bandits?"

"Oh dear, Edward . . ." Leokadia stood up and began to pace the room. In her navy-blue dress and white collar she looked like a teacher from a girls' boarding school. She spoke emphatically, like a dedicated pedagogue. "She left the house with Hanna and with her friend Jadzia Wajchendler . . ."

"I've not liked that Jewish girl for a long time . . ." muttered Popielski. "That little friend . . ."

"On the contrary," Leokadia laughed, "you've always liked the Jewish look in a woman! Are you turning into a fraternity student[†] in your old age? But listen to what I want to say and don't interrupt! Our good Hanna went to church, the girls went to the circus. That must have been what happened! What fun they must have had secretly putting on make-up in some gateway! First of all, nobody was going to recognize them; secondly, they were going to feel grown up! Maybe – and don't get worked up, Edward! – they even lit a cigarette and choked on it, the poor things! They sat in the audience at the circus. And what does it take for some fox or Don Juan from Mościska to join them? Maybe it was the strongman who noticed their admiring glances? And invited them for pastries in the cake shop. Except that the cake shop turned out to be some place frequented by ruffians that sells illicit alcohol. And that's all! The rogue you spoke to today had been buying alcohol too, and he didn't know what happened to the girls afterwards! And nothing happened to them! They left, ran away, and maybe the woman who owns the drinking-den stood up for them like Mikulik did for me once. That's all, Edward! Rita was clearly in high spirits when she talked to me. She was not dishonoured, believe you me! A girl acts differently when she loses her virtue!"

†   Student fraternities in interwar Poland often had anti-Semitic or nationalist tendencies.

At that moment the phone rang. Popielski marched briskly to the hall and picked up the receiver.

"Popielski speaking," he said, still in German, and immediately grew confused. He then wanted to say the same in Polish, but did not manage in time.

"How good of you to be expecting my call, Commissioner, and to answer in German," he heard a hoarse bass voice speaking the purest German. "So you got the message that I would be calling? When I spoke to them at noon today, the Police Administration in Lwów told me it was best to reach you at eleven at night. Oh, I'm sorry, I forgot to introduce myself. Criminal Director Eberhard Mock from the Breslau Police Praesidium."

LWÓW, WEDNESDAY, JANUARY 13TH, 1937
TWO O'CLOCK IN THE AFTERNOON

The Head of the Investigative Bureau, Chief Inspector Marian Zubik, did not like Commissioner Edward Popielski for several reasons. His subordinate reminded Zubik of his own mistakes and shortcomings. The aristocrat's manners and mysterious signet ring irritated Zubik, who tended to dress plainly and act simply. He had, in fact, heard that Popielski could be as violent and vulgar as a carter, but he had never witnessed this himself. Popielski's studies in mathematics and philology in Vienna, although incomplete, painfully belittled Zubik's education. This had been cut short when he was thrown out of school in Chyrów without finishing the fifth form because of his Latin, which his subordinate flaunted constantly and excessively. The immaculate and somewhat dandyish elegance of the commissioner reminded Zubik of his own worn-down, rarely polished shoes and too tight suit. He was even irritated by the ostentatious way in which Popielski carried his closely shaven head, while he himself tried desperately to hide his bald pate by combing his hair from just above one ear to the top of his head. And now as Popielski reported his conversation with the German police officer from Breslau, he irritated his superior with his glasses, so dark that one could not see the eyes behind them. Zubik had wanted to call his subordinate to order on many occasions, but the latter seemed unpunishable. He worked when it pleased him, attended parents' meetings during working hours and generally went about his own business, and yet he enjoyed the support of Commander Władysław Goździewski, the chief himself!

"Well, Popielski?" muttered Zubik. "Why have you gone quiet?"

"May I ask, sir, that we draw the curtain?" Popielski stared anxiously into the intense January sun which sharply defined the contours of the Polytechnic College library visible from the window of Police Head-quarters. "You know it's bad for me, sir."

"You may." Zubik signed a document brought in by a secretary and glanced regretfully at Popielski as he drew the curtain. "And what hap-pened with this Criminal Director . . . what's his name?"

"Mock."

"So what happened when Mock found out that this supposed pederast came to Breslau with the murdered girl from Lwów?"

"Mock went to the border crossing at Chebzie and found the men who were on duty on New Year's Eve. The customs officer stated that that day he had checked the passport of a girl with a ticket from Lwów to Breslau. The girl had been travelling in a private compartment with – as the man with whom I spoke said a little ironically – a very beautiful young man who, in fact, the customs officer knew very well by sight."

"A German customs officer knew a Polish lad from Lwów very well by sight?" Zubik asked in surprise as he trimmed a cigar.

"I didn't say the lad was from Lwów, but your intuition is excellent, sir." Popielski was sprawled out in the chair, the corners of his lips betraying a smile. "Yes, he knew him by sight because the lad made the journey to Breslau several times a year. Always in a private compartment. It was the first time he was with a girl. Usually he was with Germans, men much older than him who joined the compartment at the border, in Chebzie. Mock also questioned the train workers. One of them remembered the youth quite well since he returned to Lwów very frequently by the same train. No-one was with him on the way back. Since the train wasn't due to leave until the next morning, the young man spent the night in Breslau. According to the Germans he looked like a Gypsy . . ."

"What do those Germans know? He could have been a Gypsy, Armenian, Georgian, Jew . . . But does he have a name, this Gypsy? Did that Prussian tell you?" Zubik shook some ash into a massive ashtray.

"Yes. The customs officers noted it down in their reports . . . Making terrible mistakes at that."

"And?"

"His name's Alfons Trębaszczkiewicz . . ."

"It's hardly surprising they made mistakes . . . Strange name for a Gypsy . . . Well, Mr Popielski? Is there a Trębaszczkiewicz in our files?"

"Trębaszczkiewicz. I checked our files yesterday and those in the civil registrar's office." Popielski coughed. He could not stand the Patria cigars Zubik smoked. "There's no man by this name. Yesterday I sent a telegram to Warsaw. Here's their answer, handed to me by the charming Miss Zosia."

He put the telegram on Zubik's desk. Zubik took a long time to read the single line of text.

"Ah, well," he said, removing his glasses thoughtfully, "there's only one Alfons Trębaszczkiewicz in the whole of Poland . . . He's in Posen . . . A master tailor."

"The passport was forged, sir, and that's what I told Mock over the phone yesterday. He only asked me to enquire about the name, but later he also asked me to find a homosexual looking like a Gypsy in Lwów. That's when something hit me. I've got good intuition like you, sir. I said I wasn't going to look for anyone unless Mock let me in on the circumstances surrounding the case. He didn't say anything for a long time, but in the end he told me everything. The girl travelling with this Gypsy had been the victim of an abominable crime. Her name was Anna, as noted by the hotel receptionist . . ."

"A fine state of affairs in that Germany of theirs," sighed Zubik. "They only record first names in hotel registers . . . I ask you!"

"The hotel's a den, a bawdy house in disguise, sir. And now, hold tight because what I'm going to say is . . ."

"Alright! Go on!" Zubik did not wait for Popielski to find some sophisticated adjective.

"The girl was raped and her cheek had been gnawed away, devoured! And she had been a virgin before the rape."

"Bloody hell!" Zubik could not stop himself from swearing in front of his subordinate, something he had never done before. "And this also happened in a hotel . . ."

"Yes. It looks like the case of the Minotaur," Popielski said and fell silent.

The silence spread through the chief's office. Popielski removed his glasses, breathed on the lenses and wiped them with a white handkerchief on which a secret symbol had been embroidered by Lodzia, the same as that on his signet ring. Zubik rocked his hefty body back on the chair and interlaced his fingers behind his neck. A tram grated by beneath the window; the cigar smouldered in the ashtray.

Both men remembered well the unresolved case of two years earlier, reported by every newspaper in Poland and which had attracted odium to the Lwów police. The summer of 1935. Within a few days two girls had been found raped and murdered. The faces of both had been gnawed away.

One had been sixteen, the other eighteen. One had been found in Hotel Fränkel in Mościska, the other in Hotel Europa in Drohobycz. In both cases the girls had been registered under the surnames they had given, and nobody had given them a second thought. The young ladies claimed they had missed their train and had to spend the night. Both names were false. Nobody had ever identified the victims, even though the forensic pathologist from the university, Doctor Ivan Pidhirny, had proved to be exceptionally gifted at reconstructing faces. They had been buried at the state's expense. For half a year the Lwów police – secretly colluding with the criminal underworld – had searched for the Minotaur, a nickname thought up by none other than Popielski. Everyone had tried to track down the monster who ate and raped virgins. Popielski's questionable methods of hypnosis and the use of a clairvoyant were of no avail. Every one of their efforts was in vain.

"And so?" Zubik broke the silence and crushed his cigar, which now reminded Popielski of a huge, trampled cockroach.

"So I told Mock it was our case and asked him to send me all the files."

"And how did he react?"

"And he," – Popielski smiled – "behaved just as I would in his place."

"Meaning?"

"He told me to forget we'd ever had the conversation and beat it."

Zubik leaped up and started pacing around the table like a beast. He turned puce and his neck expanded two sizes.

"What does he think, that Prussian!" he yelled. "It's my case! It's our case!" He picked up the receiver. "Miss Zosia, please arrange an appointment for me to see Commander Goździewski as soon as possible! And you" – he turned to Popielski – "make a note of the conversation straight away! Very accurately! And in Polish. And translate what he told you at the end. To hop it, right? The Hun!"

"I can't translate it," Popielski said.

"And why is that?" Zubik loosened his collar, his face nearly exploding.

"Because it's obscene." Popielski smiled again. "He told me exactly what I would have said in his place. He said: 'Up your arse, you old Austrian!'"

Zubik stood glued to the spot. He had never before heard Popielski swear. He was so astounded his jaw dropped.

"Popielski, what are you saying? He addressed you so coarsely? A criminal director? Why 'old Austrian'? And what did you do?"

"I've probably got an Austrian accent. And what did I do? I replied: 'Up your arse, you old Prussian!'"

BRESLAU, MONDAY, JANUARY 18TH, 1937
SEVEN O'CLOCK IN THE MORNING

As he grew older, Mock got up earlier in the mornings. Perhaps because he no longer led as intensive a nightlife as even two or three years earlier. With a great deal of persuasion from his doctor he drank less alcohol and very rarely visited Madam le Goef's salon in Nadślężański Manor in Opperau just outside Breslau, where on Fridays he had always found great satisfaction in the arms of two girls simultaneously. Now, if ever he looked in, it was about three times a year and he often left without availing himself of female charms. To a large extent this was the result not so much of a lessening of need and libido, but rather due to a sense of alienation in that exclusive temple. At once time, when he had been an important official in the Police Praesidium, he had been greeted there most warmly; the young ladies he picked had been exceptionally engrossed in their work and constantly paid him compliments, delighted as they were by his gentlemanliness and good manners. He, on the other hand – apart from professional competence – asked only one thing of them: the ability to play chess, a game which had always preceded his erotic excesses at Nadślężański Manor. Of Madam de Goef he expected only discretion and the provision on Friday evenings of a comfortable apartment where he could eat, drink, play chess and, in the arms of Ishtar's priestesses, forget about the whole world. Unfortunately everything had changed once he deserted the Criminal Police for the Abwehr. Madame le Goef, realizing Mock was no longer as powerful and influential as he once had been, ceased to be accommodating and pleasant; the prettiest girls were ever more frequently reserved for high-ranking officers of the S.S., while the captain's virility was not helped by spy-holes hidden in the walls. He knew about them perfectly well; when he had worked for the police they had allowed him to catch men in a vice of blackmail on more than one occasion. He had decided, therefore, to forgo the madam's services. Nor did he have a permanent mistress because recently he had only happened upon women whose feigned enthusiasm for making love was obvious to him right from the start. Indeed he was not an idealist, nor did he believe that some twenty- or thirty-year-old would fall in love with a man who – according to Plato – stood on the threshold of old age, but he did like to keep up appearances. So Mock's nights were not as exhausting as they had once been, and his mornings were more rarely spiced with a hangover. He rose at six every morning, walked his beloved Argos along the old city moat, bought the *Breslauer Neueste Nachrichten* and then partook of an enormous breakfast at home, which sometimes held hunger at bay even until supper.

The head of the Gestapo in Breslau, teetotaller and vegetarian Criminal Director Erich Kraus, did not know that Mock had undergone such a transformation. By making an appointment for seven in the morning without consulting von Hardenburg about the timing, he had wanted to humiliate Mock, whom he sincerely despised – a hatred which was reciprocated. But instead of a hungover gentleman with bloodshot eyes, a fat dandy smelling of cigar smoke and the perfume of numerous mistresses, he beheld before him a healthy man with ample but not excessive fat, who smelled of frost, wind and expensive eau de cologne.

"Please do not shake your cigarette ash into the palm pot." Kraus' treble grew even shriller.

"I'm sorry, Herr S.S.-Sturmbannführer," Mock smiled derisively, knowing he was striking two blows in one, "but there's no ashtray, sir."

Kraus did not allow himself to be provoked by Mock's use of the S.S. title rather than the official police "Criminal Director". He knew perfectly well that he would never instil the habit in the old, obstinate police officer, who considered it inconceivable and shameful that the political police should be addressed as criminal police. The second blow – smoking a cigarette in defiance of the clear notice hanging on his office wall – hit its target.

"Then please extinguish that stinking cigarette butt!" yelled Kraus.

"Yes, sir," retorted Mock, and he pressed the cigarette into the earth which filled the pot of the huge palm.

Arms behind his back, Kraus strolled across the room clearly appeased. All of a sudden he spun on his heel and stood in front of Mock with his legs astride.

"How is your work with Criminal Secretary Seuffert coming along?"

"It that why you summoned me here, to ask about your Seuffert?"

"And how's your collaboration with the Police Praesidium in Lemberg going?" Kraus grinned from ear to ear.

"But you know that, Herr Sturmbannführer. I was refused the collaboration."

"Because you treated their commissioner boorishly." Kraus was still grinning. "Anyway, that's good, Captain Mock. Down with the Slav beasts! You're acting like a loyal member of the N.S.D.A.P. You're not one yet, but no doubt shortly . . . Eh, Mock?"

"You like insinuations, Herr Sturmbannführer." Mock sensed that Kraus was beginning to make him angry and decided to work on the lordly and intellectual complexes of the plebeian from *Frankenstein*. "Insinuations or verbal ellipses. The phrase 'How's your collaboration going' should be, 'How's your collaboration working out', and that last 'but no doubt shortly', what does that really mean? 'No doubt shortly you will be one', suggesting 'a member of the N.S.D.A.P.'? Can we please not use ellipses but sentences containing normal subjects and predicates?"

Kraus turned his back on Mock, walked to his desk and slowly sat down behind its wide, gleaming surface. He pretended to be calm but the appearance of a thick vein on his brow betrayed his true state of mind.

"You think you only answer to Colonel von Hardenburg, Mock," Kraus hissed quietly. "But in actual fact nobody can protect you from me. I summoned you for seven o'clock in the morning, and what do we see? Mock is here in a flash. Obediently, punctually, even though he had something to drink the night before, had it off . . . You're entirely in my disposition . . ."

"It's 'at my disposition', Herr Sturmbannführer!"

"Nice, nice . . ." Kraus clenched his fists. "So contrarious from first thing in the morning . . . Hangover, eh, Mock? A hangover takes it out of you! But to the point. Really you belong to me, and you're never going to free yourself of me. For example . . . Ah, this here." Kraus put on his glasses and began to leaf through a file lying on his table. "Yes, I've got an assignment here that's just right for you . . . Perfect, in fact . . ."

"Now you're exaggerating, Herr Kraus." Mock did not use the official Gestapo title and, lashing out blindly, unfortunately showed his unease. "You have no right to assign duties to me or give me orders. An invitation to a meeting at seven in the morning is one thing, but it's something else to . . ."

"Well?" Kraus closed the file and pushed it under Mock's nose.

"Getting worked up already are you, Mock? Take a look at this." He nodded towards the file. "There are orders for you here signed by Colonel Rainer von Hardenburg."

Mock did not even glance at the file, he did not intend to give Kraus the satisfaction.

"Yes, Mock." Kraus stood up again and walked to the window. "That's the end of getting drunk, the end of girls, the end of the comfortable five-room apartment on Zwingerplatz for a few weeks if not months . . . Yes . . . The end of civilization, of culture . . . Of insolence . . . If you look into the file you'll see a letter from Police President Schmelt to the Chief of Police in Lemberg. In that letter there's an offer to collaborate. We also have a reply in the file. Our offer of collaboration has been accepted . . ."

Mock still said nothing and did not open the file, which made Kraus furious.

"You are going, sir" – the vein on Kraus' forehead pulsated – "to Lemberg to find the Gypsy homosexual who, in his hatred of women, his hatred of the German family and the German nation, two weeks ago murdered a young German girl, Anna Schmidt, at the Warsaw Court Hotel."

This time Kraus succeeded. A knockout. With every one of his nerves Mock sensed his powerlessness. The worst of it was not that the scum von Frankenstein – as he called Kraus – was ordering him about while that coward and careerist von Hardenburg threw him at the feet of the political police. It was that Mock's mind had been raped; he had been denied the right to think; he had become a blunt instrument in the hands of political manipulators who were telling him all of a sudden that the earth was flat and a Polish girl was German; he was going to play a part in a propagandist scandal and become a herald who sang the hymn *Ad maiorem Hitleri gloriam*.

"That murdered girl was Polish," he choked.

"Here are your orders, Mock." Kraus rapped a fingernail on the file. "Signed by your boss. This week you're off – for how long we don't know" – his smile displayed healthy white teeth – "to the wild, Jew-ridden country of underpeople, where dogs are used to drag harnesses in the streets. To a country of barbarians, Mock. Just the place for you. You're going to go there, find the Gypsy homosexual and bring him here. You're to introduce yourself to the Poles using your police, not military, rank. They don't have to know you work in espionage. That's all, Mock. You're to finalize the details with von Hardenburg."

Mock got to his feet, lit up and rested his fists on Kraus' desk. Without removing the cigarette from his lips he blew a cloud of smoke across its surface.

"You can spare yourself this pitiful demonstration, Mock." Kraus moved a little away from the desk. "Dismissed!"

"How dare you, sir" – Mock's voice was somewhat distorted by the cigarette clenched between his teeth – "be so familiar with me and order me 'dismissed'! I'm Captain Mock to you, understand? I'm going to find that Polish girl's murderer not because you have ordered me to, but because it is my job!"

A column of ash fell from Mock's cigarette onto the gleaming table. The captain drew back from the desk, plucked his cigarette from his lips and threw it onto the polished parquet floor.

"And do you know what, sir?" He ground the stub beneath his shoe. "Lemberg's not so barbaric after all: Commissioner Popielski speaks better German than you do."

Jadzia Wajchendler, finding herself in the reading room of the Ossolineum for the first time in her life, sat poring over the first volume of Władysław Tatarkiewicz's *History of Philosophy*, and in her exercise book noted down the more salient information regarding Stoic thinking. Thanks to Professor Sedlaczek's influence she was in a library to which only students, professors from secondary schools, and academics had access. Initially she had been proud and overawed, but as the day wore on, she grew indifferent. She could not concentrate on Xryzyp's and Zenon's succinct and sound characterizations because the information bored her to tears. Her eyes kept wandering over the green tables, over the book-filled shelves, the librarian in his purple housecoat and the snow-covered trees on Wronowski Hill visible from the windows. More and more frequently her eyes came to rest on the slim student sitting opposite her at a table strewn with several volumes of the *Journal of Laws* and reading just as inattentively as she was, the only difference being the books he was reading. In front of him there also lay Buczym-Czapliński's *Code of Criminal Procedure*. Miss Jadzia was secretly angry at the cankerous Latinist, Professor Sedlaczek, who must have asked her to prepare the lecture on Stoics as a punishment, and thought with tenderness about the handsome young supply teacher who had taken the Latin class at the beginning of the school year.

The bell announcing breaktime rang in the stooping librarian's hand. The girl sighed with relief. Out of the corner of her eye she noticed that the student was watching her surreptitiously from beneath the peak of his black-rimmed cap. As she made her way to the corridor she contrived ways to bolster his interest, but all of a sudden a man loomed in front of her, thwarting her plan. He was hefty, bald, dressed in black and carrying a bowler hat and she immediately recognized him as Commissioner

71

Popielski, father of her close friend Rita; she had seen him only once in her life, and yet had never forgotten. Even then, when he had been summoned by the school head together with her father, he had terrified her. She imagined that someone in his line of work must almost on a daily basis meet people possessed by the dybuks with which her grandmother had so frightened her in childhood.

"Good evening, Miss Jadwiga," said the commissioner in a deep voice which sounded as though it emerged from the depths of a well.

"Good evening." Jadzia curtseyed and lowered her eyes. She felt Popielski's voice right down in her stomach.

"May I speak to you, Miss Jadwiga?" He stared at her through dilated pupils. "Here, at the table with the book slips."

"Of course, Commissioner, sir," she replied and glanced at the place he was indicating. "But there's a gentleman sitting there already . . ."

"The gentleman's a colleague of mine." Popielski took her lightly by her slender elbow. "He's going to be present at our conversation. I promise it won't take long."

She nodded and walked over to a table where there were some blank library cards. Popielski's colleague rose to his feet, tipped his hat and held a chair out for her. She was grateful for the gesture, as her legs were shaking with fright. Commissioner Popielski sat on another chair pushed towards him by what was, she presumed, his subordinate – a corpulent man with a grey, turned-up moustache and a broad, smiling face. He looked sympathetic. Everybody looked sympathetic at that moment, compared to the commissioner who was studying her with the eyes of someone possessed by a wandering spirit.

"I know everything" – she picked up the scent of tobacco and spicy eau de cologne as he leaned over and whispered – "about you and my daughter being in a drinking-den in Zamarstynowska in the company of bandits, rogues and prostitutes. I didn't hear this from Rita, but from one

72

of the cads who was there. And your father, I take it, knows nothing about it, am I right?"

He broke off as a female student approached the table and picked up a library card to fill in. There were tears in Jadzia Wajchendler's eyes.

"Your father doesn't know anything about it," continued Popielski. "And he's not going to find out if " – he pushed a business card towards her – "if you inform me of your plans and actions."

The schoolgirl burst into tears, her sobs resounding across the empty space of the corridor. The law student, who had been watching the whole scene with some concern, now made towards Popielski. Zaremba blocked his way, pulling out a distinctive badge showing an eagle and laurel wreaths. The boy leapt aside as if burned. Popielski and Zaremba left the building. The commissioner's hands shook as he lit a cigarette.

"Edek, how could you? That schoolgirl is senseless with fear!" said Zaremba, concerned. "Do you know what you've just done? You've turned the girl into a stool-pigeon, don't you see? And deprived your daughter of a good friend! That's what you've done!"

Popielski grabbed Zaremba by the shoulders and yanked him closer.

"Can't you understand, Wilek" – his faltering voice would not have terrified Miss Jadzia now – "that that beast has struck once more and is probably here again? He's chewed up a virgin in Breslau and now he's come back. He's a danger to every young lady . . . including that Jewish girl and my Rita! My Rita! That monster's loose somewhere among us." He turned and ran his eye over the passers-by, the Lubomirski Gallery and the narrow, dark street which climbed the slope of the Citadel. "Maybe he's tearing a girl's cheek apart with his fangs even now! I cannot allow it to happen!"

He left Zaremba and walked off a few paces. He took a wide swing and slapped himself on the thigh. Everyone on Ossoliński heard something which Zaremba, who had been Popielski's friend since secondary school, had heard only a few times in his life: "Fucking son of a whore!"

Getting it out of his system, Popielski ran back to the Ossolineum. He approached the empty table where Jadzia Wajchendler had just been sitting. His business card was still there. He tore it up, spat on it and threw it into the basket of blank library cards.

Zaremba was now sitting behind the steering wheel of the Chevrolet. Before climbing in, Popielski removed his bowler hat and approached the low wall surrounding the educational institution. He gathered up a handful of snow in his glove and applied it to his head and neck. Then he rested his forehead on the spiked iron railings. As he got into the car Zaremba looked at him and fired the engine. Both men remained silent. They drove along Kopernik Street by the Greek-Catholic seminary, past the police building on Łącki Street with which they were only too familiar, and turned into Leon Sapieha Street. On their left they passed the beautiful corner tenement with its huge, semi-circular terraces where the famous Helena Bodnar flower shop was located, and drove alongside the large edifice of the Politechnik. They passed the church of St Teresa, the Ukrainian secondary school and the church of St Elizabeth. Behind dirty façades stretched a dangerous world of crooks. A good many of them were standing in the doorways of the squat houses on Bilczewski Square, wafts of smoke drifting up from beneath the visors of their cloth caps. Glum eyes rested on the gleaming body of the car. Apart from their place of birth they did not have much in common with the jolly figure of Szczepcio who, to the amusement of the whole of Poland, bantered with his companion Tońcio in the programme "On Lwów's Merry Wave". There was as much merriment on their faces as poison on the head of a matchstick.

The Chevrolet came to a halt in front of Main Station. Popielski squeezed Zaremba's hand in both of his, stepped out into the snow and wind, and disappeared through the monumental entrance. He made his

74

way straight to the ticket office and bought a ticket for the Saturday train to Kraków together with a return ticket for Sunday. Zaremba watched his friend through the car window. Popielski had not told him where he wanted to be driven. He did not have to. Both knew the remedy the commissioner needed in moments of great turmoil.

THE KRAKÓW–LWÓW TRAIN
SUNDAY, JANUARY 24TH, 1937,
TWO O'CLOCK IN THE AFTERNOON

The remedy was also known to someone else: Eberhard Mock. Before partaking of it, however, he had been subjected to a thorough personal search and changed trains once. His pockets and luggage were searched by Polish officials at the border station in Chebzia and the carriages had been shuffled in Mysłowice, where the former Prussian Iron Railway of Upper Silesia came to an end. Mock and the other travellers climbed into another set of carriages which was going to Kraków and then on to Lwów. This train, the conductor informed him with pride, was being pulled by an exceptionally fast and modern steam engine which had been awarded a gold medal at a fair in Paris.

Only a few moments later Mock had the impression that he was in another world. He stood by the window marvelling at cottages with thatched roofs and little stations where timber huts with heart shapes cut out beneath the eaves caught his eye, as did the beauty of the young women who stepped onto the platforms to sell cooked cabbage and tea. He let himself be tempted by the Polish treats in Trzebinia where the train stopped a little longer, and from a peasant woman rosy from the frost he accepted a tin plate of piping-hot, aromatic and thick cabbage garnished with crackling. He enjoyed it so much that he wiped his plate clean with a slice of bread, giving rise to spiteful comments from his fellow passengers in first class, a middle-aged couple who insisted on speaking to Mock in French even though he only gesticulated in reply. The couple snorted disdainfully and kept repeating something which amazed Mock no end; they referred to him as a "Swabian".† How they had come to think that he had been born in Swabia he could not imagine, all the more so since they spoke no German and therefore would have been unable to catch the idiosyncrasies of the Swabian dialect. He tried to ask them but this only gave rise to giggles. So he abandoned all attempt at conversation with these conceited people and went and stood in the corridor to smoke and stare out of the window. At the stations his attention was riveted above all by the Jews. Easily recognizable by their gabardines, round peaked caps and long beards, they in no way resembled the Jews of Breslau who distinguished themselves from their fellow German citizens by certain physiological characteristics alone. Here in Poland their language and their dress was different, too. Mock had known they spoke a medieval German dialect, but he had never heard it before, so it was with great interest that he listened to the Jewish traders on the platforms. Their discussions and arguments were a clear indication to Mock that he now found himself in some transitional country at the border of Europe and the East, where these rather odd people used a language that belonged to the West while their gesticulations and expressions placed them rather in some Oriental marketplace.

"Outside the window it's lively even in the frost of winter," he thought, "whereas inside this luxurious express train there are only whispers, polite chatter and upturned noses." Reluctantly he considered returning to his compartment, where the elegantly dressed man kept kissing his lady's hand while she grinned, baring small, uneven teeth, and shook her head. He glanced at his watch. Six hours of the journey still to go. It

† In Polish "Swabian" was a derogatory term for a German, much as "Kraut" or "Fritz" were used in the English language.

was a good thing he had taken with him *Golem*, a fantastical novel by Gustav Meyrink. He would just have to find himself a compartment where the passengers were less garrulous and would allow him to concentrate.

The thought anticipated a situation in which he had wanted to find himself. Because there in front of him were two conductors who spoke a little German and would be able to show him to an empty compartment. He observed them with joy, but as they approached he heard something which astounded him and prevented him from even enquiring. One of the conductors uttered a familiar name: "Commissioner Popielski". When the official handed back his much-punched ticket, Mock, loathe to scare away the herald of faint hope, asked politely:

"Did you say 'Commissioner Popielski'?"

"Yes," replied the conductor, surprised, "I did. I don't see why you're asking."

"Is Police Commissioner Edward Popielski from Lwów travelling on this train?" Mock used the Polish "Lwów" because "Lemberg" would have been unknown to the train crew.

The other conductor tapped his colleague on the shoulder and said something in Polish.

"Excuse me, sir" – the man addressing Mock tried to pass by him – "but I have my duties."

"My sincere apologies," Mock said as he pulled out his identification, "I'm a German police officer and I'm just on my way to Lwów to visit my colleague, Commissioner Edward Popielski. If he happened to be on this train it would be wonderful . . ."

The conductors looked at each other and there was another exchange in that sibilant, jangling language which Mock often heard at the street market on Neumarkt in Breslau. To hasten their decision he took a two-złoty piece from his pocket, change from the Polish peasant woman along with some other coins. One of the conductors accepted it without hesitation.

"Yes," he replied. "As usual Commissioner Popielski is in the private compartment with his daughter, Miss Rita. This way, please!"

Mock could not believe his luck. He followed the conductor and laughed out loud. First of all, he would not be subjected to the refined company of the scornful, giggling couple; secondly, he was going to meet the man with whom he might be working for quite some time. He would have an excellent opportunity to explain their misunderstanding on the telephone and discuss any eventual details of the investigation if, that is, Popielski was willing to talk about any of this in front of his daughter. They stopped at the door to the private compartment.

"Ticket inspector!" called the man as he knocked.

"Come in," came a stentorian voice from beyond the door.

The conductor opened the door and said, "Commissioner, sir, what a coincidence! I met a friend of yours in the corridor, a German!"

He moved aside to allow Mock to pass. The German beheld an elegant private compartment lined with yellow and pale-blue striped wallpaper. The curtains were drawn and the lamp by the window cast a feeble light. On the table stood a carafe of red wine, two glasses and a silver tray with two covered dinner plates. On the couch sprawled a hefty, bald man with a small beard, his shirt and waistcoat unbuttoned. At the corner of his lips hung a smoking cigarette in a holder. On a side table lay a chessboard and an open book. One glance was enough for Mock to see that the book contained Latin poems, the characteristic versification of which pointed to Horace. The conductor picked up the tray and quietly closed the door from the outside.

"Criminal Director Eberhard Mock from Breslau." Mock's eyes grew accustomed to the semi-darkness.

"Commissioner Edward Popielski from Lwów." The bald man stood

78

up and held out his hand. "We're not so intimate yet, surely, as to be called friends. Especially as the manner in which our one and only telephone conversation ended suggested quite the opposite."

Mock studied Popielski and sensed that he would not enjoy working with the Polish police officer. The latter was sure of himself, repulsive to look at and not very hospitable. He had not invited Mock to take a seat in the compartment and stood there in silence as if to say: You have come, sir, at a bad time! This is my private time, a Sunday, a day of rest; we'll talk about work matters tomorrow, on a weekday! Mock even preferred the loge of mockers in his own compartment to this haughty, taciturn Pole. He glanced at the chessboard and recognised a configuration he had seen somewhere before. For a moment he forgot the bitter welcome.

"I apologize, Commissioner, for that crude description." Mock approached the chessboard and without waiting for a "never mind", which in fact never came, asked: "Checkmate in how many moves?"

"Seven," replied Popielski, still standing.

Mock admitted that the chess puzzle was difficult, but he could still use Horace's verse to make closer contact. He looked at Popielski, whose expression was part disparaging, part repulsive. Mock was overcome by a double dejection.

"Well, I'll be on my way," he said. "It was a pleasure to meet you, Commissioner. See you in Lwów!"

Suddenly a door separating the private compartment from an adjacent room opened and Mock heard a woman scream with fright. Out of the corner of his eye he saw a naked figure hide behind the door. He could not be sure whether in the semi-darkness he had seen – or only imagined – heavy, full breasts suddenly sway. The young blonde whose fashionably cut hair was held in a band poked only her head and rounded shoulders from behind the door. She said something in a melodious voice; Popielski sighed, walked over to a woman's hold-all – Mock had not noticed this in the semi-darkness – and pulled out a linen make-up bag. He rummaged for something he could not find and exclaimed vehemently in Polish something which sounded like the German for a contagious disease. The girl smiled at Mock, who was momentarily electrified. In a second he understood Popielski's bad mood and his expectant glare which said: "Perhaps you could go now!"

"Commissioner, sir!" Mock smiled joyfully. "*Homo sum et nil humani a me alienum esse puto.*"†

He listened to a brief exchange between Popielski and the girl. The Pole then looked at the German carefully, without his former agitation and tensed facial muscles.

"Politeness dictates" – he smiled faintly – "that I translate for you, sir, my brief exchange with the young lady. She asked me to translate Terence's famous saying and I told her that you said we belong to the same club of lovers of Antiquity and a woman's body. Am I right?"

"And what did she say?"

"'I like men who belong to that club.' That's what she said."

LWÓW, MONDAY, JANUARY 25TH, 1937
TWO O'CLOCK IN THE AFTERNOON

There was a throng of newspaper hacks milling around the entrance to the Provincial Police Headquarters, known as the "mansion on Łącki Street". Everyone was waiting for the meeting called by the Head of the Investigative Bureau, Chief Inspector Marian Zubik, to end. Present at this meeting – which the journalists had known about since that morning, their source of information known only to themselves – was Criminal Director Eberhard Mock. Articles referring to him as a "legend of German

† "I am human, therefore nothing human is strange to me."

criminology" and outlining his achievements in the '20s had already appeared in the afternoon papers. Had Mock been able to understand Polish and read the articles he would have been most surprised since he had never solved the cases they described. Conscious of the remunerative potential, these journalists wrote whatever came to their heads in moments of inspiration. They waited with their photographers, so that their pieces for the evening edition could be accompanied by a picture of this "star of the Breslau police".

After a good night's sleep at the Grand Hotel, a substantial breakfast and a walk along Hetmańska and Akademicka, Mock was now sitting with several Polish police officers and the forensic doctor cum psychologist, Doctor Ivan-Pidhirny in Chief Inspector Zubik's office. He listened attentively to the speech being given by the Head of the Investigative Bureau and simultaneously translated for him by Popielski.

"Gentlemen" − Zubik raised his arms and thumped the desk − "thanks to Criminal Director Mock's report we can renew our investigation into the Minotaur affair. Our chief suspect is a man whom we should surely have no difficulty finding. Commissioner," − he turned to Popielski − "I hand you the voice since you have a better knowledge of German."

Popielski rose to his feet, adjusted his dark glasses and stood behind Zubik's desk. The chief did not budge an inch, as if to demonstrate that he was handing over the proceedings only for a moment.

"The chief suspect . . ." Popielski tried to speak slowly. In fact all the Lwów police officers present in the office, apart from Stefan Cygan, had won their military epaulettes during the reign of Emperor Franz Jozef, and Doctor Pidhirny had studied at the university in Czerniowce, but the German language − as it was not used on a regular basis − could have led to a misunderstanding of the important instructions he wanted to convey. "The chief suspect is a sallow, dark-haired man of no more than thirty with leanings towards homosexuality. All this we know thanks to

81

Criminal Director Mock. On the day the unidentified Polish girl, Anna, was murdered, the suspect was dressed in women's clothing. He has associations with Breslau's circle of queers. A German customs officer in Chebzie remembers him frequently crossing the Polish-German border; he always travels in a private compartment in the company of older, wealthy Germans."

"A male dame," said Commissioner Wilhelm Zaremba in Polish. "I knew some like that in Franz's day, they used to use the trains but they were just young floozies." He glanced meaningfully at Popielski. "Not boys, though. One ride to Vienna with a wealthy client and they wouldn't have to roam around on Hetmański Embankment for a whole week."

Popielski's eyes briefly met Mock's.

"Let's not lose track, gentlemen," said Zubik reproachfully. "*Ad rem*. We now have something we didn't have before: a starting point. Please go on, Commissioner Popielski."

"Yes," continued the man being addressed. "After two murders committed in 1935 the Minotaur has become active once again. He has killed after two years of silence, and this time in Germany. How would you explain that, Doctor?"

"It indicates" – short Doctor Pidhirny stood up and with one fingernail scratched a face furrowed with acne scars, which spiteful people said had been devoured by corpses' venom – "that he is becoming more careful. Two earlier murders in the vicinity of Lwów and now far away in Breslau, Germany . . . And disguised in women's clothing. No doubt, gentlemen, you'd like to ask whether it is possible for a man with homosexual tendencies to rape a woman. I'm of the opinion that the word 'tendencies' is highly significant here. Perhaps he goes both ways and can be a passive or active participant. If the latter is the case he could be quite normal, and in the case of the former only a dispassionate and passive object who has found himself a means of making money in this particular way. He certainly has above-normal sexual needs. It's possible that there were moral disturbances implicating him at his school or halls of residence . . . That is all I have to say."

"Thank you very much, Doctor," Popielski nodded to Pidhirny as the latter sat down. "These are the important characteristics of the man we seek: sallow skin, or a Gypsy-like appearance, heightened sexuality and homosexual tendencies. With Chief Inspector Zubik's agreement I allocate you your tasks, gentlemen. Aspirant[†] Stefan Cygan[‡] is to infiltrate the world of men with Greek preferences." Popielski meticulously addressed the men by their titles and names; experience had taught him that it was difficult to remember foreign names and he wanted Mock to be well acquainted with those he would be working with. "You're to begin with the Szaniawski boys and some of the regulars at the Atlas drinking-den. Szaniawski is a well-known dancer, a ballet master with the Grand Theatre," he explained to Mock. "He surrounds himself wtih a fair number of perverts and these, if they're to be found in a larger group, congregate at the Atlas. It's where writers and actors go ‒ and sometimes homosexuals among them. The Atlas is usually . . ."

"The place of their rendez-vous," concluded Zaremba and turned to Cygan with a smile. "Well, well, Stefan, you be careful in the Atlas. You're such a pretty boy, slim . . . A tasty morsel for them . . . Like a pretzel . . ."

Everyone sniggered apart from Mock and Zubik. Aspirant Cygan, a slender young man with black hair and a scarf wrapped around his neck, did not feel at all like laughing. He bridled, snorting disdainfully at Zaremba's insinuations.

"Yes, that's where they meet." Popielski got back on track, hastened by the chief's severe glare. "Aspirant Valerian Grabski is first of all to look through the vice files at our headquarters – both municipal and provincial

† Equivalent in rank to junior officer.
‡ "cygan" is Polish for Gypsy.

– and then to follow any leads he finds there, and question the managers and porters – especially the porters because they know everything – working in men's halls of residence and hostels."

Grabski, a short, fat man with an honest countenance, squinted through the cigarette smoke and jotted down Popielski's instructions in his notebook. His dullness and lack of any distinguishing characteristics predestined him to work as a secret investigator, and he had already misled many an offender.

"The Jewish community will be infiltrated by Aspirant Herman Kacnelson in search of this sallow, dark-haired pervert," continued the commissioner. "And please don't forget about our Armenians and the immigrants from Soviet Armenia and Georgia, Officer. Criminal Director Eberhard Mock, Commissioner Wilhelm Zaremba and I will visit all the orphanages and schools in the province."

"Sorry for butting in," Doctor Pidhirny sprung up, "but you've forgotten the ethnic Russians, Commissioner."

"Who?" asked Mock in surprise.

"Ethnic Russians" – Popielski picked his words carefully – "are our fellow citizens of Ukrainian nationality. They're mainly Greek-Catholics, or less frequently Orthodox. In Lwów and the south-eastern provinces they make up a considerable proportion of the population. Doctor Ivan Pidhirny here is an ethnic Russian."

"I see," said Mock, belying what was going on in his head. "But are they important to our investigation? Are they sallow-skinned?"

"There, Doctor," Popielski laughed merrily. "You're always looking to see where ethnic Russians are being discriminated against. I'm not trying to find a murderer among them, I've simply mentioned all the other nationalities without saying a word about the ethnic Russians! And why? Criminal Director Mock has asked a very good question! No, Criminal Director Mock, sallow skin is not a characteristic of ethnic

Russians. They don't distinguish themselves from us in any way."

"I know what discrimination I'm talking about!" Pidhirny was not in the habit of giving in so easily.

"And what happened to you?" Mock said with growing interest.

"I was forced to change my name to a Polish one, you know," said Pidhirny. "To 'Jan Podgórny'! A university lecturer cannot be called Ivan Pidhirny! And that isn't discrimination?"

"Don't exaggerate, Doctor," Grabski said indignantly in Polish. "There are several ethnic Russians working at the university, after all. Take the archaeologist, Associate Professor Styrczuk, who fought with the Siczów Fusiliers! And then . . ."

"Gentlemen, gentlemen," Zubik broke in. "Let's not bore Criminal Director Mock with our country's affairs. Doctor" – he turned to Pidhirny – "you're one of the best forensic pathologists in Poland and we could not do the work we do without your expert opinion. And that is what counts right now, not the Polish–Ukrainian conflict! Gentlemen, I have a question." Zubik made himself comfortable in the armchair, which squeaked alarmingly. "Why do the three of you have to search the orphanages? To track down the suspect and his moral perversions? Surely Mr Grabski can do that by himself. And why orphanages

"Criminal Director Mock will explain everything," Popielski said, looking at the German.

Mock got up from his chair and cast his eye over the assembled men. This was what he had been missing for the past three years. Briefings, focus, pertinent questions, suggestions exchanged and spiced with political discussions. One could not discuss politics in Breslau any more. Only one set of values was permitted, and only the Austrian Corporal honoured. Mock breathed a sigh of relief. How he missed this smoke-filled world of meetings and swearing, and the quest for corpses! In distant Lwów he had found what he had longed for back in his sterile office, where he analysed information and wrote endless reports and statements.

"Gentlemen," he spoke slowly and clearly. "We're not going to be looking for traces of the suspect at the orphanages. We're going to look for traces of his victims. We have to identify them because this trail may lead us to the murderer. I had a lengthy discussion about this with Commissioner Popielski over a game of chess last night. We asked ourselves why nobody had recognized the murdered girls, despite the expertise with which their faces had been reconstructed by Doctor Pidhirny here. Why did nobody report their disappearance?"

"Because they could have been orphans! Of course!" Pidhirny interrupted him. "They could have been brought up in an orphanage."

"To work, gentlemen!" shouted Zubik. "You all know what to do."

The room was filled with the sound of chairs scraping against the floor, pages turning and cigarettes hissing as they were extinguished in the damp ashtray. Mock filled his lungs with air. This was what he missed. For the first time in his life he thought with gratitude about Kraus, who had wanted to banish him but instead had awoken in him something nobody would ever be able to eradicate: the happy excitement of an investigator who could display on his standard the slogan *investigo, ergo sum* − "I detect, therefore I am."

LWÓW, THAT SAME JANUARY 25TH, 1937
THREE O'CLOCK IN THE AFTERNOON

Mock, Popielski and Zaremba stood on the steps of the building on Łącki and fixed confident, hard eyes on the flash bulbs which kept sweeping horrifically bright light across their figures. They thrust their chins towards the lenses, stuck out their chests and pulled in their stomachs; in other words, they did everything to present the readers of Lwów's evening

86

newspapers with an image of three city cowboys, determined and ready to do almost anything to catch this cannibal and rapist of virgins.

Popielski signalled to a caretaker, who adjusted his hat and greatcoat, then willingly advanced upon the journalists with his enormous belly.

"That's enough, gentlemen, enough! That's it! There's work to be done here!" repeated the caretaker in his booming voice and, spreading his arms, marshalled them all towards the revolving door.

All of a sudden the officers heard the clatter of a woman's shoes behind their backs. They turned and gazed at the chief's secretary, each of them differently: Zaremba with a patronizing smile, Popielski with unease, and Mock with desire. Miss Zosia blushed beneath these gazes, even though she had worked in this male world for two years now and was familiar with many and varied manifestations of interest – from timid glances to covert propositions.

"Commissioner, sir," she said, holding out a piece of paper towards Popielski. "I'm sorry, but I've only just managed to transcribe this tele-gram. The chief would like you to have a look at it before he sends it out to all the provincial police stations . . ."

"Thank you." Popielski took the piece of paper and *ex abrupto* trans-lated it into German. "All heads of police investigative departments are requested to gather information regarding any exceptionally cruel murders displaying cannibalistic tendencies. Please send information to the address below. Signed the chief and so on . . ."

Popielski looked at Mock, who in a split second had metamorphosed from satyr to vigilant detective.

"It seems to me" – Mock was pensive – "that something needs to be added . . ."

"I think I know what you mean, Criminal Director." Popielski glanced at Zaremba. "Turn around, Wilek, and hunch your shoulders a little! There's no lectern so I'll use your back."

"And now I'm going to be a camel from Arabia." Zaremba started working his jaws horizontally, pretending to be the exotic animal.

Miss Zosia burst out laughing. Zaremba removed his hat and pulled silly faces at her while the commissioner scribbled a long note on his back with his Waterman.

"You are also requested to give information of any cases in which victims have been gnawed by a human being, even if not fatally, provided the injuries were sustained on or near the face." Popielski spoke as he wrote and added a full stop so forcefully that he almost pierced the paper with his nib. "Please make that addition, Miss Zosia. And tell the chief that I'll explain it to him when I can."

Miss Zosia ran off, asking them to wait a moment, and her slim calves flashed in the dark corridor. Mock could not tear his eyes away.

"Hello, Criminal Director!" Popielski scowled at Mock. "Wake up! Is that the sort of note you had in mind?"

"Yes, something just like that." Mock waved his hand as if chasing away a wasp. "You must have read my mind . . . And let's not mess around with formal addresses, alright?" Mock was still staring into the depths of the corridor. "Nobody ever told me there were such beautiful women in Poland!" He smiled lustfully.

"Let it go." Popielski removed his bowler and stared at Mock. "Miss Zosia could be your daughter!"

Mock removed his hat in turn. He ran a bone comb through his thick, wavy hair, straightened his coat, pulled his gloves firmly over his fingers and stood in front of Popielski with his legs apart, resting his fists on his hips. He was the shorter man but had a stronger build. With a jutting jaw he hissed through his teeth:

"I forbid such comments, dear sir! You have no right to play the moralist! I'm not the one who travels by train with floozies!" He used

88

Zaremba's word. "And I'm not the one who has it off with them in a private compartment, like some bull!"

Popielski's eyes remained on Mock for a long while. He had to react fast in order to show this Swabian that he was not on home territory, that here he was nothing more than a helping hand, an apprentice in the Polish State Police. But if it had not been for Mock and his evidence, Popielski would now be wringing his hands in helplessness over the monster who had crawled across the roofs of Drohobycz and Mościska and into the rooms of young girls, robbing them of their virtue, butchering their faces and throttling them. And it was not at all certain, as Mock had stressed, that he had done it in that order. If the German police officer had not come from faraway Breslau, he himself would be gazing each day, powerless and anguished, at sleeping Rita's beautiful, still-childish face, wondering whether his daughter would be the beast's next victim. Fleeting images ran through his head: the private compartment filled with Blondie's sighing and moaning, his hands grasping her hips, the Sicilian defence in chess, Doctor Pidhirny bent over the corpse and sewing up the girl's face, the receptionist at the Jewish hotel in Mościska, sobbing his heart out, Rita smoking in the drinking-den on Zamarstynów, his hands entangled in Blondie's hair, Mock smiling meaningfully, *Homo sum et nil humani a me alienum esse puto*. These images superimposed themselves on each other and heralded an attack. But it was he who had the power over his epilepsy, not the other way round! He had the authority to let it momentarily blacken yet simultaneously enlighten his mind. But not yet. He had screwed like a bull. Like a *bull*. He liked that phrase a great deal. Suddenly he burst out laughing.

"I have to tell you, sir" — he rested his hands on his knees and howled with laughter — "it's all because of you that I didn't have it away as much as I would have liked. And I had so much time left 'til we reached Lwów . . ."

"The trains are still running between Lwów and Breslau!" reposted Mock; he squinted, stuck his tongue out and, clenching his fist, pumped his forearm like a steam engine. "I invite you to the metropolis on the Oder in the company of a couple of young ladies from Poland! We'll visit this and that!"

"Gentlemen, gentlemen," hissed Zaremba. "Aren't you ashamed of corrupting the young? How old are you? Hairless, don't play about!"

Miss Zosia stood before them blushing, the telegram awaiting final approval in her hand. She did not understand German, but she knew perfectly well what Mock's gesture meant.

LWÓW, THAT SAME JANUARY 25TH, 1937
FIVE O'CLOCK IN THE AFTERNOON

Despite the heavy traffic on Słowacki, the street was drowned in silence. A blizzard was falling so thickly over the town that no eye could penetrate it further than a few metres. It muffled all sound, blocked the exhaust pipes of cars, and covered the nostrils of sleigh-drawing horses with sticky moisture. Shop windows glowed with coloured lamps. A caretaker spread sand over the pavement outside the Main Post Office, and an irritated policeman controlling traffic at the crossroads kept removing his oilcloth hat to shake off wet layers of snow as they swelled in front of his very eyes. Students from the nearby university clapped hands blue with cold as they waited for a tram.

Popielski, Mock and Zaremba sat in their Chevrolet in a long queue of cars and carts. They were silent and cold, though not as cold as the students, who were hopping up and down. Each was thinking about something different. Wilhelm Zaremba thought about the delicious dessert which his maidservant, unable to wait for him, must already be putting into the gently preheated oven; Edward Popielski about Rita, who was leaving in a few days with her Aunt Leokadia to go skiing in Worochta; and Mock about the two orphanages they were still to investigate.

They had already visited two such institutions that day. The reaction had been the same everywhere. Initial fear on seeing a delegation of three police officers who spoke German amongst themselves had given way to indignation at the questions they asked.

"No, it's impossible. The victim couldn't have come from our orphanage. Our wards are virtuous girls who continue to visit our institution throughout their adult lives, or at least send us Christmas cards. We're constantly in touch."

So spoke Mrs Aniela Skarbkówna, Director of the Abrahamowicz Educational Institution. Mr Antoni Świda, Director of the Municipal Orphanage, put it a little differently, but his words came to exactly the same thing. That time Popielski had reacted angrily:

"But those girls were virgins," Hairless had exclaimed, raising his voice, "so they must have been virtuous!" The heads of the charitable institutions had generally tried to conclude the conversation by saying: "No decent girl spends the night alone in a hotel!"

Popielski had not given them the chance. With savage satisfaction he questioned them about any wards who may have displayed certain aberrations in their sexuality, or who were unsettled or were the cause of issues of moral concern. Their indignation was then so fierce that the police officers had no choice but to leave empty-handed.

The windscreen wiper gathered layers of snow as rubber squeaked across the window. The men's breath condensed and settled on the inside of the glass. The coloured bulbs in Markus Ludwig's menswear shop began to flicker. Popielski pulled on his bowler hat and closed his eyes. Despite his glasses and tightly closed eyes, he could still see flashes lighting up the elegant hats, walking sticks and ties. He broke into a sweat. All of a sudden he opened the car door, climbed out and walked off, tripping over clods of snow.

"Where's he gone? Home?" Mock leaned out but the commissioner's massive figure had already disappeared down a side street. "Does he live far from here? What's the matter with him? Did he feel unwell?"

"He hasn't gone home." Zaremba turned and looked at Mock with a serious expresson. "I know where he's gone. You don't, and you won't for a long time. Let me tell you something, sir — just because you've played a game of chess with somebody, it doesn't mean you know everything about them."

LWÓW, THAT SAME JANUARY 25TH, 1937
HALF PAST FIVE IN THE AFTERNOON

Popielski slackened his pace once he was a considerable distance from the automobile. He passed his house and walked slowly down the alleys of Jesuit Gardens, taking care not to slip. Once he had removed his dark glasses he was able to gather speed. The feeble flicker of the gaslights was as harmless as the sputtering of a flame in a paraffin lamp.

He walked along Mickiewicz, Zygumntowska and Gródecka, passing the massive building which housed the Railways Head Office, Gołuchowski manor house and the church of St Anne. He hopped across the street's pot-holed cobblestones and a moment later arrived at the corner of Kleparowska and Janowska, the site of a taproom that went by that very name, "At the Corner of Kleparowska and Janowska". A few days earlier he had abused Felicjan Kościuk, alias Felek Dziąsło, known as "Gum", in the Sea Grotto tavern, but a different danger threatened him in this place. Here he would not have received a warning in the guise of a pig's ear skewered by a nail, but would instead have been sneered at or flogged with insults. He would have lost every brawl or argument here; he

92

would have had beer thrown in his face, or someone would have hawked and spat into his bowler hat.

This is what had happened one night several years earlier when he and Zaremba had ended a bar crawl there. He had pulled out his gun in fury and waved it about, but the laughter had been so thunderous that Popielski had immediately sensed how ludicrous the whole situation was. He had run his bloodshot eyes over the place, rammed his spat-in bowler onto the head of the student laughing the loudest, and left. He had later tried to take his revenge on the owners of the den but met with unexpected obstacles in the political branch of the Investigative Department. It had been explained to him that no harm was to come to the owners of a place that served a considerable cluster of stool pigeons. Members and sympathizers of the Communist Party of West Ukraine gathered here, as well as poor consumptive students, raving radicals and drunken representatives of Lwów's bohemia with their passing muses.

Pushing away these recollections, Popielski passed by the taproom and entered the first doorway on Kleparowska. Stepping quietly, he soon found himself on the first floor. He tapped a light bulb which glowed feebly for a moment before going out altogether. But the moment sufficed for him to catch a glimpse of a couple kissing passionately in a recess next to a small column which blended with the building about as well as gothic vaulting blends with a cowshed. He knocked loudly on number 3. Before long the door opened with a rasp, and in the doorway stood a man wearing a long white coat and holding a cigarette.

"Ah, the commissioner!" he smiled. "We haven't seen you here for a long time!"

"But it's not the first time the police have been here today, is it, Mr Szaniawski?" Popielski held out a hand which the man clasped firmly.

"Indeed." Szaniawski closed the door and positioned his slender fingers beneath his chin, in a gesture which was to denote deep thought.

"Your young partner was here today and asked about some sallow-skinned boy. I told him two things . . ."

Popielski cast an eye over Szaniawski's apartment which had been rented from the owner of the corner tavern for the past few years. It was furnished in bad taste, with the fake glamour of Lwów's suburbs. This was the style adored by a dancer who took particular delight in fake chrysanthemums and tacky ornaments from second-rate music-halls. The apartment served as a venue for his secret meetings with young bandits and artists procured for him by various go-betweens. He could not hold the meetings in his own home for fear of losing his good reputation, one he strove to maintain. Here Szaniawski allowed various boys to spend the night and bring their friends. He had been sympathetic, invariably in a good mood with a song on his lips. Until the moment when one of the street urchins had cracked open his head with a candlestick and robbed him. Popielski had found the thief that same day. Once his battle with death in the surgical clinic on Pijarów had been won and a week later he beheld his stolen wallet in which he kept a valuable piece of jewellery – his beloved late mother's ring – Szaniawski had asked the commissioner if they could meet, and in a quiet, faltering voice assured him that he was forever at his service. Popielski was not long in giving Szaniawski an opportunity to repay the courtesy. A few weeks later he requested that he make his apartment available to him so that he could give vent to his – as he called them – harmless eccentricities.

"It's a good thing you passed on the information to my younger colleague." Popielski looked around the apartment once more and it seemed quite empty to him. "Thank you, on behalf of the police. The usual brings me here today: my little eccentricity."

"Welcome." Szaniawski pointed to the door next to the entrance. "Your bathroom is free. And my Cossack boy has lit the stove. As if I'd known you were coming!"

"Thank you." Popielski pressed the door handle and entered the long dark room with its small window. In its centre stood a narrow bathtub and a rather large water closet.

Heat radiated from the stove. He shut the door and turned on the light, then stripped off and folded his clothes on the chair. He reached for the box of lye standing on the bath tub, and washed and rinsed the tub scrupulously. Then he turned off the light, drew the curtains and lit several long, thin candles. He stepped naked into the tub without running the water. And waited.

LWÓW, THAT SAME JANUARY 25TH, 1937
EIGHT O'CLOCK IN THE EVENING

Despite the keen cold Popielski's eyes kept closing. He sat in the Chevrolet which Zaremba had brought round to Zielona Street, pinched his cheeks, smoked, constantly aired the car's interior – but nothing helped. It was always like this after his sessions at Szaniawski's. After these extreme and utterly indescribable experiences full of anguish, pain and sudden muscular spasms came such deep relaxation that he longed above all to go home and do what he enjoyed most: to throw the window wide open and half an hour later crawl beneath his duvet to warm the sheets with his body. But this was never possible, because if he fell asleep early in the evening he was sure to wake up in the morning and this would disrupt his old rhythm of living and working and subject him to further epileptic fits triggered by the sharp morning light. And so after his sessions at Szaniawski's, he generally returned to his day-to-day duties but did not perform them as well as he should. Perspicacity vanished somewhere along the way, and he was drowsy and forgiving of the world.

Now, too, he was fending off sleep, trying to keep his watery eyes fixed on Queen Jadwiga's Secondary School for Girls on Zielona 8. For some peculiar reason his usual fifteen-minute nap in Szaniawski's apartment had extended to three-quarters of an hour, and he had been torn from it by a strange noise which sounded neither like a motor revving nor a dog growling. He had slept too long and had not made it on time to Rita's performance of *tableaux vivants*. He did not want to enter during the show as she would be sure to notice him and would not have spared him a string of biting comments. All he could do was wait patiently until the show was over.

Catching sight of a newspaper vendor, Popielski climbed out of the car and beckoned him over. He handed him five groszys and opened the *Lwów Illustrated Evening Express*' special supplement. On the first page was a photograph of the three police aces. "Detectives Popielski, Mock and Zaremba partnership leads investigation" stated the headline. "Yes," he thought, "that sounds excellent. A good, cadenced name for their organisation. Popielski, Mock and Zaremba." What metre was that in? He pulled out his Waterman and began to write the syllables and accents on the newspaper, on which rare snowflakes settled: Po-piel-ski-Mock-and-Za-rem-ba. A man jostled him and tipped his hat, apologizing.

Torn from his philological ponderings, Popielski noticed that parents and daughters were already leaving the secondary school. A mother hugging her radiant and happy child awoke in him bad thoughts and memories. His eyes followed mother and daughter to the end of Jabłonowska, where the pair disappeared in the dim gaslight. "There goes Rysia Tarnawska," he thought with a sneer, "top of Rita's class, the best in Latin! I wonder if the girl knows that her proud father, engineer Marcel Tarnawski, who barely returned my greetings just now, once sat on the other side of my desk in tears, and – not failing to mention the fact that we knew each other from parents' evenings at school! – begged me to hush up the suicide of a certain young manicurist?" The newspapers had

96

claimed that the woman, addicted to morphine for several years, had committed suicide because of an unhappy love affair. The engineer had feared the case would bring out into the open the months he had been carrying on with her. Now widow Zacharkiewicz with her daughter Beata – "Beanpole" – pretended not to see him. How indignant she had been when he had once explained to the tutor why he had arrived so late at a parents' evening – he had gone to class 3A, whereas Rita was in 3B! "It's unheard of," the widow had said to the woman next to her, addressing her by some title, "for a father not to know which class his child is in! No wonder . . ." But Popielski had not heard the rest.

And all of a sudden a terrible thought occurred to him, one so awful he did not want to admit it even to himself. Fortunately Rita had just emerged from the school building and swept away all bad premonitions. She was flushed and laughing, and he knew why. Her talent for acting had been appreciated by the new Polish teacher who was teaching them Romanticism that year. The previous teacher – dull, pedantic Miss Mąkosów – had not allowed Rita to take part in school productions because this would have had an effect on her already poor school marks. Professor Kasprzak, on the other hand, did not countenance such details as they were entirely irrelevant to the theatre.

"Good evening, Papa," Rita greeted him joyfully. "And did you like the whole thing?"

"Very much, my little one." He kissed her on the forehead, drawing air in deeply through his nostrils.

He breathed a sigh of relief. Not a trace of cigarette smoke.

"Oh, hello, my darling Jadzia," called Rita, holding out her hand to her good friend who approached and curtsied to Popielski.

Once the girls had kissed, he realized Jadzia Wajchendler had come out earlier, that she had stood by the little newspaper rotunda not far from him and greeted him several times, but he had not reacted. She gave him a bad conscience, and he had already had enough such scruples for one day.

"I saw you earlier, sir." Jadzia smiled at him. "But I didn't want to disturb you. You were so lost in thought, Commissioner . . . Another fascinating riddle . . ."

"Tell me, Papa," Rita interrupted, much to her father's relief, "which scene did you like most? Well, which one?"

She demanded this with the same tone of voice as when she had asked him for a toy as a child. They could not walk past Aptawag toyshop on Sykstuska without her gluing her nose to the window and her lips to his cheek. She had never needed to terrorize him, stamp her feet or throw herself on the pavement; he had always bought her everything. "You spoil her too much, Edward," Leokadia used to say. And then he used to hurt his cousin by saying: "And who's going to spoil her if not me? You love bridge, books and concerts more than my daughter!" When later he had apologized to Lodzia he saw a flash of anxiety in her eyes, but also a certain amusement inspired by, as she said, "a father madly in love with his daughter".

"Well, Papa, which scene?"

Popielski's head was in turmoil. Because of that cursed session at Szaniawski's he could not remember which *tableaux vivants* were to have been presented that day. Matejko, surely. But where do maidens figure in his paintings?

"You were so delighted," cried out Jadzia, "when Marek Winicjusz visited his beloved Ligia in prison!"

"But of course!" he said with feigned enthusiasm. "You played that so well, darling! But do you know what? I'm waiting for you to do something other than mere pantomime. You have such a harmonious, beautiful voice."

"Thank you for the compliment, Papa." Rita watched tiny flakes of snow as they fell in the lamplight.

"So, how about it, girls?" Popielski latched on to the good mood. "Shall we go to Masełko's for some pastries?"

Jadzia's smile was full of consent but Rita hesitated, which meant the suggestion did not fill her with enthusiasm. He recalled forced conversations over pastries with his daughter, punctuated by troubled silences. Each one had inevitably led to a discussion of poor school marks or unforgivable behaviour, and had ended in sulks and once even in tears. He remembered how on Sunday she had rolled her eyes when he suggested they pop out to the Europejska Café for some meringues. "Not again!" is what her expression had conveyed. Then as now.

"I understand. You're tired," he said with a false smile. "Let's go home, then. Please get into the car, Jadzia. I'll give you a lift."

"But can't we go home by ourselves?" Rita's eyes entreated. "Jadzia will see me home. Please, Papa!"

"No." He walked to the car and opened the door. "Please get in."

Once the girls had obediently climbed in Popielski started the engine and turned round.

"I have something important to say to you. Lwów is a very dangerous place right now . . ."

"So that's why you came to the show," Rita exclaimed. "Not to see me, but to supposedly protect me. Right? That's why! How many times have I heard about all these dangers lurking, just waiting to pounce on young ladies!"

"Rita, how dare you speak to me like that!" he said coldly. "And in front of your friend, too!"

"But, Rita," said Jadzia, staring at him with the eyes of a schoolgirl who is top of her class and always has an answer ready, "your father only wants what's best . . ."

Popielski turned away and the car moved off. The girls were silent. In the rear-view mirror he saw Rita gaze at the passing shops and buildings while Jadzia read the special supplement he had tossed onto the back seat earlier. Her eyes did not leave the front page. Throughout the entire journey one thought preyed on Popielski. The Minotaur murdered and raped only virgins. Rita could be protected from the beast if . . . At this Popielski shook his head to prevent the monstrous notion from entering it. ". . . if she wasn't a virgin," uttered a demon.

LWÓW, THAT SAME JANUARY 25TH, 1937 EIGHT O'CLOCK IN THE EVENING

Aspirant Cygan sat in the Atlas cursing his Ephebe-like looks. This sumptuous place on the corner of Rynek was frequented by artists and men of letters, some of whom had decidedly Greek tastes. They usually met on odd-numbered days in the Grey Room, although this was never mentioned *expressis verbis*. Except, perhaps, among officers who could not afford to let themselves be led by smug prudishness and needed to call a spade by its name. Included in the circle of men upholding the Greek habit were the ballet dancer, Juliusz Szaniawski, the rich art merchant and antique-shop owner, Wojciech Adam, and the director of the National Bank, Jerzy Chruśliński. As a cover they were often accompanied by women who were always ready for a lively discussion, and vociferously expressed unconventional or entirely revolutionary opinions on moral issues. Anyone not native to Lwów and coming here for the first time might think they had found themselves in an exclusive restaurant which distinguished itself – if at all – by its magnificence. Only once they had studied the slicked, slim waiters, with backs straight as arrows, would they realize that they were all young and striking in their exceptional beauty. An outsider would have no idea that some of the waiters had got a job at this luxurious restaurant through the influence of their wealthy lovers.

Aspirant Cygan had inhabited Lwów since birth and was not in the least surprised by the Greek preferences of some of the waiters and customers. As soon as he entered he was met by two languid glances. In a mirror he could clearly see the caresses bestowed upon him by a no longer young man with dyed black hair who was sipping alcohol from a shallow glass, and a thirty-something man with an athlete's build and booming voice who knocked back one glass after another and followed his vodka with – oh, the horror! – cream cakes.

Cygan did not return their glances or smiles but calmly smoked his cigarette, sipped slowly on a small iced vodka, ate an excellent steak tatare – which he had seasoned and made exceptionally spicy – and waited patiently. Szaniawski had told him earlier that day that two young men had appeared in his circle, and because of their swarthy complexions and remarkably beautiful black eyes they had immediately found themselves in the receptive sights of some of the Atlas' regulars. They spoke, to use Szaniawski's expression, "a mixture of Polish and Russian", which for some unknown reason added to their attraction in his eyes. So Cygan sat by the door and watched for these dark-haired young men with sallow complexions. After an hour of waiting, which he whiled away by reading the weekly newspaper *Signals*, he saw two youths who answered to the ballet dancer's description. First he heard a stamping outside and then they came in, brushed the snow off their coats and handed them to the cloakroom assistant. They walked past Cygan and sat by a window with a view of Adonis' fountain. A waiter appeared straightaway and took their order: two glasses of gin and apple cake with cream.

Cygan walked up to their table and greeted them gallantly. Without waiting for an invitation, he sat down and said something which made their smiles disappear as they stood their glasses back on the marble surface.

"Criminal police," he said in a sweet voice. "I'm not going to pull out my badge now because everyone's looking. Our conversation's to look like a friendly chat, understand? So, please raise the glasses to your lips and give me a nice smile."

Silence fell at the table.

"Your names?" Cygan asked when they had done as he requested.

"Ivan Tshuchna."

"Anatol Gravadze."

"Been in Lwów long?"

"Two years."

"Me, too, like my friend."

"Did you arrive in our city together?"

"Yes, together we came."

"Where from?"

"Odessa, then Stanbul."

Cygan was silent as he considered whether one of them might be the man sought by the police. Both were very elegantly and stylishly dressed: suits of Bielsko wool, diamond tie-pins. He had not thought their Polish would be so bad. The German customs official and the cabby in Breslau would have been able to distinguish Polish from Russian, especially by of the melodious accent. But could he himself be sure? Would he be able to tell Danish from Swedish? Probably not, but had he ever heard the languages? No. Yet the customs official must have heard Polish frequently. But one of the Russians might have spoken to the German official in Polish, in which case he would have really had to know Polish very well or else have a musical ear in order to differentiate literary Polish from that of a foreigner. Cygan decided not to bank on the musicality of German officials and instead to carefully check how well both of the men knew Polish.

"To what do we owe the honour of you gentlemen from Odessa visiting our ancient settlement on the Poltva?" he asked in a manner both courteous and convoluted, and waited for their reaction.

As if on command the two men shook their heads and looked puzzled. They obviously had not understood.

"Keep smiling," he said sweetly but emphatically. "Why did you leave Odessa?"

"Things poor," asked Ivan Tshuchna. "Here better. Play music and dance there. And to Lwów come for stage. To dance and sing. Then stay here and ask Lwów authorities if can stay. Well, get permission. And two years we here."

"And what do you do here?"

"Well, same as Odessa." Tshuchna pronounced the name of the town as in Russian: "Odessya". "Dance Cossack, sing in Bagatella two times Sundays."

"You couldn't make such a good living dancing and singing," thought Cygan. "You wouldn't be able to afford expensive clothes and drink gin at the Atlas, even though the boss of the Bagatella – known to everyone as Mr Scheffer – is no miser." He turned and immediately found his answer. Here there were several men for whom the upkeep of these two eastern princes would not prove a great cost.

"And did you dance at the Bagatella on Sylvester's night, too?"

"When?" Gravadze had clearly not understood.

"Of course," thought Cygan, "the Soviets only celebrate birthdays. They've no idea that in a Catholic country every day has its patron saint. Even the last day of the year. And don't be so bigoted," he criticized himself. "These two aren't members of the Sodality of Our Lady."

"Well, on New Year's Eve, when champagne is drunk at midnight! Where were you?"

"Oh, drink champagne at ball in Cyganeria," replied Tshuchna. "Go there with fiancées."

"Any of these?" Cygan jerked his head as if wanting to look behind. "Can any of these confirm what you say?"

"No," Gravadze said, looking offended. "We not like that. We with girls."

"Don't lie to me, you queen!" Cygan stuck out his jaw. "Or we'll go and talk at the police station and you'll be back in that Odessa of yours!"

"We not lie, Colonel, sir." There were tears in Tshuchna's eyes. "Girls dance now at Bagatella. We go with you – you talk to them. We not even go in, not cook anything up before."

"That's what you say." Cygan stood up but he was plagued by uncertainty as to the logic of his decision. "So, let's go to the Bagatella!"

He said this loud enough for others to hear. As they left the Atlas in a threesome they were followed by several pairs of envious eyes and the murmur of voices talking about the handsome dancers' new young boyfriend.

LWÓW, WEDNESDAY, JANUARY 27TH, 1937
TEN O'CLOCK IN THE MORNING

Aspirant Walerian Grabski was disheartened when he left the Police Headquarters archives. He belonged to the category of men who are conscientious, reliable and level-headed. Only once in his life had he been thrown off balance, and that was in his relationship with a certain priest who had taught him religion. He had got into the priest's bad books for aping his sermon at a retreat. Catching the boy red-handed, the priest had come down very hard on him, a true Cato the Elder to the Carthaginians. While turning a blind eye to the ignorance of the other pupils, awarding them all solely on the basis of his own perception of their religiosity, he grilled Grabski in great detail about the decrees of specific synods and ecumenical councils, about the views of the Holy Fathers, about liturgical and homiletic reforms. Grabski had learned all this by heart and recited it like a parrot, but even so he could not please his catechist. After two months of such torture he could stand it no longer. One day, when he was not praised but criticized for his descriptions of St Athanasius the Great's and Socrates Scholasticus' accounts of the Nicean Council, he was tipped over the edge. He walked up to the priest and slapped him so hard the priest fell off his chair. Thus Grabski left the Secondary School for Classics after six years of studies and almost ended up in jail. Blacklisted, he was allowed only to become an accountant, and it had been in a counting-house that he was spotted by Marian Zubik, at that time Head of Personnel at Lwów Police Headquarters. Moved by the accountant's punctiliousness and punctuality he had offered him a job in his unit, which Grabski had willingly accepted. He had then wandered through various departments and even towns as a result of his benefactor's promotions. He had the diligence of an ant and a particular liking for archival work, which is why he was a little saddened when, keeping to the order of tasks allocated by Popielski, he had to remove his over-sleeves and protective dust visor, leave the police archives and instead visit student hostels to question their caretakers. His sadness was all the greater as every man listed in the archives as having a moral transgression on his conscience was either too old to dress up as a young woman, or was in jail or had left Lwów long ago. Of the latter there were only two and neither looked like a Gypsy.

The hostel on Issakowicz Street was first on a list he had meticulously put together, beginning with establishments closest to the mansion on Łącki. He walked slowly along Potocki and congratulated himself once again for not having left Lwów for Lublin, a move offered to him along with a promotion. He would not now have been looking at such wonderful buildings as, for example, the Biesiadecki manor, constructed in the style of a medieval fortress; he would not have been walking through vast and well-tended parks; and he would not have been able to visit his favourite haunts, especially Mrs Teliczkowa's famous restaurant where they served crispy onion bread rolls and boiled ham with horseradish for breakfast, or a cup of borscht to "calm the digestive humours" of those suffering a hangover.

Aspirant Grabski regretfully cast aside these pleasant thoughts and plunged down a tree-lined street where the huge edifice of the House of Technicians student hostel was located.

The beadle sat in a duty room where there was a small settee, a basin and spirit burner. To Grabski it was plain that he was a tough old man from Lwów. Unlike the owners of the hostel, which offered shelter to young men regardless of their denomination or origin, the beadle was not very tolerant. He immediately criticized the "stubborn Rusyns whom the state allows to stay and who don't do anything but conspire against Poland". The description did not endear him to Grabski, who should have been presented at every meeting of the chiefs of the Provincial Police as a paradigm of complete and absolute apolitical standing, something which, after all, police regulations required.

The aspirant soon realised that with such a hostile attitude towards Ukrainians, the beadle was bound to answer any question about moral perversion by stating that all pupils of such origin staying at the hostel were sexually rampant and committed the sin of impurity several times a day. He decided to put this hostility to use.

"Hey, good citizen!" he said grimly. "Are you aware that you're committing an offence right now?"

"And what offence might that be?" The beadle cringed.

"Are you aware that you're stirring up nationalist hatred before a representative of the law? – before a state official?"

"But I wasn't . . . I even quite like those Rusyns . . . Some of them are good chaps!"

"And did you know that I'm a Rusyn myself?" Grabski pulled a stern face and slipped a pair of spectacles onto his nose.

"Well, I . . . There's nothing . . ." The caretaker was clearly embarrassed. "Alright, alright, Mr . . . Mr . . ."

"Żrebik's the name, christened Józef . . ."

"Well then, Mr Żrebik" – the aspirant waggled a finger at him – "let that be the last time! I don't want anything but the honest truth!"

"*Jawohl*, Commissioner, sir." The old man must have served under Franz Jozef because he clicked his heels there in the duty room.

"Well then, tell me since you know this best, Mr Żrebik." Grabski leaned over the beadle. "How do these Rusyn students and pupils behave? And not only the Rusyns . . . the Poles, Jews, maybe others . . . You know what I mean . . . With girls and that sort of thing . . ."

"I don't let anyone in, Commissioner, sir." Żrebik looked offended. "No stranger! I'm a veteran *Feldfebel*, I obey my superiors!"

"That's very good, very praiseworthy." Grabski held out his right hand. "Let me shake the hand of such a fine state official. I, as it were, am also your superior. But a gentle and understanding one . . ."

Żrebik was so pleased he even blushed as he shook Grabski's hand, while the latter prepared to hit him with more taxing questions.

"So, tell me one thing. These are young men, after all – they need the company of women. You know, when I was their age I couldn't go a day without . . . Well, you know . . ."

"Commissioner sir, there was a fellow in the army with us, a smith from Sanok who, when he woke up in the morning, could carry a bucket on his rascal! That's how hard his was!"

"There you are." Grabski laughed heartily. "We're all like that . . . Life's not easy with women but it's even worse without them . . ."

"I always tell my Mania . . ."

"There you are . . . And here are these boys . . . None of them is going to nip off to a harlot because they can't afford one, they're too expensive, right Mr Żrebik?"

"*Sicher*. One harlot costs as much as some live off for a month . . ."

"So? Surely there are times when they . . . You know what I'm thinking about . . . They have to have it off themselves . . ."

"Oh, that there are, that there are," sighed the beadle. "There are sometimes such queues to the toilet it's terrible — because someone or other is taking so long in the lav . . . Well, what could he be doing there if not wanking . . ."

The aspirant wondered for a moment whether, when asking the most important question of all, he should allude to his interlocutor's military experiences. He decided, however, that an opener such as: "Mr Źrebik, you know about life, so I'm going to ask you straight out . . ." could offend the old man if he thought he was being suspected of homosexual leanings.

"And do they ever service each other?" Grabski then asked without preamble. "It's rare but it does happen . . ."

To Grabski's surprise, Źrebik did not bridle in the least, let alone explode in righteous indignation. He merely lowered his voice a little.

"There was such a one here" — the beadle looked carefully at the police officer from beneath his bushy eyebrows — "who was exceptionally hot for his colleagues. Not a Rusyn, definitely one of ours from Zdołbunowo. Son of . . . it's a pity to have to say it but he was the son of a policeman. He'd walk the attic at night trying to persuade the youngsters to go with him . . . He's the only one I can remember."

"What was his name? How old is he? And what is he doing now?"

"That I'd have to check," said the beadle, and pulled out a grease-stained notebook. He flicked through the pages and pinned one of them down with a finger yellowed by nicotine. "He's the one, I've got him . . . Zając Antoni, born 1910 . . ."

"1910, right? That would make him twenty-seven."

"Yes, that would be right."

"And what's he doing? Where's he working?"

"That I don't know. He studied law and moved away somewhere. That would be five years ago. That's all I know."

"And what does he look like?"

"He wasn't big, but strong, sinewy . . ."

"Dark-haired, fair . . ."

"Dark . . ."

"Handsome?"

"Would I know?" Źrebik pondered. "Would I know whether this fellow or that is handsome or ugly?"

Once out on the snow-covered pavement freshly sprinkled with sand, Grabski felt a shudder of emotion run through him – something he had not felt for a long time – and realized that his regret at not working in the archives was both risible and inexplicable.

LWÓW, THAT SAME JANUARY 27TH, 1937
NOON

Aspirant Herman Kacnelson was not pleased with the task he had been allocated. He had tried to explain to Chief Inspector Zubik that the mere fact that he was of Jewish descent did not in the least predestine him to work – as his boss was wont to say – "with ethnic minorities". Kacnelson came from a Jewish family which had long been assimilated and whose members, for the past two generations, had been Lwów lawyers. Their attitude to the religion of Moses was, to put it mildly, rather cool, whereas to socialism and Polish independence it was enthusiastic indeed. The Kacnelsons spoke only Polish and had typically Polish first names. He was the only exception in the family with a name such as "Herman", in memory of a certain Austrian officer who had saved his grandfather's life at the battle of Sadowa and whose portrait hung in their living-room next to that of His Majesty Franz Jozef. In fact the name Herman was very common among Polish Jews, which was why the aspirant especially hated it. He considered it an intolerable hallmark of his Jewish roots, an unnecessary burden unworthy of a modern man who decides for himself which nation he belongs to. He could not, however, change it for fear of being disinherited, as this is how his father would no doubt have reacted. So it was not surprising that he performed these "ethnicity"-related tasks allocated to him by the chief with a certain unwillingness. He awaited better days when his boss would be – as he firmly believed – Commissioner Edward Popielski, a man who appreciated his investigative talents without regard to his nationality or ethnic origins.

The prospect of talking to representatives of the Jewish religious circles who looked after the student hostels filled him with distaste. When he saw the dirty prayer rooms adjacent to the synagogues, the boys swaying in the heder pews, the threadbare gabardines, the skull-caps of the Orthodox Jews and the wigs of pious Jewish women; when he listened to the disquisitions in Yiddish, a language he did not know, he felt that he was stepping back into the darkness of an unknown world, and that his logical, rational mind – trained during his incomplete studies at the polytechnic – was being drowned in the scum of immemorial superstition.

It was with relief, therefore, that he ticked off in his notebook every religious institution which offered the youths of Moses a roof, board and laundry. There were only a few, and in each of them he received the same negative answers to his questions: none of the superiors of the Jewish orphanages would even hear of the notion that some *meshugge* boy capable of committing the sin of Onan or – God forbid! – that of the Sodomites, could possibly be found in their boarding house. Even though he had not found a single clue, Herman Kacnelson breathed a sigh of relief, dismissed the distant cousin he had employed as a Yiddish interpreter, and made his way to Jewish lay institutions offering board and education.

110

The first of these was the House of Jewish Orphans on Strzelecki square. After some considerable time he was allowed to see the head, Mr Wolf Tyśminicer. The police aspirant officer introduced himself, pulled out his pencil and notebook and, with a heavy sigh, commenced yet another interrogation. He asked several questions and sensed his pulse beating faster, and after a quarter of an hour's conversation Kacnelson had ceased to curse Chief Inspector Zubik for allocating him exclusively "Jewish" tasks.

LWÓW, MONDAY, JANUARY 25TH, 1937
NINE O'CLOCK AT NIGHT

Aspirant Cygan and Vasilii Pohorylec, manager of the Bagatella restaurant and dancing club, walked through the labyrinth of narrow corridors at the back of this excellent and well-known Lwów establishment. Behind them traipsed Tshuchna and Gravadze. He could not leave them outside lest one of them should phone the "gals" in the back rooms to agree upon a common version of events. The men stopped outside a door marked "Changing Room", with a crêpe-paper flower affixed to its top right-hand corner.

"This is it," said Pohorylec. "Miss Stefcia and Miss Tunia from our variety show change in here with the other dancers. But I sincerely entreat you, sir, to be brief. Both ladies are about to appear on stage! When you can see for yourself what beautiful girls we have here perhaps you'll be persuaded to visit our establishment? I've never seen you here before, sir! And that's a pity, a great pity . . . Just listen to the fine singing up there!"

As he said this the manager pointed to the ceiling. They could clearly hear the words of a jaunty song coming from above:

My brothers, jig away,
Let the accordion play.
Grab the lasses by the arms
And God'll give you strength.
My brothers, jig away,
In Gródyk, Kliparów,
'Cross the hall just jig away,
There's nowhere like our Lwów.

Pohorylec nodded as if to endorse the words of the song, and without knocking opened the changing-room door. Laughter and screams of feigned fright came from within. Cygan looked sternly at Tshuchna and Gravadze who were standing in a recess by the toilets.

"Right," he snarled. "Don't move from that hole and wait for me!"

"And I'll be on my way, Aspirant, sir," said Pohorylec. "Duty calls, you know. The carnival's in full swing. I insist you keep it brief . . ."

Cygan resisted informing the manager that he was talking absolute twaddle. Instead he simply nodded, entered the changing room and closed the door behind him.

The aspirant officer was already twenty-eight, had recently got engaged and no longer remembered very well the days when, as a schoolboy, he had been troubled by erotic dreams and a longing for music-hall dancers. But now the unease and fantasies returned; the sight of a dozen semi-naked women in frills and stockings, the scent of their perfumes and powders — all this hit Cygan unexpectedly and momentarily knocked him off balance. Regaining it was made no easier by the smiles, fluttering eyelashes and flirtatious, intrigued looks of the dancers. He decided to apply his unfailing remedy against sexual arousal and brought to mind the photographs of female genitalia deformed by venereal diseases which he had seen in lessons on forensic medicine during his police training in Tarnopol. It helped. He looked at the dancers with assumed gravity.

"Which of you are Stefcia and Tunia?" he asked.

"We are." Two girls stepped forward, a brunette and a blonde.

"Full names, please, not stage names!"

"I'm Stefania Mazur," said the slim blonde. "And she's Antonina Kaniewska, our Tunia." She indicated her dark-haired colleague.

"Have you got boyfriends?" Cygan pulled out a pencil and rebuked himself for such a stupid question.

"Just one, Commissioner, sir?" laughed Tunia as she adjusted her stockings.

"Shut up, you stupid monkey!" Stefcia shouted and smiled at Cygan. "We do, but all of them pale in comparison to you, sir . . ."

This plebeian compliment had an electrifying effect on Cygan. He took his eyes off Stefcia, whose hands rested on her narrow hips as she gazed fondly at him, and laid them on the other dancer as she rolled a stocking up her shapely thigh. His imagination got the better of him, and instead of the ghastly images he saw himself in the embrace of lustful female bodies. Fortunately the bell summoning the dancers onstage resounded in the changing room.

"With whom did Miss Stefcia and Miss Tunia spend New Year's Eve?" he asked in despair.

At that moment the door opened and Pohorylec, the worried manager, appeared. Tshuchna and Gravadze were in plain view behind his slight figure.

"With them!" shouted Miss Tunia joyfully and pointed to the two foreigners. "With those beautiful Cossacks! Their dance is wonderful!"

Aspirant Grabski sat in the waiting room of Commercial Bank on Legionów and looked out of the window as he waited for Mr Antoni Zając, one of the bank's team of lawyers. The police officer was pleased with his day's work. After obtaining that important information from the beadle, Józef Źrebik, he had gone directly to the Law Department at Jan Kazimierz University. There the elderly secretary, Miss Eugenia Koczurówna, had slipped on a pair of over-sleeves and scrupulously searched through the student files. She had easily found Antoni Zając, born in 1910, and had taken down his index number to look through the graduate files. After this thorough exploration, which won Grabski's true admiration, the secretary told him that Antoni Zając of Zdołbunowo had completed his law studies the previous year and had decided to undergo a year's unpaid apprenticeship at the university bursary. Aspirant Grabski expressed his admiration for Miss Koczurówna's rigorous accuracy and set off for the bursary. There he learned that the apprentice going by that name was working at Commercial Bank, and had been for several weeks.

Now at the bank and rather pleased with himself, Grabski stood at a window in a corridor leading to the lawyers' offices and out of boredom watched workers clearing the snow in front of Bieniecki's pastry shop where, as a reward for the day's success, he intended to eat several cream cakes.

A door rattled and slow footsteps reverberated down the corridor. Grabski turned to see a young man in a dark suit approaching. The man was not tall and had a sallow complexion, black hair and large black eyes.

"Mr Antoni Zając, born in 1910?" he asked.

"Yes, that's me," answered the man. "What's this about? With whom do I have the pleasure of speaking?"

114

"Aspirant Valerian Grabski." The badge he showed impressed Zając greatly. "Which hostel did you live at when you were a student?"

"The House of Technicians on Issakowicz," replied the clerk.

Grabski tipped his hat in farewell and squeezed past Zając, rubbing against his huge protruding belly as he did so.

LWÓW, FRIDAY, JANUARY 29TH, 1937
NOON

"Thank you for your report, Mr Grabski," said Zubik in Polish and lit up his favourite Patria cigar. "Zając turned out to be an elephant, and elephants don't climb hotel gutters . . ."

Kacnelson and Grabski forced a smile while Zaremba erupted with sincere and loud laughter; only Mock remained silent, not understanding a word of Zubik's joke.

"This isn't good, gentlemen, not good at all," said the chief. "The two Russkies have an alibi; the other suspect is fat, too fat to perform acrobatics on a roof." Here he changed to German. "There's nothing from the orphanages or schools either, as Mr Zaremba has reported. And what about the ethnic minorities, Mr Kacnelson? Any clues there?"

Kacnelson grimaced at the term "ethnic minorities" and recounted his fruitless search in Jewish religious circles. In spite of his sour face, his colleagues listened eagerly because they knew that their "little yid" – as they called him behind his back – liked to spring surprises as much as he liked complex games of chess. After an innocent introduction which heralded nothing of any significance, he was capable of coming out with a real bombshell at the end of his report – indeed he had on many occasions.

"After questioning all the Orthodoxes" – that is how Kacnelson always described committed Orthodox Jews – "I set my sights on lay student

115

hostels and hostels run by Jewish welfare organisations. The director of the House of Jewish Orphans, Mr" — he glanced at his notebook — "Wolf Tyśminicer, presented me with an interesting clue. A twenty-year-old resident at the hostel, a not very tall, slim dark-haired young man called Izydor Drescher, only too readily took on female parts in school performances. After finishing merchant school he worked in the Ingber and Wiener timber company and was to stay at the hostel on condition that he left as soon as he had found alternative lodgings. Then one day Mr Tyśminicer found the lad drunk on the hostel stairs and immediately turned him out. Drescher moved to lodgings on Zielona. I asked the caretaker there about him and was told the man in question was no longer working at the timber company but was drinking heavily and working as a stage artist at Kanarienfogel's tavern nearby. The evening before last I watched the artistic programme offered at this den, and it certainly was something to behold!" He snorted in disdain. "Drescher, with an abundant beard and wearing a dress, was spinning around the stage in a Jewish dance yelling 'Ay, vay' to klezmer music, while a crowd of soldiers and non-commissioned officers from the barracks on St Jacek's hill roared in delight. I approached Drescher after the performance and questioned him in detail. Above all I wanted to check whether his beard was real."

"Why?" asked Zubik.

"The suspect is remarkable for his feminine beauty, right?" Kacnelson stared lengthily at the chief. "If he had a beard he probably wouldn't have been compared to a woman in Breslau, would he?"

"Well, what happened to the beard?" asked Mock. "Did you tear it off?"

"Something happened alright. But to my face." Kacnelson touched his cheek where a large bruise was evident. "I didn't want to explain when you asked about the bruise earlier because you know how much I enjoy surprises." He smiled sourly. "So, when I pulled Drescher by his very real beard some tough fellow, a friend of his who thought I wanted to harm the dancer, threw himself at me. And I got a fist in the eye."

"Where is this friend, and what's his name?" asked Mock.

"I don't know." Kacnelson shrugged his shoulders contemptuously. "He ran away and I couldn't detain him. I hadn't taken my gun that day, as it happens."

With every report presented that day Mock grew redder and redder, especially on the neck, but after Kacnelson's account his neck turned purple. He raised his stubby-fingered hand, the onyx signet ring glistening, and looked Zubik in the eye.

"Please go ahead," the chief nodded. "I hand the voice to you!"

"Thank you, Inspector." Mock got to his feet and cast his eyes over the assembled company. "I wouldn't like to offend you, gentlemen, but I regret Commissioner Popielski not being here. I have something important to say and he would translate it extremely well . . ."

"He's not here," said Zubik, annoyed, "because it's too early for him. The sun's out today. He could suffer an attack of an illness nobody's ever seen . . ."

"I beg your pardon, sir." Zaremba leapt from his chair. "I've witnessed it and swear . . ."

"Gentlemen!" Mock interrupted. "Forgive me for interfering, but this is no time for arguments. May I make a few critical comments about your work?"

"Please do!" said Zubik, turning angrily towards Mock and almost upsetting the overflowing ashtray.

"Firstly," Mock now spoke calmly, "all of you, gentlemen, are working on your own when you should be working in pairs. That's elementary! Mr Kacnelson was assaulted, and what would have happened if this Drescher had indeed been the murderer? He and his minder would have got away while a police officer would have lain unconscious in the corner of a room somewhere. Secondly" – he took a deep breath – "you're too gullible and, forgive me, too naive. How can you approach a suspect without knowing exactly who he is, what his weaknesses are, or how he might be pressed into a confession? You'd save yourselves masses of time if you asked the witnesses what the suspect looked like, whether he was thin or fat, had a beard or not . . ."

"Please don't lecture us!" growled Zubik. "What's that supposed to mean, 'press'? Blackmail? We don't blackmail those we question. We act according to the law! What you're proposing is some sort of . . . some sort of . . . torture." He had remembered the German word and added emphatically: "Those are fascist methods which might hold good in Germany, but not here, understand, Criminal Director, sir?"

Before Mock had managed to calm down and collect his thoughts after this biting riposte, the door opened and Miss Zosia stepped into the office. The sight of her and her gentle smile soothed each of the men. Zubik pulled his waistcoat down over his protruding belly, Zaremba began to roll his eyes, Grabski tore himself away from his notebook, Kacnelson stopped rubbing his cheek and Mock instantly forgot that indirectly he had been called a "fascist".

"I knocked," said the secretary, "but you must have been too engrossed in your meeting to hear. I have an important telegram from Kattowitz. It's just been encrypted."

"Please read it to us, Miss Zosia,"said Zubik, assuming an authoritative stance. "And you, Mr Zaremba, translate every word for our honourable guest!"

"In mental institution in Rybnik. Stop. Woman bitten on face by dog. Stop. Maria Szynok, 20. Stop. Claims bitten by count." Miss Zosia read out the contents of the telegram and looked at those present.

"Thank you." Zubik did not mask his disappointment as he took from the secretary the text with the police decoder's signature. "And so, gentlemen?" – he turned to the officers once she had left – "which of you would like to go to Silesia to question a mentally-ill woman in order to find out whether she has been bitten by a count or a tiger? Perhaps you would like to go, Criminal Director Mock? It's no distance at all to Breslau from there . . ."

"You're not going to kick me out of here," retorted Mock through clenched teeth, resting his fists on Zubik's desk, "until I find the pig! But I'll go to Kattowitz because I never ignore leads, do you understand, sir, most honourable and most moral Inspector, sir?"

"You should have said 'we find', not 'I find'!" Zubik got up and he too rested his fists on the desk. "This is not your own personal case!"

The jaws of both police officers continued to move as if they were pounding curses and insults back and forth. Both men looked like gorillas preparing to attack, and they remained like that for a good fifteen seconds. Neither of them even blinked. A heavy silence fell.

It was Mock who relented first. He walked away from the table, put on his coat and bowler hat and then said very slowly:

"Yes, you're right. I should have spoken in the plural: 'until we find the pig'. But that 'we' means me and somebody else, not you gentlemen present! With that someone, we – the two of us – are going to find the monster and bring his head here. *Per fas et nefas*. You know what that means? Judging by your faces you don't. But that someone will know, because he knows Latin."

And with that Mock left the chief's office.

LWÓW, THAT SAME JANUARY 29TH, 1937
ONE O'CLOCK IN THE AFTERNOON

On the table in the darkened living-room stood a platter with large slices of cheesecake and poppy-seed cake, and next to it, bowls with vegetable

119

salad, bread rolls garnished with coarse salt and caraway seeds, and halves of hard-boiled eggs wrapped in herring. Every Friday, year after year, Edward Popielski corrected guileless Hanna Półtoranos' description of "herrings from the barrel" with the words "I always thought herrings came from the sea". These words of reprimand said in jest belonged to the family's Friday tradition and they always provoked the same reaction from everyone else in the house: Hanna's condescending nod, Leokadia's faint smile, and Rita's bored, disdainful pout.

That day Popielski did not poke fun at anyone. He sat at the table in his cherry-coloured smoking jacket with its velvet lapels, a cigarette in an amber holder between his lips, and from his freshly shaven head there emanated the scent of an eau de cologne Leokadia had bought at the Black Dog perfumery the previous day. He did not even touch the cakes, the salad or his favourite herrings. He was fixed in the attitude of someone who is far-sighted but cannot be bothered to wear spectacles: in one out-stretched hand he held a letter, in the other, a newspaper, and he shifted his eyes constantly from one to the other.

Leokadia knew the reason for Popielski's terrible mood. A short letter addressed to him – his name had been typed – had been slipped through the letterbox at about one o'clock in the morning. As she had carried the letter to his desk she had smelled the scent of cheap perfume wafting from the envelope. At first she had thought that the sender was one of the girls with whom – for fear of tainting his already dubious reputation – he took the sleeper on his overnight trips to Kraków. She had rejected the thought, however, firstly because none of the girls used a typewriter, and secondly because all those sluts were pretty and had enough wealthy lovers to be able to afford better perfumes.

As she looked at her frowning cousin, who had not even touched his breakfast, she felt a surge of anger. She had had enough of his morning moods, his gloomy glances over the breakfast table, his neurotic outbursts and obsessive love for Rita to whom he pretended to be an overbearing tyrant when in fact he was a dog fawning for the slightest caress. But most of all she hated his feigned secretiveness. She knew perfectly well that he would reveal the reason for his mood that day in due course, but first he had to tease her a little, act out a pantomime and sigh and hiss, only to burst finally and tell her everything *ab ovo*. She was as familiar with his reactions and most of his secrets as she was with overtrumping in a game of bridge. But the letter smelling of cheap perfume had knocked her a little off balance. She feared it had something to do with a dark, unknown matter which Edward had not told her about, and probably never would. She was almost certain that the letter had something to do with his mysterious visits to the apartment of the ballet dancer Szaniawski; the woman selling artificial flowers at the shop on Halicka, who frequented the apartment for, so to speak, professional reasons, had been her informant.

In annoyance Leokadia spread out her cards which had refused yet again to be arranged in a sequence of Patience, sorted them into open heaps, then carefully rearranged them into four bridge hands. This drew Edward's attention and he set aside the letter and newspaper. For a moment he forgot about his problem, took his fork and cut a square of cheesecake, which he devoured with obvious pleasure.

"Look, Edward," she said as she laid out the cards. "This is the way they were dealt yesterday. The assistant judge bid one spade. The assistant judge's wife called 'no bid'. What would you have said in my place? These were my cards" — she indicated one heap with her slender, well-manicured hand. "Would you have agreed on spades or shown your clubs? Both are questionable . . . I'll tell you presently what happened but first take a good look at the cards."

But Leokadia did not manage to tell him anything, nor did Popielski manage to analyse the cards because the doorbell rang. About ten seconds later Hanna entered the living-room.

"Commissioner, sir," said the maidservant, greatly troubled. "There's some fatso dandy here to see you."

"How many times have I asked you, Hanna," said Popielski angrily, "not to make comments about my guests! The gentleman may have overheard!"

"God help us!" Hanna did not give up easily. "He don't understand our language, that's for sure."

LWÓW, THAT SAME JANUARY 29TH, 1937
A QUARTER PAST ONE IN THE AFTERNOON

Popielski noticed immediately that Mock did not make the best impression on Leokadia. His cousin was a bridge fanatic, and he attributed her anger to the fact that she had not been able to conclude her account of the previous day's bidding vicissitudes. Nor did the German police officer rise much in her estimation when he appeared greatly surprised on hearing Popielski say that he held no secrets from Leokadia, and that they could confidently discuss professional matters in her presence. When she saw Mock grimace in disbelief, Popielski's cousin ostentatiously gathered the cards from the table and left the room under some pretext or other. Her sulks did not bother Popielski; he remained silent while his thoughts hovered once more over the newspaper and letter which lay on the table, as if Mock did not exist at all. The German was silent too and stared intently at Popielski, unable to concentrate on what he had come to say. The reason for Mock's distraction was the plate of herrings he so adored, and which reminded him that he had not eaten since breakfast. Hanna placed a cup in front of the guest, who thanked her with a broad, insincere smile.

"To what do I owe your visit?" The clinking of a cup being replaced on its saucer tore Popielski from his reverie. "Did something come to light at Chief Zubik's meeting?"

122

"There's an old university custom" — Mock picked up a sugar cube with the little tongs and dropped it into his coffee — "hailing from a time when study was not as widespread as it is today. A student starting at a new college would visit his professors at home. That's why I'm here."

"Oh, how gracious you are today." Popielski passed him the cake platter. "But the comparison is greatly exaggerated. I'm not going to play up to you, or flatter you by saying that you are the professor and I the student. No, that wouldn't be right. We're equal. There, see? The papers say the 'Popielski, Mock and Zaremba partnership'."

"Sounds good." Mock greedily put a piece of poppy cake in his mouth. "Popielski, Mock and Zaremba . . ."

"I even wondered for a moment what metre it could be in." The Commissioner tapped his fingernail rhythmically on the table.

"It's iambic dimeter with catalexis and the last iamb is an anapest," said Mock, swallowing a mouthful.

"Does metre interest you?" A combination of astonishment and joy was reflected in Popielski's face. "I used to be a great deal interested in it too, especially the discrepancies in accentuation in Plautus' spoken verse. It seems some scholar in Breslau wrote something on the subject."

"Could be, I don't know . . ." Mock lost himself in thought for a moment. "I analysed the whole of Plautus' *Casina* and *Aulularia* metrically." He pulled out a golden cigarette case and passed it to the man he was addressing.

"Including the choruses? Really?" Popielski studied the German Juno cigarette and, full of joy, looked at Mock again. "Those kinds of analyses are particularly fascinating, like describing new plants and insects!"

For a while neither man said anything. They smiled at one another while their thoughts revolved around bygone days at school and university, when each of them dissected the verses of ancient poets with sharp pencils and from them cut pure, crystalline particles, like trigonometric equations.

"That dimeter of our names sounds good" said Mock, breaking the silence, "but it isn't accurate. We form a much larger group under Chief Zubik's leadership. There are six of us altogether: you, Zaremba, Grabski, Cygan, Kacnelson and I. Have I remembered their names correctly? That's a few too many. Such a large team is a little lifeless, it doesn't operate efficiently . . ." He inhaled and looked attentively at his colleague. "Let me tell you something . . . in confidence . . . Something occurred to me at today's meeting . . . The two of us – you know, just the two of us – should create a two-man special task force within the group. A privileged force with exceptional powers. Just you and I. Without having to report in or go to endless meetings. They're a waste of time! If the others discover anything significant, they're bound to tell us. What do you think?"

Popielski was amazed, but before he had time to give it any thought or express his opinion, the German began to relate the events of the morning's meeting with Chief Zubik until he got to their argument about "fascist methods". Popielski listened very carefully up to the point when Mock recounted numerous examples of what he called a "pressure vice". Popielski heard how this police officer from Breslau had once "pressed" a prostitute addicted to morphine, and felt his throat fill with bile. He remembered how he himself had blackmailed the innocent schoolgirl in the Ossolineum. He saw all this in a flash: the fear, the tearful, terrified eyes, his visiting card next to the box of library cards, spat upon and ripped in half. Like a torn school uniform at the scene of a rape.

"That's enough, Mr Mock!" he cut in. "In describing this hyper-effective vice to me so comprehensively and criticizing my colleagues, might you be suggesting that I resort to criminal methods? Dishonourable ones, too! And as if that weren't enough, that I withhold this from my superior! Are these the exceptional powers you refer to?"

"I didn't think you were such a stickler for rules." Mock's cufflinks clinked quietly as he placed his interlocked hands on the table. "Is the Polish police force made up of noble knights fighting with open visors?"

"Do you have children?"

"Unfortunately, no." Mock shifted nervously in his chair, angry at himself for having revealed too much with the word "unfortunately". "I don't understand your question."

"But I do." Popielski rested both hands on his high forehead and looked at Mock in irritation from beneath them. "A seventeen-year-old daughter. My beloved Rita whom I brought up single-handed. Without a mother. And I brought her up very badly. Now I have to protect her from the Minotaur and other men who would like to do to her the things he does! Well, apart from murdering and devouring her perhaps . . . I have a choice: either I enter into a 'Popielski and Mock partnership' with you and track down the beast *per fas et nefas*,† or not worry about the investigation, conduct it sluggishly and concentrate all my energies on protecting my daughter!"

Popielski drew on his cigarette so hard it looked as if he was going to swallow it, then furiously threw it onto the floor. He pulled himself together, however, and restrained himself from crushing the butt into the polished parquet. Instead he snatched the letter from the table, gathered up the tiny red embers and poured them into the ashtray.

"Listen, Mock." Popielski sat down, wiped the sweat from his forehead and looked his guest in the eye. "I've chosen the latter. I'm going to protect my daughter. I'm not going to run after the beast. And now if you'll excuse me, I have to get dressed. I'm going to work shortly."

"I have great respect for your familial feelings" – Mock pretended not to have understood Popielski's dismissal – "but instead of receiving an

† Justly or unjustly.

answer to my question as to whether the Polish police are knights of honour I have heard your fears of . . . a tragedy which hopefully your daughter will never encounter!"

"Yes, I suppose it all sounds confused . . . I owe you an explanation." Popielski slapped his bald head. "Here goes! I put one of my daughter's friends in just such a vice. I wanted her to tell me what Rita does and who she sees when she's not in my direct care. The friend, an exceptionally delicate and thoughtful girl, began to cry, she'd obviously suffered a shock. I wanted to make an informer of her, a grass! I've degraded her! It's as if I had raped her! That's what your kind of vice leads to! And now let me read something to you!"

Popielski stood up, put on his spectacles and slowly began to translate the scented letter he had just used for scooping up the cigarette ash.

Dear Commissioner, sir!

After our last meeting, when I saw your face in the newspaper, I realized what an important mission you are performing for society in your search for the beast who murders and chews up innocent virgins. I've hidden the newspaper with your photograph in my escritoire and sneak a look whenever I feel threatened. And then I gaze at you, Commissioner, sir, and feel so well, so safe . . . You look much better in real life than you do in the photograph, but even there you look better than that fat German. . .

"Show me that newspaper!" Mock broke in. "Do I really look that fat in the photograph?"

"Well . . ." Popielski hesitated and handed Mock the newspaper, "You're not all that slender in it . . . But you're much slimmer in real life . . . It's not a good photograph . . . Alright, now let me carry on reading:

126

After our last meeting, I realized how silly my qualms were about co-operating with you, Commissioner, sir, and that your suggestion, well, your demand, is an honour for me. Take this letter as my agreement. I hasten to inform you that Rita may be endangered by our Polish teacher, Professor Jerzy Kasprzak. He's the young teacher who has replaced Professor Mąkos. He leads the drama group and thinks Rita has a great talent for acting. He's always telling her so, and keeps offering her parts in school productions. In my opinion this is harmful because it distracts her from her work and more important subjects. And the fact that Rita is probably secretly in love with Professor Kasprzak is even greater cause for alarm. They often talk to each other during break, and obviously all our friends comment on this.

Respectfully yours,
Jadwiga Wajchendler

Popielski sat down in a chair by the clock. He was exhausted. Grey wisps of smoke floated in the air beneath the brightly lit chandelier. The roaring fire blasted out heat. Both men were tired and felt like ardent players who, after a whole night at cards, have no idea that a new day has dawned and continue to sit in a smoky room with curtains drawn. Popielski unfastened two buttons on his shirt and with the back of his hand wiped the sweat from his brow. Mock fanned himself with the newspaper.

"Open the window, will you," he said, "or we'll suffocate in this heat."

Popielski unhooked the vent of the casement window and fresh, frosty air poured into the living-room. Mock would most like to have opened all the windows onto the balcony but saw that this was impossible since, apart from the small vent, every one of them had been sealed with oakum and taped shut.

"Allow me to recapitulate. I'll also try to banish your anxieties," said Mock greedily eyeing the herring once more. "You're very much on edge just now. I understand your concerns about this jester – the teacher – even though I have no children myself. But one thing at a time, and first the matter of Rita's friend. She has probably turned into an informer because she's taken a fancy to you, as some of the passages in the letter indicate. And you accuse yourself of having corrupted her? Too bad, what has happened has happened. A girl has broken the sacred ties of friendship" – the irony in his voice was evident – "but thanks to that you have control over your daughter. Except that you keep having scruples. Unnecessarily! That little Hedwig would have transgressed her principles sooner or later! What is she to you anyway? It's your daughter who is important! Your own flesh and blood!"

When Mock had finished his tirade he slammed his fist on the table, making the coffee pot rattle. Popielski had the impression his guest's reaction was premeditated and a little contrived.

"And now the next thing," continued Mock. "You say you don't want to conduct the Minotaur investigation because you don't have the time. I can understand that. I've been in a similar situation – I didn't care about people being serially murdered because I was going through a very difficult time with my first wife. So I understand! You obviously feel you have to devote all your time to protecting your daughter from various Minotaurs. But for God's sake, act preventively! Remove all additional and secondary fears, such as concern about a seductive tutor! Simply dampen his ardour, catch him in a vice and put your daughter into the care of a police officer who wouldn't hesitate to use a gun or at least a fist in her defence! And then devote yourself to our case with a pure conscience and clear mind . . ." Mock hesitated. "But now . . . there's something I still have to ask you. Forgive me for being so direct . . . Are your fears for your daughter by any chance . . . ?"

A knock at the door resounded in the living-room and after Popielski's vociferous "Enter!" there appeared the slender figure of Rita, who finished classes early on Fridays. This was her last schoolday but one before the winter holidays. Beneath her unbuttoned coat she wore a navy-blue uniform with a white sailor collar, and her raven-black hair was hidden beneath a warm beret. One lock had escaped and curled in a spiral over a cheek that was pink from the cold. She was beautiful, as young girls unable to conceal constantly changing emotions can be: from joy at the end of a school term, through surprise at seeing Mock, to faint fear inspired by her father's overcast expression. "Sorry", she muttered, and disappeared into the hall. Mock stared at the door she had just closed.

"There, you see how I've brought her up?" – the sight of his daughter had brightened Popielski's mood – "A grown young lady, and she runs away like a deer instead of politely introducing herself to you! But let's conclude our conversation and then I'll make the introductions. You wanted to say something about parents always thinking their children are the most beautiful . . ."

"It's nothing . . ." Mock frowned, as if deep in thought. "That is . . . I wanted to say that I understand your fears for your daughter very well. Very well indeed. But, *but*, let's get back to the crux of the matter. Most importantly, I'm proposing a Popielski and Mock partnership. Just the two of us. But first you must eliminate these fears for your daughter."

"Right," said Popielski firmly. "But I'll do this my own way. The knightly way! Without any sort of pressure! That teacher is well respected, a professor at a secondary school! I'll do it, and you, Mock, sir, are going to observe my methods. I'll prove to you that they're better than coercion!"

"Alright." Mock gave a sigh of resignation. "But if your methods don't prove to be apt you're standing me a large vodka, agreed?"

"Agreed," replied Popielski mechanically.

"Well? A Popielski and Mock partnership?"

The German extended his right hand. Commissioner Popielski hesitated for a moment and, guided by his intuition alone, came to a decision. Had he revealed to anyone what had succeeded in persuading him to enter this singular partnership, they would have laughed. It was Mock's signet ring, adorned – like his own – with an onyx. "We belong to the same club," Popielski had thought, remembering the scene in the train compartment when they had first met. "To the club of lovers of Antiquity and a woman's body." "I like men who belong to that club," the blonde girl had said at the time.

"Popielski and Mock," said the commissioner, extending his hand. "Sounds good, too. Iamb and anapest, if I'm not mistaken. And now I'd like to introduce my daughter."

Popielski left the room and Mock slipped an egg wrapped in herring onto his spoon, greedily swallowed it and then took a bite of a bread roll. He stood up, looked critically at his reflection in the glass-fronted bookcase and forcefully pulled in his stomach.

LWÓW, THAT SAME JANUARY 29TH, 1937
FOUR O'CLOCK IN THE AFTERNOON

Professor Kasprzak was correcting homework on Mickiewicz's *Wielka Improwizacja*† in the empty staff room. It had put him in a bad mood. He hissed angrily and slammed the exercise books onto the desk. "Do these idiots" – he was thinking about his pupils – "always have to be so unbearably highfalutin when they write, so baroque and verbose! Those stupid habits pumped into them by that old sclerotic Mąkos, I've been trying to

† "Great improvisation", from Adam Mickiewicz's poetic novel *Dziady*.

wean them off them for half a year now. They used Rej's language to write about Rej, and now Mickiewicz's to write about Mickiewicz! But I'll get it out of their heads! They can read a few of Kleiner's analyses and write in his style!"

At moments such as these the Polish teacher would recall his own thesis, which he had written on Romantic drama and defended, *summa cum laude*, to Professor Juliusz Kleiner himself ten years earlier. Those praiseworthy moments made him immensely proud and had been, as he realised years later, a prelude to his bright career. On completing his studies at twenty-three, he had immediately obtained a position as Professor of Polish Literature at Queen Jadwiga's Secondary School for Girls, thanks to Wilam Horzyc, director of the Grand Theatre, whose assistant he had been on several occasions. Horzyc's influence had proved exceptionally effective, for it broke down the resistance of the headmistress, Ludmiła Madler. She would have preferred to take on an elderly, solid person for the vacancy rather than a handsome young man draped in a Hidalgo coat, who would turn the head of many a schoolgirl. To the headmistress' great relief, Professor Kasprzak had married a year after starting work at the school, and his wife, a Jewish-Christian convert who was older than him, had given birth to four children in ten years of married life. His teaching achievements, especially where the theatre was concerned, were so great that Headmistress Madler had agreed to his request to teach Romanticism and Modernism to the lower and upper sixth forms. In order to maintain his growing family, the teacher had also begun to work with several well-known theatre directors. This was a semi-clandestine collaboration which involved providing theatres with an audience. Kasprzak took his pupils to shows – and sometimes to the same ones – twice a week, and the theatre managers paid him a fee on the side: one zloty per head. So the Polish tutor made a fair profit and kept in with excellent acquaintances in theatrical circles, and on top of that was held in high regard by the educational authorities because of his untiring extra-curricular activities, namely, staging several plays a year at Queen Jadwiga's Secondary School for Girls. These successes had changed him to a large extent: he had become haughty, self-confident and arrogant, could not see the world beyond theatre, and had begun to neglect his teaching duties. For months on end he neglected to mark tests or home-work, to which Headmistress Madler, troubled by complaints from the parents, politely yet firmly drew his attention. Then Kasprzak began to despise the parents and his work as a teacher, and looked forward to the end of the school year and the holidays, after which a cosy position on the Board of Education awaited him.

With relief he threw the last exercise book on the pile, knowing that there was only one day of work still ahead of him and then two whole weeks of winter holidays! He would devote them to planning his new show which he had been promised would be premiered in a real theatre even though the actors were schoolgirls, and would be seen by the whole of Lwów. He got dressed, grabbed his walking stick and hat and left the school, barely acknowledging the caretaker.

On Piłudski Street he jumped onto a moving number 3. Noticing the conductor's severe expression he realized that leaping onto a tram did not befit the dignity of a school professor. He got out at Halicki Square and made along Hetmańska towards the Grand Theatre whence stretched his true destination: a labyrinth of small streets inhabited almost exclusively by Israelites. Here too was Krakidały, the flea market where everything could be either lost – by playing various gambling games, of which "three cards" was the most popular – or bought, from horsemeat to unbreakable combs. On Friday afternoons, however, these streets were almost deserted due to preparations for the Sabbath, and in the gathering dusk they seemed rather dangerous. This sense of danger was heightened by the presence of a few gloomy traders who had failed to sell their goods and blamed the entire world for their misfortune. They glowered at passers-by as they dismantled their stalls. But this did not discourage the professor; he had arranged to meet a second-hand book dealer, Nachum Rudy, whom he had commissioned to find for him old editions of Romantic plays and theatre programmes. Kasprzak passed his beloved Grand Theatre, crossed Gołuchowski Square and plunged into Gęsia, a narrow street on the other side. From here it was not far to Zakątna, where Nachum had his stall. He glanced at his watch and quickened his pace. At that moment he heard a loud voice behind him:

"Professor, sir! Excuse me, Professor!"

Startled, he turned to see a breathless man he recognized immediately: Commissioner Edward Popielski, father of Rita, one of his pupils. The man rested his hands on his knees and panted for a few moments. Kasprzak did not like him; he was irritated by his masculinity, and by his reputation as a brute and alcoholic as well as a vanquisher of crooks. There was yet another reason why the teacher did not like the commissioner; he suspected him of informing on him to the school authorities. Besides, it was not at all to his liking that anyone should meet him on Krakidały which, because of its gambling, prostitution and the underhand sales of pornographic postcards, did not enjoy the approval of the learned circles to which he aspired.

"I sincerely apologize for daring to accost you in the street, Professor," began Popielski. "I was at the school and the caretaker told me you had made your way towards the theatre. I ran and managed to spot you. I have an exceptionally urgent matter. I'm the father of your pupil Rita Popielska. Do you recognize me, sir?"

"How can I help you, Commissioner?" said Kasprzak dryly, glancing at his watch.

"I won't take up much of your time, Professor." Popielski had straightened up and was now towering over the teacher. "My daughter has told me that you're planning to put on a performance of Euripedes's *Medea* in the near future. Hence the urgency. To put my request to you before the winter holidays. I kindly ask that Rita does not take part in the performance. For her acting is a reward, and she doesn't really deserve one, bearing in mind the report she got this term. That's all, I won't take up any more of your time. May I count on your kind agreement?"

Kasprzak was speechless with astonishment. He could not absorb the absurdity of the whole episode: the famous Commissioner Popielski accosts him here on Krakidały and makes demands! He looked about him as if searching for witnesses to this unseemly and grotesque scene. His offended gaze was wrongly interpreted by a shady character in an old Austrian army coat, lugging a basket from which poked the shaggy heads of several puppies. The character looked at both men and asked:

"All due respect, would either of you kind gentlemen fancy some near-pedigree pups?"

"No," growled Popielski, knowing it wasn't easy to shoo away a desperate salesman on Krakidały.

This growl, this blunt, self-confident growl, irritated Kasprzak all the more. "*What?*" he thought, "Does this bald prick think he can impose his will on everyone? This degenerate whom the whole town says is living with his own first cousin?"

"Commissioner, sir," said Kasprzak, barely controlling his annoyance, "this performance is to be a great theatrical event. And do you know why, Commissioner? Apart from anything else, because your daughter is going to play Medea. She is a phenomenally talented actress. You ought to be proud of her!"

"My superior, Chief Zubik, has already mentioned the performance to me." Popielski smiled sweetly. "They talk about you a lot, Professor, in the official high circles of Lwów . . . A lot . . ."

"Well, I'm not surprised." Kasprzak brushed the snow off his coat-

134

sleeves and for a moment forgot Nachum Rudy. "I've done my bit for the town . . ."

"You have such a great talent, Professor," Popielski gushed in admiration, "that it is even marvelled at by police officers who, according to *opinio communis*, are thick and rarely go to the theatre . . ."

"Well, I don't know, I don't know," said Kasprzak, wallowing in the compliments. "Come to think of it, I myself wonder whether police officers go to the theatre at all. I don't know anyone in those thrilling spheres of higher authority apart from you, Commissioner, and I've never seen you at a theatre . . ."

"Yes, a great talent" — Popielski grabbed the professor by the elbow and tilted his head in admiration — "which is bound to be appreciated by exactly those higher authorities with whom I'm on very good terms . . ."

Kasprzak looked at the police officer carefully, his brain working fast. Popielski's eventual support would definitely not outweigh the near-certain success of *Medea*. "Besides, he might start making fresh demands," he thought, "for example that Kasprzak should pull some strings with other professors so that his silly — though certainly pretty — little goose might pass her final exams in a year's time. Oh no! Was he, Professor Jerzy Kasprzak, to have dealings with police types who probably have the blood of more than one man on their hands? Certainly not!"

"She's going to perform in the play, Commissioner", said Kasprzak firmly. "It would be a failure without her. And a man in my position cannot allow failure."

"She will perform" — Popielski stopped smiling —"if I let her. Who has the final say in my child's upbringing? Do I, or does the school? The father or the teacher?"

"Please don't get upset, Commissioner," said Kasprzak, changing his tone as he prepare to deliver the final blow. "Agree to your daughter taking part in this play! You can have no idea of the gratitude that will come your

135

way. You'll win Rita back completely! She's told me a great deal about you, about her late mother whom she never knew . . ."

Kasprzak broke off as he saw Popielski's jaws moving beneath taut skin. The Commissioner leaned towards the teacher and whispered in his ear:

"You've debased me now, but you're not going to debase Rita."

Popielski walked away. He held his bowler high in his outstretched right hand as a dusting of snow settled on his bald head.

LWÓW, THAT SAME JANUARY 29TH, 1937
FOUR O'CLOCK IN THE AFTERNOON

Eberhard Mock rubbed his eyes in amazement. He had never seen anything like it. If it were not for the snow and frost he would have been certain that he had found himself at some Turkish or Arabian market. Bearded Jews, reeking of garlic, were closing their stalls and shoving various objects under his nose. Efforts to repel these pests with curses in German had the opposite of the desired effect. The pedlars simply switched to a peculiar German dialect, began to praise their wares even more ardently and there, before Mock's eyes, extended a veritable panorama of shoddy goods: cigarette lighters, metal tape measures, cufflinks, calendars, whetstones for razor blades, elasticated braces, watches, contraptions for tying neckties and holding trouser legs in place, suspenders, scented soaps and clothes hangers. Mock felt completely helpless in the face of these traders, and so he decided to allow them to gather around and touch him, in the hope that they would eventually tire of it.

They tired of it faster than he had anticipated and before long there were no more pedlars nearby. So he gazed with fascination at the dirty houses with their Hebraic signs, at the dogs running from doorways and the screaming children in round caps with long ringlets dangling at their ears. For a change, two musicians – one playing an accordion, the other a mandolin – now appeared at his side. Despite the cold they wore only jackets, and instead of ties had colourful scarves wrapped around their necks.

Clouds of mist drifted in from the narrow streets, dusk began to fall, and the musicians came closer and closer. They gave off the smell of alcohol, and their eyes shone with insolence. The lively tune, combined with the dusk, the fog and the men's wicked intentions, created a sinister atmosphere. All of a sudden Mock remembered something: a waltz on a deserted, rusty, spinning merry-go-round in Breslau, beneath the merry-go-round a murdered child. He felt ill at ease, looked around for Zaremba and at that moment caught sight of Popielski disappearing down the street. The commissioner was bare-headed, his bowler hat held high in his hand.

Mock pushed the surprised musicians aside and made after the man to whom Popielski had just been speaking. The brisk footfalls of the two angry drunk men were soon drowned out by the roar of an engine. Mock looked round.

Kasprzak did the same and saw, a few paces away, a man of medium height, stocky and square-shaped. Behind him were two irate musicians. And even further behind, in the snow flurry, yet another man came running. All these people were heading in his direction, while a black car crawled alongside the pavement. Anxious now, the teacher turned abruptly into Bóźnicza, where the synagogue was, and tried to cut quickly across the road.

He did not have time. The automobile stopped and blocked his way. The square-shaped man came up close and made a swift movement with his leg. Kasprzak felt pain pierce his shin. He seethed with unbridled anger that someone should have the audacity to assault him in the centre

137

of Lwów, and instead of attending to his agonizing leg he threw himself at his assailant. The latter raised his other leg and propelled a heel into Kasprzak's knee. Kasprzak groaned and took a swipe with his fist. The assailant ducked and the professor struck the roof of the car. The passenger door opened. Instinctively Kasprzak lowered his head and peered inside. Just then he received a blow to the back of his head which nearly threw him into the car. Then he got another in the face from the driver, close-up. His mouth filled with blood. As he was dragged into the car by his tie and the lapels of his coat, the stitching of his over-tight jacket ripped. Suddenly he felt pain everywhere: in his shin, his knee, his hand, on the back of his head and his nose.

"Help!" yelled Kasprzak. "Help! Murder!"

At that moment he heard Popielski's voice:

"Police! Disperse! Can't you see we've caught a thief?"

Kasprzak raised his head with difficulty and through the rear window watched as one of the musicians spat at Popielski's feet. Then the driver who had dragged him into the car threw a blanket stinking of oil over his head. Somebody grabbed him under his arms, pulled him back out of the car, opened the back door, pushed him onto the seat then tumbled in heavily beside him. The last thing the teacher heard was the odd pronounciation of "hairless-s-s" with double or even triple the number of "s"s. He thought the word came from the lips of the musicians.

LWÓW, THAT SAME JANUARY 29TH, 1937
FIVE O'CLOCK IN THE AFTERNOON

The Chevrolet passed the crossroads of Kleparowska and Janowska and stopped. Kleparowska was lit only by the feeble light coming from apartment buildings and the yellow glow of one solitary streetlamp which swayed in the wind three metres above the uneven cobblestones.

Sitting next to Zaremba, Popielski glanced anxiously at the windows of the drinking-den. The raised voices and the singing confirmed his fears that there must be a large number of customers – both drunk and politically minded – who would react angrily at the sight of the police officers.

"Wiluś," he said to Zaremba, "Mock and I are going to take this citizen, and you, brother, will drive home as quickly as you can so that the rabble in the tavern don't recognize our car. Wait there for my call. We'll certainly be needing you again today" – he gestured to Kasprzak who was being held down in the back seat by Mock – "to get rid of his carcass somewhere."

Zaremba nodded and waited as Popielski climbed out, opened the door, grabbed Kasprzak by the legs and tugged hard. The latter yanked his handcuffed hands taut and spluttered something, despite the gag. "Mock's done a good job of incapacitating him," Popielski thought with a certain admiration. The German drew up his legs, rested the soles of his feet on the teacher lying next to him and, cursing his own belly and panting loudly, he pushed the delinquent out. When almost all of Kasprzak's body apart from his head was on the cobblestones, Mock jumped out of the car, walked around it and grasped the prostrate man – who hung thrashing about like a fish between the car seat and road – beneath the arms. Popielski took him by the legs and nodded. At this mute command they just about managed to pull him towards the doorway. Once inside, Mock felt the slippery leather of his gloves and the material of Kasprzak's coat lose contact. He tried to push one hand deeper into the man's armpit, but the attempt was in vain.

The collision of Kasprzak's head with the first wooden step was as loud, or so it seemed to them, as a small explosion. The door to the ground-floor apartment opened, and Popielski realized that the worst possible thing was about to happen – they were going to be exposed. A vision appeared to him in a flash: he was standing in Commander Goździewski's office being handed his dismissal along with a life-long injunction which forbade him from carrying out state duties. Both he and Mock froze in anticipation of how the events would develop.

Meanwhile, in the doorway to the apartment stood two men with their coats unbuttoned, swaying on their legs. The peaked cap of one had slid to the back of his head, the wire glasses of the other to the tip of his nose. Both were drunk.

"Yeah, Józek, give us a kiss," yelled one of them.

"You gorgeous hunk," yelled back the other. "Just us two in the world, you and me!"

The men fell into each other's arms and their drunken kisses were like slaps on a cheek. Popielski winked at Mock. Both grasped Kasprzak beneath the arms and began to drag him up the stairs, soon disappearing from the patch of light cast by the open door. Kasprzak mumbled something. The sound and the commotion on the stairs did not go unnoticed by the two drunks.

"Wha's happenin'?" One of them pushed his glasses up his nose and tried to make out the dark silhouettes on the stairs.

"Ay, my pal's gone and got plastered," said Popielski in street lingo, "and I'm bringin' 'im 'ome!"

Kasprzak's shoes thumped up the stairs, the tails of his coat wiped the dust and dragged through the cigarette butts. They found themselves on a landing between two floors. A button rolled down the wooden steps. A rusty nail protruding from a banister caught on the pocket of Kasprzak's trousers, digging fast into the material and making it impossible to carry him any further. They tugged. Nothing. The drunks were still staring up at them, but semi-darkness and vodka blurred their vision. Popielski tugged once more and heard the ripping of material, but the body did not budge another inch on the turn in the staircase.

"Close that door!" yelled someone from inside the apartment. "It's cold and there's flies comin' in!"

"I'm just closing it!" The bespectacled man peered up at the landing. "But there's one needs lightin' up 'ere, 'e's draggin' a sozzled mate."

"Lightin' up for who?" Chairs and shoes scraped across the sawdust covering the floor of the tavern. "Show us who's been dragged then! Maybe it's Tadzio? He's never been one for appearances!"

Popielski and Mock tugged. In vain. DISTINGUISHED SECONDARY-SCHOOL PROFESSOR BATTERED BY FAMOUS POLICE OFFICER was the headline Popielski already saw before his eyes. Downstairs, the voices of those annoyed by the cold coming through the open door now grew in volume. "Life-long injunction not to carry out state duties". Popielski experienced a peculiar itch in his gums – the sign of imminent fury. He reached towards Kasprzak's stomach and grasped his belt, then jammed his heel against a stair, clenched his teeth and heaved. At that moment he noticed the nail caught on the professor's trousers, and without un-hooking it glanced furiously at Mock. They tugged and the nail tore Kasprzak's trousers, piercing his underpants and skin. Through the gag came a painful groan, and the body moved upwards as the point of the nail slashed material and ploughed through skin. Kasprzak's head thumped against the ground on the first floor.

The door slammed below. Darkness fell. Mock and Popielski caught their breath while Kasprzak lay still on the floor. After a while Popielski straightened up and kicked one of the doors, which opened onto Juliusz Szaniawski standing in a strip of red light. He was wearing a luxuriant wig, tight underpants and the stiff skirt of a ballerina. The scent of Turkish incense and a red glow emanated from the apartment, in which the "Czardas" from *Swan Lake* was playing loudly on a gramophone.

"You didn't warn me of your visit, Commissioner." The dancer waved his hand, and smoke from his cigarette whirled in the demonic glow. "Or of your friends . . ." He glanced indifferently at Mock and at the man lying on his doorstep with a sack over his head. "But welcome, welcome as always. Your little nest is free."

The light was on in Szaniawski's bathroom, which he grandiloquently called the "bathing room" or "Popielski's little nest". Kasprzak lay in the bathtub undressed down to his underwear; his clothes had been rolled into a bundle and shoved in a corner. Mock was sitting on a chair, Popielski on the closed water-closet. They sat in their shirtsleeves, cuffs rolled up and ties loosened, smoking and staring at Kasprzak with heavy, fixed eyes. It was stuffy, they found it hard to breathe, and a moment earlier they had almost been exposed. They glared darkly at the man in the tub, their eyes filled with an anger they did not have to feign.

"Kasprzak," said Popielski slowly and emphatically, "you said you'd never seen me at the theatre. True, I rarely go. And do you know why? Because the actors shout too loud and stamp their feet too hard on stage. I've got a limited imagination and somehow can't be persuaded I'm in Capuletti's palace, for example, when some floorboard on the stage keeps creaking . . ."

Kasprzak seemed not to hear Popielski's words. He sucked in air and groaned in pain, licked his finger and gingerly touched the wound on his thigh. Blood ran to the bottom of the tub in a little stream; his long johns hung in tatters on either side of his leg, revealing a thin, hairy shin. One none-too-clean sock had sagged down over his ankle and below his knee flapped a rubber garter. He shivered as if he were in an Eskimo's igloo, not an overheated bathroom.

"You're to write a letter which I'm going to dictate to you." Popielski lifted the lid of the water-closet, threw in his cigarette butt and pressed the handle. "I'll keep it as a souvenir. And if I hear that you're talking to my daughter outside school hours, if I hear that you still want to use her in your plays, if I hear that you're gushing about her acting talent, I'm going to go to Headmistress Madler with it. And if that doesn't help I'm going to show the letter to the municipal authorities and *Sprawiedliwosc* will print it the following Saturday under the headline 'Belated flirtations of a schoolteacher'. And the first thing you're to do is dismiss my daughter from her role in *Medea*. Do you understand?"

Kasprzak did not respond. Popielski winked at Mock who got up heavily from the chair and leaned over the tub.

"Yes, I do!" yelled Kasprzak, looking at Mock. "I've understood every-thing!"

Popielski got to his feet and pushed his colleague's chair towards the tub. From the pocket of Kasprzak's jacket he pulled a visiting card and a fountain pen. He then passed him the jacket.

"Wipe your hands on this!" he muttered. "Or you'll stain the card. Now write!"

"What am I supposed to write?" Kasprzak pushed himself up in the bath with a hiss of pain and uncapped the pen.

"I'm about to dictate." Popielski was so astounded by how readily Kasprzak had agreed that for a moment he could not collect his thoughts. "'Dear, beloved Rita! I can't stop thinking about you. Your talent is magnificent, unique. Oh, how I dream of touching your hand! Your lips I don't dare to touch, even in my dreams . . .'"

"There's no more room after 'even in my dreams'." Kasprzak's eyes revealed the eagerness of a class toady. "May I have another card, please?"

Popielski deliberated for a moment. The very thought of Rita being kissed by this thin, hairy goat repulsed him. His gums were still itching. Neither Kasprzak's blood nor his fawning readiness to obey any order

143

had diffused his anger. He could still picture the sunny September after-noon when Rita had rushed happily into the house after her first day at school and shouted joyfully, "Papa, that old fogey Mąkos doesn't teach me Polish any more. I've got a new teacher who gives such wonderful lectures, and he loves the theatre!" Leokadia had smiled over her cards and asked, "And is he handsome, this new Polish teacher?"

Popielski approached the bathtub. Kasprzak did not even groan when the side of the commissioner's hand struck his jaw. The Bakelite pen fell to the tiled floor and shattered into several small pieces.

"So, handsome, are you then, Professor?" hissed Popielski, raising his hand once again, despite the sharp pain shooting along it from the previ-ous blow. "Casanova, are you?"

He did not have time to strike, however, because Mock caught his wrist in one strong hand, and with the other pushed him against the wall.

"Calm down, damn it!" Mock squeezed Popielski's wrists and watched his face contort. "Do you want to beat him to death? We've achieved our aim. He's in our hands, locked in a vice from which he won't escape until your daughter's final exams. That's how the Mock and Popielski partnership works!"

"I'm corrupt, I'm corrupt," said Popielski, only half conscious.

"We're all corrupt!" yelled Mock. "Here, take a look at real corrup-tion!"

At this he opened a hatch in the wall which Popielski had not even known existed. This little window gave onto the living-room, from which incense smoke and music now flowed into the bathroom, and through it they saw a contemporary Sodom and Gomorrah. Szaniawski had already discarded his pants and was performing the "Dance of the Cygnets" on the table amongst the empty wine bottles wearing nothing but a tutu and wig. Beneath the table three naked men were crawling about on all fours, each with a peacock feather pinned in his hair.

Popielski collapsed into the chair. Mock pulled out a cigarette, lit it and passed it to the commissioner. Professor Kasprzak wheezed in the tub. Mock wiped the sweat from his brow.

"High time we had some vodka, don't you think?" he sighed.

LWÓW, THAT SAME JANUARY 29TH, 1937
ELEVEN O'CLOCK AT NIGHT

They clinked glasses and swallowed Baczewski's cumin vodka with pleasure, along with a bite to eat; Mock had chosen herring roll-mops, Popielski a terrine with lingonberry sauce. They sat in the Palais de Dance near the Grand Theatre and watched the slowly revolving circular dance floor on which couples were dancing the playful "Lambeth Walk". On their table stood a bowl of meat jelly and a platter of herrings, terrine and goose necks stuffed with liver. A bottle of champagne peeped from an ice-bucket and a slender, iced carafe of vodka towered over the plates.

They were silent. The fact that Popielski had just dismissed two young hostesses who had wanted to sit at their table irritated Mock. Popielski, on the other hand, was thinking over the day's events, and quite dispassionately now: Kasprzak's humiliation, Zaremba's arrival at Szaniawski's apartment, their throwing the teacher out with a sack over his head at the corner of Rzeźnia and Starozakonna, followed by four fruitless hours at the Investigative Bureau interrogating representatives of Armenian and Georgian minorities whom Herman Kacnelson had not managed to deal with before being beaten up at Kanarienfogel's tavern. Popielski and Mock had put Rita and Lodzia on the sleeper to Kołomyje, and then had been politely greeted by Mr Zehngut, owner of the Palais de Dance himself, who had offered them the director's loge. Mock spoke first:

"Let's have another drink. I feel like some of that delicious aspic." He waved at the meat jelly. "But I can't have any without vodka."

"Why?" said Popielski mechanically, without looking at him. "Don't you like it?"

"On the contrary." Mock reached for the bottle. "I like it too much. But I don't want to put on any more weight."

"And what's vodka got to do with it?" Popielski shouted over the music.

"A forensic pathologist I know," said Mock, leaning towards the commissioner's ear, "a *doctor rerum naturalium*, claims that fat dissolves in alcohol. With alcohol it doesn't settle around your waist, but dissolves harmlessly somewhere else in your body." He patted his belly and burst into affected laughter.

Popielski did not join in. From the height of their loge he watched the dance floor without the least interest, tightly gripping his glass and with it drawing small circles on the tablecloth. Mock felt anger gathering within him, not because the festive evening was dragging in unbearable silence, but because something else was bothering him. He simply could not believe that this man, whom he had almost caught red-handed frolicking with a beautiful woman, had taken him to a cave of Sodomites where he felt at home and even had his own "nest". He did not know how to tell Popielski that their partnership could not exist without total trust, without their revealing to each other even their darkest secrets. Yet he was afraid that Popielski would confess to something terrible about his sexuality, which Mock did not want to know for fear of it ruining their police partnership.

"I have something to confess." The orchestra had stopped playing and in the silence Popielski stared at Mock, as if reading his thoughts. "A shameful secret of mine . . ."

"There's something I forgot to tell you," Mock cut in. "We got a tele-

146

gram from Kattowitz today. A twenty-year-old woman in a mental hospital. Face gnawed. She claims she was bitten by an aristocrat . . ."

"Please don't interrupt!" Popielski threw back a vodka without taking a mouthful of food. "What do we care about some mad woman from Silesia! Listen to what I have to say . . ."

"We've got to go there," Mock did not let him finish. "It could be important!"

"For God's sake, stop interrupting me!" yelled Popielski, springing up and loudly scraping his chair, much to the waiter's alarm.

"I don't damn well care," said Mock, on his feet now too and leaning over the table, "about your intimate relationship with that 'soft brother' Szaniawski! He's got nothing to do with our investigation! Don't play at being Hamlet, damn it! First you despair about some teacher, and now you want to disclose your sexual proclivities to me! I do not want to hear about it, I tell you! Concentrate on the investigation and get yourself some balls!"

Mock's words rang out across the room during the interval in the music. The silence brought Popielski to his senses. He regained his wits and hoped that the speed with which the German had hurled his insults had made it impossible for anyone to understand them, all the more so as the most suggestive of them were not clear even to him. The orchestra started up a tango and Popielski calmly sat down at the table.

"I don't understand." He got out an Egyptian cigarette and tapped it on the table. "What do you mean 'soft brother'?"

"Isn't that what they called homosexuals in Austria?" Mock was still on his feet, but had changed his tone of voice.

"Listen to me." Popielski drew deeply on his cigarette. "You'll find out in a moment what ties me to Szaniawski." He raised his hand when Mock wanted to interrupt once more. "In fact nothing ties me to the man, but a great deal ties me to his apartment. He makes his bathroom available to

147

me whenever I should want it. And I want it when I feel an attack coming on. Yes, my good man, I suffer from epilepsy – you must already know. But what you don't know is that sometimes during my attacks I get visions. Have you ever used a clairvoyant in the course of your work with the police?"

"No, never."

"Neither have I. I don't have to. I'm a clairvoyant myself, although I must be the worst in the country. I sometimes get visions during an attack, but I can never interpret them correctly, or straightaway. Well, that's an exaggeration, I've managed on a couple of occasions. But generally it's when a murder has been committed, or there's already been a kidnapping, that I hit myself on the forehead and say: 'I've seen that before!'"

The orchestra played on, and Mock remained silent. Popielski pushed aside his shot glass, poured some vodka into a water glass and in one go downed what must have been two thirds of it. He wiped his lips and looked at Mock with clear eyes.

"I suffer from a minor form of epilepsy, Mock. The medication I'm on counteracts it almost completely. But when I want to have a vision I don't take the medication to bring on an attack. And for that I need Szaniawski's apartment, or to be precise, his bathtub."

Mock was agape and Popielski sighed with relief. He cut a large triangle of meat jelly with his fork and squeezed a segment of lemon over it. He put half the triangle in his mouth and chewed, shutting his eyes in bliss.

"And can't you bring on the attacks in your own apartment? Your own bathroom?" Mock's eyes were round with amazement.

"No." Popielski swallowed a bite of aspic and looked at Mock with a certain amusement, even though this was the moment at which he would have to admit to the most ghastly truth about his epilepsy.

"Unfortunately, I sometimes lose control of my bowels and my bladder during an attack, then fall asleep. The sleep usually lasts about a quarter of an hour but it can be longer. Imagine, Mock, the following scene: I'm in the bathroom for a long time, my cousin and daughter start to get worried, then knock or bang on the door. I don't let them in so they call the caretaker. He prizes the door open and what do they all see? Popielski asleep in his own shit."

He broke off and anxiously studied Mock for signs of derision. He saw none, and breathed a sigh of relief.

"That's why I sometimes need a discreet bathroom. Now do you understand? You're the only person apart from Zaremba who knows why I go to Szaniawski's. My cousin doesn't even know, and I've been living with her for twenty years!"

Mock refilled their glasses, to make up for lost time. They drank, took a bite and Mock immediately poured some more. They drank before the alcohol had even managed to run down into their stomachs. Both now felt the effects of the vodka: a slight burning of the cheeks, lethargy and a pleasant tiredness in their muscles.

"I'm honoured that you've told me," said Mock, breaking the silence. "I shall certainly keep your secret. I understand you perfectly well and apologize for my suspicions. I find those visions of yours fascinating. What did you see during your last session at Szaniawski's? Tell me, maybe there were colours, symbolic figures? We'll work them out together. After all, that complex Latin syntax we unravelled couldn't have been any harder!"

"Nothing." Mock was sad to hear this. "It happens. I didn't see anything, although I did hear something."

"What? I believe you. A few years ago I had this case in Breslau with a clairvoyant Jew who, in a trance, would foretell when people were going to die."

"Since you believe me I'll tell you. A dog growling. It came from beneath the bathtub. And Szaniawski hasn't got a dog. He hates all animals. There was no dog, it must have been part of my vision."

Mock pushed himself away from the table and clicked his fingers.

"The bill!" he shouted.

"Hold on, why the hurry?" Popielski put a hand on Mock's arm in a friendly gesture. "I've told you my secret so we can have a proper drink! And now you want to run off!"

"We've got a train to Kattowitz in an hour." Mock was still looking around for the waiter. "I checked at the station today."

"And what are we going to go to Kattowitz for? And why so suddenly? To see some madwoman who says she was chewed up by an aristocrat? They could verify everything in Kattowitz on the spot and send us a detailed report."

"They said her injuries looked as though they had been made by a dog," said Mock emphatically, "and you dreamed about a dog."

Popielski studied Mock's face, looking for any hint of mockery or irony. He saw none. The German waited for his colleague's decision; he sat sphinx-like, as if turned to stone, with only his fingers moving as they tapped out a rhythm on the table.

"It defies logic," said Popielski, and rested his elbows on the table. "Those visions of mine have nothing to do with the logistics of the investigation."

"You have your methods, I have mine. You believed me today, then I believed you. That's all." Mock looked at the man he was addressing with an impish grin. "Popielski, don't ramble on! Don't expect me to convince you of your own methods! You've gained a significant position in the police world – even if you got there by gazing into a crystal ball. To cut it short, let me say one thing: I want a crystal ball like that. Anyway, do you have a better – what am I saying! – a different trail to follow from the one in Silesia?"

"Let's go to Kattowitz, then." The commissioner glanced at the dance floor, inhaled the scent of perfume, closed his eyes and gave a slight nod. "But not alone, eh? We've bored ourselves enough in each other's company today."

THE LWÓW–KATTOWITZ TRAIN
SATURDAY, JANUARY 30TH, 1937
EIGHT O'CLOCK IN THE MORNING

Popielski, Mock and two Jewish prostitutes whose names they did not remember sat in the private compartment eating breakfast. The girls were resting, a little drink-sodden and dispirited, and their conversation kept falling apart. The men sat in silence. They were tired and short of sleep. They were both over fifty and their bodies did not recuperate as quickly as they had ten or twenty years earlier. They were not, however, suffering from post-alcoholic spleen – Baczewski's vodka was of the very best quality and the food that went with it sumptuous and full of fat – or from debauchery-related scruples. Nor was the sight of the two girls – who the previous day had seemed desirable and attractive, but whom the sharp pale light of the morning revealed as having open pores, eye-lashes caked with make-up, greasy hair, an over-abundance of curves and gaps in their teeth – the reason for their morose mood. They were troubled by something entirely different. Two hours earlier, at Kraków station, they had been visited in their compartment by Inspector Marian Zubik, who just happened to be taking his sons for a winter holiday in Zakopane by the very same train.

This was the last thing they would have expected to see after the stormy events of that evening and night. The previous day, on leaving the Palais de Dance, they had immediately gone to Main Station to buy tickets to Kattowitz. Unfortunately the private compartment had already been taken, and the single sleeping compartments too. They therefore had to make do with a compartment with two beds, one above the other. To make matters worse the festal night had swept all the prostitutes from the station and they had left for Kattowitz alone, frustrated and disappointed. In Przemyśl, however, Chairman Bronisław Bromberg, an industrialist returning from the winter fairs in Romania's Chernivtsi, vacated the private compartment. Mock and Popielski had immediately transferred to the empty and luxurious quarters in the company of two young ladies, which the enterprising and generously remunerated conductor had found for them at Przemyśl station. Then the alcohol had not stopped flowing and the compartment appeared to burst at the seams; clothes flew about, the young ladies poured champagne over their naked bodies, shrieking and groaning, while Mock and Popielski had risen to the very peaks of their virility. Towards morning they had swapped partners and drunk to their brotherhood.

Up to the moment which had put them in the aforementioned mood. The obliging conductor had come at six in the morning to report that he had just spoken to Inspector Zubik, who wished to visit their compartment. The inspector, as the conductor reported, had got off in Kraków and by chance had caught sight of Popielski standing in the window, relishing a morning cigarette. The visit was to be a short one, the conductor assured them, as the train was about to leave.

Mock and Popielski had tidied the compartment in a flash. They were not worried about the girls since both of them were next door, fast asleep. Zubik had entered, greeted his colleagues ceremoniously, enquired about the purpose of their trip, praised their diligence and then was struck dumb, his eyes fixed on the ceiling. Popielski's eyes had slowly followed.

From the chandelier hung a stocking and two used condoms.

152

The deputy director of the psychiatric hospital, Doctor Ludwika Tkocz, hated men adoring her, which is why she was resolute, taciturn and rather brusque with them and put a prompt, effective and irrevocable stop to any flirtation. She had made a rule of this as far back as her days at the Jagiellonian University in Kraków, where she had studied medicine. One of her colleagues had once coarsely joked in front of some students that Professor Władysław Heinrich had published her thesis in the *Psychiatric Review* not because of her light pen, but because of her light morals. Apart from the fact that this was nothing more than nasty, unfounded slander, Doctor Tkocz had realized one thing: to resort to sex in matters of scientific discourse was an act of desperation on the part of impotent, mediocre and envious individuals. She had kneed the student hard in the genitals, and as he writhed in pain, pronounced to everyone her personal manifesto condemning the limitations of sexual differences. And she had acted on it to this day: she had not married, so as not to be anyone's slave; she used no eye make-up or lipstick, so that no man should slobber at the sight of her; and she dressed in men's fashion so as not to be given special treatment as a woman.

In the ten years that followed university she had made a brilliant career for herself. She had completed three supplementary years studying psychiatry at the Sorbonne with great success, passed her doctoral thesis with flying colours, and after taking up the position of deputy director at the psychiatric hospital – though not without a tiny bit of help from friends in high places – she was now working towards a professorship. She had never met the man of her life, who would need to be both resolute towards others, yet patient and yielding with her, brilliantly intelligent and at the same time capable of becoming merely a background to her disquisitions when the need arose. And yet she attracted weak, lost individuals who looked to her for support and a degree of care which was verging on the maternal. She could not abide such men. Once she had realized that she would never find her Platonic other half she ceased to care about relationships with the ugly sex. She snorted derisively at all rumour and spitefulness — which included no shortage of suppositions that she harboured Sapphic passions — and saw them off with a Silesian curse: "May lightning strike you!", which she had often heard used by her father, a foreman at the Emma coalmine in Rybnik. She grew even more determined and sure of herself, definitively changed her skirt for a pair of trousers, and threw all her cosmetics — apart from soap and tooth powder — out of the bathroom.

Despite her "anti-beauty" care regime and the relentless passage of time, Ludwika Tkocz had not succeeded in concealing her fine looks. The worst cataclysms in a woman's appearance — hormonal tempests as well as ante- and post-natal fat deposits — passed by this delicate blonde with her porcelain complexion. She was not, therefore, surprised that the two men entering her office had devoured her with their eyes; she was used to it. But she *was* surprised that they were still staring at her now, despite the brusque manner in which she had greeted them, tearing her hand away from one as he had raised it to his lips, snapping that she hated such affections. These two must have been hopeless cases who would never understand the essence of a man—woman partnership. Two typical police officers who thought the world belonged to them, and that women were only waiting for them to beckon. Two puffed-up peacocks more than fifty years old, smelling of the best eau de cologne and flashing their signet rings, cigarette lighters and diamond tie-pins in front of her. Stuffed wallets were their guiding principle, and the wrinkled worms in their long johns their only concern! Worst of all was that she had immediately sensed a sudden change come about in the men when they found themselves in her presence. Discord between them grew with every word; they began to criticize each other, and make increasingly spiteful jokes at each other's expense. She tasted bitterness in her mouth. Subconsciously they were competing for her, and she was supposed to be taken in by the chintz and beads of their mediocre intelligence! She looked at them with undisguised disdain, but held back. She did not want them to decipher her true feelings; she did not want to be helpless. Out of professional habit she began to register various details of their dress and behaviour.

The bald man, after what no doubt seemed to him to be a well-aimed riposte directed at his stouter, dark-haired colleague, gazed at her in the hope that she would approve of his words. His beautiful, slender fingers were ready for any action, his well-built body was taut and his hazel-green eyes full of perverse anticipation.

"My dear sir," she addressed the bald man in German, a language she particularly disliked, "before you even attacked your colleague with that poor joke about biting out of passion . . . before you showed how bright you are, you asked whether the patient Maria Szynok has a family. Well, she doesn't. She has no family. She is a ward" – she peeped into a cardboard file – "of the Mielęcki Orphanage in Kattowitz. It is so typical of this state and its welfare institutions!" She looked sternly over her glasses at the men she was addressing, as if they were the very state she was criticizing. "Brought up by nuns to hold her own body in contempt! Taught that her only goal is to get married and have five children . . . It's not surprising that when for whatever reason she did not manage to achieve this goal she took to daydreaming. For some that would be as far as it goes; in her case the daydreaming turned to paranoia, and severe paranoia at that, revealed straightaway by the stress of that mysterious event which occasioned the arrival of the police. Perhaps it was rape? Hence these fabrications of hers about being married to some mythical count, some prince on a white horse. I simply cannot work out those wounds on her face . . ." She lost herself in thought for a while. "I wouldn't entirely believe the local forensic pathologist, who has concluded that she was bitten by a dog. He's irresponsible. He didn't even examine her internally, so we can't know whether she was raped or not. My interpretation of her injuries is completely different . . ."

"In what way?" The dark-haired man had hazel-green eyes too. "How would you interpret them? We'd be curious to know!"

"Don't be so inquisitive!" the bald man delighted in scolding him. "Or you'll provoke the doctor into giving us another scientific lecture like the one we had when we arrived. If I hear one more thing about affective illness and manic depression I'm really going to go mad . . . On the other hand, that wouldn't be so bad. To be a patient of yours and see you every day . . ." His lips parted to reveal strong, even teeth.

"My interpretation" – only now did Doctor Tkocz notice the bald officer's carefully tended beard – "is as follows. These wounds were self-inflicted as a form of self-punishment, or as a prelude to future reasoning. In other words, she harmed herself as it were for the future, so as to explain her failure to find a husband: I can't find a husband? Not surprising – I'm so ugly . . . That's how she's going to explain it to herself when she gets out of here and is at least partially cured – which could take ten years!"

"And then she'll find herself one more reason." The bald man crossed his legs and displayed his shiny brogues, on which there was not even a trace of the snow and mud which covered the streets after the recent thaw. "She'll say to herself: I'm old *and* ugly . . ."

"I don't believe a woman of thirty is old!" Doctor Tkocz felt herself grow red, something she hated above all.

"There, you see, Edward" – the dark-haired man adjusted his pearl-coloured tie, which contrasted beautifully with his dark, pinstriped suit – "your suppositions have proved correct. This Maria Szynok is insane and her story about some count is pure fantasy . . . You were right, we could have ascertained all this in Lwów without coming all the way here, although I" – and here he smiled at the doctor – "don't regret having made the journey at all . . ."

"Nor do I." The bald man's tie beneath the snow-white collar of his shirt was, so the doctor noticed, very neat and tied in a Windsor knot. "But I don't agree with you. I think we can believe the patient."

"Are you joking?" His colleague raised his hands in a gesture of despair and bared his amber cufflinks. "I know you had a dream about a dog, but believe me, Edward, this is a false trail! If this gnawing had been the work of the Minotaur, he'd have killed her afterwards! So why didn't he kill her? Why did he run the risk of such danger? She could have recognized him, after all!"

"He probably didn't come from here." The bald man got up, reached for an expensive fountain pen and used it as a pointer. "After the murders in Mościce and Drohobycz he became more cautious. Now he's killing in different towns, even different countries. Breslau, Kattowitz . . ."

"Gentlemen! Gentlemen!" broke in Doctor Tkocz. "Perhaps you could clarify something for me! What dog? What Minotaur? The one the newspapers wrote about a few years ago? If that's the case, then there has never been a murder committed by the Minotaur here in Kattowitz!"

"There, you see?" The dark-haired man laughed triumphantly. "He hasn't murdered anyone here! And still I ask myself: why did he supposedly gnaw her, and yet not kill her?"

"Let me answer that." The bald man began to pace the room, sweeping his eyes indifferently over Doctor Tkocz's diplomas hanging on the walls. "Maybe she was no longer a virgin? The Minotaur only murders virgins, after all!"

"Was she or was she not a virgin?" The dark-haired man looked at Doctor Tkocz.

The deputy director laughed out loud.

"Was she a virgin? Follow me, gentlemen. Let me show you something! It's time you met the patient you're so interested in!"

RYBNIK, THAT SAME JANUARY 30TH. 1937
A QUARTER PAST TWELVE IN THE AFTERNOON

They accompanied Doctor Ludwika Tkocz down a long corridor of the red-brick building. The deputy director went ahead at a brisk, energetic pace and her well-defined backside swayed beneath her ample trousers. As he listened to the doctor's commentary, Popielski thought about daily life in a mental asylum; passing room after room, Mock asked about the history of the hospital, which reminded him very much of the buildings belonging to public service organizations in Breslau. A hospital had also existed here, when this was Germany, so he learned. Both then and now one could hear the hoarse yelling of the patients, their loud discussions and monologues, insults and curses; one was even challenging God to a duel. Then as now there was the clatter of metal plates of groats and crackling, and male nurses stood along the walls.

"Lunchtime," said Doctor Tkocz. "We're in the canteen, and beyond are the solitary cells for particularly dangerous inmates. Please follow me!"

"Is Maria Szynok dangerous?" asked Popielski.

Doctor Tkocz ignored the question and summoned a stocky male nurse with three folds of fat on the nape of his neck. He traipsed after them across the canteen, which was separated from the kitchen by a serving counter. Fantastical stains flowered on the ceilings and walls of the rooms, and there was no shortage of them in the small corridor where they now found themselves after descending some narrow stairs.

"Here are the solitary cells," said Doctor Tkocz, and with her hand indicated the first door. "Meet the patient Maria Szynok, gentlemen. Through the peephole for the time being."

Popielski opened the flap and peered into the depths of the room. He retreated and shook his head.

"There's shit in the judas hole again," said the nurse to the deputy director. "Shall I open it?"

"Are you strong, gentlemen?" asked Doctor Tkocz, smiling mockingly at the police officers. "Strong, self-confident men who have seen a great deal in life, and whom nothing will horrify? Then let me tell you something first. The wounds on Maria's cheek were badly operated. The cheek got infected, resulting in proud flesh. Pus sought a way out. Small perforations and fistulae appeared in the vicinity of the wound. The odour from her mouth can be detected from a distance of two metres. Are you strong, gentlemen? If so, we'll open the door. If not, it's better not to open it. Shall we open?"

Mock and Popielski looked at each other in surprise.

"Please open it," they replied almost simultaneously, a hint of offence in their voices.

"Open it, Peter," she said to the nurse.

The door opened with a screech. The stench of secretions took their breath away, and both officers held their noses and breathed the air, poisoned by the miasma, through their mouths. Only Doctor Tkocz remained unshaken, as if the scent of her favourite carbides and not the stench of urine and excrement reached her from the room. Nurse Peter appeared amused by the sight.

The woman within started dancing, lifting her legs high as if climbing over a low fence. With one hand she pressed the hem of her shirt to her temple, hiding a breast and half her face. The rest of her body was uncovered. Her reddened pudenda was starkly on view, and abundant pubic hair, sticky with something, spread over her thighs. A full, hefty breast swung heavily in rhythm to her singular skipping. Around her nipple sprouted three long black hairs. All of a sudden she let go of her shirt, as if shy. The stiff material fell over her body to reveal a mass of round, dark-yellow stains. The patient shoved both hands between her legs and began to back away until she was leaning against the wall. Even at a distance they could see the hole in her cheek. The skin was purple-brown at the edges, glossy and rigid, even when Maria Szynok smiled and closed her eyes as she pushed her fists between her legs, faster and faster.

Popielski turned from the door and moved aside. Mock immediately did the same. He rested his hands on his knees and breathed heavily. Doctor Tkocz gestured to the nurse, who slammed the door.

"You wouldn't bat an eyelid at the sight of a decomposing corpse." Doctor Tkocz yanked up her trousers which were slipping down. "But you can't bear to see what contempt for her own body has done to this unfortunate woman! This is the result of our hypocritical society, of which you are the guardians!"

"Now you're going to go and say that I'm the one who did it!" Mock glared at the doctor with the same dislike as he had glared at Zubik that morning. "I'm supposed to feel guilty, am I?"

"And you, Doctor," said Popielski, moving close to the doctor so she could smell his scent, "were you by any chance brought up in an orphanage? With contempt for your own body?"

"No!" Confusion was reflected in the psychiatrist's eyes. "How dare you! What's it to do with you anyway?"

"Because you dress" – Popielski moved in even closer, and Doctor Tkocz leaped away as if burned – "as if you disdain your body. And I'm sure that it's not to be disdained . . ."

He nodded to Mock and they made their way back to the canteen, where they were met by the unbearable din of metal bowls. Doctor Tkocz stood in the corridor burning with anger.

Popielski sat at a window in the corner apartment of Hotel Monopol, translating for Mock the report of Maria Szynok being found with a gnawed face exactly five months earlier:

"'On August 30th, 1936, Police Constable Pampusz Karol, of Police Station III, was alerted on his rounds by Rabura Józef, aged twelve, that Szynok Maria, aged twenty, subtenant and home help of Mrs Wozignój Gertrude, aged sixty, residing at 4 Mieroszewski, in Kattowitz, was found at her employer's in a serious condition. Miss Szynok, wearing only her underwear, was unconscious and had suffered numerous bloodied injuries to her face. According to Mrs Wozigóra Gertrude, Miss Szynok Maria had been found in this condition by the aforementioned on the threshold of her abode. Apart from this, the injured woman had with her a handbag, the contents of which are described below. Miss Szynok Maria was still conscious when she declared that the wounds on her face had been inflicted by "a count who had bitten her". Necessary action was taken.' The signature's illegible."

"Is that it?" Mock was lying on a chaise longue with both legs propped up on the armrest.

"No, there are three further annotations. The first is from the pathologist. 'Serious injuries to the right cheek and numerous bruises and contusions to the entire body were discovered. The untidy wounds to the cheek, combined with injury to the tissue were most likely inflicted by an animal, perhaps by a dog's teeth. After regaining consciousness Miss Maria Szynok has been displaying symptoms of mental illness. Doctor Zygmunt Mierzejewski, Forensic Pathologist.' The following annotation is dated October and comes from Investigative Judge Manfred Dworniok, and it reads: 'Due to an inability to communicate with the sick woman, who since the incident has been residing at the Institution for the Mentally

161

Ill in Rybnik, and conflicting information from the neighbours and acquaintances listed below, the investigation has been discontinued.' And the last annotation. 'Contents of handbag: comb, rosary, needle and thread, fake-leather pouch containing coins to the sum of four złotys, fifteen groszys and a shaving block, also a picture of Our Lady of Piekary, lipstick, matches, handkerchief and three Grand Prix cigarettes.' That's all, Ebi."

"What did that unfortunate woman need a shaving block for?" Mock wriggled around on the chaise longue and settled with his arm beneath his head.

"Maybe she wanted to pass off as a virgin?" Popielski interlocked his hands on his bald head and rocked gently on his chair.

"And how was she supposed to pass herself off as a virgin?" said Mock, growing animated.

"I don't know. It's the first thing that came to mind." Popielski continued to rock and his unbuttoned waistcoat rippled. "All this reminds me of something . . . I once knew a young lady who rubbed her pubes with an alum shaving block. The skin somehow shrunk and tightened, and penetration of her *antrum amoris* was rather difficult."

"Wait, wait." Mock leaped to his feet. "We have the following situation. Maria Szynok pleasured herself before our eyes in a horrible, lamentable and provocative manner. That is not the way a virgin behaves. That's the behaviour of a woman who is debauched . . . That, if I may say so, is what one of our companions did on the train. . . But to the point. That's the first thing . . ."

"What you say is not at all certain." Popielski got up, approached the window and stared for a long time at the covered market, from which horse-drawn carts were departing. "She is insane, after all. And insanity can turn a nun into a courtesan."

"Secondly, she uses alum." Mock obstinately pursued his reasoning,

162

as if he had not even heard Popielski's reservations. "Let's assume she uses it to fake virginity . . . The most important question is: why would a woman fake virginity?"

"Non-virgins are in a difficult situation on the marriage market. The answer's straightforward: the woman was twenty and wanted to get married!"

"Good. She had some alum in her handbag. What was it for? Well, let's say it was to fake virginity. And what does a woman carry in her handbag? The bare necessities: cigarettes, handkerchief, needles, a rosary . . . Alum sticks out like a sore thumb. It's not a bare necessity, unless she was a prostitute pretending to be a virgin at a client's request, like your one . . ."

"You're right, Ebi." Popielski turned away from the window. "Alum sticks out like a sore thumb. And yet it was in her handbag, meaning she needed it for something. A handkerchief is something you always carry with you because you don't know the day or the hour when your nose is going to start running, but you don't always carry a condom, surely – you only have one with you when you're out to get girls! You can't always predict a runny nose, but canoodling you certainly can! She had some alum with her because she was out to have sex and play the role of a virgin!"

"That's it!" Mock slapped his thigh. "You're right! And the Minotaur bit her but didn't kill her, because she had already been deflowered. And he only murders women who are untouched."

The men began to pace nervously around the table, and several times bumped into each other. The pale-green wallpaper turned darker; dusk spread slowly over the couch, chaise longue, table and the clock that stood in the corner of the parlour. This did not bother them. Mock had a headache from thinking so hard; Popielski chased around the table as if wanting to catch a vital premonition which had been sparked but then

163

immediately extinguished during his German colleague's last utterance. Without warning he came to a standstill.

"Was she going to see someone? Yes. Was she going to have sex? Yes. With whom? With some beau, let's say. And now the most important question: where did they come across each other? Where did she meet this man? If she called him 'a count' then he must have been introduced as 'a count'. And where can a simple girl meet a count?"

"In a brothel." Mock sat down at the table, lit a cigarette and automatically pushed the cigarette case across the table with such force that it fell on the floor. "That's it! A brothel! And that's where she passed herself off as a virgin! We'll have to scour every brothel in the city."

"They might not have met in a brothel," said Popielski, deep in thought. "Remember what that smart-arse at the mental hospital said? She said that Szynok fantasized about getting married to a count, a knight on a white horse . . . Remember?"

"Yes, I remember."

"Perhaps they didn't meet in a brothel, but in a marriage bureau. Maybe that's where the Minotaur searched for his victim."

"Let's go!" Mock got up, straightened his tie and put on his jacket.

"Marriage bureaus are closed at this hour," said Popielski. He turned on the light and looked at Mock, who was bursting with energy.

"We'll check the bureaus on Monday," grunted Mock, slipping on his shoes with the aid of a long shoehorn. "But brothels can be visited at any time."

"Still not had enough?" asked Popielski with a smile.

"Poland, my dear man" – Mock grinned broadly – "is famous for its beautiful women. May I finally savour this speciality or must I be satisfied with poor ersatz, those two gap-toothed sluts from the train?"

A droschka carried Mock and Popielski down Marszałek Piłsudski. The cabby had thoughtfully covered their legs with a fur-lined overcoat, their cheeks burned a healthy pink, and their brains were functioning in totally differing gears. Mock, glutted with alcohol, tobacco and the debauchery to which he had devoted himself the previous night, now sat in silence beneath the sheepskin, gazed at the buildings and tenements they passed and was amazed at the increase in warmth he felt for the city. It was extra-ordinarily similar to Breslau. The Zdrój Okocimski beer hall on Stawowa, where they had begun their Saturday tour of the temples dedicated to all manner of immoderation, reminded him of Kissling's on Junkernstrasse in Breslau. Both there and here, there was a discreet garret with rooms on offer where gentlemen could spend a few ravishing moments in the arms of a lady; both there and here they could savour frankfurters in mustard sauce; and both there and here, an excellent Pilsner was served. But the similarities Mock had noticed were not only in all eleven bawdy houses, some of which he had visited with Popielski on Saturday, and some alone on Sunday. He also noticed them in the vicinity of his hotel: a building on Piłsudski Street reminded him deceptively of a tenement on Tiergarten-strasse; the secondary school on Mickiewicz was like a twin of the Elisabethgymnasium, differing only in colour; and the brick school on Stawowa was built in the same style as hundreds of schools in Breslau and across the whole of Germany. Mock felt at home in Kattowitz; more than at home because the women here were far prettier. In one of the brothels he visited, the criminal director was so taken by the beauty of one young lady that he did not limit himself to routine questioning.

Popielski had no such appreciation of Kattowitz, since none of the towns he had seen to date – well, apart from Vienna perhaps – could compare to the greatest garden of all, his beloved Lwów. Let alone this mining-town of houses that may be comely, but were covered in black dust which got into every nook and cranny. He was in a bad mood anyway, because usually at this time of day he was in bed.

Unlike Mock, he had spent his Sunday decently and diligently. He had eaten his breakfast alone, because his German colleague had slept the sleep of those greatly wearied by alcohol. On Saturday night the commissioner had been greatly incensed by the entire Kattowitz investigation, which they were conducting at an insane speed and had not in any way co-ordinated with the Silesian police. He now reproached himself for having told Mock about the dog he had heard growling during his epileptic fit. He had drunk little, and did not share the merriment of Mock, who, at the sight of any and every dog, would ask if this was the one from his vision. On Sunday, therefore, Popielski was as fresh as Lwów's Kajzerwald wind and after an afternoon walk, while Mock was recovering, the commissioner had set about furthering the investigation. He had found an address directory for the Province of Silesia and noted down the details of two marriage bureaus in Kattowitz. He and Mock had then eaten a generous dinner at a German restaurant, Zur Eisenbahn on Dworcowa, and had gone separately to the remaining brothels. Mock had stayed in one of these until morning.

Popielski sat there a little gloomily; he was not observing the town as they passed through it, but thinking instead about the next steps in the investigation and the participation of police officers from Kattowitz. He had just had an extremely unpleasant and agitated telephone conversation with Commissioner Zygfryd Holewa, who had used strong language to condemn their inspection of the bawdy houses of Kattowitz without his knowledge and had threatened to throw the two pests – neither of whom were officials of the Silesian Provincial Police – out of town! Only Popielski's promise to acquire special authorization in the future had pacified Holewa. To make matters worse the investigation had not progressed an inch despite their visits to the temples of debauchery. Nobody in those houses of ill-repute had ever heard of an aristocrat paying a visit; the highest spheres of society with which Kattowitz courtesans had any physical contact were office workers from the plants and mines, or agents and travelling salesmen. In Hestia marriage bureau, where they had been that morning, a very pleasant and polite clerk had merely rolled his eyes and was even a little moved when he heard about some count and a poor girl from the lower classes. He was sorry that nothing like that had happened in his establishment since he would have made good use of it in his publicity. Now that they were on their way to the second bureau, Matrimonium, it was not surprising that Popielski was gloomy about their results to date and thinking about the no doubt hopeless course of action he would have to take alongside the reluctant Commissioner Holewa. "The Silesian is going to undermine everything for me," thought Popielski. "After all, he's the one who closed the Szynok case. There's absolutely nothing in it for him to open a new investigation which might uncover some error he's made in the past."

Thinking about the words he would use to placate Commissioner Holewa, whom they were to meet at precisely noon, Popielski jumped out of the now-stationary droschka and onto the snow-covered pavement. Mock awoke from his light nap and blinked. They were parked in front of a tenement on Stawowa. Above the door marked No.10 hung a sign which read MATRIMONIUM MARRIAGE BUREAU, with a drawing of a dove wearing an absurd lace collar and holding interlinked wedding rings in its beak.

The office was located on the first floor and its windows gave onto a small courtyard. Miss Klementyna Nowoziemska, informed over the telephone of their visit by Popielski, was already waiting for them. She was a corpulent lady of about fifty, with carefully styled hair and neatly painted lips, and wearing an expensive suit of striped wool. At her neck was a lace collar similar to that worn by the dove. Her voice was quiet and soothing, her smile subtle, yet full of dignity. It was hard to imagine a more suitable person to run the Matrimonium bureau. She sat at a solid mahogany desk, behind her a large cabinet full of files, their corners reinforced with elegant gilded ferrules. The official atmosphere was sweetened by two vases of carnations.

Since Miss Nowoziemska did not speak German, Mock wanted to leave right away to wait for Popielski in some nearby tavern, and there extinguish the flame of his hangover with an Okocim beer, which he found greatly to his taste. Even though they had drunk to eternal friendship, Popielski did not know Mock very well and could not be sure that he could trust him to stop at one or two beers. On the contrary, he believed the German might really get going and disappear off again somewhere as he had done the day before. He therefore entreated Mock to stay. Miss Nowoziemska, noticing Popielski's concern, had the brilliant idea of interesting his "German friend" with the offer of single women. Mock willingly agreed, sat down in the small, bright parlour filled with the scent of perfume, and began to look through the announcements and photographs of available women with great interest.

"Thank you for such an excellent idea," smiled Popielski, truly pleased.

"Oh, men are just like children," said Miss Nowoziemska, reciprocating with a beautiful smile. "Give them an album full of attractive women and they immediately calm down like little boys browsing through a stamp collection."

"Yes . . . yes . . ." Popielski crossed his legs. "You know what brings me here, don't you? I explained over the telephone. Criminal Director Eberhard Mock from Breslau and I are looking for a dangerous criminal who, calling himself an aristocrat, charms modest, decent working-class girls. Has anyone like that visited your establishment?"

"I've possibly misunderstood." The smile disappeared from Miss Nowoziemska's face. "But when you called I deliberately didn't raise your hopes that I'd betray confidential information concerning my clients. And in spite of this you've come to ask about them! Well, let me put this clearly to you now: I am not going to give you any information. That's it."

Miss Nowoziemska stood up, indicating to Popielski that she considered the meeting at an end. The commissioner rose too, certain that he had asked the wrong question. It was stupidly long and vague; he should have made it briefer, and simpler. This is what he now did.

"Was Maria Szynok, a woman of twenty, one of your clients?"

"I don't think you've understood what I said, Commissioner, sir," the owner of the bureau replied coldly. "I am not going to pass on any information regarding my clients, male or female! Goodbye, sir!"

"Is that so?" Popielski could barely control himself. "Then I won't ask; I'll just requisition the files. I'll take them to police headquarters, look through them and find out everything I need. That's what I'll do" – he raised his voice – "and right this minute! I can tell by your reaction that you're hiding something! And I'm not going to continue this conversation any longer because I suspect you would lie! I'm taking the files, and that's it! And all this could have been quite straightforward and peaceful . . ."

"If you're going to requisition my files" – Miss Nowoziemska did not raise her voice one decibel, but barricaded the glazed cabinet with her plump body – "you'll have to use force. Because I'm not going to give you anything of my own free will! And I'll call the police! Any police officer not from Silesia has nothing to say here!"

Popielski slapped his freshly shaven head. He did not know what Commissioner Holewa looked like, but he could well imagine. He was no doubt fat, glum, and quick to fly into a fury. He wore collars which were too tight for him and carried a gold-plated watch chain. Right now he was probably wiping his whiskers after a glass of beer with his breakfast and sharpening his teeth in preparation for a police officer from Lwów who was poking his nose into what was not his business on what was not his territory. Popielski imagined the following scene: he and Mock enter Commissioner Holewa's office. They are laden with Miss Nowoziemska's files and she, no doubt a highly respected citizen, follows them, yelling and flinging herself at the throats of her persecutors. Then Popielski says to Holewa: we're going to conduct this investigation together. He shook off this grim vision. Nowoziemska was smiling triumphantly and Mock was craning his neck to peer in from the parlour, intrigued by his colleague's raised voice. On his knees lay an album containing details of the women on offer. Popielski looked at Mock and sat down on the couch. He lit a cigarette and smiled at Miss Nowoziemska through the smoke.

"What's your fee, Madame?" he asked. "The fee for finding a match for someone like me."

"Are you trying to bribe me?" The owner of the bureau sat down too, despite her stern expression.

"No. I want to be your client. I'm a very good party. A lonely, rich widower, fifty-two . . ."

"And then what?" A faint smile appeared once more on Miss Nowoziemska's face.

"Precisely! Then what. . ." Popielski blew smoke at a palm standing in the corner. "I propose a deal. I'll allow you to put me on your books and I look through the album which the criminal director is browsing at this moment. Maybe I'll chose a woman. Maybe I'll meet her here, in this tastefully furnished parlour. I'm well placed. I'll pay well for future marital happiness . . . But first you'll have to know a bit more about me. Please, go ahead and ask! But after each question you ask I'm going to ask one too, and you're going to reply. A question for a question, my dear lady."

"But you're not going to believe me anyway! I'll say: I don't know,

I don't know, to all your questions. And what are you going to do to me then?"

"I'll be your client only if your answers are going to be in the affirmative. You're not risking anything. Either you help me and I give you the opportunity to find me a match, or you don't. It's as simple as that."

Miss Nowoziemska stared at Popielski in silence. Meanwhile the telephone on her desk began to ring but she did not pick up the receiver. Mock was bored at this stage, and set aside the photo album. Snow was falling outside, covering with a white shroud the heap of coal which a man was shovelling through the cellar window. The telephone rang again. Nowoziemska picked up the receiver and spoke briefly in French.

"Excuse me, Commissioner, but I must make a phone call. I have a very important meeting today." She dialled and again spoke the language of Descartes for a few minutes. She then sat down and clasped her hands.

"I'm terribly sorry, Commissioner. A certain foreigner has just arrived in Kattowitz. He's looking for a Polish wife and I think I've got something for him." She smiled coyly. "I also have something for you. Important information, I believe, about Maria Szynok. But I won't disclose it until tomorrow evening at six. After the three meetings you're going to have with my three clients. We have to give Cupid a chance."

"But you don't know anything about me," Popielski protested. "How are you going to introduce me to those clients?"

"I know all I need to know about you, Commissioner." Miss Nowoziemska was once again sweet and gentle. "Do you think that after twenty years of working in this profession I don't know men? Well, how about it? Come at three o'clock tomorrow afternoon. The first lady is Doctor Fryderyka Przybilla, a forty-year-old dentist. I'll just show you her photograph, and those of the other ladies."

Popielski got up, extinguished his cigarette and approached the owner's desk. Like a dog, he could raise his upper lip and bare sharp teeth;

171

he could squint so that his face looked like a mask of fury; he could even flare the nostrils of his broken nose so that his face was like that of a gorilla. He could do all these things at a moment's notice, something which had often amused little Rita. Now these skills presented themselves involuntarily.

"There's one thing you don't know about me, Madame." The voice emerging from his throat sounded like a strange wheezing. "And that is that I'm not going to leave here now. Either you tell me everything, or I'll smash this cabinet to pieces! Understand me, you old bawd?"

So Miss Klementyna Nowoziemska told him about Maria Szynok and the man who was interested in her. She knew what would happen if she refused. In her twenty years of working in the field, she had certainly got to know men.

KATTOWITZ, THAT SAME FEBRUARY 1ST, 1937
NOON

There were many similarities between Mock and Popielski: both were prone to anger and were pedantic; both spoke Latin and Greek, and adored chess, bridge and gluttony, and neither avoided the company of fallen women. They had yet one more characteristic in common: impatience. This usually manifested itself when they had to wait a long time for their orders in a restaurant. They would then huff in annoyance, smoke numerous cigarettes, drum their fingers on the table, keep calling the waiter, scratch themselves nervously on the back of the neck – in a word, they would be on the verge of exploding.

Now, however, as they sat in the Eldorado Restaurant on 3rd Maja Street, they had not only forgotten about the passage of time, but did not even remember what they had ordered. Mock stared at Popielski, trying not to miss a word of what he was saying:

172

"Maria Szynok brought Miss Nowoziemska some savings in her pouch and asked that her name be entered in the register and an announcement along the following lines be put into the national press" – and here Popielski glanced at one of two sheets of paper which the owner of the marriage bureau had lent him – "'Cinderella seeks fairy-tale prince. Modest, hardworking and handsome maiden aged twenty seeks stable, wealthy and well-mannered gentleman to whom she is willing to give everything most valued by a lover of the family hearth.' Two weeks later this letter arrived at the bureau." He began to read a page from a letter pad covered with typed text. "'Dear Madame, I was greatly interested in Cinderella's announcement, entry 142/37. I would very much like to meet this maiden. Since I have been searching for several years for the right candidate to be my wife I am well acquainted with the many forms of deception to which crafty and determined young individuals resort in order to win a husband like myself, a man with connections, a fortune and a noble title. This would not, in all certainty, apply to your reputable marriage bureau, yet I would rather save myself a long and tedious journey and future disappointment. I am therefore obliged to put to you, dear Madame, two questions. One: Is 'Cinderella' an orphan? Two: Is she pure and untouched physically? In order to have the pleasure of beholding your own countenance and making Cinderella's acquaintance I would need to receive a positive answer to both these questions. Otherwise I will be forced to forego this tremendously interesting offer of marriage. Please forward your reply to *poste restante* at your nearest post office. Yours faithfully, Count . . .'" – and here Popielski pronounced a peculiar, German-sounding name, then smacked his lips in surprise.

"Why so surprised?" asked Mock.

"Nothing, nothing . . ." said Popielski, pondering a while.

"Where was the letter sent from?"

"We don't know. Miss Nowoziemska found it under her office door. Somebody had slipped it in from the corridor.

"'Long and tedious journey . . .'" Mock pensively repeated the words in the letter.

"Wait, this is where it gets going." Popielski pushed himself up from the chair like a sprinter on the starting line. "Nowoziemska replied to both questions in the affirmative . . ."

"And how did she verify the girl's virginity? Did she ask the caretaker for a favour?"

"No." Popielski burst out laughing. "I asked her the same question. She told me that this was the least of her worries . . . I think we can take her word for it. In spite of her immaculate manners she looks like a brothel madame . . . So she wrote to the Count saying that the girl was an orphan and a virgin and he arrived a few days later . . ."

"And?" Mock was concentrating so hard he did not so much as glance at the waitress as she stood a tankard of Żywiecki beer in front of each of them.

"Short, thin, about forty years old, elegantly dressed . . ."

"The perfect Mr Nobody," interrupted Mock. "A man without qualities."

"You're wrong." Popielski took a sip of beer. "Miss Nowoziemska was worried beyond words when she saw him. When he entered her office she realized straightaway that she would make no money on this man. 'Incredibly ugly', that's what she said. Let me quote her again. I noted down everything she said. So: 'A man doesn't have to be beautiful. He should be a little better-looking than the devil, but he shouldn't *be* the devil.' That's how she characterized him. And here's a more accurate description: 'Thick, greying hair that started just above his brow like a hat. Bluish shadow from shaven facial hair reached right up to his eyes, which were small and sunken. Square jaw, uneven teeth, narrow lips.' She

174

took his registration fee and arranged for him to meet Maria Szynok that same day, not believing for a moment that the meeting would result in a successful marriage. She even breathed a sigh of relief when he didn't appear, and she never saw him again."

"He didn't come . . ." repeated Mock, deep in thought.

"Now listen carefully: the meeting between the Count and Klementyna Nowoziemska took place on 30th August, 1936 . . . He was to meet Maria Szynok that same afternoon. Does the date mean anything to you?"

"That's when she was found. Gnawed."

"Yes!" Popielski thumped the table, spilling their beer. "It's him, Ebi! He went to that meeting but he didn't go into the office. He waited until the girl left and followed her. And maybe she was crying, because she was disappointed that he hadn't come. She walked out, unable to see anything through her tears, and in her shabby bag she carried alum, which was to restore her lost virginity. That monster followed her . . . and attacked her somewhere . . ."

The waitress came and set down their plates. The men broke off their conversation, but did not take their eyes off each other. They were not interested in the crunchy skin that parted a little from the pink, moist meat, nor the pale heaps of Silesian dumplings, nor the little mounds of peas and thick, steaming red cabbage. Neither so much as gave a glance to the waitress, who had not left their table and was waiting expectantly.

"What does she want?" Mock could not bear it. "A tip? Give it to her, Edward, I don't have any change!"

"I'm not waiting for a tip," said the waitress in German, her face full of umbrage. "I've found out what you wanted." She now addressed Popielski in Polish. "My colleague, the one who once served that ugly gentleman, has just arrived."

"Could you call him?" Popielski handed her a fifty-groszy tip.

175

"Helmut!" she called. "Oh go yourself, sonny!"

"What's this about?" Mock speared a dumpling with his fork and held it in mid-air. "I saw you discussing something with her when we entered . . . I thought you were asking for an empty table . . . Maybe you could finally explain . . ."

Popielski shifted his eyes to Helmut the waiter, who was nearing their table. He was a broad-shouldered young man with a pox-scarred face.

"At your service, sir." Helmut stood officiously next to them.

"Have a drink to my health, Helmut," said Popielski, handing him fifty groszys too. "Can we speak in German?"

"Speak yes, drink no," the waiter stammered in German, looking around the room, and he slipped the coin into his pocket. "I'm not allowed to drink right now."

"Who said anything about right now?" Popielski cut himself a thick slice of pork knuckle and slid a knife over it, leaving a thick layer of horseradish. "You can have a drink later and tell us something now instead. Your colleague mentioned that six months ago a customer came here who was repulsively ugly. And you served him . . . This could be extremely important; the man might be a dangerous murderer . . ." Popielski almost whispered these last words and showed the waiter his police badge. "You could be in possession of exceptionally valuable information. Would you like to share it with us?"

"There's one word I don't understand. What's 'repulsively'?" Helmut was clearly perplexed.

"As ugly as an ape," interrupted Mock.

"I remember him." The waiter's face lit up. "He really was as ugly as an ape, and he dirtied the whole tablecloth . . . He wrote something on it . . . I gave him a talking to. He apologized and even paid for it to be washed. That's all I remember."

"Eh, my good man," said Popielski, smiling amicably. "I'm sure you remember a good deal more . . . Sit down with us, have a beer, or some vodka . . ."

"I'm not allowed to sit with customers." Helmut looked towards the bar again.

"What did that customer order?" asked Mock.

"I don't know, but probably the usual. Silesian dumplings and meat roll. And then he left. I can't remember any more. It was such a long time ago . . ."

"And what did he write on the tablecloth, can you remember that?" Popielski brought a piece of quivering skin, brown with mustard, to his lips.

"No, no I don't. He wrote all over the tablecloth. We couldn't use it any more."

"Well, what? A letter? Words?" Unlike Popielski, Mock had not swallowed a mouthful.

"Nothing like that!" Helmut rubbed his forehead. "No, he was working something out. Jotting numbers down! And using ink, too! It didn't want to come off the tablecloth!"

"And you threw it away, no doubt?" asked Mock, resigned.

"Well, yes. What were we supposed to do? Excuse me, but I have to see to other customers."

Helmut bowed and left. Mock sighed, ate a dumpling and dug his fork into the pork knuckle. He did not, however, manage to bring it to his lips. Popielski, completely tense, was pressing his arm firmly to the table. The German stared at him, his mouth — into which the piece of meat was fated not to disappear — gaped open. Fat now ran down the pork and dripped onto the tablecloth.

"The fake count came here from afar, I repeat, from afar. He met matron Nowoziemska, who recommended this restaurant to him. He jotted down some figures on the tablecloth"— Popielski pressed Mock's hand to the table as the veins on his forehead swelled – "and in the interim gnawed the face of Maria Szynok. And the first two victims were found in the vicinity of Lwów. Do you know what the European capital of mathematics is?"

"What's that got to do with it?"

"Do you or don't you?"

"No, I don't . . . Probably Gettingen. Or Paris, Berlin?"

"No, my friend." There was pride in Popielski's voice. "It's Lwów. My city."

"I know what you want to say. That the Minotaur is a mathematician who scribbled some formulae on the tablecloth. And that in his letter to the marriage bureau he wrote that he'd be coming from far away. You've linked the two facts. But he could just as easily be a businessman living in Warsaw who was working out his profits in a spare moment . . . Your capital city is also far away, surely. And let me finally eat this pork knuckle, damn it!"

"Did you know there's a famous café in Lwów called the Scotch House, where mathematicians meet?" Popielski let go of Mock's arm. "And did you know that for years and years they used to write on the tablecloths there, or even the tables themselves, just like that fake count? Perhaps he used to go there, too, and hasn't got out of the habit?"

"Maybe . . ." Mock chewed on the pork knuckle with relish. "I can understand that you want to go back to your home town . . . And that you don't feel like explaining yourself to this Commissioner Holewa or whatever his name is . . . But you're relying on only two pieces of information and your intuition. And we're to go back because of that? We've still got a lot to do here. Question the girl's neighbours, for example . . ."

"You're saying I've randomly linked two pieces of information. But there's still a third fact, and it's the most important. I should have started with it. And it's the reason we're catching the next train to Lwów. Do you

178

know what our count is called? How he introduced himself in his letter? Count Hugo Dionizy von Banach. And do you know who Professor Hugo Dionizy Steinhaus and Professor Stefan Banach are?"

"No."

"Exactly!" said Popielski, carefully arranging his cabbage on the remaining pieces of pork knuckle. "They're mathematicians from Lwów and regulars at the Scotch House. Let's go. We'll just pop into Matrimonium and perhaps get some more information from there. I regret not having asked Miss Nowoziemska about the gorilla's accent – I'm sure that observant woman would have detected a Lwów ring to it."

KATTOWITZ, THAT SAME FEBRUARY 1ST, 1937
TWO O'CLOCK IN THE AFTERNOON

Miss Klementyna Nowoziemska was in the habit of eating lunch at about two o'clock in the nearby Theatre Restaurant. She would then lock her office and hang a notice on the door which read: LUNCH BREAK. BACK AT 15.30. And this is what she did today. She donned her sable-fur coat and little hat with a flower fastened on a fancy loop, then made towards the door with her handbag beneath one arm and the notice beneath the other. The door opened, and there stood a short man wearing a coat and hat and carrying a walking stick.

"I'm just on my way to lunch." Miss Klementyna tapped a red fingernail on the varnished notice. "Would you like to accompany me? We can talk just as easily there."

The first blow almost fractured her eye-socket. Warm blood covered the eye and a red mark appeared on her forehead which soon turned blue. The knock threw Miss Nowoziemska against the wall. She slid down it on rigid legs and fell heavily on her tail bone. Her assailant unscrewed the lower part of his walking stick to reveal a ten-centimetre-long steel spike.

179

He raised his hands and rammed the spike into her head, pushing it through the woman's hat and skull with equal ease. He pressed on the spike and twisted it as far as it would go. He was merciful. He did not want her to see him lean over her, dig a knife into her cheek, make a deep incision and into the cut slip his upper teeth. He did not want her to see him tip his head back and the red pulp slop onto the parquet floor.

PART II

The Minotaur's Chamber

"All negligence is deliberate, every random encounter is a planned meeting, every humiliation a punishment, every failure a secret success, every death a suicide."

From "Deutsches Requiem", Jorge Luis Borges, 1942

WOROCHTA, MONDAY, FEBRUARY 8TH, 1937
FOUR O'CLOCK IN THE AFTERNOON

Rita Popielska schussed down the slope which led from the recently built chalet to a dark strip of beech trees. Her shapely figure, porcelain complexion, and cheeks which in the frost and wind had turned the colour of rosy apples, drew everybody's attention. Older women looked at Rita with a slight disdain during meals at the chalet, taking it as understood that every beautiful girl will sooner or later become a street-walker or a kept woman; younger women looked with envy; men, on the other hand, with either lust or helpless resignation. Rita, not even realizing that she provoked such assorted emotions in others, threw herself into snow-related pursuits with passion, as if every day was the last of her winter holiday. The only contact she had with Aunt Leokadia, who was forever playing bridge, was at mealtimes in the restaurant. Even then she did not have to put up with her aunt's sardonic glances and smart comments, however, because from the very first day two men had fought their way to her table: the Krzemicki brothers, the younger of whom, Adam, was a student at Lwów Polytechnic and the older, Zygmunt, a cadet with the Kresowy Fusiliers at Stanisławów. During meals Rita launched herself joyfully into bright, flirtatious conversations with both young men,

183

especially when Aunt Leokadia, after swallowing a couple of mouthfuls, hurried off to the palm-filled foyer from whence came the scent of cigars and the rustle of cards being dealt. With a carefree smile, Rita, a flighty and fickle lass, would often break off her conversations with the brothers — who blushed in turn like schoolboys — leave them mid-sentence and run to her room to change into a pair of warm knickers, thick stockings, narrow ski-trousers and two Zakopane jumpers; she never wore a hat since wool irritated her and made her itchy. She then rushed off to the slope with her skis and whizzed down at a crazy speed, her black hair blowing in the wind, leaving behind both the brothers and several other schoolboys and students, who tried in vain to prove equal to this fit young lady. It was almost impossible to catch up with a girl who had been skiing since she was five years old and spent every winter holiday in the Carpathian Mountains.

Anyone who thought that Rita Popielska was throwing herself into the whirl of wind and snow purely from an atavistic need to burn off her youthful energy would have been mistaken. Her motive was entirely different. She had decided, quite rightly, that the faster the day passed and the more tired she was when she buried herself in her cool, scented sheets in the evenings, the faster her two-week holiday in Worochta would fly by and the quicker she would return to Lwów. And that is where she wanted to be, come what may. Because somebody was waiting for her there. A mysterious man who had passed a letter to her via the train conductor when, wrapped in a thick, quilted dressing gown, she was on her way back from the toilet to the sleeper compartment she shared with her snoring aunt. The conductor had tipped his hat, handed her an envelope smelling of a man's scent, and told her that a masked youth at Lwów Main Station had requested the favour he was now granting.

Apart from anything else, Rita was freeing herself of the company of various admirers because she wanted to be alone. She longed to stand among the old spruce and beech trees and for the hundredth time read the letter which had left her in a pleasant state of confusion.

Disconcerting Miss Rita!

Before I beheld you in a certain forbidden place in Zamarstynów in the company of another young lady and some circus strongmen, I was an entirely different man, a bored and cynical *bon vivant* who thought he had experienced and seen everything. A man who knew both evil and good in their purest form. In order to prove to you that these are not empty words, I will simply say that I have been sought by the police of three countries, spent time in jail and acquired a great fortune. To counter this I would add that I am highly educated and twenty-seven years of age. At present I do not have to work for a living; I do not have to do anything. An overwhelming sense of boredom had crept into my life. Until that day in January when I saw you. If previously I had known evil and good in their purest form, then now, in your person, I saw the highest beauty. A weak man would write: "I cannot sleep or eat, I dream of one glance from you, one smile of those wonderful lips." I am not going to write that, I am a strong man, the kind of man who conquers, who can lay the whole world at your feet, and that is why I am going to say something bold and impudent: I dream of the whole of you. Your presence in the drinking-den in Zamarstynów is proof that you, too, are someone who is determined and sneers at society's concept of decency. Rita! If you could just bring yourself to take a daring step and agree to receive another letter from me (to which I will attach my photograph), stand one Sunday at precisely midday beneath the clock of the Viennese Café on Hetmańska. Every Sunday at midday I will stand close by and watch people pass. I know that one Sunday you will be one of them.

185

For some time now Popielski had been a regular customer at the Scotch House café on the corner of Łoziński and Fredro Street and had already managed to accustom the staff to his eccentricities. He never ordered anything other than countless glasses of unsweetened, strong tea since, as he announced the first time he went, he was undergoing a diet which was to cleanse his body of unnecessary toxins. He did not add that these toxins were chiefly of an alcoholic nature, because why should he be on such familiar terms with waiters and waitresses who already demonstrated a considerable lack of deference towards their guests? With every day of his fast he felt the weight fall off him, and his irritation at the entire world rise: irritation at Hanna, whose singing of her morning prayers woke him with increasing frequency when he had only just gone to sleep; at his colleagues in the Investigative Bureau who were too sluggish in their search for people of remarkable ugliness; and at mathematicians, the regulars of the Scotch House, who looked down on him and treated him with a touch of irony.

He had already managed to meet most of them and find his way around the problems which preoccupied them. However, his erstwhile knowledge of mathematics – acquired in Vienna from the excellent Wielkopolanin, Franciszek Mertens and gruff Wilhelm Wirtinger – had now lost its freshness, and the enthusiastic outbursts of Lwów's mathematicians over problems which had peculiar and sometimes even poetic names seemed to him nothing less than childish. When Professor Stefan Banach raised his hands – often with a smoking cigarette in each – and fell into raptures about a new contribution to "Steinhaus' sandwich", "Mazur's game" or "Hilbert's tripod and cube", Popielski thought he had been transported back to his schooldays when he had played chess with his cousin Leokadia and they had given various moves the names of heroes from books they were reading, which resulted in "Winnetou's check" and "Kmicic's gambit". While Stanisław Ulam, with one leg on a chair and the other on the floor, explained the "densification of singularity" or "supposedly dense spaces", while Hugo Dionizy Steinhaus and Stefan Kaczmarz poured coffee and sometimes vodka, while each of them voiced their criticism of the latest French paper on octagonal sequences and Stanisław Mazur stunned everyone with his linear methods of summation, the commissioner – perhaps influenced by pangs of hunger – succumbed to ever greater misanthropy and to a deep-seated complex about his misspent opportunities. He remembered happy days in Vienna and the mathematics he had once so loved, and which, because of his health, he had abandoned in favour of philology; lectures and seminars in philology at the University of Vienna were generally held in the evenings, which meant that he had been able to avoid sunlight. He had not, therefore, managed to learn about the complex problems these men were discussing.

He came to the Scotch House at lunchtime, sat alone and in mournful silence by the curtain at the front door, and carefully observed those who entered. He knew the murderer would be well acquainted with his appearance from the newspapers, and so he waited for fear to register in one of the faces. This occurred only once, but in a face which was not ugly, unfortunately, and besides, it belonged to a woman; it was the face of a prostitute who had once painfully ridiculed the commissioner's post-alcoholic impotence. So Popielski sat there, dreadfully bored. He did not read the newspapers, nor even did he set out a game of chess for fear that one of the mathematical geniuses should want to play with him, and thereby bring him immediate and inevitable defeat.

Something he noticed on the first day undermined a common Lwówian myth which he himself had also believed, namely that these scholars wrote on tablecloths. This was not so – the mathematicians used their indelible pencils to blacken either the marble surfaces of tables or the pages of a special book which could always be found with the cloakroom attendant. This observation disappointed Popielski a great deal because the myth had, after all, been one of the pillars to support his reasoning that the gorilla-faced man who had written on a tablecloth at the Eldorado Restaurant in Kattowitz was a mathematician from Lwów. However, he quickly pulled himself together after this momentary setback and began his carefully planned investigation.

For the first four days he observed the mathematicians and kept demanding that the waiter give him their names. For a little variety he doggedly summed up the investigation to date, analysing for the thousandth time the circumstances in which he and Mock had found Klementyna Nowoziemska murdered, and talking to a woman of easy virtue who, at his request, came to the café in order to judge the ugliness of a man "from a woman's perspective".

When after a week he had got to know the luminaries and pretenders to the upper reaches of mathematics, and to his regret had not found any of them strikingly ugly, he started to look for those among them who stood out for having a linguistic imagination rich enough to invent the ingenious fictitious name of Hugo Dionizy von Banach. With this in mind he abandoned his undercover operation and held long and boring conversations with the scholars on the basis of which he formed a reliable opinion as to the wealth of their vocabulary and linguistic constructions. After another four days he identified a main suspect whom, however, he had quickly to erase from his list. This was Hugo Dionizy Steinhaus, a man who used exquisite Polish language, full of unusual and highly apposite word play. Firstly, he was not ugly, and secondly, it was hard to imagine that the murderer would make use of a pseudonym comprised of two of his own names.

When Popielski had crossed out all the Scotch House regulars from his list of suspects, he began to question them individually about "ugly" colleagues or students. Which is when things got going.

"In what sense 'ugly'?" asked Meier Eidelheit.

"I know, Commissioner, the relationship that plane geometry has to the aesthetic or artistic representation of space in works by the Italian masters," Kazimierz Bartel fell to thinking. "And from there I deduce what is beautiful. But when speaking of ugliness I would have to adopt a converse reasoning."

When Popielski tried to narrow down these speculations by comparing the man he was seeking to an ape, the men to whom he spoke drew him into deep waters of abstraction.

"Can the noun 'ape' be definable by a finite number of words?" asked Mark Kac, growing dispirited.

"My dear sir," said Leon Chwistek, sprawled at the table, "I can define ugliness only as a lack of beauty. And beauty I see in art which has shaken off the insupportable burden of imitating nature. Consequently, a picture of an ape and one of Venus de Milo are equally ugly because both are elements of nature; however, there is no beauty in artistic representations of nature."

After three weeks Popielski gave up his diet and resolved to leave the Scotch House, never to return. The famous café had led him nowhere. What he had planned for the days that followed was even less absorbing: he was to attend the next few meetings of the Lwów circle of the Polish Mathematical Society and look for the Minotaur there. There were not many such meetings: one in March, one in April, two in May and one in June. But how to continue tracking down the beast in the meantime? He was conscious of the terrible vacuum he would be feeling the following day, when he returned to his office at the Investigative Bureau. He wanted to push as far away as possible the thought of his furious colleagues wandering about Lwów, asking after "ugly" people and laying themselves open to ridicule. He could not bear to think of Marian Zubik, who would be asking him about the progress of the investigation. He decided to deaden all this with alcohol. End of diet, he told himself. After a few vodkas he set out the chessboard and, in a flush of courage, decided to challenge one of the conversing mathematicians to a game. He approached their table, but they did not so much as glance at him. They were too busy debating the existence of machines which could give an automatic response if a quantity of inert matter was introduced into their environment.

Popielski gave up, sat down alone to some chess puzzles from the *Deutsche Schachzeitung*, to which the Scotch House subscribed, and ordered yet another glass of vodka. He missed Mock. He would gladly have played him. But Eberhard was not there.

KATTOWITZ, THAT SAME FEBRUARY 17TH, 1937
SIX O'CLOCK IN THE EVENING

After they had found Klementyna Nowoziemska's body, Mock had remained in Kattowitz for three reasons: first of all, he did not believe in the Lwów lead so strongly advocated by Popielski; secondly, it was not far from Kattowitz to Breslau, and therefore to Karen, whom he missed more and more in proportion to his bad conscience, which plagued him after his erotic excesses; thirdly, and most importantly, the murder of the owner of the Matrimonium marriage bureau demanded an explanation, and the circumstances pointed to the Minotaur, whom Mock was beginning to hate as much as Popielski did. Admittedly, in killing Nowoziemska, the Minotaur had not murdered a virgin, but the mutilation of the victim's cheek was his signature. Besides, it could be the copycat act of a madman, or the virginity of the previous victims could have been coincidental. The investigation promised to be exceptionally tedious since all the files from the marriage bureau had disappeared. The police had two choices: to investigate the criminal underworld in search of any contacts the murdered woman may have had, or to look for shady elements in her past. Neither of these seemed all that important as Miss Klementyna Nowoziemska was well respected and enjoyed an immaculate reputation. But one thought did not leave Mock in peace, namely, Popielski's suggestion that the owner of the bureau must once have been a brothel madame.

Having served for many years in the Vice Department, the police officer from Breslau knew the world of covert prostitutes only too well; often they were poor working-class women who provided carnal services on the quiet while working at entirely different professions, as workers or maidservants, for example. Covert prostitution proved lucrative. On the one hand, these women did not risk being on the records of the Vice Police, which would ruin their reputation and result in them losing their job; on the other hand, they could put a fair amount of money aside as an eventual dowry. Since they never walked the streets, they would make use of various intermediaries instead. Admittedly, Mock had never before heard of a marriage bureau acting as a go-between, but the comparison of Nowoziemska to a brothel madame gave him no peace, and it seemed to him an exceptionally tempting lead to follow. He was almost certain that the "ugly count" was not some mathematician from Lwów, but an ordinary Silesian industrialist who secretly made use of Nowoziemska's mediation and spent his money on crypto-prostitutes. Although this was just an intuition, it was one he had to explore. Mock would be the last person to disregard his own intuitions.

So Mock had something to do and, most importantly, he could act with confidence. Nor did parting company with Popielski hinder him in any way; people in Kattowitz generally spoke German, even the common folk. Besides, Popielski had endeavoured to obtain for him appropriate authorisation, which allowed him to act independently on Silesian territory as a representative of Police Headquarters in Lwów. It was with a certain reluctance that Mock had said goodbye to Popielski, but then he had eagerly thrown himself into the metropolitan hustle and bustle of the Silesian capital. He felt wonderful in a town which reminded him so much of Breslau.

Right from the very start, however, Commissioner Holewa had poured a bucket of cold water over Mock. The police officer from Kattowitz – who turned out to be totally irascible, and for all the world just as Popielski had imagined him – coarsely told him where he had Mock's authorization and categorically forbade him to conduct any investigation into the case of Maria Szynok. He knew the German would be in no position to appeal to the Polish police authorities and resume the inquiry. In order to prevent him from attempting to pursue it of his own accord he allotted him an assistant in the person of Senior Sergeant Franciszek Wybraniec who was to inform his superior immediately of any instances of Mock's insubordination.

As Holewa's informant, Wybraniec watched Mock's independent activities very carefully, but he did not attribute the least importance to any enquiries they undertook together, believing that Mock would not be so bold as to lead a private investigation with him at his side. When the German informed him over an evening beer that the following day they would be visiting a man called Michał Borecki, who was Nowoziemska's messenger, he nodded in agreement without even asking how Mock had come to know of the man. Of course Mock did not mention that before Holewa had placed the restrictions on him he had questioned Gertruda Wozignój, at whose lodgings Szynok had rented a bed, and from the landlady had learned of a certain Michał Borecki, apparently the girl's betrothed. The role of messenger was a figment of Mock's imagination.

The questioning of Borecki was the last task they had set themselves for that day. After visiting Matrimonium's financial auditor, Mr Jan Sławiński, who had nothing interesting to tell them, they stood outside the police station on Młyńska Street from where they were to go to the Bogucice district. There wasn't a droschka in sight and all the police Chevrolets were in use. At that moment Sławiński, who was just passing, suggested they borrow two bicycles. The weather was frosty and dry — the snow had long since blown off the pavements — so it seemed like a good solution.

They rode their bicycles into the cobbled street. It was a long time since the criminal director, a man of considerable weight, had ridden one, and to begin with he had to be very careful to maintain his balance. He quickly ascertained, however, that the locally constructed Eboco bicycle was extemely solid, and that the Dunlop tyres made it even more reliable. He therefore stopped worrying about his conveyance and looked about him as he rode.

They arrived in Kattowitz's poor mining district, entirely different in appearance to Lwów's slum quarters with which Mock had acquainted himself a little. These streets were densely lined with two- and three-storey, unplastered, red-brick buildings, whose recessed windows were by and large painted green. Both here and in Lwów entire families tended to live in one-room lodgings with a shared toilet in the yard, but the living quarters in Polish Silesia were much larger, the streets paved and wide, although few trees grew in the town, unlike in Lwów.

They passed a large church and a hospital, and then, turning into a narrow street, stopped at the first house, the address of which Mock had copied from the Szynok report as belonging to Borecki. No. 1, Piotr Street. Groups of people speaking what Germans disdainfully called *Wasserpolnisch* were walking along the main avenue, the men in long black cloaks and hats, the women in full, coloured skirts and lace bonnets. They were on their way somewhere in herds, watching the two men on bicycles with curiosity. Wybraniec quickly worked something out and struck his forehead.

"Ash Wednesday," he informed Mock. "Today's Ash Wednesday, we might not catch him in right now, damn it!"

"So we'll wait in some tavern until he gets back," said Mock. "Would you like a small schnapps? It's cold today!"

"You don't know the local customs," said Wybraniec, a little annoyed. "Taverns here don't open on Ash Wednesday."

Mock shook his head in disbelief and peered at the dark windows. It certainly did not look as though there was anybody on either the ground or the first floor. He went through the main entrance – scrubbed clean and smelling of detergent – approached the door to No. 1, and put his ear to it. Smiling to himself, he stepped outside and nodded to Wybraniec. The latter entered and stood at the door next to Mock. He listened and a moment later his broad face also lit up in a smile.

"The wench moaning in there isn't going to make it to church today, that's for sure," whispered Mock.

"So what are we going to do? Knock and go in?" asked Wybraniec.

"Wait until they've finished." Mock put his ear to the door once more. "Ever been interrupted at a moment like that?"

KATTOWITZ, THAT SAME FEBRUARY 17TH, 1937
A QUARTER TO SEVEN IN THE EVENING

Michał Borecki sat in the room wearing a pair of trousers, braces and a vest. A saucepan stood on the tiled kitchen stove, blazing with heat. Across the floor a child's toys lay strewn. On the wall hung a wedding photograph in which Borecki sported a walrus moustache. Now his moustache was thin and its owner reminded Mock of Adolf Hitler. In spite of the unpleasant association Mock was smiling from ear to ear. Senior

Sergeant Wybraniec kept peering through the window at the bicycles they had left in the yard.

"Gave her a good one, eh, Borecki?" Mock shoved an index finger in the ring formed by the fingers of his other hand and pumped it a few times. "The only question is, who's the woman? I don't see anyone here in the kitchen." Mock bent to look under the table.

"I don't understand German," replied Borecki in Polish.

Mock got up and made towards the door leading to the only other room, but Borecki was faster and barricaded it with his body. He was well built. The powerful muscles of his arms tensed beneath tattooed skin. Mock moved away, walked over to the window and studied the frame. It was stuck down with tape and sealed with oakum — just as in Popieski's apartment. Anyone wanting to escape through it into the yard could not do so without making a noise. Mock approached the kitchen stove. He lifted the lid off the saucepan and sniffed.

"Ah, tasty. Garlic smells good," he smacked his lips. "And I'm so hungry . . ."

To Borecki's and Wybraniec's total consternation he poured some soup into a metal bowl, placed it on the table and began to eat. When he was half finished he stopped and looked at Borecki.

"If your wife's in that room, Borecki," he said slowly, waiting until Wybraniec had translated, "she'll get dressed soon and come out and say hello. And if your wife *isn't* in there, then we'll wait for her, won't we, Wybraniec? We'll wait until she comes back from church with the children."

"What do you want?" asked Borecki.

"I want to know everything about Maria Szynok."

"But, sir," protested Wybraniec, without translating what Mock had said, "you've no authority to pursue the investigation!"

"Go and keep an eye on the bicycles!" the criminal director shouted at him angrily. "I'm your superior, and that's an order!"

195

"I'll go then." Wybraniec looked offended. "You won't find anything out anyway – he doesn't speak German!"

"It'll come back to him." Mock slurped the aromatic soup with pieces of bread floating in it. "You're the one who's making him so anxious he's lost his tongue!"

Wybraniec went out, red as a beetroot. Mock ate his soup and poured himself some more. He placed two zlotys on the table.

"I don't want to deprive your children," he said, and continued to ply his spoon energetically.

Something moved on the other side of the wall. The clock struck half past six. Mock pulled out a packet of Egyptians, Polish cigarettes which he particularly liked, and pushed it across the table towards Borecki. A rustling came from the other side of the wall and the door squeaked quietly as it opened a little.

"Welcome!" shouted Mock. "Please come and join us, Mrs Borecki!"

"What do you want?" the man in the vest asked in German.

"There you are!" Mock grinned even more broadly. "And didn't I say it was that idiot who was making you uncomfortable? You can speak German like nobody's business!"

"What?"

"I heard you were Maria Szynok's betrothed. A funny kind of betrothed who's married. But maybe 'betrothed' means 'lover' in Polish?"

Borecki did not say anything, and Mock continued without waiting for an answer:

"It's not important whether you were her betrothed or she was your mistress. What's important is that you had it off with her, right?"

"Yes."

"Finally you've said something!" Mock clapped his hands. "Well now, tell me just how much she wanted to get married, how she went about looking for a husband – whether she went to a marriage bureau, whether she met anyone who wanted to marry her. What do you know?"

"She wouldn't have dared to tell me," said Borecki, smiling to himself. "She knew I'd beat the shit out of her. She was mine or nobody's!"

"The first time you had her, was she a virgin?"

"Come on!" Borecki burst into loud, forlorn laughter which echoed around the kitchen. "She'd already had the scrape several times!"

"In a hospital?"

"No, not a hospital. You'd be nicked for that in Poland."

Something struck Mock. He was revisited by his intuition about the crypto-prostitution to which Szynok had submitted herself. His heart began to pound. He had never before heard of a respectable marriage bureau acting as a go-between for carnal services. But he had heard often enough that women who performed abortions acted as such, and he had even encountered it on several occasions. These women could easily persuade their desperate and generally poor clients that one night with a wealthy gentleman was nothing to be ashamed of.

"So where did she get rid of the foetus?" Mock saw that Borecki did not understand the question and so, with some disgust, he used the previous formulation. "Where did she have the scrape? Who did it?"

"How should I know? It was before my time!"

Mock removed his coat and hat, gestured to Wybraniec, who was standing by the bicycles, to come in, and spread his arms as if to say he had not learned anything. He looked at Borecki calmly and coldly. Without smiling.

"Give me the name of the woman who does the scrapes here in this town, in this area. I'm not going to throw her in the nick. I just need to talk to her."

"I don't know! I don't know the name of anyone doing scrapes!"

"We've got time. We've got plenty of time."

The Viennese Café on Mariacki Square was busy on Sunday mornings. On that day the café was filled mainly with wealthy Jews who, unlike their Christian fellow citizens, were not hurrying off to church where High Mass was being celebrated. At this hour the café's regulars were drinking hot chocolate and eating cakes and fruit with their families, on the whole members of the wealthy, liberal intelligentsia. There were not many devout Jews among them, because they generally avoided all dealings with their free-thinking kinsmen. Nor were there merchants, as merchants tended to spend their Sunday mornings in the Grand Café on Legiony. There was, on the other hand, an abundance of doctors and lawyers.

Edward Popielski was not looking for a representative from any of these professions. For almost three weeks the only professionals he had been interested in were mathematicians. Now he was whiling away his time in the café solely in order to behold the face of a lawyer, Eisig Nussbaum, whom a certain informer had described as: "a fellow with a mug like a monkey's". The lawyer's name was the last on a list compiled by Aspirant Kacnelson, and it differed from the others in that it had not been underscored. The list was the result of two weeks' painstaking work by Kacnelson and Cygan and comprised the names of people who were mathematically gifted, but who had not chosen that line of study. In order to acquire this information Kacnelson had done the rounds of all the Jewish schools, while Cygan had taken on those run by Christians or the state. They had spoken not only to the headmasters and teachers of mathematics and physics, but also questioned librarians about past pupils who had shown a particular interest in charades or logical problem solving. Grabski, in turn, had carried out the titanic job of gleaning information about various private tutors who made their living by working in the homes of the rich. All the officers had asked about physique, and a consid-

erable list of fifty-two names had emerged, which they divided equally –
like dealing cards at bridge. The thirteenth name on Popielski's list was
the lawyer Eisig Nussbaum, whose countenance he was yet to behold as
on Saturday the gentleman had left for Tarnopol on a business trip.
Popielski's informant, the one who had compared the lawyer to a monkey,
assured him that the lawyer always appeared at the Viennese at midday
on Sundays, come what may. And indeed, as the clock in the room struck
twelve, a short, slender man entered the café, his evident ugliness contrasting with the striking Mediterranean beauty of his companion. The
waiter winked to Popielski to let him know that the lawyer about whom
the commissioner had just enquired, and whom he had promised to point
out for the sum of twenty groszys, had just arrived. The police officer
stood up to approach the lawyer, but immediately abandoned his intention with a heavy sigh. Instead of a left hand, the man had a prosthesis
which ended in an expensive suede glove.

Popielski swore to himself. He should have told his men when they
were compiling their lists to ask not only about physique, but also about
anything which could disqualify the suspect from being the acrobat who
had leaped from roof to roof in Breslau. Annoyed, he looked through the
window and instantly calmed down. In a split second he had forgotten all
about his investigation.

"God, she's so beautiful," he muttered.

His daughter was slowly walking by and looking about her dreamily.
She truly was the epitome of beauty. All of a sudden it occurred to
Popielski that the clock by the Viennese Café was a meeting place for
lovers. He hid behind the curtain and waited for an admirer to appear.
After a while Rita walked off towards the Grand Theatre and Popielski,
rushing out of the café, ran after her. He needed to know the reason for
her walk even though, deep down, he knew she would not tell him the
truth.

The true reason was known to the author of the seductive letter who, from beneath the statue of Hetman Sobieski, was carefully observing father and daughter through a pair of binoculars.

LWÓW, FRIDAY, FEBRUARY 26TH, 1937
HALF PAST SIX IN THE EVENING

The Lenten psalms at St Nicolas' church always brought in a sizable group of schoolgirls. They were drawn not only by unquestionable devoutness, but also by the priest, Konstanty Kierski, who gave magnificent sermons. Apart from a fiery talent for preaching, nature had not stinted the young priest on masculine good looks. Standing in the pulpit and tossing his head in anger so that his black hair fell over his forehead, or shedding heartfelt tears of sorrow which flowed down the cheeks of his soulful, gaunt face, he inspired both fear and fascination in most of the young girls. It was not surprising, therefore, that the schoolgirls flocked to Lenten psalms and, much to the delight of their catechists, filled their exercise books with holy pictures handed out to mark their presence at the Lenten rites.

Rita Popielska did not share her peers' view of the priest's spiritual and physical beauty. Once, unable to bear a friend's near-ecstatic rapture, she had even sharply retorted that Father Kierski must be a "queen". Still, despite her negative attitude, she visited St Nicolas' for social reasons; it was here that most of her friends gathered, and they could dawdle home together afterwards.

That day, however, she had no intention of walking home with her friends. She stood close to the entrance, scrunching in her pocket the holy picture she had won with a charming smile before the end of the service, and waited for the right moment to outsmart their catechist, Sister Bonifanta.

200

At the cross her station keeping,
Stood the mournful Mother weeping,
Close to her son to the last.
Through her heart, His sorrow sharing,
All His bitter anguish bearing,
Now at length the sword has passed.
O, how sad and sore distressed
Was that Mother highly blest,
Of the sold-begotten One.

As the words of Stabat Mater came to an end, Sister Bonifanta approached the group of young schoolgirls to restore order, which had been momentarily disrupted. At that moment Rita, squeezing the hand of her new friend Beata Zacharkiewicz — nicknamed "Beanpole" — to say goodbye, hastily left the church, ran down the road and turned right. Here Sister Bonifanta would no longer see her.

Dusk had fallen over Mochnacki Street, cut through here and there by yellow shafts that beamed from the gas lamps. Beneath an old chestnut tree on the corner stood a rogue with a hat pulled down over his eyes, smoking a cigarette. Rita felt uneasy. She climbed the steep street, slipping on the icy paving stones. The man abandoned his tree and made after her. The street was deserted, the university library already closed. At the top of the street, beneath another tree that was battered by the wind, stood another man. Rita wanted to turn back to the church, but the first man was already nearing it. He stood staring at her for a moment, then slipped into the shadow of a doorway. Rita breathed a deep sigh of relief and quickened her stride up the street. She would turn off very soon, and a few minutes later find herself beneath Fredro's statue on Academy Square in the friendly urban hum, the lights, the window displays and amongst trustworthy people.

The man standing by the tree at the top of the street suddenly started towards her. Again a spasm clutched at her throat. She could do one of two things: walk towards him, or return to the church where the other rogue, the one in the hat, might still be waiting for her. She chose a third solution and turned into Chmielowski Steet. Here the street lamps were few and far between. Drizzle glanced against the few lit windows. Rita looked back and saw the man from the tree standing still, his eyes searching for her. Quickly she ran towards Kalecza Góra. She leaped into the little street, then into a doorway reeking of cat's pee, and wrapped herself in darkness.

When she was little she had prayed in moments of great fear. Now she no longer believed in prayer and remained quite still in the darkness. An impudent thought flitted through her mind. Her father would certainly not worry if she was murdered here because for him all that counted were good marks in Latin and German! But he would be furious at the photograph she had hidden in the pocket of her school coat. On it were inscribed the words:

"I saw you beneath the clock. So you have taken the first step. The next lies ahead. Do you want to find out something about me? Write to me. *Poste restante*, number 192. I have beautiful eyes. It's a shame they aren't any clearer on the photograph."

The photograph showed a young man dressed only in trousers and a vest. He was slim but perfectly muscular. His stomach muscles undulated beneath the taut material. He wore a hat, and his face was covered by a white headscarf.

The man following her reached the little street and passed Rita's hideout. He walked around the tenement building and a moment later found himself in the courtyard. For a while he stood perfectly still beneath a huge oak, then from the side of the yard entered the doorway where Rita was crouching and sniffed. He hated cats. He pressed the handle of the cellar door. It was open. He walked past it and quietly climbed the steps to the landing. Now he could see her. Feeble light fell from a doorway, casting light across her back. She was shaking all over. He made towards her.

At that moment he heard heavy footsteps in the street.

"Rita, how could you take such a risk and walk down forbidden streets!" he heard a loud voice cry. "What would your papa say!"

"Were you following me, Mr Zaremba?" screamed Rita. "I hate my father! He never leaves me alone, and he's always having me followed!"

A moment later the girl was no longer there. On a stair lay one of her gloves. He picked it up and sniffed it for a long while.

LWÓW, SATURDAY, MARCH 13TH, 1937
A QUARTER TO FOUR IN THE AFTERNOON

Popielski left the Scotch House where, for perhaps the first time ever, he had spent time solely as a customer and drunk an entire pot of scalding tea flavoured with raspberry preserve and fortified with a glass of vodka. He did not feel very well; the 'flu which had already mowed down his entire family, including the serving girl Hanna Półtoranos, had finally caught up with him. He had, therefore, taken the alcoholic raspberry mixture as a prophylactic measure, considering it an effective remedy for everything.

He followed a group of mathematicians down St Nicolas towards the university, and in order to avoid small talk kept slowing his pace, which had been exceptionally brisk since childhood. As it was, meeting them would be unavoidable since they were going to the same place, but he did not see the need to precipitate the irksome situation. He walked very slowly in the rain and mud, gazing about in the hope of looking like someone who was truly interested in this remarkable oasis of learning in the very heart of Lwów. Unfortunately, he did not sense any spirituality in the atmosphere and instead associated everything with past and fairly recent criminal cases. Instead of the university library he saw the massacred body of a student who had jumped from its roof; instead of the trees on Mochnacki Street – leafless at this time of the year – he saw the horrified face of a young nurse who had been raped in one of the street's courtyards; and instead of the Trinitarian Monastery, a frozen infant left at its gate. Everything that surrounded him was evil. He did not even see the greatest luminaries of world mathematics in the hunched and gesticulating men who were walking in front of him, but only malicious, absent-minded men with sick ambitions.

He followed the men into a building – known as the "old university" – adjacent to the Church of St Nicolas. Like them, he left his overcoat and hat in the cloakroom and climbed to the first floor where a meeting of the Lwów circle of the Polish Mathematical Society was to be held in one of the lecture theatres at four o'clock. Besides current issues there was to be a lecture by Bronisław Kulik entitled "Logic of names and logic of sentences".

Popielski sat by a window and leaned against the sill. This way he could clearly see anyone who entered. The mathematicians glanced at him with absent eyes and sat down on the benches. Some eyed his carefully chosen outfit with envy: the snow-white shirt, the black tie with white polka dots purchased in the Gentleman, and the suit made by Dajewski on Akademicka. He, in turn, looked at them through tired eyes and knew what would happen at this dull hour on such a rainy day: he would presently close his eyes and the sough of ominous phrases such as "interdependent operators" and "dual spaces" would lull him to sleep. Suddenly he started. He had caught sight of a small squat man with a nose turned up like a piglet. Slovenly dressed and unshaven, he had been the last to enter the lecture theatre and had not closed the door behind him. Popielski's heart pounded.

The stranger looked around, arousing general interest, then his eyes rested on Popielski's bald head. He walked up to him quietly and handed him an envelope.

"I'm the brother of Józef Majda, the caretaker." Popielski recoiled at the strong reek of garlic that wafted from the mouth of this man who resembled a pig. "My brother's sick and told me to pass this on to you, Commissioner."

The hum in the lecture theatre had died down. Everybody, including Professor Stefan Banach, who was chairing the meeting, stared at Popielski and the garlic lover.

"May we commence?" said the chairman, clearly vexed and addressing Popielski.

"Thank you," whispered Popielski. He backed away from the messenger in repulsion and waved his hand as if chasing off a fly.

"A warm welcome to you, gentlemen, at this, our March meeting of the Lwów circle of the Polish Mathematical Society," began Banach. "Today we have the pleasure of listening to Doctor Bronisław Kulik from Kraków, who will be talking to us about formal logic in a lecture entitled 'Logic of names and logic of sentences'. As the very title suggests, we are dealing here with an interesting methodological proposition. Welcome, Doctor Kulik."

Muted applause reverberated around the room and a slim, elegantly dressed and good-looking man of under thirty took the chair. He began by assuring everyone that it was a great honour for him to be standing in front of such excellent scholars and that he would note down all their comments, although he was not certain that he would be able to respond to them immediately. Two men sitting behind Popielski struck up a conversation.

"Who is this Kulik anyway?" Popielski heard them whisper. "Someone from the Jagiellonian? One of Leja's?"

"No," replied his companion. "No, Leja doesn't deal with logic. It's one of Łukasiewicz's new doctors. I think he's a private reader in Kraków, passed his Ph.D. recently and goes around Poland giving lectures. He wants to worm his way into the circle. Apparently it was Łukasiewicz who intervened with Banach about today's meeting. He's some kind of layabout, like all those logicians!"

Popielski smiled to himself, noting that gossip and envy also find their way into the world of abstraction. He threw a discreet glance behind him and saw two mathematicians he had never spotted in the Scotch House. In front of one was a file spilling over with exercise books. School teachers, thought Popielski, and pulled the letter out of its envelope. As usual, he was happy to see Mock's neat, even writing. He had a fast track for correspondence with the police officer from distant Breslau. Mock would hand the letter to the conductor on the Kattowitz–Lwów train who, on arriving in Lwów, would send the station messenger with the letter to Popielski's house on Łącki. There the caretaker would deliver it personally, or knew where to find him. Popielski began to read the letter in the hope of news, happy in the knowledge that he would have something to do during the boring meeting.

Kattowitz,
12th March, 1937

Dear Edward,

Let me relate what has happened since my last letter. As I wrote to you, I caught Maria Szynok's so-called betrothed – a certain Michał Borecki – in a vice, and he revealed the name of a woman who performs abortions in the area where the wretched madwoman lived. You will probably ask why I needed it. Well, I am pursuing the trail of "carnal mediation". I believe Szynok was a covert prostitute. First I thought that the murdered Nowoziemska was a bawd, even though I could find no evidence to confirm this. But this thought became an obsession. I called it the "trail of crypto-prostitution". While speaking to Borecki it occurred to me that women who perform abortions are often bawds. He himself made me aware of this unwittingly when he revealed that Szynok had had lots of lovers before him and — as he put it — had "had the scrape several times". So I put pressure on Borecki and he gave me a name. Monika Halaburda. As it turned out there did indeed live a woman of that name in the area, except that she was a respected seamstress, and in her private life the mother-in-law of this suburban Don Juan. He had played a cruel joke on me and my vice is now probably no more useful than scrap iron. I have not, however, been put off, despite Commissioner Holewa poking spokes into the wheel. For the time being the drone is ineffective, and I'm conducting my private investigation under his nose. How so? Well, I'm obstinately pursuing the "crypto-prostitution" trail, visiting Aphrodite's priest-esses in Kattowitz and asking them about women who perform abortions. I'm visiting them as a client, of course, so my shadow in the form of that nark, Senior Sergeant Wybraniec, does not accom-pany me. Holewa is furious with me and spouts moralistic tirades, but he cannot in the end forbid me my harmless weakness. And I can already see light at the end of the tunnel. I feel I am going to discover something soon. You know I know how to talk to girls and I'm generous with them. Besides, I don't pay them just to talk. Remember, dear friend? *Homo sum et nil humani* . . . That is all the news for today.

My best wishes,
Your Eberhard

P.S. Nothing new as far as Nowoziemska's murder is concerned.

Popielski read the letter three times and looked up at the lecture theatre. The lecturer must have been nearing the end of his talk, and the listeners were fidgeting impatiently. A muted hum had broken out. Popielski, who even then had not entirely given up Latin and frequented scholarly philological meetings, knew what the noise meant. The lecturer would meet with either admiration or crushing criticism.

"What on earth is he saying?" he heard a stage whisper behind him. "That's methodological treason!"

"Are you going to take the voice, Professor?" said the second whisperer.

"I'm not even going to stoop to taking part in the discussion!"

"Oh, don't exaggerate, Professor! You spoke up once at a similar lecture . . ."

"Never!" The professor flared up. "Never! What are you talking about, dear colleague!"

"What about that time the amateur gave a lecture, eh? Did you not debate then, Prof? Did you not take him to pieces?"

"What amateur?"

"I don't remember his name . . . Short . . . you know, the one who was as ugly as the devil himself! That eccentric, who looked as though he had escaped from a madhouse. The one who took Auerbach's hat by mistake!"

"Hat? Auerbach?"

"You don't know the anecdote? It's beautiful!"

"Gentlemen, gentlemen!" responded Banach *ex cathedra* as he glared at both teachers and rapped his pencil on the table. "Our lecturer is nearing his conclusion. Please allow him to do so!"

Popielski's heart was thumping again. "An amateur as ugly as the devil himself," he thought quickly, "they don't remember his name . . . Auerbach's hat . . . Steinhaus' sandwich . . . Hilbert's tripod . . . Ugly as the devil himself . . . ugly as an ape, like a monkey . . . Looks mentally ill . . . As if escaped from a lunatic asylum." These feverish thoughts quickened his pulse. He felt a twitch at his right ear. Auerbach's hat. He looked around the theatre. The lecturer had finished and Herman Auerbach, sitting in the front row, put himself forward to be the first to speak. Popielski left his seat noisily. Everyone turned to looked at him.

"Please wait for your turn," Banach reprimanded him, somewhat startled. "Reader Auerbach has the voice now."

The twitch at his ear became a thudding. Popielski approached Auerbach and grabbed him by the elbow. The grip was firm.

"You'll ask your question presently," he said in the silence of the theatre, "but there's something I have to know straightaway!"

"What is this supposed to mean?" yelled Leon Chwistek. "How dare you disrupt our academic freedom? How dare you drag us down from our crystalline heights of logic into the cesspool?"

"Let's go!" Popielski said to Auerbach. "It's a matter of the greatest importance!"

"As you can see, gentlemen" – Auerbach was clearly amused – "I am *vi coactus*."†

"*Cloacus*,"‡ sighed Steinhaus looking at Chwistek.

Popielski stepped into the corridor with Auerbach and then lost his self-control. He grasped the mathematician by his feeble biceps and pressed him to the wall.

"An amateur once held a lecture here. Very ugly. You'll remember him because he took your hat by mistake! Tell me all you know about him!"

† Under constraint.
‡ Arsehole.

- "Yes, I know who you mean," replied Auerbach calmly. "But first let me go. He's a logician and mathematician — self-taught, in fact. He didn't complete any studies. I don't know where he comes from or whether he studied anything at all," he continued once Popielski had let go of him. "His name is Zdzisław Potok. I saw him in the Scotch House only once. There was me and Staszek Ulam, who left for America a few days ago. Potok spoke to us for a while, he even had an interesting idea regarding Dirichlet's theorem, and then he left. He took the wrong hat. The rascal took my new one and left his old. Then he disappeared. So I wore his old hat. Better that than nothing at all. About a year later he approached me at the university, returned my hat with his apologies, and asked whether he could give a lecture there on logic. A lecture by a foreign guest, Professor Lebesgue, had just been cancelled and we were left with a gap to fill. I questioned him in detail about his lecture. It seemed to make sense and was coherent. So I agreed. He spoke to a practically empty theatre. I remember there was only Ulam, myself and one other person. Afterwards I got a hard time from my boss for allowing an amateur in and practically nobody turning up. That's all I know about him. Oh, and I know where he lives too because I sent him back his old hat. Żulińskiego Street 10, apartment 12."

"Was he ugly?"

"Must have been, because he even frightened one of the female students who was taking a test with me at the time."

"Why did you send him the hat and not give it back straightaway, when he came to return yours?"

"It was summer and I didn't have it with me."

"I have one last question." Popielski felt something tear in his body and he himself grow lighter and lighter, as if he had been on an exhausting diet. "Why didn't you tell me about this ugly man when we spoke at the Scotch House?"

"Because you didn't ask about the hat, you asked about some repulsive monster" smiled Auerbach. "The word 'hat' can be defined whereas 'repulsive monster' cannot. Goodbye, Commissioner. I'm going to go and ask my question."

He shook hands with Popielski and turned towards the door. As he was pressing the handle he felt the commissioner's hand on his arm.

"This really is going to be my last question." Popielski's face was as full of joy as those of Auerbach's students when they passed a difficult exam. "What is this anecdote about the wrong hat, where you played the hero?"

"Oh, that." Auerbach took his hand off the handle. "I wore Potok's old hat for almost a year and didn't clean it once. One of my colleagues asked why I never cleaned it. 'Why should I clean it for a thief,' I answered."

KATTOWITZ, THAT SAME MARCH 13TH, 1937
SIX O'CLOCK IN THE MORNING

Mock patted some eau de cologne onto his freshly shaven cheeks, poured a few drops into his hand and smoothed down his hair. He twanged his braces against his belly and left the bathroom, whistling quietly. Despite the early hour he had had enough sleep and felt relaxed. He put on his shirt, slipped on his amber cufflinks and fastened his tie in front of the mirror. He sat down at the table in the little parlour and pulled out his notebook. On the first page in a woman's neat writing were the words: Ernestyna Nierobisch, 4 Żogała, apt 1. He tore the following page from the notebook. Squinting against the cigarette smoke, he wrote: *I'm not going to wake you because you sleep so beautifully . . . Make yourself at home. Trust in exchange for trust.*

He approached the bed and placed the note on the pillow where there was still a warm impression of his head. The blonde he had met the previous day muttered something in her sleep. Mock wanted to stroke her damp forehead, but abandoned the thought for fear of waking the girl.

He turned off the bedside light, silently closed the door, stepped out into the corridor and pressed the button for the lift. The liftboy, familiar with his generosity, greeted him humbly and profusely.

"Here's two zlotys." Mock handed him the coin. "Buy a zloty's worth of roses and the other zloty's for your trouble."

"And what shall I do with the flowers, sir?"

"Take them to my room and stand them next to the bed." He wagged his finger threateningly. "But make sure you don't wake the lady!"

KATTOWITZ, THAT SAME MARCH 13TH, 1937
HALF PAST SIX IN THE MORNING

Mock went to the address jotted down by the girl with whom he had spent the night. Żogała Street was in Bogucice, the district where Borecki lived. The door was opened by a stout, slovenly woman of about sixty. She wore a pink dressing gown and a dirty-yellow velvet belt encircled her prominent stomach. Above her forehead, at what was almost a right angle, her long hair stood on end. It looked as if someone had gathered it from the back of her neck and thrown it over her head. Traces of mascara were lodged in the wrinkles around her eyes.

"What is it?" she growled.

Mock took a two-hundred-zloty note from his pocket and showed it to the woman.

"I've come on an important practical matter." He waved the note in front of her eyes. "I'm a rich industrialist from Germany, and I'm looking for a pretty girl for a few days!"

"Don't understand!" she yelled. "This ain't Germany any more! Speak our language!"

She slammed the door in his face. Mock sighed and went out into the dark street. He walked away slowly, and then suddenly spun on his heel. A net curtain stirred in Ernestyna Nierobisch's apartment. He went back to the main road and whistled down a passing droschka, then climbed inside and told the cabby to go down Żogały and make a U-turn. The latter did as he was asked. As they were nearing the doorway to Nierobisch's apartment, Mock ordered him to stop and wait. The cabby made sure his client was aware of the fact that he would have to pay for the wait and settled down to nap in the box.

Mock lit a cigarette and pulled up the collar of his overcoat. His good spirits had evaporated. The commissioner had of course considered that he might meet with such a reception from the abortionist, but he was so pleased with himself that morning that he had not worked out an effective strategy and eventually had decided to act ad hoc. And now he did not know what to do. He was angry that he had approached the situation so casually. No woman who performed abortions and procured clients would be so gullible; she wouldn't be taken in by some shady referral or a large banknote and she would be risking too much if she revealed her business. All this Mock knew perfectly well. He also knew that for lack of any other avenues he would have to do the rounds of the clandestine abortionists, put the fear of God into the right madame and force her to reveal Maria Szynok's probable client. He did not want to allow the thought of failure to enter his head, but his great satisfaction at having got to the first bawd was eclipsed by his usual scepticism. Only then did he realize that there was no tool he could use to force her to disclose the name of Szynok's client. Mock had no vice to hand in Kattowitz. "But have I got anything better to do?" he thought bitterly. "Go back to Breslau and present myself to my angry superiors? Or to Lwów, to track down some alleged mathematician? I might as well sit in this cab and see whether that old witch goes out. And then search her apartment . . ."

The cabby yawned. Żogały Street was utterly deserted. This was the dead hour of the morning when the men had long since gone to work in the mines and their wives had not yet woken the children for school. Mock felt tired to the bone, proof of his considerable physical activity in the night. He adjusted his collar. He did not even notice when his cigarette slipped out of his fingers and his heavy eyelids closed.

"Hey, my good man!" The cab driver shook Mock awake. "Are we going or aren't we? This isn't a hotel, you don't sleep in here!"

"Did an ugly fat woman go out through that doorway?" Mock rubbed his eyes, angry at himself.

"That she did!" The cab driver stared at him in surprise. "A good ten minutes ago."

Mock pressed a coin into the cabby's hand and ran across the muddy pavement. He stood at Nierobisch's door and listened. Minutes passed. A woman's angry shouting resounded on the first floor along with the high-pitched entreaties of a child. Mock took out a pick-lock from his outer coat pocket and turned it at various angles in the lock. More minutes passed. The old bag could return at any moment if she had just popped out to the shop, for example. Despite the cold, Mock's head grew damp beneath his bowler hat. The building became noisier and noisier. Plates clattered, children bickered. The steel pick-lock caught against something and he heard the lock click. Somewhere upstairs a door opened, and children thumped quickly down the stairs.

The hall gave straight onto the kitchen, just like in Borecki's lodgings. Mock moved carefully between various obstacles on the floor. There was a powerful stench and an indescribable mess. Woodchips and coal lay scattered on the floor beneath a stove on which stood a saucepan. Mock lifted the lid and sniffed. Even though he had not yet eaten, he would not have tasted the soup in that pan for anything in the world. Not only was there a pungent reek of soggy garlic, but the vessel itself looked as though it contained dishwater. On its sides, glistening with grease, a thick liquid had hardened into hideous tongues. The smell of the dishcloth thrown over the stove reminded Mock of the Great War, when in the trenches of Dyneburg he had wrapped rags around his feet for want of socks. On the floor was a basin full of dirty water. As he passed it, Mock leaned on the table and felt his hand stick to the oilcloth. He was furious.

"I have the luck to get in here," he said to himself, "then . . . shit, what a hole! All of Holewa's men put together wouldn't be able to search it!"

Panting with anger, he looked around for a cabinet or a chest, without knowing what he was supposed to find there. He walked past a bed on which lay a red duvet without a cover. He pressed the handle of the door leading to the other room.

It was probably here, with windows looking out onto the brick wall of a small courtyard, that Ernestyna Nierobisch carried out her procedures. In the centre of the room stood a single couch, and from beneath it poked a dustpan. Mock pulled out the *Kattowitzer Zeitung* from his pocket and laid it out on the stained carpet littered with strips of cotton wool. He lifted the edge of a throw that covered the couch and saw a small, chipped basin shaped like a kidney. Its sides were encrusted with dried, rusty-coloured liquid. He straightened up quickly, held his nose and took a moment to breathe rapidly through his mouth.

Just then he thought he was experiencing déjà vu. Facing him in the glazed cabinet stood a file. It was black and its corners were adorned with elaborate gilded ferrules. Mock raced to the cabinet and seized the file. In it were thick sheets of cardboard to which postcards from exotic locations had been affixed. One of them, with the caption "Greetings from Breslau", showed zoological gardens familiar to Mock. He shuddered with excitement and looked at the file's spine. Information as to its contents had disappeared from beneath the elastic band but an imprint of the writing which had probably appeared there remained on the soft spine.

"Gen-tle-men," syllabized Mock.

It was one of the few words he knew in Polish. It appeared in lots of places to convey important information about gender, for example at the entrance to the men's toilets. Or on the files in murdered Klementyna Nowoziemska's marriage bureau.

LWÓW, THAT SAME MARCH 13TH, 1937
A QUARTER TO FIVE IN THE AFTERNOON

Popielski was well acquainted with the area around Żuliński. He used to frequent the tavern on Ochronki, which was full of veterans and prostitutes so old the streets of Lwów sang about them:

> *A genital louse*
> *Roams thro' this house*
> *And is good for nought else*
> *'cept Babiczek's dripping*

Popielski remembered the song and it was no secret to him – or to anyone else from Lwów – that Babiczek sold horsemeat and cured meats of the worst quality. To compare anyone to this butcher's produce was, therefore, an insult. Although the song still rang in his ears, once he found himself in Łyczaków he thought of nothing but the course of action which was to be the culmination of a complex and time-consuming investigation.

Żuliński, a street on the outskirts of Łyczaków, was short and started at Łyczakowska, a hundred metres from the Church of the Order of St Clare. Its gateway was formed by two corner taverns – Einstein's and Krebs' – and the road ended at Piekarska. It was lined with two- and three-storey houses and was almost devoid of trees. The two-storey tenement numbered 10 and 10A was in the middle of the street and very run-down, with flaking plaster here and there; its owner must have saved a great deal of money on caretaking, because in front of the doorway lay all kinds of kitchen waste which some heedless housewife or mischievous child had thrown out of the window. Disgusted, Popielski pushed aside the potato peelings and apple cores with the tip of his brogue and entered. Stefan Cygan and Herman Kacnelson followed right behind. Popielski directed Kacnelson to the courtyard, where the dull thump-thump of carpet-beating could be heard; then he nodded to Cygan and they made their way upstairs, passing a door from which emanated the sounds and smells of Saturday chores: pans clattering, water sploshing as it dripped from rags into buckets, and the penetrating smell of turpentine floor polish. Intermittently they heard the cry of a baby or an irate voice fortified by alcohol.

They climbed to the second floor. There was no door marked 12, but Popielski did not appear concerned. He knew the mathematician could not have mistaken the number. Access to the lodgings must be by way of the courtyard. Popielski looked through a window. Kacnelson, standing by the carpet horse, caught sight of his boss and pointed at the garret. A moment later they were at the place he had indicated, the highest gallery in the courtyard. The door to number 12 was warped and in several places there were large gaps between the door and its jambs. Popielski knocked lightly. Silence. He knocked again. Still no sound from within. Popielski grasped the door handle and pressed. The door was locked. He peered through one of the gaps. Darkness.

"Go and ask the neighbours, Stefan," he whispered. "One of them might have a key. That's often the case where there isn't a caretaker. Pretend you're Potok's brother. He mustn't know the police have been enquiring about him."

"Yes, sir." Cygan turned and made towards the neighbouring door.

217

Popielski stepped aside into the semi-circular stairwell and observed the whole scene. He realized that with the appearance of a film star, Cygan was not an especially credible brother to Potok, whose striking resemblance to an ape was general knowledge. Popielski would have been even less credible in the role, however, with his dandy looks, or Kacnelson with his Jewish heritage engraved on his face.

The door was opened by a short man in a jacket, whose lack of teeth was apparent to Popielski even at that distance.

"Good afternoon." Cygan tipped his hat.

"Aye, a good one, a good one," replied the man, looking warily at the stranger.

"I'm extremely sorry, sir, my name is Kazimierz Potok and I'm Zdzich Potok's – your neighbour's – brother. He's not home at the moment and I've come a long way. Do you know where he might be?"

"He never said he had a brother." An unkempt woman leaned out from behind the man's shoulder.

"He never says much," laughed Cygan.

"That's right enough," answered the neighbour. "He doesn't talk much. But he's not here, he left today, didn't say where for. . . He'll be back next Sunday."

"I knew he was leaving today but didn't know what time . . . And I didn't make it," said Cygan with a concerned expression. "Oh well . . . Next Sunday, you say . . . That's not very good . . . I thought I'd spend some time with him before my train for Przemyśl. It doesn't leave for another two hours . . ."

"Well then, come inside." The man opened the door wide. "We don't have much but we can always find some tea, bread and onions for Mr Zdzisław's brother."

"I wouldn't like to put you to any trouble . . . Maybe you know who's got the keys to his apartment . . . I can wait there . . ."

"Oh, what a dunce!" The neighbour slapped himself on the forehead. "I've got the keys! Come on, I'll let you in."

The man returned with the keys and opened the door to Potok's apartment. He accompanied Cygan in. Popielski heard the hospitable neighbour do the honours by telling Cygan to "take off his coat, hang up his hat" and "sit at the table". A moment later he returned to his apartment. As he was closing the door his wife said:

"That fellow's far too handsome to be Mr Zdzisław's brother."

"Maybe it's his stepbrother," Popielski heard, and the door clicked shut.

Silence fell. A minute later Popielski was in Potok's apartment. It was an ordinary bachelor's flat with a dark kitchen separated from the hallway by a thin oilcloth curtain hanging on a wire. In the main room was an iron bed, a table, two chairs and a small wardrobe. All these were buried beneath sheets of paper covered in untidy writing. Here and there the ink had run on the poor-quality paper and the annotations were totally illegible. But it was clear that the pages were covered in mathematical notes and calculations.

Apart from this scholarly mess, the apartment seemed neat and tidy. There was nothing in the kitchen besides a cast-iron sink, a spirit burner, small work surface fixed to the wall, a cupboard for plates and provisions and a bucket for waste. Popielski checked the cupboard and saw a few scraps of bread and a jar with the remains of some dripping. He went into the other room and opened the wardrobe, in which he found a few dirty shirts and some removable collars. Evidently Potok had only one suit and one coat, and that was what he had been wearing when he left. At the bottom of the wardrobe stood a thick cardboard binder. Popielski untied the ribbons and took out a wad of about a hundred pages covered in typewriting. It was a thesis on logic, written in French. Popielski was astonished to see that it contained numerous Ancient Greek quotations.

219

He thought hard; a vein pulsed in his temple. The work was typed in French, in *French*. He browsed a few pages. Neither the accents nor any other French diacritical marks or abbreviations had been written by hand.

He handed Cygan the binder. "Please send this to Breslau for them to establish whether this paper was written on the typewriter found next to the murdered woman on New Year's Eve. Phone me at home in an hour and I'll give you the exact address."

"Yes, sir." Cygan was rummaging absent-mindedly through Potok's bedclothes. "Oh, naughty, naughty," smiled the young police officer as he reached under the pillow. "Keeping some pretty dirty things here, I believe . . ."

Cygan tossed some rolled-up photographs onto the bed. They were not what he had expected, not pornographic postcards at all. The play of light and shadow as well as accessories such as a fan, sabre and sombrero indicated that the photographs had been taken in a photographic studio. They showed a face – always the same – taken in profile and *en face*. Teeth bared, pouting or with pulled-back lips.

"Commissioner, sir," Cygan was no longer smiling, "he really isn't very good-looking."

LWÓW, SATURDAY, MARCH 20TH, 1937
NINE O'CLOCK IN THE MORNING

As she entered the gateway Rita found herself on an axis where light meets shadow. The axis, which was exceptionally, even unnaturally sharp, bisected her face along the nose. The light came from a skylight cut into the roof above the steep spiral staircase. She stood erect and motion-less between the white, glaring light of the morning and the dense, damp darkness. Suddenly her face moved a centimetre forward, her muscles relaxed, her chin dropped and her eyelids started to close. Sleep appeared to have overcome her. From beneath one eyelid a forked tongue of blood began to ooze and spread. Within it flowed bile and what remained of her eyeballs. Her body collapsed onto the floorboards but her head remained hanging in the air, swaying imperceptibly, suspended by Rita's plaits held in a clenched fist.

A sound resembling a sob, a cough and vomiting all at once emerged from Popielski's lips. The commissioner sat up in bed and placed a hand on his chest beneath his silk pyjamas; he felt his heart pounding beneath the skin. He glanced around his bedroom as if he were seeing it for the first time. A moment passed before he finally surfaced from the dark gateway where Rita's head had been hacked off and returned to his own apartment next to Jesuit Gardens. Despite the heavy, drawn curtains the room was a pale grey. Outside, the sun must have been blazing, bringing joy to all those longing for spring, but within his brain it stirred epileptic nerves. He looked at his watch. It was only nine o'clock.

"Why have I woken up?" he asked himself.

His body, for many years accustomed to rigorous sleeping hours, had hardly ever rebelled with bouts of insomnia or abrupt awakenings. Popielski always fell into a deep oblivion at five o'clock in the morning, and at precisely midday raised his head, which ached from sleep and the tobacco-rich stuffiness of his bedroom. Occasionally the headache would be caused by night terrors, or rather morning terrors. These nightmares rolled through Popielski's dormant mind without inflicting any harm, and the first cigarette of the day effectively dispersed any recollection of them. But several times in his life they had caused him to wake with a jolt, and these instances of awakening had taught him to treat them as a warning. That is what had happened during his exile in Russia, when a gang of old peasants – bearded and crazed on the pure spirits they had drunk – had burst into the inn where he had been resting after a night of cards, and

221

with axes red with blood had begun to cleave wedges in the skulls of the sleeping Tsarist officers. That is what had happened during his days in Vienna, when a mad chess opponent, having wagered his mistress and lost the game to him, had broken into his miserable student lodgings with a shard of glass in his naked hands raised like a battleaxe. And that is what had happened when he was ten and sleeping heavily in his aunt's house, and a messenger had arrived with the news that Tatar bandits had beaten his father to death with flails near Kijów, and the following day his mother had hanged herself at Kijów station.

Dreams like these were invariably warnings or heralds of impending misfortune. They usually featured bestial creatures which emerged from the corners of his room and sat on his chest, rolling their long muzzles. This time – and this had never occurred before – he had dreamed of a person he knew: Rita had appeared in his nightmare. Hair stuck together, head severed from body, eyes gouged out.

He leaped out of bed and began to dress, spurning the clothes he had arranged – as he always did before going to bed – on a clothes horse. He did not so much as glance at the shirt and suit jacket for which he had chosen a suitable tie. In order to save the time he would have needed to fasten the tie and struggle with cufflinks, he threw the jacket of his dress uniform over his pyjamas and buttoned it up to the neck. Shoes in hand, coat over his arm and sunglasses on his nose he raced out of the apartment. The only thing he forgot was his hat.

With the servant's whining and Leokadia's exclamations of surprise still in his ears, he jumped into the Chevrolet parked in front of the building. He drove quickly down Kraszewski Street and turned right into Słowacki. He flashed past the Main Post Office and the Ossolineum then headed into Chorążczyzna. The people drinking water at the old well on Dąbrowski Square gawped at the car, as if it were some fantastical vehicle. On Sokół Street Popielski beeped at a group of youths who were blocking the way, clearly heading towards the gymnastics hall. The young men fled with loud and hostile comments. He turned left into Zimorowicz and glanced up at the Towarowa Stock Exchange building and the statue of Ujejski. Overtaking a coal cart, he shot down Akademicka. He passed the Scotch House and Fredro's statue and a moment later pulled up at 8 Zielona – Queen Jadwiga's Secondary School for Girls.

LWÓW, THAT SAME MARCH 20TH, 1937
HALF PAST NINE IN THE MORNING

The headmistress of Queen Jadwiga's, Miss Ludmiła Madler, did not like Commissioner Edward Popielski. She had got to know him over the course of several unpleasant meetings concerning his exasperating daughter. On those occasions he had sat sullen and pensive, as if absent, and the headmistress had sensed the fury rising within him. She had seen many similar reactions during her long career as a teacher, but in Popielski – and this she sensed perfectly well – the anger was not directed at his daughter, nor did it herald a just rebuke of the unruly little madame; no, the fury was directed at her, at a meritorious pedagogue and highly experienced teacher who had dedicated the best years of her life to bringing up girls, and who understood their anxieties and innermost thoughts better even than her own! Popielski would listen to everything she had to say with a gloomy calm, then quickly leave her study. Through the window she would see his impressive figure – in bowler hat and gleaming white shirt – pacing around the small square in front of the Protestant Church of St Ursula, which was encircled by trees and squeezed in between two tenements, like some wild beast. Surrounded by a cloud of smoke, he had excited the young art teacher, Miss Helena Majer, whom the headmistress had once caught staring intently at the police officer.

"Such a strong man!" Miss Majer had said admiringly at the time,

223

thinking it was her friend, the sports teacher, who had come up behind her. "He must be working on an important criminal case!"

"No, dear colleague," the headmistress had replied, greatly disconcerting her employee. "He's thinking of placing a bomb beneath our school. Best of all when I'm here!"

Now Popielski stood before the headmistress, unshaven, in dark glasses and with his coat buttoned up to the neck despite the springtime warmth. Miss Madler remembered the ill-repute that surrounded him — all those rumours about his brutality and numerous romances — and she did not find him exciting at all. Looking at his tired face and the glasses which hid his eyes, what she detected in the rumours — if there was any truth in them — was instead an indication of practical ineptitude and loneliness . . .

"It's a good thing you've come, Commissioner," she said severely. "Your daughter has decided to play truant today! Her tutor, Professor Paklikowski, has just told me he's seen her on Piłsudski Street! She was with . . ."

Popielski behaved uncharacteristically. Up until now he had listened to the headmistress' pedagogical tirades to the end. Up until now he had always said "Goodbye!" on leaving. And he had never slammed the door so hard.

LWÓW, THAT SAME MARCH 20TH, 1937
A QUARTER TO TEN IN THE MORNING

If Rita Popielska were asked to say honestly what gave her as much pleasure as skiing, she would reply "truancy in spring". She never felt better than when she had succeeded in escaping the vigilant eyes of her teachers, the caretaker or other oppressors at Queen Jadwiga's. She would burst with joy as she sneaked out of school and a quarter of an hour later would disappear into Stryjski Park to hide among the bushes and share secrets with a fellow truant. Until now this had been Jadzia Wajchendler, but Rita had taken a great dislike to her as, on the occasions she recounted the conflicts she had with her father, she noticed that Jadzia always seemed to side with "Mr Commissioner". For some time now her confidante and accomplice had been Beata Zacharkiewicz, a tall and unattractive girl with the unflattering nickname of "Beanpole".

Some of the more courageous pupils celebrated the first day of spring by playing truant. This year it fell on a Sunday, so Rita decided to mark the day a little earlier and persuaded her new friend to join her celebration. At first Beanpole resisted, but gave in as soon as Rita promised to reveal to her the greatest secret of her life.

The girls had made careful preparations. Rita had stolen four cigarettes from her father, while Beanpole had filled a small jar with wine from a bottle standing in the cellar. Both had taken more than the usual provisions to school that day. A few days earlier Rita had typed out a document authorizing them to be absent from school that day on the pretext of organizing a school trip. They had both forged the signature of their tutor, Professor Paklikowski, and armed with all this they met up before eight in the morning at Stryjski Bazaar.

From there they had quickly arrived at the park. In order to avoid any busybodies at the main gate, they had walked up Stryjski and approached the west gate, near the gardener's house. They had gone down into the park and raced past the statue of Kiliński, then walked up the hill. Before long they had found a hiding place in the bushes. Although the weather was glorious and truly spring-like, there had been nobody amongst the shrubs or along the half-wild avenues, and so, untroubled by anyone, the young ladies had sat down on a log, eaten a ham roll, smoked a cigarette and taken a large gulp of wine. Since early morning Beanpole had tried in vain to persuade Rita to reveal her secret, but Rita was unyielding. She said firmly that she would tell her everything on the way to a certain mysterious place where she was expected at ten o'clock. Beanpole's eyes boggled with curiosity and she resolved to be patient.

Rita was not able to disclose her secret on tram No. 3, which they had taken in the direction of Łyczaków, because it had been too crowded. Nor could she disclose it on Piekarska, because she had been prevented from doing so by students from the nearby Department of Medicine, who must have pulled out of lectures en masse that beautiful day and were drifting along the pavements accosting all the young ladies. It was not until they got to Żuliński Street that they were almost alone. The sun hid behind some clouds and only a pale light settled on windows and balconies. The girls walked briskly arm in arm, constantly looking about them in case they were being spied upon, and exchanging whispers and sighs.

"And, you know, I wrote to him *poste restante*."

"Then what? What happened?"

"I showed a cool interest in him. In fact I wrote: 'Surely you think too highly of your eyes. You may seduce other young ladies with them, but not me.'"

"And what did he say then?"

"In the next letter, a week ago, he again mentioned the beauty of his eyes. He must be very sure of himself. I mean, what man would send a woman a photograph, with a written dedication, which displays his torso . . ."

"What?"

"Torso, torso, Beata, why are you so surprised? Have you never seen a man's torso?"

"Of course I have," Beanpole sulked. "But carry on. What else did he write?"

"He wrote suggesting that we meet, in a public place of course, where I would be able to – just imagine! – where I would be able to admire . . ."

"What, his eyes? Or his torso?"

"Not in public, come on!"

They stopped talking for a moment because their words were drowned out by the cries of a street vendor who was going from door to door, laden with sacks, and yelling at the top of his voice: "Handełe! Handełe!"[†]

"So where is this public place!"

Rita stood still and looked at her friend with a smile. She revelled in her friend's burning curiosity.

"That's just where we're going, silly."

"What? We're going there now?"

"Don't you want to?" Rita grew serious and pointed to the inside pocket of her coat. "I've got the address here. I carry all his letters with me so the old man doesn't find them. The public place is a billiard club . . . I want you to come with me . . . Not because I'm scared of going by myself, of course, but so that we can exchange opinions about his so-called beautiful eyes . . ."

"Thank you, sweetheart!" Beanpole kissed her on both flushed cheeks. "Thanks so much for trusting me!"

"Quiet," hissed Rita. "We need to see what the time is because we're almost there. But first let's take a look at the tenement."

They passed the doorway to number 10, then to 10a, and a moment later they were on the corner of Łyczakowska. They entered Krebs' tavern. The windows were shuttered and it was dark within. All they saw was some drunkard and a barman with a face so gloomy and downcast he could have been a main character in a dark urban ballad. The drunkard, who had clearly gone too far in his attempt to cure a hangover, stood swaying over a shot of vodka and tried to take a bite of the herring he held by the tail between two fingers.

† Yiddish: "Come and buy! Come and buy!"

227

"And what brings these two young ladies here?" boomed the barman in a powerful voice.

"We'd like to know what the time might be," said Rita, much braver than Beanpole.

"It might be midnight but it's just before ten," laughed the barman.

"Thank you," said Rita, curtsying politely.

The street outside was empty. They left the tavern and Rita pulled her friend into the nearest gateway.

"Go on, Beata, give me a bit of wine!"

"Right away!" answered Beanpole.

They each took a large mouthful. Squinting, they leaned out of the doorway and looked up and down the street. It was still empty, except for a black automobile which was just parking a few metres away.

"Which building is it, Rita? Which building?" Beata was pale with excitement. "The one where the car's parking?"

"No!" Now Rita was pale too. She grabbed her friend by the elbow. "We've got to go back. Right now! This way, through the yard!"

"What do you mean 'go back'? Now? Don't you trust me any more?" With tears in her eyes, Beanpole ran after Rita as she strode quickly towards the back door and into the yard. She caught up with her only after some twenty metres. Startled by the girls, the vendor stopped his cries of "Handełe" and was staring at them.

"How could you?" sobbed Beata. "Do you know what it feels like to be pushed aside, trampled on? You'd given me so much hope!"

"My old man was driving that car, understand?" Rita's eyes were full of fury. "I don't know how he discovered my secret, but it's a piece of cake for him!" She broke into derisive laughter. "That ace of the Polish police . . ."

"Listen, Rita." Beanpole suddenly calmed down. "Maybe your father's come to get that man? He wrote to you himself that police from

228

many countries have been looking for him. Maybe your father's on his trail?"

"Oh, my God." Rita buried her long, slender fingers in her hair. "That could be true! I have to know! Come on, we're going back to the tavern to watch through the window!"

"But there's the drunk and that terrible barman!"

"Don't be scared, if anything happens . . ."

"You'll call your father?"

Rita stared at Beanpole for a long time, as if wanting to burn out her eyes with her glare.

"Don't dare even think it!" she said slowly. "I'm never going to ask that rat for help if he keeps following me at every step! He's made my life hell! Did you know that I'm not going to have a part in *Medea* because of him? Kasprzak has taken it away from me and given it to Jadzia! When I asked why, he said I ought to ask my dear father! Now do you understand? Do you think I'm ever going to ask him for anything?"

LWÓW, THAT SAME MARCH 20TH, 1937
FIVE TO TEN IN THE MORNING

Zaremba heard footsteps on the stairs. He put his eye to the little hole in the net curtain that hung over the toilet door. A man in a hat with a ruck-sack on his back was slowly coming up to the small gallery. He was dressed in a worn overcoat that was too large for him. He passed the toilet, looked carefully at the OUT OF ORDER notice and dragged himself up to the top floor. He was young, yet he moved like an old man. He was slim, yet panted like a fat man. He was human, yet looked like an animal.

Zaremba, disguised as a plumber, sat down on the closed toilet seat and wiped the sweat from his brow with the tail of his workman's

229

overalls. He heard a key grating in a lock and a door slamming. He had no doubt it was Potok. He had just entered his apartment.

The police officer tried to collect his thoughts. The raid on Potok's apartment was to have taken place the following day. The neighbour had clearly said Potok would be coming back on Sunday, and yet he had returned a day too soon. Zaremba went cold at the thought of what might have happened had the man appeared half an hour earlier when, in breach of regulations, he had popped downstairs for some cigarettes.

If something were to go wrong with their intricate plan, it could only be due to human error. Every precaution had been taken. The toilet had been set up as an observation point, and Wassermann's nearby haber-dashery on the corner of Żulińska and Łyczakowska Streets – equipped with a telephone – was to act as a centre for communications. In order to ensure immediate contact, a special line had been installed between the shop and headquarters. The trap set for Potok in his tenement was to be infallible. The toilet had been locked under the pretext of plumbing repair work, but in fact this was so that the stench would cause no problem to the detectives on their watch. An officer was to keep an eye on the suspect's apartment day and night until Sunday, checking identification papers and questioning anyone who visited him. The police were keen to hang something on Potok on the basis of these reports, something which would allow them to apprehend him, even if by some sixth sense he caught on to the swoop and did not return to his apartment. On Sunday it was all to come to a head. At four o'clock in the morning Żulińska would be swarming with police, including all four officers from the Investigative Bureau and twelve plain-clothes men from Station IV on Kurkowa. Six plain-clothes officials were to wait at the train station. But now Potok had returned a day early!

Zaremba slowly composed himself and pondered what to do. He could not leave his vantage point to call headquarters from Wassermann's shop since this would involve a huge risk. Potok might in the meantime visit his neighbour and discover that his brother had come to see him – who knows whether he even had a brother – and simply run away. Zaremba could either wait for his replacement – Kacnelson was to come at half past ten – or arrest the Minotaur himself. He chose the latter. He felt for the Browning beneath his arm and began to take off his plumber's overalls.

At that moment he heard footsteps on the stairs. Popielski was on the small gallery, unshaven and strangely attired in his dress uniform jacket. On his neck flushed a raspberry-red patch. Zaremba opened the door and Popielski slipped into the toilet cubicle.

"He's here, Eddie, the Mino . . ." Zaremba began feverishly, forgetting that his colleague hated the diminutive "Eddie".

"Wait," Popielski broke in. "Tell me where you saw Rita a couple of days ago when she left the church. Quick, I've had a dream, and she's not at school. I've got to find her . . ."

"Stop babbling." Zaremba's whisper sounded like a shouted order. "Potok's home."

"Let's go." Popielski immediately calmed down but the red flush on his neck began to spread. "We're going to get the beast."

They left the toilet and Zaremba buttoned up his overalls on the way. They stood silently for a moment at the door to number 12, and then Zaremba knocked.

"Who's there?" A strange, high-pitched voice came from the apartment.

"The plumber," said Zaremba. "Something's broken in the lav. I've got to check your pipes."

Slowly, the door opened a little. One eye appeared – small, round and set far back in its socket. The upper part of the eye was surrounded by formidable eyebrows, the tortuous tufts of which curled over a swollen, red eyelid. Below, on the cheek, appeared stiff clusters of unshaven bristles among which erupted whitish seborrhoeic scabs. The eye rolled in its socket and caught sight of Popielski with his Browning.

From the side, Popielski struck the eye with the barrel of his gun. His aim was inaccurate, but the sharp metal cut into the skin of Potok's forehead. Potok clasped the wound with both hands and blood dripped from between his fingers. Just as in Popielski's nightmare it had dripped from Rita's eye. The commissioner pushed Zaremba aside and rushed into the apartment as Potok tried to escape, thrashing around between the narrow walls of the hallway, bleeding profusely. Popielski tripped on the partially torn-down curtain that separated the kitchen from the hallway, by which time Potok was already on the threshold. He turned to look at Popielski and grinned. Blood was running down his nose and cheeks and dripping from his lips onto his teeth. Popielski caught sight of bloodied gums and fangs. Potok gnashed his teeth, as if wanting to show the commissioner how it had been at the scene of crime – this is how I gnawed my victims, how I tore at their flesh, devoured the tissue in their cheeks.

Popielski pulled down the oilcloth curtain. Metal rings rolled across the kitchen. In one swift move he kicked the beast between the legs with the tip of his brogue. Potok fell to his knees, grasping his testicles. Popielski wrapped the oilcloth curtain around his head as if to suffocate him.

"Let him go, Eddie!" shouted Zaremba, grabbing Popielski by the arms. "You kill the swine and you'll get locked up! Let him go, damn it!"

Popielski caught a glimpse of Potok's blood mixed with some sort of secretion on the sleeve of his jacket and moved away from the wheezing body in disgust. But he forced himself to grip Potok's wrist and pinned his leg to the bed. Still wrapped in oilcloth, the beast's head rose and fell with his broken breathing.

Popielski sat on the bed and lit a cigarette.

"Go to our communications centre, Wilek, and phone for a van," he said, releasing a cloud of smoke. "I don't want him fouling up our car with his gore. I'll keep an eye on him."

"Best you go, Eddie," said Zaremba with a smile. "If I leave you alone with him you might just kill him! Do you really want to move into Brygidki prison?"

Popielski wiped his bloodied sleeve on the bed sheet and got up. The red flush on his neck had disappeared. He grasped the bed frame and shook it several times, laughing like a madman.

"We've got him!" he yelled, and then said with a smile: "I'll be back in a minute, you keep a good watch over him! So, how goes it, handsome sir?" He gave Potok a light kick and ran out to the stairwell.

Potok tossed his head and threw off the oilcloth. He looked at his immobilized wrist. The handcuffs were certainly an obstacle, but the leg of the bed was not fixed to the floor.

LWÓW, THAT SAME MARCH 20TH, 1937
A QUARTER PAST TEN IN THE MORNING

In the dark tavern Rita sat alone by the window looking out onto Żulińska Street and wondered what to do. She could not even ask Beanpole's advice, for Beanpole had run off home, scared by both the gloomy barman and the blind-drunk customer who had sucked the salty meat off yet another herring. Neither bothered Rita. The barman was drying a tankard and listening to Hanka Ordonówna's hit "A kogo nasza miłość obchodzi?"† on the radio. The drunk snoozed, his forehead resting on his hands.

Rita squeezed the glass of luke-warm tea standing in front of her. She had caught sight of her father, and he was walking in her direction. She

---

† "And Who Cares About Our Love?"

felt weak at the thought of him finding her there, but instead he turned into the haberdashery twenty metres from where she was sitting. Rita stepped out of the tavern, crept up to the shop and from behind a corner peered in through the window with one eye. She glimpsed her father's bald head. He was wiping his neck with a handkerchief adorned with a monogram she had once embroidered – in days gone by when, sitting on his knee, she had confided her childish secrets to him. She was saddened at the memory, and at the sight of her father's helpless gesture as he wiped away the sweat. Shaking her head to dispel such sentimentality she ran quickly down the road; she had to discover whether her father was after her stranger.

Once in the gateway she looked about her. There was no sign to indicate a billiard club. With a pounding heart, she began to climb the stairs, her shoes ringing out on the steps. She reached the small gallery on the top floor. One door was ajar. She pushed it open, and it squeaked a little. All at once she felt scared. She wanted to back out and run from there, but she could not. There was somebody behind her.

LWÓW, THAT SAME MARCH 20TH, 1937
TWENTY PAST TEN IN THE MORNING

Popielski dabbed his neck and tucked the handkerchief into his pocket.

"Two uniformed men from Station IV will be there soon, as well as Kacnelson who's going to relieve Zaremba," he heard Aspirant Cygan's voice over the phone.

"Good, Stefan. I'm going back to Wilek."

"Wait a moment, Commissioner." Cygan was excited. "I've got some important news for you from Breslau. The technicians there say the thesis was written on the same typewriter as that found near the murdered woman."

"Well, I'll be . . ." Popielski was lost for words. "No parrot's going to defend him now!"

"And one last thing: Mock called. He's got some sensational news about the brothel madame from Kattowitz . . . The old woman's mixed up in human trafficking . . ."

"Stefan," laughed Popielski, "do you have to bother me now? We've got the Minotaur, understand, we've got him!"

"But Mock's going to phone in a moment. What shall I tell him?"

"Tell him to come to Lwów! It's time to celebrate the end of our investigation!"

Cygan wanted to say something more, but Popielski had hung up. He winked cheerfully at the embarrassed shop girl and left, squinting in the bright sunlight. As he put on his sunglasses he saw Kacnelson enter the gateway at 10 Żuliński Street with two uniformed policemen. None of them had noticed Popielski.

The small gallery echoed with the sound of heavy footsteps. A door on the top floor squeaked. The police had entered Potok's apartment. Holding on to the banister, Popielski went up the stairs with a smile. He was a floor beneath them. A dirty rug was hanging over the banister, and when he touched it he immediately wiped his hands. He looked down at his brogues, rested one foot on the step above and from the tip of his shoe wiped some cabbage in a thick sauce that someone had spilt on the stairs. He glanced upwards and felt distinctly uneasy. He heard no greetings or conversation, no jokes exchanged between police officers who, after two years, had finally succeeded in apprehending the beast. He rushed upstairs.

Kacnelson burst out of the apartment.

"Don't go in there, I beg you!" Kacnelson extended his arms as if wanting to push Popielski away. "You mustn't see this!"

The commissioner shoved his colleague aside and ran in. The bed had been moved diagonally across the room and the window was wide open. One of the uniformed men was leaning out and, after looking upwards and down, shook his head. The other passed Popielski and made towards a side staircase and from there onto the roof. A moment later his heavy footsteps thudded over their heads and disappeared. Kacnelson grasped Popielski by the sleeve to lead him out of the room, but Popielski tore himself away. He stared and stared. Somebody was lying under the bed. The body was covered with the oilcloth up to its neck. The head remained uncovered. But it was not Potok's.

LWÓW, THAT SAME MARCH 20TH, 1937
ELEVEN O'CLOCK IN THE MORNING

Zaremba's head lay on Popielski's knees, his cheeks resting in his friend's hands. Popielski was afraid the head would sever from the neck completely. He was crying. Zaremba tried to smile. He opened and closed his eyes and even moved his head a little as if to say: It's alright, Eddie.

All of a sudden his cheeks shuddered, like those of a diving swimmer. He opened his eyes once more, but could no longer close them. Popielski did this for him.

LWÓW, WEDNESDAY, MARCH 24TH, 1937
SIX O'CLOCK IN THE EVENING

Eberhard Mock got out at Main Station, put down his suitcase and cast his eye along the platform. He was searching for a tall figure dressed in black – Popielski. But his bald head, dark glasses and white scarf were not to be seen. Porters, baggage handlers, newspaper and lemonade vendors loomed out of the smoke and steam bursting from the locomotive. The steam subsided, but still there was no Popielski. Mock pulled up his

236

gloves and extracted a cigarette from his packet of Egyptians with his teeth. An obliging porter jumped to his side, lit the cigarette and took his suitcase.

Mock followed, worried and deep in thought. He had not known Popielski for long, but he was absolutely certain that the Pole was one to keep his word, not only in important matters but in small things too. His absence at the station, even though he had assured Mock a few days earlier that he would be there to meet him, could indicate that something unexpected had happened, something bad. The tragedy that had befallen Popielski on Saturday circled in Mock's thoughts. He had heard the story in detail: Zaremba's death and Potok's escape across the roofs. He knew that Kacnelson and two uniformed policemen had chased the murderer in vain, while Popielski had turned to stone over Zaremba's dead body. Popielski had telephoned him that same evening. His voice had sounded strange even then; he seemed lost in thought, kept breaking off and searching for words as if he were only just learning German instead of speaking it like a native Viennese. Mock put Popielski's unexpected difficulty with verbalization down to failure, and to the shock of Zaremba's death. This too could have been the reason for his absence at the station. But for how long could one be in shock when the beast was still at large? How long could one brood over defeat when the animal was still hiding somewhere in the narrow streets and drinking-dens?

He climbed into a droschka, paid the porter and thrust a card with Popielski's private address on it under the cabby's nose. The cab pulled away. Mock stopped admiring Main Station, whose harmony and perfect balance of architectural ornaments he felt outclassed its grandiose equivalent in Breslau. Nor did he study the churches or the façades of schools and colleges along the way. The only thing that drew his attention as they turned off the main road towards the park adjacent to Popielski's apartment was the Latin inscription on a building which looked like a library.

237

Hic mortui vivunt et muti loquuntur. Here the dead live and the mute speak. "If the dead could speak," he thought bitterly, "there'd be nothing for me to do in this world." Mock felt to some extent consoled.

He recalled recent events in Kattowitz and still failed to understand the role of Zdzisław Potok. The investigation had kicked off after they had found the file from Klementyna Nowoziemska's marriage bureau in Ernestyna Nierobisch's apartment. Commissioner Zygfryd Holewa, sensing that he had a case which might seal his promotion, had immediately forgotten the injunction issued to Mock and instead launched a vigorous operation of the kind that Mock liked. He had not stood on ceremony when speaking to Nierobisch in the interrogation cell; within two days he had received all the information he needed from the woman, who would still be aching from the blows and kicks she had received. Mock and Popielski's intuition had proved correct: the abortionist had turned out to be a bawd just like Nowoziemska, and both had worked hand in hand. Nierobisch had sought out desperate girls – servants who had allowed their masters to get too intimate, waitresses and dish washers whose employers had made them an offer they could not refuse, or ordinary prostitutes, for whom pregnancy would be a hindrance. Nierobisch knew full well that, for all these women, abortion signified an even greater devastation of their principles and values. She scrupulously noted down their details and passed them on to Nowoziemska who, after a suitable interval, would visit the girls posing as a respectable priestess of marriage and promise them an exotic journey to Argentina, or a less exotic one to Germany where a much older, wealthy man would be waiting for them, yearning for their Slavic beauty. This rich man would of course turn out to be the owner of a brothel, and the girls would sooner or later submit to their fate as slaves.

After a time many of them proved surprisingly happy with this change in their lives and would send Nierobisch postcards with heartfelt greetings. Nowoziemska paid Nierobisch generously for each of the girls, and often gave her additional presents, for example a set of – admittedly second-hand – luxury binder files. She herself made an extraordinary profit on these dealings, although she did not always manage to deceive the women and send them off to Germany or Argentina. She had not succeeded with Maria Szynok. Nierobisch herself did not know what had happened to the girl, and was not apprised of the real or invented names of any of her betrothed. All she knew about this mad unfortunate on whom she had performed an abortion was that – for Nowoziemska – Szynok constituted valuable goods destined for marriage and not a brothel, and that she was to be matched for an enormous sum to a wealthy client who had taken a particular liking to her. Despite threats and beatings, Nierobisch had said nothing more.

Having discovered all this, Mock had said goodbye to Holewa, Wybraniec and Silesia itself – later he was to think of the region with some fondness – and bought a ticket for the next train to Lwów. He was certain Popielski would now be needing him. Together they would find the beast and investigate this gang of human traffickers who must have international connections, seeing as the girls were landing up in Argentina and Germany. Potok was somehow tied up in all this, and this – in view of his last victim – led the investigation towards Breslau and Baron von Criegern. After all, he still hasn't been found, thought Mock, this beau who brought Anna Schmidt to Breslau! The case appears to be a gigantic affair, on a European or even global scale! Popielski and I will think everything through over two or three days' time; we'll make a precise plan, and then I'll be able to go to Breslau for Easter. And after the holiday everything will start anew! *Investigo ergo sum!*

Mock paid the cabby and climbed out. In the gateway to the tenement, the caretaker blocked his way and asked him something politely. Mock showed him Popielski's business card, and when he noticed the look of dismay on the man's face he hurried past him, ran up to the first floor and pressed the bell. Miss Leokadia Tchorznicka opened the door, her eyes swollen from crying. She left it ajar and retreated without a word. As he entered the apartment, Mock felt as though he had stepped into a crime scene, except that instead of the stench of a corpse the air was permeated with the smell of valerian. A sudden, sharp cry reached him from the kitchen, then a wrenching, choking sob. Somebody seemed to be choking, wheezing and coughing all at the same time.

Mock was there in a flash. At the table sat the maidservant, her forehead resting on its surface and her body shaking with sobs. Mock looked about him, horrified. The door to Popielski's study and bedroom was open; he approached it quietly and peered in.

Edward Popielski was sitting in an armchair by a table on which stood a huge ashtray full of cigarette butts. He had several days of stubble and was wearing an unbuttoned pyjama shirt beneath the navy-blue jacket of his police uniform. He did not even glance up at Mock, but stared at his hands resting in front of him on the table.

"Rita didn't come home on Saturday," he said in German. "And this is what was dropped onto my balcony on Sunday."

He waved his hand at the desk. There lay Rita's school uniform, carefully folded, and on top of it her stiff, snow-white sailor collar.

"Hanna had ironed the collar so beautifully." Popielski raised his head and in his bloodshot, sleepless eyes there appeared tears. "She had ironed it as if for a funeral."

He lowered his head so that Mock would not see him crying. His bald head turned purple and spasms shook his entire body. Tears flowed through the fingers which he pressed against his cheeks and eyes. Mock sat on the armrest next to him and just about managed to put his arm around his friend's broad back. He sat there for a long time, until Popielski grew still, then got up and went to the parlour. Leokadia was staring at the face of the grandfather clock. A cigarette smoked in front of her.

"I'll stay with you for a few days," said Mock quietly.

"Aren't you going to see your wife for Easter?" asked Leokadia.

"No. I'll stay here, with Edward."

"You have no idea what will happen here! You don't know what his attacks of despair can be like!"

"I don't? Then I'll find out," said Mock, and he returned to the study.

PART III

The Minotaur's Head

Theseus is passing through a sea
of bloody columns leaves restored
in a clenched fist he holds a trophy
— the scalped head of the Minotaur

Bitterness of victory An owl's shriek
measures dawn with a coppery stick
so that he will feel the sweet defeat
to the end a warm breath in his neck

"Head", Zbigniew Herbert

LWÓW, WEDNESDAY, OCTOBER 13TH, 1937
SEVEN O'CLOCK IN THE EVENING

Edward Popielski sat in the Sea Grotto and sipped at his second large glass of vodka. The place was almost empty. The small number of customers glanced surreptitiously at the commissioner and knew perfectly well what he was thinking about.

There had been no news of Rita for half a year now. The whole town was weighing up whether she had been kidnapped or murdered, and whether her disappearance had anything to do with the Minotaur's escape. Such speculation was dangerous in Popielski's presence, as Kacnelson had once discovered the hard way. Every officer knew that Popielski blamed himself for Zaremba's death. And everyone knew that shackling the beast to the leg of a bed which could easily be lifted was an act of inexcusable negligence. Popielski interpreted the coincidence of Potok's getaway and Rita's disappearance simply and personally: if he was responsible for the Minotaur's escape and it had something to do with Rita's disappearance, then he was also responsible for his daughter's disappearance. When Kacnelson once analysed this coincidence, Popielski had seen it as a personal attack. He had leaped at his friend like a raging bull, thrown him to the floor and set about kicking him. He would even have hurt him had Kacnelson not shouted: "Do you want to kill me like Zaremba?" That had calmed Popielski straightaway and he had slumped into a chair, where for the next hour he held his face in his hands and said nothing. The following day he had apologized publicly to Kacnelson, who had been perfectly understanding, and Inspector Zubik did not even think of initiating disciplinary procedures.

Since Palm Sunday, when the bundle with Rita's belongings had landed on his balcony, Edward Popielski had been a different person. The changes which had occurred in him manifested themselves differently at home and away. At home he was unusually affectionate and thoughtful towards Hanna and Leokadia. When she spoke to other maids the former praised him to the heavens, while the latter sensed a certain falseness; Leokadia could not believe that her cousin, who until then had concentrated almost exclusively on his own thoughts, hypotheses and investigations, was all of a sudden interested in everyday matters. He talked to her incessantly about her games of bridge and her reading, and had become exceedingly polite and obsequiously helpful. He never lost his temper, and this seemed unnatural. Only sometimes would his eyes, reddened by insomnia and alcohol, flash dangerously. Leokadia had heard it said on many occasions that suffering ennobles a man, but her cousin's false smile was not a sign of noble-mindedness; rather it was some kind of mask beneath which Edward hid his true feelings.

Away from home Popielski's behaviour was completely different. If up until then he had been hot-headed and irascible, now he had developed into an irritated hornet who attacked anyone around. His fury and aggression were most keenly felt by the rogues and chancers from the suburbs, since Popielski was convinced that the Minotaur was hiding somewhere in their midst — and most likely in Łyczakow — waiting for the right moment to leave town unnoticed which, with his likeness posted on every announcement pillar, would prove very difficult. But the beast was not the main reason for Popielski's fury at the bandits of Lwów. He was tormented by another obsession: Rita's abduction. Popielski was certain that she had been snatched by certain elements from the criminal underworld for a ransom. The fact that no ransom had yet been demanded indicated that they wanted to push up the price – at least that was his view. The commissioner firmly believed that Lwów's bandits would soon be asking for something that would ruin his life – his resignation from the police force.

Thus began the commissioner's personal and – what was worse – solitary crusade amongst Lwów's criminal classes, conducted in his very own way. He would drop into a dive – whether public or illegal, with or without a sign outside – order vodka and something to eat, then cast his aching, sleepless eyes over the clientele, who would more often than not then disperse. Not all of them, however. Some he stopped and sat down at his table. He would offer them vodka and ask courteously about Rita and the Minotaur. When they refused a drink and helplessly shook their heads at his questions, Popielski would pour vodka down their throats and manhandle them in front of the assembled company.

It is not surprising, therefore, that black clouds had gathered above him – ever thicker, and ever more ominous. Only a few months earlier, straight after Rita's disappearance, a delegation of the legendary kings of the underworld, Mosze Kiczałes and the Żelazny brothers, had paid him a visit. Kiczałes, wearing an immaculate pale suit, had offered his sincere condolences regarding the disappearance of his daughter and had sworn that no criminal group from Lwów had anything to do with it; he had even promised to help catch the abductors. Popielski had accused him of lying and thumped his fist on the table with such force that he had spilt coffee over Kiczałes' suit. Kiczałes and the Żelazny brothers had been furious when they left, but despite this they ordered their men to tolerate Popielski's whims for a while – at least until they had come to a final decision about him. Not everyone listened to the kings, however, and the commissioner's excesses were becoming intolerable for the bandits. In tavern after tavern he received warnings in the form of a pig's ear trans-fixed by a nail, but he scoffed at them. He would remove the ear now and again and shove it under everybody's nose, shouting: "Did you give this to me, you son-of-a-whore?"

The pedantic dandy with the ironic sense of humour and polite manners who smelled of expensive eau de cologne had become a vulgar sloven. He forgot to take medication for his epilepsy and he no longer visited Szaniawski. One day he had collapsed, shaking, on the tavern floor and had wet himself. The street urchins had thrown him into the yard in disgust, and one of them had shoved his face into horse shit, hoping the commissioner would choke on it.

He did not change his shirt for weeks on end and wispy tufts of hair sprouted at the sides of his bald head. He drank vodka by the glass, but his strong body stubbornly resisted it; the commissioner was not able to drown his sorrows and sleep like a log afterwards. Instead he would come home towards morning, swaying on his feet, and smile mockingly at Leokadia, who was terrified. He would ask the sleepy woman about household affairs and her bridge games, kiss her respectfully on the hand, then go to his room, tumble into his sheets and lie awake until midday. He would then get up, splash his face and go to work, having thanked Leokadia profusely for a delicious breakfast which he scarcely touched. Letters from Mock piled up unread on his desk and the telephone was, on his orders, picked up only by Hanna who would simply replace the receiver when she heard German spoken.

Had Zaremba been alive he would have known how to take care of his friend. He had seen him in such a state once before, when his wife Stefania, a well-known actress from Lwów, had suffered a postpartum haemorrhage and died after bringing Rita into the world. Unfortunately, like Stefania Gorgowicz-Popielska, Zaremba now rested in peace in Łyczakowski cemetery, and the others whom Popielski would have allowed to approach him – Leokadia and Eberhard Mock – either did not know how to speak to him or were too far away.

On this sad and rainy October afternoon he was out on one of his escapades, which he described in his reports as "reconnoitring". He was sitting in the Sea Grotto, waiting for he knew not what. On this occasion his clothes were exceptionally clean. He wore a striped shirt from a shop called Poland on Gródecka Street, given him that morning by Leokadia as a name-day present. And because it was his name day – which looked to be marked by a sad dinner for two – he had been coerced into having a bath and shaving. He was not, however, wearing a tie, his signet ring or cufflinks, and nor had he polished his shoes. He sat sipping his second glass of vodka and waiting. As people entered he studied them carefully, but without aggression, while they looked at him and nodded. Those with a lighter conscience sat down, those with a heavier one left, not wanting to have anything to do with a guardian of the law.

Two men who entered when Popielski had already drained his glass behaved differently to the others. Neither sat down, and neither beat a hasty retreat. With their boots ringing loudly against the stairs and dirt floor, the men approached the table at which the commissioner sat alone. They stared at him for a moment through their motorcycle goggles, then one of them reached into his long leather coat, pulled out a photograph and placed it on the table. On it appeared a younger, smiling Popielski. Rita, perhaps seven years old, was smiling too, her head resting on her father's shoulder. She had always carried the photograph with her.

"We found this on your daughter," said one of the men, indicating the photograph. "You want to see her? Come with us!"

Without waiting for an answer both men made towards the exit. Popielski gazed at their military boots for a moment, then left the table.

Popielski had no idea where he was. He recreated the events from the moment he had tipped back his second vodka and met the motorcyclists. When he had seen the photograph and the mysterious men left, he had sprung to his feet. He wanted to tell everyone that these two were his daughter's kidnappers and should be arrested, yet something stopped him. It was not so much the indifferent expressions on the faces surrounding him as the voice of reason: it was more important for him to see his daughter than to catch her kidnappers. He stepped out into the yard, pale and shaken. The men were waiting for him, one seated behind the other on a Sokół motorcycle. The driver pointed at the sidecar and handed Popielski a pair of goggles, which the commissioner pulled over his eyes. They were lined with black velvet.

"If you try to see where we're going," he heard one of them say, "we'll throw you out, understand?"

They rode for a long time. Popielski counted twenty turns, got confused and stopped counting, and after about half an hour the motorcycle rumbled into a yard and the engine was switched off. He felt himself being taken under the arms and pulled out of the sidecar. They entered a place which stank of chemical reagents. He was set down on a chair which creaked dangerously beneath his weight and felt his arms being slipped under the backrest. When they handcuffed him from behind he did not protest, he simply waited.

The goggles were then removed, and at first he thought he was in a theatre. He was sitting in darkness and before him stretched a spot-lit, dark cherry-coloured curtain. But when he looked around him he saw that there was no audience; his chair was the only one there. The curtain was not very large and hung on a free-standing semi-circular screen. Lights on tripods, cameras and flashlights were ranged around the curtain. He

250

heard the rattle of hooks and the curtain parted. The young man seated on a chair in the spotlight seemed familiar to Popielski. He wore a pale-grey suit of expensive wool and a contrasting wine-coloured tie, with a red rose in his lapel. His feet were clad in golf shoes. The young man's facial features were exceptionally regular, his lips full, and his face oval and slender. If it were not for the short hair combed to one side, the masculine body and faint five-o'clock shadow, he could have passed for a woman. A beautiful woman.

"Do you want to see the Minotaur, Commissioner?" His voice was deep and expressive. "We've got him. He's alive and waiting for his Theseus. And you, sir . . ."

Popielski could not place the man. Could it be possible that it was Father Kierski, the youthful chaplain who set alight the hearts of girls with his strong preacher's voice? It seemed impossible, and yet . . .

"Are you a priest? Father Konstanty Kierski?" he interrupted him mid-sentence.

"As far as I know I've never been a priest," the man replied solemnly. "Although I used to know one very well. Do you have any more questions, or are you going to let me continue?"

"What do you mean 'we've got the Minotaur'? I haven't come here for the Minotaur! Where's my daughter?" Popielski strained at his chair.

The man rose and picked up a long object from the floor. A golf club. He approached Popielski, leaned over him and studied his earlobe for a moment. The commissioner did not register the movement but felt a pain which pierced his head like a thorn. His ear throbbed and quickly swelled and a dreadful ringing vibrated in his skull. The man walked round to Popielski's other side and began to examine his other ear like an otolaryn-gologist. He took a swing. A second blow threw Popielski's head to the side and the commissioner toppled over with his chair. The ringing grew louder. There was only one way to drown it: he had to scream. Howling

251

with pain like a wounded beast, he convulsed on the floor and thrashed his legs. Instead of ears he had two hot, damp, aching jellies.

He caught the scent of perfume and opened his eyes. The man was crouching over him, golf club in hand. Popielski expected another blow and stopped yelling; he had to reserve some strength for further beatings.

"You're not going to interrupt me any more, are you, Commissioner?" the man said quietly. "What you're going to hear now is the story of a certain boy who became a young man. As coherent as a sequence. As true as the extremum of a parabola."

The man pulled out a thick notebook with an elephant-skin cover, and began to read:

The boy was born in 1910 into the wealthy, aristocratic Woroniecki family on the Baranie Peretoki estate in Sokalski district. He was a late child to his parents. His father, Count Juliusz Woroniecki, a large landowner, was a mathematics alumnus of Jan Kazimierz University in Lwów. He harboured a great passion for community work, which he put into practice by teaching mathematics to peasant children. When he discovered a child with a scientific mind he would look after it. He paid for the child to go to secondary school, so that its talent should not go to waste. The boy's two older, grown-up brothers were also mathematicians. Both had perished at Gorlice during the Great War. The boy could hardly remember them. From an early age he was brought up to be an outstanding mathematician. Instead of fairy tales he had mathematical puzzles read to him at night; instead of toy soldiers he arranged geometrical figures on the floor; instead of sandcastles he built rectangles on the sides of a triangle; instead of flying kites he played with square trinomials. He was magnificently talented. At the age of six he solved sets of equations, and at the age of ten he studied function graphs.

All this ceased to mean anything when a certain Rusyn peasant girl revealed to him the world of physical sensations, a world which he found utterly absorbing. To sets of equations he preferred carnal sex; exponential functions he now associated with nothing other than a woman exposing her breasts. In Sokal, where he went to school, he spied with his friends on the manager of the Dawn cinema, Mr Karol Poliszuk, as he crushed local courtesans against the wall of his little office. One day he was caught spying. The manager of the cinema wasn't at all angry with him and suggested he join in.

The boy grew increasingly bored with mathematics and kept interrupting his lessons to run to the school lavatory. He had to repeat a year twice, and was treated for gonorrheoea. His father would often fly into a rage, but in between times he assumed that adolescence, this rebellious age – which he took to be the reason for all this misfortune – would sooner or later pass and his son would once again fall into the arms of "the Queen of the Sciences". He decided to remove him from all bad influence and handed him over to the iron care of his brother, Count Stanisław Woroniecki, a veteran officer who was now the owner of the large Palus umbrella and walking-stick factory in the Silesian town of Skoczowo. Unfortunately, Uncle Stanisław had a twenty-year-old son, Janusz, who was no less depraved than his cousin. Through Janusz, the boy – now a young man of eighteen – met Klementyna Nowoziemska, a wise and worldly woman, former brothel owner and now boss of a marriage bureau. She soon suggested a way in which he might make use of his exceptionally good looks and how he could prosper at something which, to cap it all, he greatly enjoyed doing.

The young man obeyed the madame. He generously bestowed his charms on both men and women, and all repaid him in kind.

When he was nineteen he moved out of his uncle's house and in with Miss Nowoziemska. Miserable and in despair, his father disowned his only son and broke off all contact with him which, as it turned out, did not worry the guilty party in the least. Without the slightest regret he forgot all about his father, who represented to him the personification of mathematics, and his mother, for whom nothing existed apart from her migraines. He lived as he wanted to. He had no shortage of money since – thanks to Miss Nowoziemska's contacts – he granted sexual pleasures to and frequently accompanied rich German eccentrics on their journeys along the Kattowitz–Breslau–Berlin line in luxurious private compartments. Usually he travelled from Breslau with Baron von Criegern, who confided various plans to him, one of which the youth found particularly to his liking. Baron von Criegern intended to open a brothel for the rich in Breslau. According to the baron the biggest problem was the turnover of personnel, since prostitutes frequently changed their place of work. There was only one effective way of holding on to them permanently: smuggle them in illegally and keep them locked up, half-enslaved. Since Polish and Czech women were extraordinarily beautiful, and bringing them in entailed crossing only one border, they naturally became the most suitable merchandise. When Baron von Criegern first introduced the idea to him, the young man's eyes lit up. The men quickly came to an agreement: the baron would put in the money and give his associate a two-year interest-free loan, while the youth would contribute his invaluable contacts. A few days later the forwarding company Woroniecki und von Criegern was registered in Breslau.

Their activities were not complicated. Hand in hand with Ernestyna Nierobisch, Klementyna Nowoziemska found the young women. They largely looked for orphans or women who mixed with the demi-monde; nobody would notice their disappearance, nobody would worry. Woroniecki contacted each of them, offering himself as a potential husband. Few could resist the seductive charms of the beautiful count, so they rarely refused to go on a romantic trip to Germany. There the enterprising Baron von Criegern awaited them.

The company prospered wonderfully. Von Criegern established international contacts, especially with his counterparts in the Argentine, many of whom came from his home town. A crack appeared in the blossoming business after two years, however, when the baron asked for his loan to be repaid. Woroniecki was earning such a large income that if he had put aside even a tiny amount of it, he would have accrued a large sum within a few months. But he did not understand the concept of "saving"; he threw his money about as indecently as he behaved, and when the baron asked for repayment of his loan, he had just gambled away all his monetary reserves at the casino in Kattowitz. The impatient baron kept pressing the young man. When Woroniecki applied for credit, the bankers, who knows why, turned up their noses at the solvency of the forwarding company of which he was owner. Meanwhile, von Criegern surreptitiously got in contact with Nowoziemska and confronted the young man with an ultimatum – if he did not return the money within one month, the baron would dissolve the company and look for another seducer. What was worse, the baron demonstrated his resolve very firmly. One day two Germans paid Woroniecki a visit and broke his hand. The men threatened to break the other too if he did not return the money. On top of that, Nowoziemska severed all contact with him and the young man was at rock-bottom. He was forced to sell his body once more, but circumstances had changed a great deal: now he was thrown out of elegant restaurants and cafés, and clients in the rougher localities – both male and female – did not pay so much. His hand healed badly and caused him considerable pain. One day Woroniecki learned from his cousin Janusz that his father was dying. Scattering ash over his head, he set off for Baranie Peretoki.

The father, who was surely nearing the end of his years, greeted the prodigal son with tears in his eyes, and without a murmur handed him a cheque for the sum demanded by Baron von Criegern. The young man was delighted, not only because he was finally going to repay his debt and free himself from the gangster, but above all because the revelries were coming to an end and a stable life was approaching. His father would die and he, as sole inheritor, would take over the administration of a prospering estate, turn over a new leaf, marry, settle down in Baranie Peretoki . . . well, with the occasional visit perhaps to some secret club in a large city . . . Count Juliusz Woroniecki saw through his son's plans straightaway and showed him his will. A codicil specified that the estate would go to his offspring only if the latter obtained a Ph.D. in mathematics or logic within two years. 'Your exceptional talent cannot go to waste', were the count's last words.

Woroniecki lifted both chair and Popielski without great effort. He stood it back on its legs and climbed once more onto the improvised stage. He turned his chair back to front and sat astride it, then rested his chin on its backrest and gazed at the commissioner's purple ears.

"I was a broken man," he said, "but there must be something of a priest in me, as you identified, because God was watching over me. One of my father's former pupils, a country boy who had shown a great talent for mathematics, came to his funeral. He was one of those village pearls whom the noble count had fished out and provided with an education. Yes . . . it was then, at my father's funeral, that I met the Minotaur."

Woroniecki stood up and disappeared through a door which Popielski could not see, hidden as it was by the screen. A moment later the floor-boards thudded and the count re-appeared on stage, but this time he was not alone: at his feet crouched a beast.

In his left hand Woroniecki wielded a thick chain, the other end of which was tied around Zdzisław Potok. The naked prisoner's hands were bound at his stomach, his legs at the ankles, and a gag had been wedged into his mouth. A large helmet of thick hair was covered with some sort of unguent. Red abrasions, scabs and skin eruptions were visible on his pale, hairy body. Beneath the skin tensed powerful and well-defined muscles. Bent double, Potok scowled at Popielski. The gag moved a little in his mouth and the Minotaur let out a laugh. For a moment the com-missioner forgot about Rita. He felt the blood pulse in his temples. He could stand it no longer and in a rage threw himself forward with his chair.

"Don't get excited, Commissioner," smiled Count Woroniecki, "the monster will soon be in your hands. But first the story of the young man whose life is proof of God's providence. As I was telling you, I met Potok at my father's funeral. His ugliness intrigued me – I like all sorts of freaks. I invited him to the wake and we had a long chat. I learned all there was to know about him: that he had studied mathematics in Kraków; that he had wanted to devote himself to the study of logic; that the scholars in Kraków had not appreciated him and had ridiculed his ideas. They did not want to step beyond their narrow field of learning. Potok, on the other hand, following Łukasiewicz's school of thought, had intended to study the texts of ancient logicians while applying mathematical instrumentar-ium to his theories. The Kraków scholars had directed him to philologists. These, in turn, not knowing anything about mathematics, had not wanted to speak to him. Potok was greatly disappointed, broke off his studies, left Kraków and became a tutor at an estate near Brodów. But let's get back

257

to the matter in hand. After my father's funeral I talked to Potok long into the night and suggested he write the doctoral thesis for me. I promised him heaps of gold, but he did not want it. All he wanted was women. Mentally, I burst out laughing. This wasn't going to be the slightest problem for me. But I stopped laughing a moment later. Potok only wanted virgins. He asked for three: one on starting the thesis, one half-way through, and one as a dessert, so to speak" – Woroniecki laughed at his joke – "once he had finished writing. Anyway, he did not explain these whims, but I'm tolerant. I've seen a lot of strange stuff in my life."

He paused, sat in the armchair and lit a cigarette.

"I see you're fascinated, Commissioner." He smiled at Popielski. "Just listen. This is where things really get going! I rented some lodgings for Potok on Żuliński Street, not far from the bachelor flat where I held discreet meetings from time to time. My old acquaintance, Klementyna Nowoziemska, promised to help in the whole enterprise, but of course not for nothing. The price she demanded stunned me. But I didn't haggle. A month later she had found me the truest of virgins from Tarnów. I met her several times and – I might as well be honest – I had her fall in love with me pretty quickly. I proposed we went together to the Carpathians Mountains and took her in my car. On the way there, near Mościska, I pretended the car had broken down. Evening approached. I sent her off to a hotel, telling her to register under a different name, for the sake of propriety. She was to wait there for me. But it was the Minotaur who turned up."

Woroniecki's expression changed. He leaped up, grabbed the golf club and began to beat Potok with it. The latter fell on his face. The blows pounded against his ribs , then the end of the club sank into his body as if into dough. Blood and froth appeared on the gag.

"A cannibal visited her, a monster, a man-eater!" yelled Woroniecki, striking Potok on the head. "And devoured her instead of just screwing her as he had promised! Right, you animal? Is that what you did, you freak, you eyesore?"

A good quarter of an hour passed before Woroniecki calmed down. Potok lay on his side, panting heavily into his gag. Red marks appeared on his naked, whitish body.

"I had no way out." Woroniecki sighed deeply. "Of course I could have handed him over to the police. But who would have written my thesis for me then? Even if I had found somebody, there would always have been a shadow of doubt that he would give me away . . . But this swine would never give me away, or he'd be giving himself away. Whichever way you look at it, I was dependent on him." He wiped the sweat from his forehead. "He soon brought me half the thesis and demanded another virgin. I no longer had any illusions. I knew what would happen to her . . ." Again he sighed. "And we repeated everything, the one difference being that the girl was from Kielce, and Potok . . . he killed her in Drohobycz. The whole of Poland was up in arms; everybody was looking for the Minotaur." He smiled at Popielski strangely. "It's you who thought up the name, am I right? Smart. Mythical. Anyway, that's what happened. Meanwhile the Minotaur wrote the rest of the thesis and claimed his last victim. And here something jarred in our efficiently oiled machinery. Nowoziemska couldn't find a virgin. Then Maria Szynok turned up at her office, sent there by old Nierobisch. Nowoziemska, as a former brothel madame, knew exactly how to simulate virginity. I met that Szynok woman. . . She wasn't bad . . . I even fancied her . . . Ah, well. I offered her up as the next and – as I imagined – last sacrifice. And here a problem cropped up. Potok discovered her virginity was feigned . . . He could not possess her, because that would have gone against his principles" – Woroniecki's laugh rippled – "so he only took a nibble!" Suddenly he grew serious, as if changing his mood were his speciality. "We were all terrified. The girl had survived, after all, remembered my face and Potok's. We had to do away with her.

Fortunately for us, she went mad. Well, sir, what do you say to that! Isn't providence watching over me?"

For a moment he looked at Popielski, but the latter was silent.

"But the little pet wanted some more yummy-yummy." Woroniecki smacked his lips as if blowing kisses. "The last girl really was a virgin. She came from Silesia. A ward from an orphanage. A timid, slightly tearful child . . . One to hug, to console . . ."

Woroniecki began to pace around Potok, now and then kicking him lightly with the tip of his shoe and jabbing him with the golf club, which amused him beyond measure.

"Nothing could stand in the way of the last sacrifice," he said. "I had to anticipate absolutely everything. It couldn't happen in Poland. That would have been too dangerous. I got in touch with Baron von Criegern and forgave him my broken hand. See how magnanimous I was! I took the virgin to Breslau in a private compartment, and a few compartments away from us sat Potok. As we approached Breslau I changed into a woman's clothing — I don't find it difficult to pass myself off as a woman." Flirtatiously he adjusted nonexistent hair and pretended to make advances at Popielski. "I accompanied her to a hotel recommended by von Criegern and took the opportunity to get rid of the typewriter Potok used for my, or rather his thesis. Just in case . . . I had also been using it to write my idiotic letters to Nowoziemska as the fictional Count von Banach. Shrewd woman, she had instructed me to write those idiotic things to set any eventual investigations on the wrong track . . ." Suddenly he changed subject. "But it was extremely pleasant in Breslau. I spent the New Year at von Criegern's, and Potok spent his with his last victim."

Woroniecki started shaking his head and pulling childish faces like a poor actor.

"Oh, how frightened she was!" he said in a high voice. "She kept asking why I was dressed up as a woman . . . And I replied: 'We're going to a fancy dress ball, darling. Just wait for me at the hotel. I'll come and fetch you shortly.'"

Popielski closed his eyes. He could not look at Woroniecki, could not listen to his modulated voice, which went from strangled bass to sheering falsetto.

"So I did my Ph.D. with Łukasiewicz," he heard as if from afar. "But, but! Let's get back to what we were reading!"

None of this would have come about without certain essential undertakings on the part of the doctoral student. Before initial talks with his supervisor he changed his name. He took the first that came to mind. In no way should it be associated with Count Juliusz Woroniecki, who was well known in scholarly circles and highly respected on account of the grants he had bestowed on impoverished youngsters. The son did not want to be linked to his father. It could have caused a sensation, aroused the interest of the press, and so on, while he wanted to obtain his degree on the quiet, without any publicity. First of all he had to eliminate the threat of disclosure, and so the sham doctoral student could not allow himself one-to-one discussions with his supervisor while his thesis was *in statu nascendi*. Such meetings could have betrayed his ignorance. In the few discussions he had with Professor Łukasiewicz in Warsaw, Woroniecki tossed his head, laughed to himself, clapped – in other words, he pretended to be eccentric and absent-minded. He said very little, but diligently noted down all his supervisor's comments. "Let my work speak for itself," he repeated. Since in these circles there was no shortage of eminent scholars whose behaviour was even stranger than his student's, Łukasiewicz and the two examiners took the motto at face value, as the thesis was indeed excellent, and even groundbreaking.

And everything ended just as he had planned. Woroniecki became a Doctor of Philosophy in mathematical logic. The executor of his father's will, a famous lawyer from Lwów, Doctor Przygodzki-Nowak, found no problem with the inheritor's new identity, all the more so as the change of name had been processed at his office. The prodigal son became sole heir to a huge estate, therefore. He decided to settle in Baranie Peretoki and start a new life. And that's what he probably would have done, had it not been for a fear which initially made itself felt as a slight tingle, then grew like a cancer. Woroniecki was terrified that the crimes would one day come to light. The greatest threat was posed by three people, the three most important dramatis personae: Nowoziemska, Nierobisch and Potok. First, he pierced Nowoziemska's head with a deadly spike concealed in his walking stick. He intended to do the same to Nierobisch, but this wasn't so easy; there were always people coming to see her. Somebody even broke into her apartment when she was out. And then finally, when Woroniecki had the perfect opportunity, a police van drew up outside Nierobisch's tenement on Żogały Street and the would-be victim was arrested. The whole of Kattowitz hummed with rumours about the woman who had performed abortions in some hovel. Many women trembled at the thought of what she might reveal when interrogated. Woroniecki trembled too. But Nierobisch did not tell the police anything about him, for which he rewarded her handsomely by secretly transferring a substantial sum of money, thanks to which she saw that her time in prison was not too hard after all.

"I got a telegram from von Criegern recently." Woroniecki's voice was close by. "Your friend in Breslau, a certain Eberhard Mock, keeps pestering him. But von Criegern has dealt with harder cases; he will personally put this friend of yours off the investigation once and for all." He waved his hand contemptuously. "The only danger that remained, therefore, was that hungry virgin-fancier. But here, too, God watched over me. When Potok killed that police officer in his room, he had one way of escaping the ambush: over the roof onto the neighbouring tenement, then a leap into a small gallery where I, in turn, was renting cheap lodgings. I just happened to be there since I'd arranged to meet a certain charming young lady. So I invited Potok into my bachelor flat and he stayed for two weeks without going out, not even to the toilet. He filled a bucket with his shit, and the sink with his piss. Yeuch! You can imagine how it stank! Germans say: 'It stinks bestially.' The beast stank bestially!" Again Woroniecki laughed. "After two weeks I moved him out under the cover of darkness and brought him here. He's been living here for half a year now. And today I'm handing him over to you, Commissioner. End of story. It's time for Theseus."

After this long speech Woroniecki caught his breath and was silent for a while. He then went to the screen, moved it a little and directed the light at a chopping block with an axe embedded in it. The floor beneath the chopping block was laid out with rubber aprons.

"You know what I've worked out, Eddie?" The count looked first at one, then at the other bound man. "I've worked out how to resolve the Potok and Nierobisch problem in one go. I am, after all, a Doctor of Mathematics, I can reason logically and inventively. Do you remember how Theseus killed the Minotaur in the myth? Yes, you do. He decapitated him, Eddie. And now we're going to re-enact the myth. You're going to be the new Theseus and I'm going to immortalize it on film."

He went about excitedly lighting more spotlights, like a director before a stage premiere, and then switched on the camera. As it started to roll, he turned the lens now on Popielski, now on Potok.

"You'll do it, Eddie, oh yes, you will," said Woroniecki almost to himself. "And I'll record it all. I'll have a beautiful Theseus and a beautiful

Minotaur on film. And then I'll hide the film in my safe and then I'll be able to issue you with orders. And you'll obey them. If you don't, you'll hear a curse which will work like magic. It goes: 'I'll send the film to Marian Zubik.' You're going to be mine, Eddie . . . You're going to obey my orders and ask for more. And here's the first: you're going to get Nierobisch out of prison and hand her over to me as a gift. I've had enough of paying that filthy old witch . . ."

"I won't kill anybody," Popielski croaked.

"Won't kill anybody?" Woroniecki extracted the axe from the chopping block with ease. "Well, that's too bad. My men, my loyal friends from my days in Kattowitz are going to take you to Brzuchowicki forest. They're going to dig a hole, throw you into it and cover you with our fertile humus. And your beloved Rita won't come to your grave . . . She won't light a candle for her papa, who she cuddled up to so sweetly, like in the photograph . . ."

Popielski stared at Woroniecki as if turned to stone.

"She won't come . . ." – the count ran his finger over the blade of the axe – "because she'll be far away. She'll be a beauty queen. In a Buenos Aires brothel!"

He approached Popielski, took a swing, and the axe hit the floor at his feet. Over its handle he tossed a rubber apron.

"But if you kill the Minotaur," he said, "you'll see Rita, who's quite nearby. She's grown even more beautiful over the past six months. She's, she's here . . . She so wanted to wish you a happy name day! If you want, you can even take her home with you. But is she going to want to go? She could become an actress with me, while you wanted to turn her into a Latin scholar! You think I don't have friends in the film industry? Many of them made naughty films on the quiet, and some of my girls took part. But don't worry! Not Rita! She's a true artist! Well, what do you say? Put the apron on, the axe is waiting."

He then shouted: "We're starting!", and the two men who had brought Popielski appeared. One aimed a Browning at the commissioner, while the other undid his handcuffs. Popielski's head was empty; he acted like an automaton and put on the apron.

"I'm starting to roll! Action!" yelled Woroniecki from behind the camera.

Popielski grabbed the chain wrapped around Potok's neck and dragged the beast towards the chopping block. The Minotaur thrashed about in every direction, like a fish out of water. The aprons on the floor bunched up and squeaked terribly as they rubbed against his sweaty skin.

"Stun him first!" shouted the count. "Otherwise you won't get his mug on the block!"

Popielski raised the axe. Beneath him writhed a human body, not an animal. This was no beast, it was a human being who could not be slaughtered like a porker. He ought to be judged fairly and hanged with legal sanction. And what if some golden-mouthed cunning fellow, some lawyer with a double-barrelled name, succeeded in defending him? The court would pronounce judgement: the accused is to be handed over for treatment to a secure mental institution! And Popielski would have to listen to all this with the gnawed faces of those girls in front of his eyes, the lesions on Maria Szynok's body and the bubbles of blood on Zaremba's lips. He raised the axe and struck Potok's temple with its head. Potok jerked and went limp. Popielski tried to pull his neck over the block, but the flaccid body fell to the ground. He kicked the block in anger and raised his arms with the axe over his head.

"Wait, wait!" screamed Woroniecki. "For God's sake, don't move out of frame!"

A moment later Popielski no longer heard nor felt anything. Apart from the beast's blood on his legs.

Rita Popielska was in her sumptuous apartment in the Rohatyn tenement on the corner of Kościuszko and 3rd May Street. She paced nervously across the luxuriously furnished room, the interior of which Dionizy Czyczkowski, reknowned architect and designer, had conceived on a peaceful and elegant cream-coloured scheme. She strode between the clock and the table, between the modern sideboard and antique armchair, which featured as an intended extravagance in the modernist, ascetic style of the apartment. Her heart rose to her throat when she heard the door-bell. The servant entered the room and opened his mouth to announce the arrival of a guest, but he did not have time. He staggered, thrust forward by a strong hand, and leaned against the wall before Rita's father burst into the room and drove him away. Rita fell to her knees when she saw him; the earth gave way beneath her. Her slender waist swayed as if she were in a trance, and the girl would have collapsed to the floor had she not been held up by her father's hand. Rita pressed her lips to it. She cried silently, without sobbing or spasms. Tears ran down Popielski's hand. He kneeled over his daughter without saying a word and stroked the hair above her ears. This was where he had loved to kiss her most when she was a child. He would breathe in, and in her locks pick up the scent of the forest near Sokolnik where they used to spend their holidays, or the salty tang of the sea and Baltic beaches. He wanted to kiss her there now, but refrained. He had picked up an unfamiliar scent, a sharp perfume he did not recognise. "She'll be a beauty queen. In a Buenos Aires brothel!"

Popielski rubbed his eyes, gently pushed his daughter aside and sat down at the table. He interlocked his fingers as if wanting to fence himself off from the feelings that tormented him. Rita sat opposite her father and laid a slender hand – an expensive diamond on its finger – over one of his.

"I beg you, Papa, forgive me." Two large tears fell onto her cheeks.

"Forgive me, it was your name day yesterday! I must hear your words of forgiveness today!"

"I forgive you," he whispered, squeezing his eyes, but he did not manage to hold back the tears which forced their way through his thick eyelashes.

"I've been a terrible, stupid egoist." Rita pulled out a lace handkerchief and dabbed her eyes; she could control herself in a split second, just like her mother. "But don't think, Papa, that I left home because I thought you were an unbearable tyrant, no, that wasn't it at all! Father, listen to what I have to say! Bronisław wrote to me, seducing me with his letters. We corresponded: he charmed me. He sent me his photograph with a dedication . . . That day, the first day of spring, I went to meet him as we'd agreed. Beanpole came with me. I was frightened of going by myself. This was on Żuliński Street. We were supposed to be meeting in a billiard club! Suddenly I saw you and I was annoyed, I thought that you were following me. But you were after the Minotaur. I saw you quite by chance! Beanpole ran off, scared, and I ran to the club, which turned out not to be any kind of club at all!"

She stood and drew the curtains so that the sun did not dazzle her father. She studied him in silence. He had changed, lost weight; he no longer dressed with care. His head and cheeks were badly shaven. It made her heart ache.

"He fell in love with me at first sight." She swallowed bitterly. "Then he abducted me, carried away by his feelings. He's of noble stock, the owner of vast estates, heir of an aristocratic family. He said his ancestors had also been guilty of *raptus puellae*."

"You're speaking Latin." Popielski shuddered and smiled feebly.

"No, I'm simply repeating Bronisław's words. He abducted me and took me to his manor, forbidding me to make contact with you. But don't think he took advantage of me, Papa . . . Oh, no! He's too much of a gentleman for that! He gave me two months to decide whether I wanted to stay with him and make a career as an actress – he's got friends everywhere, he's going to make it possible for me! – or go home to that cursed school . . . He visited me every day; we took walks in his parks and forests . . . After two weeks the servants stopped keeping an eye on me. They didn't have to, I didn't want to leave . . . I wanted to be there, listen to his words and look into his eyes." Rita stirred. "Oh, I'm sorry, Papa! I'm describing all this in such detail, as if you were a woman!"

"Why didn't you write to me?" he asked hollowly.

She hurried over to her father, kissed him on the head and rested her cheek on his bald skull.

"I'm sorry, Papa, I'm sorry . . . I wasn't myself . . . It was as if I were living in a dream. Nothing was important to me. But I've recovered my senses. I'm composed again, and reasonable! We're always going to be together now, Papa, always . . . I won't give you any more reason to worry . . ." Tears once again appeared in her eyes and ran down his head. "Father, I always carried that photograph with me, the one taken years ago. . . I love you, Papa!"

Popielski stood up and gave his daughter a tight hug. Suddenly he pulled away and gripped her by her delicate shoulders. Red-pink appeared patches on his neck.

"Yes, father," she said firmly and emphatically. "I'm pregnant. And Bronisław is the father of my child."

The commissioner sat down at the table and fixed his eyes on the clock. Only now did Rita notice that his ears were unnaturally large and purple.

"But Papa, you don't care about bourgeois conventions." She ran to her father and grasped his hands. "You lived with mama without getting married, and the whole town was indignant and disgusted! What are you worried about, Papa? The most important thing is that Bronisław and I love each other! Here's the wedding invitation. It's in the cathedral in three weeks' time!"

The commissioner glanced at the invitation. "Rita Popielska and Doctor Bronisław Kulik have the honour of inviting the Honorable Mr . . ." He read no more and went back in time. He is at the meeting of the Lwów circle of the Polish Mathematical Society. Professor Stefan Banach says: "Today we have the pleasure of listening to Doctor Bronisław Kulik from Kraków, who will be talking to us about formal logic in a lecture entitled "Logic of names and logic of sentences".

Rita ran around the room like a little girl and clapped her hands.

"Papa, I'm sure you're going to have so much to talk about with Bronisław! I've got that feeling! He's a mathematician like you, and he's very good at chess! Now that I'm independent I realise how much I love you, Papa! We can all go on trips together! You Papa, Auntie, your grandson, Bronisław and myself. He loves the Carpathian Mountains!"

LWÓW, NOVEMBER 22ND, 1938

Dear Eberhard,

I apologize greatly for my silence, broken only by trite seasonal greetings. I have lived through a great deal in all that time, especially between Rita's death and her resurrection. Your letters piled up on my desk like pangs of conscience and, as you know yourself, a bad conscience muted by work or alcohol grows quieter, and eventually becomes completely silent. And I wanted to rid myself of these pangs. One day, drunk and irritated, I collected all your letters in an ashtray and burned them. I didn't want to know anything about your investigation, or about the affairs of some baron. They didn't interest me in the least because I had locked myself up in my

269

own problems. But I hear that my cousin Leokadia corresponded with you and told you everything: pregnant Rita's return and her marriage to a doctor and count all in one — Bronisław Woroniecki-Kulik. Rita loves him, Leokadia likes him, and I detest him. I don't know why my daughter fell in love with him. Perhaps it's because they're both similar; both have disappointed their parents. Or perhaps he was the Satan and tempter who possessed her. I won't write any more about him because the very thought of his degeneracy fills me with repulsion. I'll say only one thing: he is a monster, an insane criminal. No, Eberhard, I have not gone mad. I repeat, and I'm fully aware of what I'm saying: he is a crazy murderer who will never be judged for his crimes. Do you know why? Because I am the only one who knows about them, apart from his two praetorians. And I'm never going to speak up against him! After all, I'm not going to take Jerzyk's father away from him, from my beloved grandson happily born in February of this year. No doubt you're curious to hear how I know about my son-in-law's villainy. From his very own lips! He told me about it, and he was fully aware of what he was doing. To hear him out and not lock him up is like being his accomplice. This is what I have become. I listened to him and I let him go free. Do you know why? Because he blackmailed me. When Rita had been gone for half a year, when in my mind I had already buried her, the right honourable count appeared and said: your daughter is with me, you can win her back when you've heard me out or lose her if you spurn my story. You choose. I chose my daughter. He told me of his horrific crimes, and I have to remain silent.

My dear friend, I want to retire. Zubik won't even hear of it and begs me to stay. I've grown even more famous and enjoy the favour of the commander of the provincial police himself. And that's because Zdzisław Potok has been found: it is my doing, supposedly, that the police hit upon his trail. Yes, he was found in the village of Strzelczyska in the Mościska District, department of Lwów. Dead, decapitated. Polish news probably doesn't reach you, so perhaps you don't know about it – unless Leokadia told you. Our forensic pathologist and psychologist, Doctor Iwan Pidhirny, found an explanation for Potok's perversion and cannibalism. The doctor believes that the criminal, damaged by his monstrous ugliness, was ridiculed by women and took his revenge on them. By depriving them of their virginity and disfiguring them, he simply branded them. But this is only Pidhirny's hypothesis. Potok took his secret to the grave.

Eberhard, I'm writing to thank you for your help. For the fact that I could always depend on you. I'm also writing to say goodbye. I cannot see or correspond with you because I have to banish from my memory anything which reminds me of the case of the Minotaur. For me it was a blood bath, Dante's hell and purgatory. It has left memories from which I must free myself. In bidding you farewell, I bid farewell to all police work – as I mentioned above. I cannot be a police officer, cannot represent the law and at the same time assure a murderer of his immunity. He killed the police officer in me, demoralized me – for ever and with no forgiveness. Farewell, my dear friend, and forgive this Hamletizing.

Yours,

    Edward

P.S. I sincerely wish you a peaceful and blessed Christmas. Do not wish the same for me. I will be spending Christmas in the presence of a murderer. What doesn't one do for one's own child?

BRESLAU, DECEMBER 20TH, 1938

Dear Edward,

Your letter has greatly saddened me. It pains me above all that you should wish to break up our relationship for reasons which I understand, but which cannot be absolute. Because time heals all wounds and one day you will laugh about the Minotaur case. For the time being I ask only one thing of you. I was even prepared to convince you on the spot, in Lwów – I was worried about you – but because of the multitude of urgent matters could not do so. I beseech you not to leave the police force. Please trust in your slightly older colleague: to sit at the same table as the murderer paradoxically gives you the opportunity to be an even better police officer than you are. Keep looking at him, remember his face well – impudent, sure of itself, unpunished. That face has to be irrevocably engraved in your memory just as irregular Greek verbs were impressed on it once. You have to be able to recall it at any moment. And particularly when you're hunting another murderer. When you hesitate, when your hands fall helplessly to your sides and the criminal keeps eluding you, bring to mind the face you now see next to your daughter's. Let that mug be the mug of all the murderers in the world, let that mug be Satan's or the Minotaur's mug – as you prefer. And thus experiencing the apex of hatred you will become Satan's vanquisher, a real bloodhound who will either gnaw the murderer to death or choke on his gore. Heed my instructions, Edward, but do as you wish. If old Ebi reminds you of the case of the Minotaur, then forget about old Ebi for a while. But not for ever, for God's sake! Who am I going to drink vodka and go for girls with, if not you?

Yours,

    Eberhard

P.S. And remember — you can always depend on me.

LWÓW, CHRISTMAS EVE, 1938
SIX O'CLOCK IN THE EVENING

The entire Popielski family sat around the table on Christmas Eve: Edward, Leokadia, Rita and her husband, Doctor Count Bronisław Woroniecki-Kulik. There was one other, the smallest member of the family — ten-month-old Jerzyk Woroniecki-Kulik whom the servant, Hanna, called her "sweetest pony". The child was developing as it should and had probably inherited its appetite from its grandfather, because everything it met in its path it considered food. And since Jerzyk usually moved around on all fours he ate anything that was within half a metre of the ground. Like a little puppy he attacked all the chair and table legs as well as the tablecloths that dangled from various cupboards and tables. It was unfortunate when the "countling" — because that is what the trusty, loving servant also called him — pulled down a dish along with the tablecloth. When this was a plate of cakes which were instantly eaten, it was not so bad; far worse when the little one took to the contents of his grandfather's ashtray with equal eagerness.

During his first ever Christmas Eve dinner the child was restless. No doubt the general atmosphere of hurry and tension and all the scuttling about had knocked him out of his usual daily routine, because he refused to take a nap in the afternoon and was peevish and exasperating as a consequence. He would not even be calmed by his grandfather, who normally had a soothing effect on him. It was not, however, so much the grandfather himself who had this effect as his bald head. Jerzyk usually grabbed his grandfather's head with such passion as if he were discovering foreign lands. The growls emitted by Edward during all this made the baby squeal with joy and bare his gums in a smile, at first toothless, then adorned with two sharp milk teeth.

Unfortunately, neither his grandfather's bald head nor his growling had the same soothing influence on Christmas Eve. Wearing a dress with lace collar like a girl's and sitting on his grandfather's knees, the boy arched his back, screamed, shoved his podgy hand into his mouth and lashed out until, in the end, he kicked the tureen of red borscht. A fountain of droplets spurted from the dish, most of them falling on the tablecloth, but a few landed on his grandfather's snow-white shirt. Popielski did not even notice; he took his grandson into his arms and began to pace the room, which seemed to calm the little one a bit.

As those gathered there watched the idyllic scene, all their thoughts were elsewhere. Rita was smiling. Increasingly she harboured a hope that in the end her father's relationship with her husband would work out. After a dismal wedding day from which her father was absent, after those first icy months when he chose not to see his son-in-law in the street, after that Christmas Eve, which they had spent away from each other for the first time in their lives, everything had changed once his grandson was born, and Edward was besotted with him. Finally the much-longed-for invitation to Christmas Eve dinner arrived. She was as happy as a child when her father phoned her to invite them "beneath the Christmas tree", as he had always called the celebration. She did not know that the invitation had come thanks to her husband mentioning the name of Marian Zubik.

Leokadia rubbed her eyes in wonder. Childless herself, she was not able to kindle as much love for Jerzyk, whose crying and frequent mood changes annoyed her. Never, therefore, would she have thought that a child could change a man so much. Popielski, who at the sight of a drop of soup on his tie or jacket would once have had a fit, left the table and raged in search of a cloth, stifling coarse oaths along the way, was now not paying the slightest attention to his stained shirt. He was dancing across the room with his grandson while the little one, cuddling up to him, was also dirtying his grandfather's collar. Leokadia was happy to see how Edward had changed. But after his destructive escapades to the taverns and his unnatural smiles after another sleepless night, she would have been happy with any behaviour.

Even though he sat calmly, Bronisław Woroniecki-Kulik was infuriated at heart. He remained silent as if under a spell, head bowed and smiling maliciously, and glowering all around. He could not forgive Popielski for his evident ill-will, nor could he understand why he was not pleased with his daughter's happiness; she lived in such opulence and – more importantly, and thanks to his connections – she had begun to make a career for herself using the pseudonym "Rita Pop". She had already had a small role in the film "Fire in the Heart", directed by Henryk Szaro himself. And this bald son-of-a-whore still didn't shake hands with him when they met or hug him when they exchanged Christmas greetings. He had simply nodded and growled something, like he was now growling to that bloody brat who was still screaming his guts out!

The child quietened down and Popielski once again sat at the table with his grandson.

"Maybe we can finally fetch the presents from beneath the Christmas tree." Woroniecki-Kulik forced a smile. "The little one can get his present and be quiet, eh? Shall I give it to him now?"

"Bronek" – Rita glanced uneasily at her father and stroked her husband's hand – "that'll only pacify him for a moment. The main problem is he's tired. He didn't sleep this afternoon. I'll put him to bed in a moment and Hanna can sing him a lullabye. We'll tire him out a little longer, then he'll be quick to fall asleep."

275

Jerzyk was no longer interested in his grandfather's bald head; he spat his dummy onto the floor and began to scream again at the top of his voice.

"Give him that present" – the count glared furiously at Popielski – "or I'll give it to him myself!"

"You do not know the customs of our house, young man." Popielski bounced his grandson on his knee. "Here we eat dinner first, then the oldest member of the family, meaning me – I repeat, *me* – distributes the presents. And that is how it will always be."

"One moment . . . one moment . . . Customs may be customs but . . ." Woroniecki-Kulik gripped his spoon so hard that his knuckles turned white.

"Give Jerzyk to me, Papa" interrupted Rita. "Maybe he'll calm down a little with me . . ."

"Did you have something to say, young man?" Popielski passed his grandson to his daughter. "Something about the customs of my house?"

"Papa, please," whispered Rita, taking her son from her father's hands.

The count pursed his lips and used his spoon to cut a mushroom ravioli floating in his borscht. He raised it to his lips and chewed slowly. He did not, however, swallow, but spat it back into the spoon. Leokadia watched him in disgust. Jerzyk was again screaming shrilly, and when his mother hugged him, he hit her in the face with his fists.

"Are you going to give him that present or not?" hissed Woroniecki-Kulik at Popielski.

"How dare you speak to my father like that?" shouted Rita. "And what in God's name are you doing with that ravioli?"

"Probably has a toothache." Popielski sneered and put down his cutlery. "He has to eat things which are soft . . ."

"Don't get worked up, Eddie." Leokadia looked at him beseechingly. "It'll do you no good . . . Your blood pressure's too high . . ."

"Please don't call me 'Eddie'!" With a face of stone, Popielski out-yelled the hullabaloo caused by his grandson. "I don't want anyone calling me that now Wilhelm is dead . . ."

Woroniecki-Kulik tipped his spoon and slid the chewed mush into his hand. He stood up, approached Popielski and pressed it under his nose. Jerzyk quietened down and watched his father.

"Eat up, baldy!" said the count, grinning broadly. "I did tell you you'd be eating out of my hand, after all!"

Everyone froze. Jerzyk saw his opportunity. In a flash he climbed from his mother's knees onto the table and reached for the crystal bowl of dried fruit salad. The bowl toppled over onto the tablecloth as if in slow motion, and its contents poured over Leokadia's beige dress. When he saw what he had done, the child burst into tears, rubbing his eyes with his fists. The screams reverberated. Never before had there been such a level of decibels in Popielski's apartment. Even the grandfather put his hands over his ears, deformed as a wrestler's.

Woroniecki-Kulik flung the chewed ravioli onto the carpet and held the child down on the table. He grabbed its head with both hands and began to push his thumbs into his son's eyes.

"What are you rubbing your eyes like that for, you bastard!" he hissed. "I'll gouge those peepers out for you . . ."

Popielski threw himself at the count. In surprise Woroniecki-Kulik turned his head towards his charging father-in-law and received a fist on his temple. He staggered, everything was dark before his eyes, and then felt such a hefty punch on his chin that he collapsed onto the grandfather clock in the parlour. He heard the mechanism chime a false carillon as he fell to the floor. Ripped open by Popielski's signet ring, his chin burned with pain and bled. The commissioner leaned over Woroniecki-Kulik to grab him by the collar of his suit, and yanked him into the hallway. Without paying attention to the weeping Rita as she clung to his sleeve, he opened the door and threw out his son-in-law's slight body; his coat, hat and walking-stick followed.

Woroniecki-Kulik sat by the banister and sneered at Popielski.

"Get ready for the nick, Eddie!" he shouted.

"I'll take you with me" yelled Popielski.

The stairwell resounded with the voices of carol singers.

> *In deep silence of the night, a voice is spreading thus*
> *Awaken you shepherds, God is born to us . . .*

Popielski closed the door, went back into the demolished parlour and sat down heavily in the armchair next to the overturned clock. Leokadia and Rita were in tears. Hanna, who was carrying Jerzyk to and fro across the room and singing him the lullabye "Bałam-bałam", was also in tears. Only Popielski's eyes remained dry.

LWÓW, MONDAY, MARCH 13TH, 1939
TWO O'CLOCK IN THE MORNING

Rita was woken by the sound of a door closing. For a year, ever since Jerzyk was born, she had been a light sleeper – like a bird. She would wake when the child sighed in his sleep, the wind blew outside or when some drunk was making a racket in the street. She knew Bronisław was home. She shut her eyes, not wanting him to catch her awake. She did not feel like fulfilling her marital duties that night, but her husband was eager, always and everywhere, and especially when he returned late from various business meetings, as he called them. He would watch her attentively, strip down to nothing and demand things of her which she disliked.

So for some time now she had pretended to be asleep, even snoring, and with her acting skills she was easily able to deceive her indefatigable husband.

She could hear him undress, dropping his clothes randomly. She felt his eyes on her as he stood by her bed, and she carried on snoring quietly. Bronisław walked away. She heard a chair creak lightly beneath him. The creaking then became rythmical. She opened her eyes a little – and froze. Her husband was sitting on a chair, one hand between his legs, and pleasuring himself. But it was not this that horrified her. One-year-old Jerzyk had woken and was smiling at his father.

"What are you staring at," Bronisław's whisper grew more and more feverish. "You want to see how a cow is milked?"

"What are you doing!" screamed Rita, and Jerzyk began to cry.

"Well?" Her husband stood up and put on an innocent face. "It's only human . . . You know I need this twice a day . . . I had to relieve myself . . . And you were asleep . . . But you're not asleep any more."

LWÓW, SUNDAY, APRIL 16TH, 1939
ELEVEN O'CLOCK AT NIGHT

Rita sat at her dressing table applying cold cream to her face and neckline. She was happy because, now that Easter was over, they were going to leave Lwów to spend the summer at Baranie Peretoki. She had come to realize that it was not acting which mattered to her, but her son. When she returned exhausted after her rehearsals and auditions, Jerzyk would stretch out his arms and cry instead of being happy to see her. It was as if he bore her a grudge for leaving him all day in the care of his Ukrainian nanny who, although she loved the boy dearly, could not replace his mother.

Lwów seemed to have a bad influence on Bronisław. He had grown increasingly gloomy, secretive and cruel; he could not spend a moment with his child without either hitting or yelling at him, and at every meal he dragged Rita's father through the mud, just to observe her reaction. At Bronisław's side Rita was slowly losing her former spontaneity and independence. She knew that any sudden or decisive actions would be to no effect; they would clash with those of a far more hot-headed and dangerous element, one which terrified her and which she could not understand. So she tried to explain her husband's attacks in various ways. She looked at him lovingly as he shouted and seethed with fury, and she remembered his childhood, saying to herself: "What a terrible burden, to be brought up as a genius from an early age! It can have a disastrous effect on your whole life! I'm not going to bring Jerzyk up like that! My father made the same mistake, but on a smaller scale. He didn't want me to be great; he only wanted me to pass my final exams, whereas my late father-in-law demanded greatness of Bronek. No wonder my husband is a nervous wreck! Now that winter is over we'll go to the country and everything will get back to normal. Bronek will find relief in nature's bosom, and Jerzyk will breathe cleaner air."

As she combed her long, thick hair, she wondered when it would be best to see her father before they left. She forgave him the assault on Bronek, who had been exceptionally bad-tempered on Christmas Eve. Since then she had seen her father several times, usually on their walks through Stryjski Park. Sometimes she had visited him as he was having breakfast, at around midday, and had coffee with him and Aunt Leokadia while Jerzyk played with Hanna. The subject of Bronisław did not even arise. Rita had to come to terms with the fact that they would never go to the Carpathian Mountains together; and Popielski had agreed to see her only during moments stolen from his detested son-in-law.

Rita smiled at the thought of seeing green fields and the still leafless beech trees at Baranie Peretoki the following day. She heard the bedroom

280

door rattle. "Wait for me naked," he had said when he left, "and I'll be naked too when I come to the bedroom. Today we're going to celebrate the rite of spring!" She adjusted her hair and slipped off her dressing gown. She never felt any false modesty at the sight of her naked body; she knew she was beautiful.

She entered the bedroom, swaying her hips. And then she screamed. Bronisław was lying naked on the bed; an equally naked young man she did not know was lying next to him. She ran out to her boudoir and threw on her dressing gown. She heard a murmur. Both men were standing in the doorway.

"I can't do this," she said quietly but firmly. "Get out of my boudoir!" she yelled at her husband. "You perverted swine!"

Woroniecki-Kulik made towards her, a golf club in his hand. He slapped it rhythmically against his open palm.

"Either you do it with the two of us," he said, "or you do it with the club."

LWÓW, MONDAY, APRIL 17TH, 1939
FOUR O'CLOCK IN THE MORNING

Popielski resolved to go to bed early. He had an important meeting the following day with the manager of the Ukrainian Land Bank, Mr Mykoł Sawczuk, who suspected one of his employees of embezzlement. A long and boring conversation about financial transactions was in store, much of which Popielski would not understand anyway.

He sighed and replaced an old edition of Horace's *Odes* on the shelf. He was angry with himself. He had already forgotten a large number of Latin words and had to look them up too often in the dictionary. He lit his bedtime cigarette and entered the bathroom to apply some cream to the still firm skin of his face. As he crossed the hallway, the doorbell rang.

Popielski walked to the door in surprise, peered through the peephole and opened his mouth in horror. The cigarette fell from his lips and rolled on the floor.

He opened; in stepped Rita, Jerzyk asleep and wrapped in a blanket in her arms. She herself was dressed in a Zakopane woollen jumper thrown hastily over her dressing gown. She walked slowly, dragging her legs. A dark streak of blood trailed after her.

BRESLAU, THAT SAME APRIL 17TH, 1939
SEVEN O'CLOCK IN THE MORNING

Mock sat in the armchair struggling to put on his shoes. He found it especially uncomfortable due to his belly, which he had filled the previous evening with delicious but heavy *Wiener schnitzel* in the Świdnicka Cellar. Although he had overeaten, he thanked Marta resolutely for her good intentions and insisted on taking Argos out for a walk himself. Panting heavily, he wove the shoelaces through his fingers. Out of the corner of his eye he saw his German sheepdog by the door, the leash between its teeth.

"We're going for a walk in a minute, doggo." Mock smiled to see Argos stand on his hind legs and wag his tail at the sound of the word "walk".

He had almost finished tying his laces when the telephone rang. Cursing all matters so urgent that they could not wait until after nine o'clock, Mock let go of the laces and picked up the receiver.

"International call," announced a woman's voice pleasantly. "I'm putting you through!"

"Thank you," he muttered and pressed the receiver to his ear.

After a few seconds of crackling and high-pitched squeaks he heard a voice: it was male and not very friendly.

"Can I still count on you, Eberhard?"

"Of course," he replied, delighted, but soon checked his joyful tone; hearing Popielski's voice he knew there was bad news to come. "What's happened?"

"You have to know the whole truth," said Popielski after a long silence. "But not over the telephone . . . As soon as possible! Where shall we meet? And when?"

"When? Why not tomorrow!" replied Mock.

"Where?"

"That's not so easy" Mock pondered and stroked Argos on the head. "I know! I know!" There's a place where friends meet over pork knuckle and a bottle of iced vodka. Do you remember the Eldorado Restaurant in Kattowitz?"

LWÓW, FRIDAY, APRIL 28TH, 1939
THREE O'CLOCK IN THE MORNING

Platform 3 of Lwów's Main Station was empty. Apart from a sleepy stationmaster and a newspaper vendor arranging papers on his stall, only one man was in sight. He was dressed in black, with a bowler hat on his head and a white scarf wrapped around his neck; the only other pale element of his clothing was a pair of suede gloves.

He gazed, lost in thought, at the fog which curled over the railway tracks and beneath the glazed steel roof above the platforms. Half an hour earlier, on his way to the station, he had passed the Church of St Elizabeth looming in the darkness. The monumental building, a replica of St Stefan's Cathedral in Vienna, momentarily awoke in him happy memories of youthful days in the city on the Danube. Now he found himself in a city on a subterranean river, and his most recent memories were as dead and unreal as the Styx of Lwów. Popielski glanced once more at the information board to make sure the long-distance train from Berlin via Breslau, Oppeln, Kattowitz, Rzeszów and Przemyśl would indeed be arriving at the platform in five minutes.

The train emerged from fog swollen with the engine's steam, as if it were a phantom. Popielski started when the engine roared and hissed past two metres away from him. He stood and waited. Soon the train came to a halt and doors began to slam. People climbed down, lugging chests and suitcases. A lady cast her eyes about in search of a porter, complaining profusely about their absence. Stacks of luggage piled up on the platform. Only one man of medium height yet of massively broad build had no luggage other than a small valise resembling a Gladstone bag. He approached Popielski and they greeted each other warmly. In fact they had met in Kattowitz just a little over a week earlier, but they were inordinately happy to see each other again.

Popielski had no time to enjoy Mock's company before he caught sight of a hefty man behind his back. He moved away from his German friend and observed yet another man, short and with a narrow, foxy face.

"Allow me, gentlemen" – Mock turned to both men – "Edward, may I introduce Mr Cornelius Wirth and Mr Heinrich Zupitza, my men for special affairs."

LWÓW, TUESDAY, MAY 9TH, 1939
MIDDAY

Popielski finished his story, heaved a sigh and got up from his armchair. Leokadia sat dumbfounded, afraid to look at her cousin. Never before had he caused so much anxiety in her. She could not believe that aside from the world she knew so well – bridge on Thursdays at the home of Assistant Judge Stańczyk and his wife; her reading sessions in the morn-

284

ings; ancient home routines; Holy Hours sung by Hanna; Juraszki ginger biscuits and Zalewski's cake shop – there was another world of dark and hidden places full of sadists, lunatics and morally warped madmen given to brutal appetites, monsters who gnawed the cheeks of virgins or masturbated over the cot of their own child. Her cousin was acquainted with this world of minotaurs, hybrids and sodomites, and even tried to set it right. Like Theseus he had entered the labyrinth, but unlike the mythical hero, he had not returned triumphant to his homeland with Ariadne at his side; instead he had come home to an icy loneliness, shared with a whimsical spinster.

Leokadia jumped as the telephone rang.

"Good day again, sir," she heard Edward's voice. "I must apologize for my behaviour earlier when I took the liberty of hanging up on you."

" . . ."

"I know, it's terrible what happened to that boy . . . Henio Pytko. Yes, it's awful, and extremely dangerous politically. . ."

" . . ."

"Yes, I know . . . Unfortunately I'm obliged to stand by my decision . . . No . . . I'm not going to change my mind . . . I'm resigning and retiring . . ."

" . . ."

"I have to help my daughter, and look after my grandson since her husband – my son-in-law – Doctor Woroniecki-Kulik, was found in the underground passages on the Poltva . . . You don't have to remind me, sir. I know, I do know . . . A family scandal . . ."

" . . ."

"This really is my final decision! I'll bring in my written resignation tomorrow. Farewell, sir. *Adieu!*"

He uttered these last words almost jokingly, replaced the receiver and returned to the parlour. He moved his chair to sit down next to Leokadia, placing his hand on her frail shoulder.

"I'm no longer a police officer, my dear." He kissed her on the temple. "I've become a judge and executioner. And one can't be judge, executioner and police officer at one and the same time."

"So now you're only going to work in the first two professions?" She looked at him with interest.

"Not entirely." Popielski got to his feet and began to pace around the table in a sudden spurt of energy. "No, I'm going to do something different now. I'm going to be a tracker and a hunter, a kind of private detective. That's all I know, apart from Latin. And am I to teach Latin at my age?"

"And who's going to be your first prey?" Leokadia stared intently at her cousin, as curious as if she were playing bridge and waiting for his answer on the aces.

"Who do you think?"

"Little Henio Pytko's murderer?"

"That's going to be my first case. Even if nobody pays me . . ."

"And what are you going to do with the murderer when you catch him? The same as you did to your son-in-law?"

LWÓW, FRIDAY, APRIL 28TH, 1939
FIVE O'CLOCK IN THE MORNING

Doctor Bronisław Woroniecki-Kulik had heard many extraordinary stories about the Poltva, Lwów's invisible river which had been covered over by the Austrians and now ran silently beneath the city. It was said that the riverine underground was a secret world of criminals, a colony of lepers and harlots, an asylum for murderers and sodomites. As a child he had imagined that bloody Furies sat there by flaming rivers, and dogs of hell filled the abyss with their howling. As an adult he had often wanted to go and acquaint himself with the cursed place which was, according to the town's legend, worthy even of Dante's pen.

When he did at last find himself there, he was disappointed. This was no hell on earth, but rather an enormous, foul-smelling latrine from whence paupers crawled now and then, only to hide themselves again. Seeing all this by torchlight, Woroniecki was curious to know whether the people living there were, as was rumoured, in the last stages of syphilitic putrefaction. He could not see for himself, however; there was no time. The men who led him mistook his passion for learning for an attempt to delay their progress. For his part, he was not able to explain his interest in this underground world because there was a gag in his mouth.

He was not in the least bit frightened by the three men who had burst into his Rohatyna apartment during the night. He was convinced it was all a practical joke played on him by a friend who betrayed a weakness for peculiar pranks and had once crept through the window of his apartment disguised as a ghost to tear him from his sleep. So Woroniecki-Kulik walked quite calmly, and despite his gag and bound hands he was in good spirits. He was waiting for his friend, the joker, to loom out of the darkness at any moment. It would not have occurred to him that anyone in this city would dare lift a finger against Commissioner Edward Popielski's son-in-law. Besides, one of the abductors had taken Bronisław's walking stick with him. Anyone wanting to do him harm would surely not worry about such details.

They came to a halt behind a turn in the wall and switched off their torches. Total darkness. Woroniecki-Kulik felt somebody's breath on his face; it smelled of nicotine and alcohol. The fourth assailant. Then he picked up the scent of an eau de cologne he recognized. This was not the scent his friend used. It was then that he began to feel afraid. Nobody in

Lwów would dare lift a finger against Commissioner Edward Popielski's son-in-law. Save Edward Popielski himself, perhaps.

A shaft of light fell onto the mathematician's face, but it did not blind him. He clearly saw an elegantly gloved hand emerge from the darkness, his walking stick between two of its fingers.

"Is this what you injured my daughter with?" he heard Popielski's voice say. "Did you push a walking stick like this into her womb?"

Woroniecki-Kulik began to shake, which surprised him because he was not in the least bit frightened. His analytical mind was working impeccably, without a shred of emotion. But his body was not listening to his mind; it shook with panic and fear, and was bathed in sweat. It seemed to him that the entire stench of that underground cesspool emanated from him.

"Did you shove a walking stick into the womb which bore your son?"

Another hand loomed out of the darkness and tore the gag from his mouth. He heard a splash. He knew he would live for as long as he refused to answer the question in the affirmative; he felt relieved. He would refuse, and he would live. His logical mind was infallible.

All of a sudden he felt his coat being torn off him, then his pyjamas. The silk tautened and split. He felt cold. A firm pressure on the nape of his neck made him kneel, then fall on his face. The stench of the sewers grew even stronger. Somebody sat on his back; somebody else parted his bare legs.

"You're going to suffer as she did" – Popielski's voice again – "except that your suffering will be worse. It will be hopeless, and final."

Woroniecki-Kulik heard the tapping of his walking stick. Out of the corner of his eye he glimpsed torchlight on his shins. His hands were bound tighter. And then he realised he had overestimated his mathematical mind. He had not foreseen that Popielski knew the answer to the question he had already asked twice. And then he no longer thought of anything. He was one burning pain.

When, a quarter of an hour later, he was thrown into the Poltva with his hands bound, and the foul-smelling water filled his lungs, he considered it a liberation.

MAREK KRAJEWSKI was for many years a lecturer in Classical Studies at the University of Wroclaw. His Eberhard Mock series, which includes *Death in Breslau* (2008), *The End of the World in Breslau* (2009) and *Phantoms of Breslau* (2010), have enjoyed huge success in Europe and have been rewarded with Poland's premier literary and crime novel prizes. *The Minotaur's Head* is the fourth in the series to be translated into English.

DANUSIA STOK is the author/editor of *Kieslowski on Kieslowski* and the translator of a range of modern Polish literature and language books, including the rest of the Breslau series.